ON THE EDGE

NEW YORK TIMES BESTSELLING AUTHOR

K. BROMBERG

PRAISE FOR
K. BROMBERG

"K. Bromberg always delivers intelligently written, emotionally intense, sensual romance . . ."

—*USA Today*

"K. Bromberg makes you believe in the power of true love."
—#1 *New York Times* bestselling author Audrey Carlan

"Always an absolute must-read."
—*New York Times* bestselling author Helena Hunting

"An irresistibly hot romance that stays with you long after you finish the book."
—#1 *New York Times* bestselling author Jennifer L. Armentrout

"Bromberg is a master at turning up the heat!"
—*New York Times* bestselling author Katy Evans

"Supercharged heat and full of heart. Bromberg aces it from the first page to the last."

—*New York Times* bestselling author Kylie Scott

ALSO WRITTEN BY K. BROMBERG

Driven Series

Driven

Fueled

Crashed

Raced

Aced

Driven Novels

Slow Burn

Sweet Ache

Hard Beat

Down Shift

The Player Duet

The Player

The Catch

Everyday Heroes

Cuffed

Combust

Cockpit

Control (Novella)

Wicked Ways

Resist

Reveal

Standalone
Faking It
Then You Happened
Flirting with 40
UnRaveled (Novella)
Sweet Cheeks
Sweet Rivalry (Novella)
Sweet Regret
What If (Part of Two More Days Anthology)

The Play Hard Series
Hard to Handle
Hard to Hold
Hard to Score
Hard to Lose
Hard to Love

The S.I.N. Series
Last Resort
On One Condition
Final Proposal

The Redemption Series
Until You

The Full Throttle Series
Off the Grid

Holiday Novellas
The Package
The Detour
Forever More

Paperback: 978-1-942832-78-2
Special Edition Paperback: 978-1-942832-86-7

Editing by Marion Making Manuscripts
Cover by Indie Sage PR
Formatting by Champagne Book Design
Printed in the United States of America

ON THE EDGE

PROLOGUE

Cruz

"**Y**OU DID IT. YOU FUCKING DID IT, MAN."

Thumps on my helmet. Pats on my back. Quick hugs teem with astonished excitement.

I blink back the tears that threaten and allow the moment to soak in.

I did it.

I really fucking did it.

A lump of emotion lodges in my throat, and pride swells in my chest. My third race in Formula 1, and I place on the fucking *podium*.

That's right. I'm a goddamn Navarro. To those who thought I was riding on the coattails of my legacy, I just proved them wrong.

And me right.

My crew celebrates around me as they push me toward the staging area for the trophy ceremony, but I search the crowd for only one set of eyes.

For one man.

For the giant I've spent my life seeking approval from.

And when I see him, when I lock eyes with the quiet steel in them, my smile freezes . . . then fades.

He gives the subtlest shake of his head as he walks toward me. "Third?" he says under his breath, disappointment and disgust edging his tone. "That's all you could get with all the wide-open space you were given? You're a Navarro. Perform like it."

The minute the words are out, his smile reappears for everyone around us to see. The Dominic Navarro façade firmly in place. He shakes the hands held out to him. He accepts the congratulations on my behalf. He shows the world the only side of him they've ever known.

And when I take the podium later and look out through the sting of champagne in my eyes, he's nowhere to be found. Not with my crew. Not with the other families of the podium holders. Not even mixed somewhere in the back of the crowd.

"You're a Navarro. Perform like it."

It's my third race in Formula 1, asshole.

I am a Navarro. On track to live up to my *grandfather's* greatness. And in the process?

I plan to beat every fucking milestone you ever held.

I've only just begun.

If you're jealous of my talent now? Just you fucking wait.

CHAPTER ONE

Cruz

"I NEVER CLAIMED TO BE A SAINT," I say and slip my sunglasses down to take them off only to push them back up the minute the sun hits my eyes.

A fucking kick drum is pounding in my head, and the bright sun isn't doing me any favors in quieting it down.

"How long ago was your IV?" Lennox Kincade, my agent, asks. When I don't respond, she prompts, "*Cruz?*"

"That was you?" Question of the morning answered. Not that I wondered about it too long.

Too many people depend on me. No doubt one of those people sent the nurse to my hotel room to make sure I recovered. Now, I know who ordered it.

"Who else do you think sent a nurse with a saline IV to sober you up for this meeting?"

"I didn't need sobering up." *Yes, I did.*

"Then call it a simple precaution based on your previous *non-saint*-like behavior," she says wryly. Clearly, she's lost her sense of humor this morning.

"Give me a break, Lennox. It was the summer recess," I say of FIA's mandatory two-week break period. "You sent me to Austin for these meetings. Nowhere in the itinerary did it say I couldn't enjoy my time here in the States."

"You're free to do as you please, but I'm also fully aware we're in the midst of the Cruz Navarro downward spiral we lapse into every three months or so."

"You're full of shit, Kincade. There is no spiral. No cycle."

"And yet I knew to send the saline to flush your system this morning," she says sarcastically.

"It's not a crime to meet up with old friends. To make new ones. God forbid I had a little fun. You should try it sometime."

"Summer break is over as of midnight last night, and you're about thirty minutes away from one of the biggest meetings of your life." She pauses. "Wait. You are at the offices, right?"

I look up at the office building for Genesee Capital in front of me. It's about ten stories tall with walls of windows for its employees to look out at . . . what? A lot of flat land and odd-shaped water towers dotting the horizon? Who knows. Who cares. Because all I can focus on is how I'm going to muddle through these meetings with a clear head.

That last bottle was *definitely* a mistake.

And that's on me.

"Yeah, I'm here," I murmur as a curvy brunette with big hair and an even bigger ass walks in front of my rental car. She sways her hips like it's her sole purpose in life. No complaints on my end.

"I need you on your best behavior in there," she warns.

"I'm always on my best behavior."

"I'm fucking serious, Cruz. You made demands—"

"Your point?"

"You wanted a deal bigger than any your father was ever offered. You wanted a brand partnership that goes beyond the sport and your time actively being involved in the sport—a brand partnership that would set you up for life with an income stream—and I've delivered on both in a big way."

"Is this the part where I'm supposed to kiss your ass for doing your job?"

"No. This is the part where you knock that fucking chip off your shoulder. I'm not your dad. I don't set impossible expectations for you to meet. I just try and deliver on whichever ones you throw at me. Now, can we get back to what's important? You know, *the meeting?*"

"Ah, yes. *The meeting,*" I parrot.

"Genesee Capital is the private equity firm you *want* to be in business with. Its holding company owns some of the largest brands out there. *That* holding company is willing to give you a lifetime contract that includes five percent of earnings on every product sold. We're talking a Michael Jordan with Nike type of deal."

I squeeze my eyes shut, willing the Motrin to kick in, and nod to my empty car. "They're really banking on that Navarro legacy shit, aren't they?"

"They're signing you, not Dominic. So no, they're banking on the *Cruz Navarro legacy shit*. Your skills. Your looks. Your charisma. Your reputation. They want you to be the face of Body Strong's new sports drink, Revive, among other products."

"Let's not forget they're also using my capital to invest in this drink."

"Exactly. That's why they need to know their new partner is exactly who and what they think he is. Cruz Navarro, F1 driver. Not Cruz Navarro, Nightclub Playboy, who's so hungover he can't take off his sunglasses and meet their eyes during the meeting."

Guess that throws that plan out the window.

I grunt in response. Is this the deal that I asked for? *Yes.* Do I like when things are shoved down my throat? *Nope.* That's the quickest way to turn me off.

"This is momentous, Cruz. There's not another driver on the grid—past or present—who has a deal like this."

Fuck. Credit's due where it's due.

"Thank you. I mean it. Sincerely."

Lennox's sigh is heavy, the soft spot I know she has for me weakening for the briefest moment. "Taking care of you and your future is my job. Just like keeping your ass in line is. And apparently, I'm not doing terribly well considering word has gotten around about the numerous bridges you've burned with some of your other brand deals—"

"I didn't burn shit. I fulfilled my obligation to each and every one."

"You did do your part. But you've also earned a reputation for being difficult to work with."

"That's such bullsh—"

"Cold, hard truth, Cruz? Companies don't want to touch you," Lennox says, never one to beat around the bush. That's great when it comes to negotiating on my behalf. Not so great when it's being directed straight at me without a buffer. "Genesee has been wavering on this. You're a liability to their squeaky-clean image. The partying. The drinking. The simply not giving a fuck when you're one of twenty drivers in arguably the most revered sport on earth. They don't know what's going to be in the press from one day to the next and frankly, don't want to have to fucking worry about it."

"I'm no different than every other driver out there."

She snorts.

Even I don't buy my own lie. My father is Dominic Navarro. Son of Sergio Navarro, a motorsports legend. The former, a man who expects nothing less than perfection from me on the grid to make up for his shortcomings. *Off the grid?* That's my own time. My own place. It's where I can live on the edge. Where I can cut loose from the pressure that comes from being tethered to my fucking last name.

But this deal? This deal can give me something he never had. A name beyond our F1 motor racing bubble. A chance at global recognition and success.

And then when I win a championship, he'll know I am better than he ever aspired to be.

"Like I said, word gets around." She tsks out of habit. "You've already had a fair share of sponsorship deals not renewed because of the press, but I've gotten Genesee to overlook all that. I've gotten them to commit to something they've never considered offering before."

"Can the lecture be over now?"

"Sure, once you hear me when I say that this company has far-reaching arms that hold many lucrative opportunities with other products and brands. If you mess this up, then everything under their umbrella will be off-limits to you in the future. Is that enough of an incentive for you to walk the straight and narrow?"

"Sure. Fine." I say the words but am looking at the text on my phone from Heather and reliving certain parts of last night . . . *and* early this morning spent tangled in the sheets with her and her friend.

> **Me:** Same time tonight?

I type the text referring to the nightclub we were at last night and send it to her, needing something to look forward to.

"You have exactly twenty-one minutes to sober the fuck up, to chew some gum so it doesn't smell like last night's gin is oozing out of your pores—"

"It was whiskey."

"Do you think I care?" she snaps.

"I know how much you like your facts to be straight," I counter and receive a frustrated sigh in return.

"Figure out how the fuck you're going to charm them."

"Relax." She's so goddamn uptight sometimes. "I'm here to sign the papers. Pretty sure the charming has already been done. The deal is essentially set in stone."

"Exactly. It's *essentially* set. You're the only one who can fuck this up now, Cruz."

"Thanks for the vote of confidence," I say, sarcasm dripping in my tone.

She makes a noncommittal sound that says she's far from convinced. "You know as well as I do that your life can change in a second in your sport. I prefer not to jinx it and go into the details regarding how. And we're both aware of your family's legacy in this industry. But wouldn't it be liberating to know that no matter what, you are set for life outside of racing and free of the strings *that* legacy ties you to? That's what this deal would do for you. Autonomy in every aspect of the word."

"I make enough money. My family money is—"

"I know you do, but wouldn't this obliterate any question about that when it comes to your father?"

Her question hangs on the line. She's really the only one who has ever seen the true Dominic Navarro and who therefore, has the knowledge to make that statement.

"Hey, that's them on the other line," she says. "I have to take this, but I'll see you in there."

"What? You're here?" I whip my head up to look around the parking lot and regret the action immediately as the sky keeps moving when my head stops.

"Via Zoom," she says and then ends the call before I can respond.

Fucking perfect. Didn't realize my babysitter was going to be present too.

I groan, lean my head back against the seat, and close my eyes. The pounding in my head is slightly better. Now if I could just get the churning in my stomach to ease, I'd call that a win.

Fifteen minutes and counting.

I'll play the game.

I'll sign the deal.

I'll play the part they need.

I'll live my life the way *I* want.

I'll earn the money.

No one controls me.

And no sooner than the thoughts cross my mind does my cell ring again.

"Papá" lights up the screen.

Speaking of controlling me. My father never can resist any opportunity.

"Not today," I mutter.

I'd rather face the blinding sun without glasses and a whole marching band right now than talk to him.

Sliding out from behind the wheel of my car, I take a fortifying breath. The fresh air does wonders to clear my head.

Each step toward the building has snapshots of the past two weeks of break flashing through my head.

Hiking the hills with the guys in the mornings.

Weight training during the early afternoons.

Meeting up with my sister, Sofia, a few times.

Nights spent at one club or another. Bottle service and velvet ropes.

Women . . . Christ, *the women* alone have been a bender in and of itself. *Thank you, America, for that.*

I pull open the door with a crooked smirk and thoughts of Heather and those lips of hers filling my head.

I'd say I'm at about seventy percent now. The moving about did me wonders. The sunglasses will stay on a bit longer though.

I'm not ready for the light yet.

"Mr. Navarro?" a pleasant voice asks to my right.

"Yes?" I turn to see a guy about my age wearing a security guard uniform and a smile. I go to take my sunglasses off out of courtesy but stop myself. I'll let the Visine have a few more minutes to clear the red from the whites of my eyes.

"They're expecting you upstairs. Ninth floor. Down the hallway to the very end."

"Yeah. Um. Thanks." I start heading toward the bank of elevators. America is a funny place. Formula 1 is starting to gain traction here so it's weird to not be recognized for who I am like I would be if I were at home in Europe.

"And, Mr. Navarro?" I stop and turn back to look at him. "I'm a huge fan. Like you're the one my whole family roots for. Every race day." He shifts on his feet, his grin widening. Guess that blew my thought out of the water. "Um, just wanted to say, good luck the rest of the season. I feel a championship year coming. If not this year, then next."

My smile is genuine when I flash it. "Thanks. I appreciate it."

"I'm not supposed to ask." He looks over his shoulder. "But maybe on the way out, after your meeting, can we take a picture?"

"Of course. You'll be here?"

He nods, his eyes wide. "Yes. Right here. Until tonight. Until you come back down." He all but bounces on his feet. "My dad will lose his mind when he finds out that I met you."

My phone alerts a text as I step into the elevator. Before I can even look at its screen, it sounds off several more times.

Ah, the Dominic Navarro love bomb texts, no doubt. Never one to be ignored for too long, he utilizes his favorite MO.

"To what do I owe this pleasure?" I murmur as I look at my texts only to be met with picture after picture of last night.

Images that don't exactly paint me in the best light or that I even remember.

Clearly drunk. My lips on one woman one moment and a different one the next.

A half-filled glass in one hand and a bottle in the other.

A series of shots that clearly show me stumbling into a group of people before landing on my ass with a grin on my lips.

Fuck.

Can't get away with shit these days with all the fucking phones everywhere.

One thing's for sure, I was having a *great* time. *And I don't really give a flying fuck what my dear old papá thinks of this.*

But the texts don't stop coming. And when my phone rings shortly there-after—just as the elevator hits the ninth floor—I know that I either have to answer the call or be prepared for him to track me down through Genesee's phone lines and make a scene.

I wouldn't put it past him to do it. Everyone answers when Dominic Navarro asks questions—the loving, doting father that he is to the public. He's only looking out for my best interest, after all. Or at least that's the shit he peddles.

"I'm surprised you could dial in between firing off all those texts," I say by way of greeting.

"Do you actually think what is in those pictures is befitting of someone who has Navarro blood in their veins?" His deep baritone echoes through the line, my own lips mouthing each word as they come. Each word like a tiny cut laced onto my skin.

Just adding to the thousand other cuts he's slashed in secret over the years.

"Hello to you too, Papá."

"Cut the crap, Cruz. This isn't funny. This isn't a game. You stopping this behavior isn't up for discussion. You are a Navarro. Our family is the oldest and most successful legacy in this sport."

"Some of us, anyway." I'll take a jab any way I can make one.

He clears his throat, and I can all but hear him grit his teeth. "It's just like you to screw up before you even sign the papers. Genesee's going to walk from the deal because you're a liability. You always have been. Apparently, you always will be."

Fuck you.

The words are on my tongue, but my sick sense of respect for a man who has none for me holds it back.

"The deal isn't in jeopardy at all. But then again, you think my business is your business even when it isn't."

"You're a Navarro. Everything is my business."

"You keep thinking that and I'll keep disappointing you. Or is that what you want? The disappointment? The screwing up? That way you have something to hold over my head, right?" I ask. Anything to use against your son as a justification as to why he's twice the driver you ever were and the only Navarro to ever come close to el patriarca's reign in Formula 1.

"When are you going to stop tarnishing our name?"

When you stop trying to make me live up to your unrealistic standards.

"Work hard. Play hard. Isn't that the motto?" I ask. "Last I checked—not that I need to or anything—I'm allowed to have fun."

Silence hangs on the line, the smart-ass smile on my face fading with every second it stretches on.

A slow response is never good when it comes to him.

"El patriarca," he says, referring to my grandfather, my idol, and our affectionate name for him—*the patriarch.*

"What about him?" I readjust my sunglasses and stop in the middle of the hallway, my chest starting to tighten.

"El patriarca said not to bother coming home to visit before heading to Zandvoort."

CHAPTER TWO

Maddix

"WOW. UM." KEVIN'S EYEBROWS KNIT TOGETHER AS HE LOOKS at me from across my cubicle. The CEO of Genesee Capital isn't exactly used to employees, tiers below him, asking him something like this. "Maddie, is it?"

I'm surprised he's even that close. "Maddix."

"Right." A tight smile. "Yes." A glance around as if he's waiting for someone—my manager—to rescue him from my question. Good thing my manager is out sick. "I stopped to ask you to run these folders to the conference room and now you're . . . I guess I didn't think you'd be interested in something like this."

I grit my teeth and smile despite my irritation. "Of course, I am. Isn't that why I'm here? To learn and—"

"Sure, but . . ." He scratches the side of his head as he angles it and narrows his eyes at me.

It was ballsy to out and out ask the CEO of the company if I could join the big meeting every intern here is talking about in hushed tones. It's one thing to be hired by a company as a low-level staffer tasked with every job no one else wants while trying to gain experience in branding and marketing. It's a whole other thing to request to be in on one of the biggest deals this company has ever facilitated.

While it's expected for my male counterparts to request to take part in events like this, it's quite different when one of us females do, as is quite apparent by the look on Kevin's face.

Well . . . guess there's a first time for everything. And that first time is right now.

I'm not going to further any part of my career by being satisfied with taking the back seat. Isn't that the realization I had come to last night as I sat across from Michael? That I was nowhere near where I had planned to be at this point in my life?

I love him, but not in that soul-owning, heart-fulfilling way I thought love was supposed to be. I enjoyed my work, but felt like I was on the hamster wheel, continuously chasing my tail, with no upward growth in sight. I adored my town and where I grew up in the outskirts of Austin, but it was over a thousand miles away from Manhattan where all the top opportunities to become a branding or creative manager are located.

I'd marked today for action. *I'm acting.*

"You've never taken interest in this sort of thing before, so why start now?" Kevin asks.

This sort of thing? As in the reason I'm here to learn and gain experience?

I blink several times as if it's going to make his comment make sense. For a savvy, forward-thinking CEO, who I do happen to like, sometimes I think he's so busy with what's in front of him, he can't see anything else around him.

He's not dense, he's just . . . *a man.*

"Kevin, this is what I'm here for at Genesee. To learn the marketing aspect inside and out and grow so eventually I can move up the ladder."

He looks out over the dozen or so cubicles of who we call the first years—me, being one of them—and I can see the indecision coloring his expression.

"A lot of people are wanting in on this meeting."

"I know. Everyone's talking about it."

"I've already assembled a team," he says and checks his watch.

"What does one more person hurt? I'll sit along the wall. Observe only."

"Why should I pick you?" he asks, back to his decisive, calculating self we all know and expect.

I may be offering to be a wallflower, but being subtle has never been my strong suit.

"Because I know shit about racing."

He chuckles. "It's Formula 1. Saying it's 'racing' is an insult to the sport."

I offer him a droll look. "Correction. *Because I don't know anything about Formula 1.* Hell, I don't even know the first thing about it or its racers."

"Drivers."

"Fine. Okay. Drivers," I say to appease him. "I don't want in on this deal for the clout of saying I know the racer—"

"Cruz Navarro is his name," he says, stifling a chuckle.

"Sure. Fine. Case in point—I don't even know his name. I mean, Aaron or Macey only want in on this so they can have clout with their friends or post pictures of themselves at races or in the . . . whatever it's called where they have the cars."

"You mean the paddock and garage?"

"Does it really matter?"

"Yes."

"Look, this job is my ticket to the next step. I have my degree but I'm not getting any chances to gain experience. I'm nowhere near getting to the next step."

"The next step always takes sacrifices, Maddie—"

"Maddix," I correct, to which he waves his hand in irrelevance.

"Sure. Maddix." His smile is quick and stoic. "What are you willing to sacrifice to get to the next step is what you should be asking yourself."

"All I'm asking is to be in on the meeting that sounds like it might be one of the most influential branding agreements for the past five years."

"So you're telling me that your lack of interest and knowledge is to your benefit?" He crosses his arms over his chest and purses his lips in that way he has that we're not sure if he's going to explode or smile.

It's always extremes with him, which is partly why asking this is such a big deal.

I nod. "I am. You know I want to be in there for all of the right reasons."

His sigh is heavy as his eyes skitter over my head and around the room. "It might be a shitshow."

"I thought the deal was—"

"It is done, but a few parameters need to be refined but . . ." He pauses. Then sighs. There's a lot of weight in that sigh, and I stare at him with fingers figuratively crossed, hoping that weight is in my favor. "Fine. Sure. Yes. What the hell. The more the merrier, right?" He looks down at the stack of papers in his hands and then back over to Aaron who is eyeing him with uncertainty. "But just a warning. There's going to be some serious jealousy over you getting to sit in there."

"I can handle that."

"The knives are pretty sharp around here." He chuckles and lifts his eyebrows seconds before holding out the papers to me. "Run these to the conference room on the ninth."

"Yes. Okay." *Holy shit, he said yes.* "But isn't that floor closed for improvements?"

He nods. "That ensures privacy then, doesn't it?"

Don't question him. Just go with it.

"I'll run those down right now." I point to the red folders tucked under his arm. "Those too?"

He pauses before he responds. "Not yet. I'm still finalizing . . . these." But the way he says it—his brows knitted together and irritation etched in the lines of his face—has me taking a step back and calling this a win before he changes his mind.

"When does the meeting start?"

"Thirty minutes. Make sure everything is set up as it should be."

Like I have any clue what that means. Guess I'll pull the whole *fake it until I make it.* "Sure thing."

Kevin turns to walk away but then stops and looks back at me. "You still haven't answered the question."

"Which one is that?"

"What are you willing to sacrifice to get to the next step?"

The question sticks with me as I take the elevator up to the ninth floor, past all the closed doors, and down the empty hallway to the largest of all our conference rooms. Whatever needs to be in place seems to be in place.

I think.

Green portfolio folders are already at each seat. A fancy pen box is open in the middle of the table. I'd assume it's for the signing of the contract, but there doesn't seem to be a pen inside. I scrunch my nose, a tad confused with worry that someone took what I can assume is the "deal-signing pen." Definitely something I need to suss out before everyone arrives.

There's a pitcher of water at the center of the table with glasses on a tray beside it. Prototypes of the Revive packaging and overall marketing campaign blanket the easels that are propped around the room.

I'm not one hundred percent sure what exactly the conference room is supposed to look like, but it looks fine to me, so I distribute the packets of paper to each seat as directed. It's when I head out of the conference room to go back and figure out the pen situation that I see a man about twenty feet away down the hallway.

Other than the whole wearing his sunglasses inside thing, it's clear the man is flustered—or is it panicked?—as he jostles the handles on a couple doors only to find them all locked. With the last denial of access, he groans in frustration.

Stuck between heading upstairs for *Pen Gate* and backing away slowly so he doesn't see me, I stand there and watch him.

He tries another door and a strangled sound comes from deep within his throat when he finds that one locked too.

"Damn it," he mutters, his hand gripping his phone so tightly his knuckles are white.

It's then that he notices me. A baseball hat sits low on his forehead, and his eyes are hidden behind dark sunglasses, but I know he's staring at me.

"I just need a minute." He labors the words out.

"That one's open," I say without thinking and point to the door midway between us that leads to a break room of sorts. It's one of the only unlocked doors on this floor.

There's a sudden change in the set of his jaw. That along with the sagging of his shoulders tells me the reprieve I'm offering is what he's looking for. With a curt nod, he moves into the room, leaving the tension to dissipate in the air around me.

Common sense would tell me to walk away and use the precious few minutes I have left before the meeting to take a quick bathroom break, gather my computer so I can take notes, and find out why the pen is missing. *Surely it's not on purpose, right?* But there is something about the man that has me walking toward the door and making sure he's okay. A draw that has me stepping a few feet into the room.

He could be a serial killer, Maddix. He's on the ninth floor of an office building when the floor is, for all intents and purposes, closed. And here you are, following him into a room when it's desolate.

Not one of my smartest ideas to date, but that doesn't stop me from standing and studying him.

He moves about the room. His breathing is labored. His hands are trembling. His mouth is pulled tight, and his entire body's tense.

I open my mouth to ask him if he's okay several times but then close it.

It's only when he stops at the window, braces his hand on the ledge, looks outside, and exhales a rather shaky breath that I speak.

"Can I help you?" I offer.

His body tenses again—almost as if he didn't realize he had an audience. "No. I'm fine." He grits the words out in the subtlest of accents, but when he looks over his shoulder at me, he plasters on the most disingenuous smile I've ever seen.

Clearly, he's not okay.

"It doesn't look like you're fine," I say, taking a few steps toward him.

"I said I'm fine." It's now that he stands up to his full height and turns to look at me. His sunglasses are off, and I'm met with the lightest set of amber eyes I've ever seen. Although a bit bloodshot, they have flecks of gold in them and are framed by a thick set of lashes I'd kill for. His well-defined jaw is set, the muscle ticking on one side, and his full lips are pulled in a straight line. His nostrils flare as he breathes in sharply but tries to appear that he isn't.

Jesus. If this man is a serial killer, his looks alone are enough to lure any woman to their demise.

"I don't believe you," I say, to which I get a lopsided smirk. The act is laden with sarcasm but only serves to make him more attractive.

"Whether you believe me or not isn't my problem." His phone alerts a text and no sooner than it does, he tosses it onto the table beside him. The clatter eats up the silence in the room.

"Lie to yourself, then. It's no skin off my back." I shrug and move toward the refrigerator. I pull out a bottle of water and hold it out to him. He doesn't look anywhere near fine. In fact, there's sweat on his brow, and the bronze tone of his skin has paled. "But I know a panic attack when I see one, and it kind of looks like that's what you've got going on there."

He grabs the water bottle from my hand and downs half of it in one tilt of the bottle. When he lowers it, his eyes meet mine. The tendons in his neck are still taut, and his shoulders continue to rise and fall with a fervid desperation. "Thanks."

"Sure. It's just water."

He nods, his throat working as he does.

"When I have one, it helps if I do box breathing."

His brows furrow, but his chest continues to rise and fall rapidly as if he's drawing in air but it's not abating his need for oxygen. "When you have one what?" he asks, annoyance tinging the edges of his tone.

"A panic attack."

"I'm not having a panic attack."

"Okay." I smile sweetly. *Why deny it when we both know that's what's going on?* "But when I do, it helps if I breathe in slowly to the count of four. Hold it for the count of four. Then exhale slowly to the same count." My shrug is pure indifference despite taking note of his slow inhale in as if he's doing what I've instructed. "It's called box breathing. It forces you to—"

"Breathe. Got it. But I'm not having a—I'm fine," he says, but I notice the tension in his body fading with each second—with each breath—that passes.

His phone alerts again from its spot on the table. The screen lights up but he doesn't give it a glance. His whole body stiffens again though, and he closes his eyes momentarily before lifting the bottle and drinking the rest of the water.

Silence permeates the room just like my awkward indecision does. "More water?" I ask.

He shakes his head as my own phone buzzes in my hand like a reminder about the huge opportunity I'm getting and how I need to get back to it.

"So, uh, I have to get back to work. Are you sure you're okay?"

Our eyes meet again. He opens his mouth and then closes it before slipping his sunglasses back on and finally responding. "I'm fine."

So you've said.

"Well, uh, this floor is technically closed right now, but you're welcome to stay in here until you feel less . . . whatever it is that you're feeling. I'd say to take your time, but you'll probably want to get to whatever floor it is you're wanting to get to before the CEO gets here."

"Why's that?" he asks.

"He's busy trying to make everything perfect for a big client. He might not be too happy to see some random man wandering the halls."

"Got it." He tosses the water bottle in the trash can beside him. "He'll never know I'm here."

"Good. Great." I take a few steps back and hook a thumb over my shoulder. "I need to get back."

"Hey . . ." he says, causing me to turn and face him. "Thanks."

My smile is quick but sincere. "Of course."

CHAPTER THREE

Maddix

C-R-U-Z.

I trace the lines of the four letters over and over and then doodle clouds around them. It's so much easier focusing on this yellow lined pad of paper and my scribbling than the uncomfortable discussion being had at the table in front of me.

"I'm confused." Cruz Navarro blows out an exasperated sigh and looks from Kevin to the other representatives of Genesee Capital—or rather the ones seated at the conference table around him—not the other lone member of the team sitting against the wall like she doesn't exist. That person being me. "I thought we were here to ink the deal."

With the pen that's purposely not on the table.

The empty box will make a statement, Kevin had said. I don't think Cruz noticed at all.

"That was the plan, but as I told Lennox before we started," Kevin says, motioning to the screen on the wall where Cruz's agent stares back at him from wherever she's calling in from. There's a crease in her brow and a very serious expression on her face. "We're having second thoughts at the moment."

Cruz chortles in what I can only read as disbelief. "All because of some pictures?" he asks, the question more of a statement than anything, before looking toward the monitor, his jaw working, and irritation evident.

A last-minute request from Kevin had me shuffling into my *wall-flower* seat several minutes after the meeting officially started. To say I was surprised to find that the man from the hallway seated across from our CEO was the same man he'd said was some big-name superstar is an understatement. That explains the slight accent at least.

Maybe because he seemed so . . . *normal?*

Get over it, Maddix, because he doesn't seem so normal now.

Normal people don't have paparazzi follow them around after a late night of partying though. And clearly—by the crude collage of paparazzi pictures that plaster the second screen in the conference room, Cruz Navarro does.

But it's his indifference to these pictures on the screen that sets him apart in this conference room. His complete *I don't give a fuck* attitude to them that's making things a tad uncomfortable and has me shifting in my seat.

"It's not just these pictures," Kevin says as he leans back in his chair. "It's the whole of the pictures. What they imply. What they say about you and the things you embody and represent."

"And what *exactly* does it say about me?" Cruz folds his arms over his chest. I notice the flex of his biceps as he does. How can I not? But I also notice his irritation.

"Revive is interested in promoting a healthy lifestyle. It's for—"

Cruz's laugh is rich and sarcastic. "Should I give you a rundown of my regimen? The cardio. The weights. The endurance training. The nutrition protocols. It's all wrapped in a prettily packaged schedule that I get every day, every week, down to the minute. I assure you, Kevin, that my supposed health isn't something to question."

Kevin clears his throat. The man never has qualms over confronting the hard things and now is no different. "We are set to invest a vast sum of money into a partnership with you. One your people approached us about. One we've haggled and negotiated and worked on for months. One I'd like to think would alter how you act when in the public's eye, knowing this was in the works."

The curl up of one side of Cruz's lips says, *how do you know this isn't my normal?* He's confident bordering on arrogant, and I fight my own smile at his blatant defiance.

The balls on this guy. They must be huge to know you're one signature away from making more money than you could ever spend in ten lifetimes, and you're acting like you don't give a fuck.

Maybe he doesn't. Just like maybe what I mistook for a panic attack earlier was just Cruz being hungover, which is completely rational considering the timestamp on the pictures currently on the screen.

He leans back in his seat, one forearm casually perched on the table, the other on his armrest as he looks at the photos of himself and has the gall to smirk—almost as if he's reliving the moment—before meeting Kevin's eyes again.

"I'm part of a sport that makes a living cheating death. It's a rush like nothing you could ever imagine. If you're telling me that you're more worried about a night out on the town with friends than me surviving the next race when it comes to how I can contribute to our partnership, then I think maybe I'm the one who needs to rethink this deal."

Kevin's back straightens the same time that Lennox warns, "Cruz."

Definitely, big balls.

"Mr. Reynoso," Lennox says to Kevin. "Would you mind giving Cruz and me a moment to—"

"I don't need a moment," Cruz states, both hands flat on the table in front of him. The watch on his wrist is understated but most definitely costs more than my car. It cuffs the bottom of some rather impressive forearms that flex with the action and definitely hold my attention.

I have a weakness for strong hands and forearms and the watch just adds another dimension to the visual porn that I force myself to pull my eyes away from.

"In our initial conversations, we voiced concerns about all of your . . . activities," Kevin says, his shoulders squaring. "We were assured by your team that things would change . . . that you'd be more reserved in your public persona but . . . stumbling out of bars? Street racing down the strip in Monaco? Doesn't sound like you've taken what we've asked for in our partnership very seriously."

"And yet we're still here, aren't we?" Cruz asks.

"What he means," Lennox says. "Is—"

"I don't need an interpreter, Ms. Kincade. I'm well aware what he means," Kevin says and then turns his attention back to Cruz.

"I have what you need to make this a success. The looks. The charisma. The following. The last name. The money. It sounds like a win-win all around, doesn't it?"

"Exactly." Kevin's voice is monotone as he taps the papers in his hand to square them up on the table. Just like someone would do before they're about to walk out of a meeting. "But what I know and what the board sees are two very different things. And they're not liking what they see to approve this deal."

I see it and I'm pretty sure Cruz sees it by the sudden startle of his neck. "What is it you're asking for, Kevin?" Cruz asks, face impassive, eyes searching. But it's the flicker of his eyes over to Lennox that tells me he's now concerned about this deal. It's the briefest break in his façade, but I notice it.

"I need some guarantees before we move forward."

Cruz's throat works and he clearly bites back whatever protest is on the tip of his tongue. He glances at his agent and then back to Kevin. "What do you need from me? What's it going to take?"

"The board needs you to show us that you're serious."

"You have to give me more direction than that."

"No more crazy antics in clubs. No more outrageous parties trashing whatever place you're at. You need to show us that you have a moral compass. That you're settling down."

"Settling down?" Cruz snorts.

"Yes." Kevin doesn't flinch. "As in with a serious girlfriend."

"What the . . ." His laugh finishes his sentence followed by the roll of his eyes and a hand scrubbed through his hair in obvious disbelief. But it's when he looks back at Kevin and sees the expectation in his eyes that Cruz's body reacts. His chuckle is flippant until he meets the eyes of everyone around us and realizes this isn't a joke. "Wait. You're serious?"

"I am, in fact, serious."

"That's total bullsh—you can't mandate that I have a girlfriend. You can't—"

"We can mandate anything we want. As a private capital firm, we can create whatever parameters, rules, whatever you want to call them, that we see fit. It's our money on the line too."

"What if I don't agree to this?"

"I'm pretty sure you're not going to like my answer." Kevin glances around for dramatic effect. Indifference as apparent on his face as it was on Cruz's moments ago. Clearly two can play this game. "Then again, maybe you don't want this deal as badly as it was relayed to me that you do."

"What the fuck?"

"It's that or nothing. With multi-million-dollar investments, there is always compromise for both parties." And the way Kevin says it, there is no room for discussion.

"Both parties? What exactly is Genesee compromising on when it comes to this deal?" Cruz asks.

"Cruz," Lennox warns, her stare unrelenting.

Cruz huffs out a sigh, clearly resigning himself begrudgingly to the idea.

"So let me get this straight. I sign the papers. I pretend I have a girlfriend to clean up my image. I walk the straight and narrow. And how long exactly do I have to keep up with these pretenses?"

"There is no signing anything, Mr. Navarro, until the board in fact sees that you will take this brand partnership as seriously as we do."

Cruz thumbs through the stack of papers in front of him, and I think we both realize at the same time that there isn't a contract mixed in there to be signed.

Oh. Shit. That's harsh, Kevin.

And the reason why there's no pen on the table.

A disbelieving smile paints Cruz's lips as he pushes the stack of papers back toward the center of the table, his demeanor more stoic than moments ago. "I don't like this."

"Liking it isn't a requirement. Simply understanding it and Genesee's reasons behind it are though," Kevin says.

"Did you know about this?" Cruz asks Lennox as if no one else is in the room.

She nods. "I did. I spoke with Mr. Reynoso after we talked earlier. I tried to get back in touch with you after, but you didn't answer your phone."

No doubt his phone buzzing on the table, I bet.

He nods, almost as if he's fortifying himself before he says his next words. "Okay. Fine. So I'll pretend I have a girlfriend."

"We've already taken care of that for you."

I think both Cruz's and my head whip up simultaneously.

Genesee does that? What the hell? How did I not know that? Since when have we become an escort agency?

Cruz snorts. "That's funny."

Kevin's hands clasp in front of him as he meets the eyes of everyone else around the table before landing back on Cruz. "No one seems to be laughing."

Cruz gives a desperate look toward Lennox who simply meets his gaze and nods in approval.

"I don't—"

"Here are the three candidates we've selected for you," Kevin says and pushes the three red folders he was holding earlier across the table.

Cruz skeptically eyes the solid red covers with the small Polaroids paper-clipped to the top of each before pressing his broad hands across the three of them and pushing them back toward the center of the table.

There's no way he could have looked closely enough at all of the images to make a decision that quickly.

"Her," he says, pointing to me and meeting my eyes.

What the what?

I open my mouth and then close it. This is a joke, right? I glance around the room to see if there are smiles cracking on everyone's lips and fingers pointing my way, but I'm met with nothing but uncomfortable stoicism.

No one knew I'd be sitting in on this meeting. Not even me. But now Cruz is motioning my way like he actually means me.

That's funny. I might even snort but the way heads slowly swivel my way, I can't.

"What?" Kevin looks over his shoulder at me, confusion etched in the lines of his face much like mine has to be.

"Her. *The wallflower. That's who I want to be my girlfriend.*"

The wallflower? I look over my shoulder, forgetting that there is an actual wall there so he *has* to be talking about me.

"You mean . . . *Maddix?*" Kevin asks, completely dumbfounded.

"Maddix. Yes," Cruz says, leaning back and crossing his arms over his chest. "*Her.*"

"But I don't—" Kevin holds up his hand to stop my comment, but I keep going. "This is absurd."

Kevin looks me up and down as the entire room weighs heavily with the moment. Chairs creak as people shift to look my way, but there are no papers shuffling or nails clicking on keyboards. It's silent but for the anticipation of his response.

My cheeks heat and I swear a bead of sweat trickles down the line of my spine despite the air conditioner blasting in the room.

There's no way they can be serious. Cruz for saying it. Kevin for remotely considering it.

I draw in a slow, even breath under the room's scrutiny.

"I'm flattered, but I'm not—"

"Fine," Kevin says with a resolute nod. He barely meets my eyes before turning back toward Cruz. "That'll work perfectly."

CHAPTER FOUR

Maddix

"**T**HIS TURNED OUT EVEN BETTER THAN I ANTICIPATED," KEVIN rambles as I practically jog a few steps to catch up with him, my mind swirling and disbelief mounting.

"Better for whom?" I ask. "*You?* Because last I checked I should get a say in this."

"You're well aware of the culture here at Genesee. We take care of our partners. Meeting their needs for ultimate success is our number one goal."

Stop blowing smoke up my ass, Kevin. You just gave me away like I was an escort . . . like I'm yours to give.

"Again, shouldn't I have a say in this?"

He stops in the vacant hallways and narrows his eyes at me. "Are you saying you don't want to do your job?"

"I'm not an actress. I can't pull this off." The words are a stuttered excuse.

"Yes, you can. You'll do just fine. You'll easily sell this whole new image for us." He shrugs. "The player who fell so head over heels in love with you that you reformed him into the doting boyfriend."

If the quick Google search I was able to do while they were buttoning up the meeting is any indicator, there is no way in hell anyone is going to believe this schtick or that I'll be able to pass as Cruz Navarro's girlfriend.

For one, I look nothing like the women he normally dates. I have blond hair and green eyes while he prefers the more exotic Salma Hayek type. And two, there are a million different women in the photos. The man sure as shit knows how to be seen—and *always* seen with stunning women on his arm in designer threads and shimmering diamonds.

My wardrobe consists of department store deals and thrift shop needle-in-a-haystack finds.

"This isn't going to work." Maybe if I repeat it enough, he'll start to believe it. Maybe I will too.

"No?"

I stare at him and his furrowed brows. At his piercing eyes. I hear his sigh that says he's exasperated and isn't going to take much more of this. "What do you plan on getting out of this job? You asked to be in on this meeting because this is what you wanted. But what is it that you want? A promotion? A leg up over everyone else on the same playing field? What are you willing to sacrifice, Miss Hart?"

"I don't—wait, you're offering me a promotion if I do this?"

There's a glimmer in his eyes. He dangled the carrot, and like an idiot I just took it.

An idiot? Maybe more like an opportunist.

"I'm guaranteeing you one, yes, along with a bonus to cover the things you'll need to play the part."

"What do you mean?" I'm still struggling to wrap my head around this.

"Cruz Navarro's girlfriend can't be seen wearing knockoffs from Target, shoes from Famous Footwear, and a purse from a store in a mall."

I glance down at my jeans and generic sandals, offended but too intimidated and embarrassed to speak up. "Wow. Okay."

"I'm not trying to hurt your feelings. This look works for Austin, for your everyday, but it does not work for the glamorous lifestyle you'll be stepping into."

What the fuck is happening here? He's talking like I've already said yes. "I appreciate the vote of support, but I can't just pick up and go to wherever I'd have to go. I have things and obligations and—"

"Things?" He narrows his eyes. "You have something more pressing than being the girlfriend of a millionaire who is arguably one of the best drivers in the world? Of traipsing from continent to continent, country to country via private jet, and hanging with the who's who of racing and Hollywood? I mean . . ." He holds his hands up nonchalantly. "I don't know about you, but I doubt there will be many times in your life when you're asked to pick up at a moment's notice and get a chance to be someone you most likely would never get the chance to become."

The red folders he's holding peek out from under his arm. He came to the meeting prepared with three candidates for this role, so I know he has a budget for this fiasco. And if he has a budget, that means he most likely has board approval.

But this is madness. For me. To become someone I'd never get the chance to become.

"A chance to be someone?" I ask, but . . . *Jesus.* Now that he puts it that way. Isn't my goal to get out of this town and see the world? To learn and grow and not be here, stuck in the same rut my parents have comfortably and willingly lived in their whole lives?

But reason has me holding back.

I don't belong in Cruz's world.

All I asked for was to sit in on this meeting.

This is crazy.

"A chance to be someone," he repeats.

"But I have a boyfriend," I blurt out, uncertain what else to say.

"Then break up with him," Kevin deadpans.

"Easy for you to say."

He nods resolutely. "Yes. It is. Quite easy. You've worked here how long? Eighteen months?"

He knows how long I've been working here? I glance over my shoulder to see if there is someone, somehow getting him up to speed on me. Or maybe that already happened. Maybe that was what his flurry of texts were as the meeting ended.

"Yes. Something like that." I glance around the empty hallway and try to figure out what he's getting at.

"And in that year and a half, I've never seen a trace of that boyfriend. Not at our Christmas party. Not at our summer picnic. Not flowers on your desk on your birthday. Not a peep about him to your co-workers."

I blink slowly almost as if that will help me process what he's saying better. How in the hell would he know—

"I know everything that goes on in my offices, Maddix." He smiles, and I'm not sure if I should be reassured by it or worried by it. "I can't be an effective boss if I don't."

I'm too flustered to argue with him or compute the fact that he knows all of this. That he's actually right.

Michael and I are . . . casual. Comfortable. *Boring*. But maybe after a year and a half we should be more than casual and yet, neither of us have felt strongly enough to ask for more or do something about it.

Another conclusion I came to last night that is somehow perfectly timed with today's unexpected events.

It's like I'm hit by lightning as I stand here, looking at my boss's boss. How was I wondering one minute what I was going to eat for lunch and the next minute realizing this strange opportunity might just be a way to get out of this town? Out of this rut? And on to the life I have pinned on my vision board on my wall in my apartment?

I shift on my feet as a thousand thoughts race through my head. I could quit. It's not like I couldn't find another job to give me marketing and brand experience to make ends meet. They are a dime a dozen with the same shitty pay scale. But . . . it wouldn't be this job. With this company. One that has endless opportunities and connections if you can make it through the lower-level grunt-work phase.

But any other job wouldn't have the base of my spine tingling. It wouldn't have goosebumps on my skin and anticipation mixed with excitement pumping in my blood.

I've traveled. Not much. Not outside the United States other than Mexico. And this . . . this is a chance of a lifetime.

Holy shit.

I can't believe I'm about to do this.

"Yes."

"Yes?" he asks.

"Yes." I nod, my heart all but jumping out of my chest.

"And the boyfriend?" He cocks his head to the side.

"He'll understand."

"Not understand. You have to break up with him."

My body has a visceral reaction to the comment but only because I don't want to hurt Michael's feelings. Not because I actually think there's a future with him.

"I'm aware."

"No. I don't think you are. If you don't make a clean break, if you contact him and continue to play nice with him, the media and armchair detectives on social media will find out. They'll have it plastered all over every site about how you're cheating on their beloved driver. So you need to end the relationship before you leave for both the company's and your sake." He crosses his arms over his chest. "People are obsessed with their driver. They have no mercy for anyone who wrongs them. And the perception of you cheating on him?" He whistles in response.

"Jesus," I mutter more to myself than to him. He has to be exaggerating. *Has to be.* "There were people in the conference room who know differently. Won't they say anything—"

"They've all signed NDAs. They know our legal team and that it's better to be tight-lipped than to say anything."

I stare at him blinking. "But—"

"And the story you'll tell everyone is that you've been asked to travel alongside Genesee's prospective client, Cruz Navarro. You're there to document his day-to-day so that we know how to better market the new, top-secret deal we're working on. And naturally, all this time you've spent together over the past few weeks preparing for this trip, for this deal, has led you to become close. Close enough to let feelings blossom and evolve."

Blossom? That's a word I never expected to hear uttered from Kevin's mouth.

"And people are going to buy that?"

"It doesn't matter if they do or they don't because actions speak louder than words, and yours won't give them any reason to question the suddenness of your relationship. To those hopeless romantics out there, love at first sight exists. To the others, for all they know, the two of you have been fighting your attraction during these past couple of weeks but now that you've been thrust together for work reasons, you just couldn't hold back anymore." There is a mocking singsong to his voice that has me wanting to roll my eyes.

"And you think that's going to work?"

"You bet your promotion and raise it will." He winks.

Shit. Shit. Shit.

I mean, the only other thing I can say is *fuck, fuck, fuck,* but that's not going to make me feel any better.

"But my parents. My . . ."

"They're welcome to sign an NDA. Or they can stay in the dark like everyone else. By the time you come back home, the 'relationship' will be over and there will be no need to explain why you fake-dated a man in trade for a promotion."

Jesus. This sounds so bad.

"You have this all planned out, don't you?"

He raises the red folders under his arm as if it's an obvious question. "I do. Yes. Have you ever known me not to be prepared?"

I pinch the bridge of my nose. Lie to everyone I know about a boyfriend that's pretend? Because clearly nothing can go wrong with that scenario, right?

You wanted to take action today, Maddix. Here's your action being served up to you on a platter.

"So?" Kevin raises his eyebrows to essentially ask if I'm in—*again*—before he folds his arms over his chest.

"Yes. Okay. I'll do it."

A slow smile plays at the corners of his mouth. "Well, look who just stepped onto the playing field. Nice to have you on the team."

Why do I get a weird sense of pride from his fucked-up praise?

"Thanks," I mutter, uncertain what response he's expecting.

"Cruz is heading out tomorrow. I'll get you the details on time and how to get runway access for the private jet. Make sure you're on the flight."

"Yes. Sure. I mean—" A private jet? I've never even flown first class. "Where—"

"My assistant will send you all the details. Take the rest of the day to"— he looks me up and down again—"shop and freshen up your wardrobe. To make those clean breaks, tidy up affairs, and go tell your friends and family you're heading out for a while on a job *field trip.*"

"Okay." This is real. Really real. "When do I tell them to expect me to be back?"

"The board votes quarterly." He glances at his watch. "Three months should be a vague enough time frame."

Three months?

My eyes practically bug out of my head. How do I pack for three months? What have I gotten myself into? My thoughts spiral out of control. "What about my rent? My car payment? I mean you're giving me a day's notice to pack up my life—"

"There's no need to pack up anything. It can all stay where it is. Coverage for your rent and bills will all be included in the compensation package. As I said, my assistant will be in touch. She'll have a company credit card to give you to cover your clothing and expenses abroad. She'll also have you write down the bills that need to be covered while you're gone, and she'll get those funds direct deposited into your account for you with your paycheck."

"Right. Thanks." The words don't sound so certain.

He nods, a smug look on his face. "Well, Hart. I'm glad you said yes. I wasn't too keen on firing you and having to retrain someone new. Besides, I've had enough drama for one day."

CHAPTER FIVE

Cruz

THIS IS BULLSHIT.

Utter and total bullshit.

I press the clutch and shift gears, the engine revving with the change.

I watch the speedometer rise slowly as the trees and fields around me become one massive blur of color.

A fucking girlfriend?

Another shift. A subtle lurch of the car as it clicks into place.

A goddamn babysitter?

"How far are you going to let me push you? Huh?" I croon to my rental Ford GT as I eat up the asphalt of the open road before me.

El patriarca not wanting to see me?

The wheel shudders under my grip. The power—pure intoxication.

This blessing and curse of a last name.

Push. Push. Push.

That's all anybody wants to do to me. All anyone wants from me is to see how far they can push me before I snap.

Just like I am this fucking car.

Sofia: Are you okay? I'm here. You can need me, you know?

Sofia. My little sister gets it. The text she sent me earlier says as much. And no, everything isn't fine. Far fucking from it. No matter how much she wants it to be, it isn't. It can't be. Not when I'm forced to live by his ridiculous standards. By his need for me to live up to what he never could be. Not when she never has had to.

The car shifts again as I add more pressure to the pedal.

I need to get back home to Monaco. Back to my car. To my team. Back to the feel of the track beneath my ass and the power of the engine whining all around me. To the roaring crowds. To the synchronized actions of my pit crew.

To the one place where I feel the most in control of everything. Ironic, really, when that is where I technically have the least control.

My chest aches like my rib cage is closing in.

El patriarca said not to bother coming home to visit before heading to Zandvoort.

My grandfather. My idol.

This goddamn deal. The doe-eyed woman who didn't know who I was. *Maddix.* Who treated me with compassion when I don't fucking deserve it.

The speedometer hits one eighteen. I ease up as tears burn the backs of my eyes and the pit of my stomach churns. As the car slows back down. No need to break it. I've already broken enough things that need fixing.

Fucking Kevin and his board don't think I can do this. Walk their razor-thin line. But I will. Just to spite my father who thinks I'll screw this deal. Simply because this is a challenge I refuse to prove him right on. I'll walk both of their lines so damn fine, teetering on the edge of what they want and what I need.

And I'll win them over. The contract. Genesee Capital. The hundreds of millions that will come with it.

And I'll prove to my grandfather I'm the man he thinks I am. A true Navarro.

And when the time is right, I'll . . . *I'll take control.* Live my life. How I truly want to.

My radar detector begins to beep, and I let up on the gas completely before I get caught. No doubt going one hundred miles per hour on a straight road in Podunk, Texas would land me in jail.

And I don't want to miss my flight.

Don't want to piss off Genesee and risk this deal. Because this is the deal I want. This is the deal I pushed for, pushed Lennox to chase.

This will be my ultimate legacy. My name everywhere. My likeness ingrained in day-to-day culture.

An ultimate fuck you to my father.

An unending homage to the only man I aim to make proud—el patriarca.

CHAPTER SIX

Maddix

"**W**HERE IN THE WORLD IS ALL THIS MONEY COMING FROM TO buy all this?" my dad asks as he flattens the shopping bags to keep them for whatever he thinks he'll need them for but will never use. Much like the flattened wrapping paper my mom keeps from years past—*just in case*. "Nordstrom, huh?" He lifts his eyebrows. "*Fancy.*"

Not fancy. In fact, I feel like an imposter with all these new clothes. I guarantee that Cruz Navarro's woman wouldn't be caught dead in a Nordstrom store—too mainstream, too mass market—but on a moment's notice and with a new company credit card, the five outfits I bought are the best I could do.

"Just mix and match them with your usual stuff," my mom says as she smiles from the doorway, arms crossed, not having a clue about the world I'm stepping into other than having to travel abroad for work. "This is all so exciting. You getting to traipse around working with a real-life race car driver."

Traipse and working. Yes, well . . . clearly she's bought the lie, and she's the first person who normally can see right through me. Just because this might work doesn't mean my conscience over lying is any cleaner.

My internal debate over telling them was endless. But considering my mom can't keep a secret to save her life and the fact that my dad would repeatedly tell me how I'm out of my damn mind for agreeing to do this—I chose not to.

When a man's motto in life is *an honest day's work for an honest day's pay,* there is no way in hell he'll even remotely understand his daughter faking a relationship to the world for money.

Besides, telling them the truth would jeopardize the lies I had to tell Michael. And Michael . . . there isn't a vindictive bone in his body, but then again, I've never seen him dumped and then replaced rapidly by another, very famous man.

Do you hear yourself, Maddix? How ridiculous this sounds? Fake dating, a famous man, a vindictive ex, and everything in between? What next? You're going to be in tabloids in Europe?

Oh God.

I am, aren't I?

"What's that look on your face for?" my dad asks, bringing my head back into the here and now. It shocks me out of my sudden—and seemingly recurring—panic.

"I'm pinching myself that this is real. That I'm getting the chance to do this—travel, assist Cruz. I mean . . . all of this is so sudden," I say as I open my carry-on and double-check that I have my power adapters and charging cords for all of my devices.

"It is, but it's also so very exciting. Now don't you worry about a thing. I'll come by and water your flowers. I'll make sure your mail is picked up. I'll just take care of everything," my mom says. Not like it's a hardship considering I live in a cottage-like granny flat about a football field length away from their main house on this big plot of land. Property that has been passed down from generation to generation outside of Austin.

Sure my place is older and it's near my parents, but the rent is cheap and when you're saving up to buy a house—or move to New York City someday—you suck it up and pretend like living near your parents is no big deal.

"Thank you. But . . . I probably would have killed them anyway."

"Shush. I'll tend to them." She stares at me as her eyes well with pride. "I can't wait to tell everyone that my baby is a bigwig now."

My dad rolls his eyes behind her back, and I fight back a smile as he clears his throat loudly. His way of saying, *let's get the show on the road before she starts blubbering.*

"Mom, I'm twenty-four. I'm not a baby. And I'm far from a bigwig."

"I still don't understand why you had to break things off with Michael," she says and then holds her hands up. "Not that I'm one to meddle with your affairs."

Remember that in the coming weeks. *Pretty please.*

I sigh. "I know you guys like him, but . . . we weren't going anywhere and thought this might be the best time for a clean break."

"Oh, honey—"

"No. It's a good thing. It's . . . best if we use this time to figure out what it is we actually want." And it's true. Was it hard to break things off with him? Definitely. Did I catch a slight startle of relief flicker through his eyes when I brought it up last night? Yes.

"Wow. So mature," she muses.

I lift my eyebrows as I catch the slightest of smiles and the quick glance between my parents. One they still think I don't catch despite not being a little kid anymore. My mom and dad have tolerated Michael. They didn't dislike him . . . they were just indifferent about him.

Much like I was, if I'm honest with myself.

"I'll be traveling a lot. I'll be super busy with my work schedule while there." Work I don't exactly want to define right now. "Maybe all of this happening is Fate's way of telling me I need to shake things up a bit."

"Agreed. One hundred percent." My mom gasps and holds her hand to her chest, startling both me and my dad. "What if he falls for her, Gavin?" she asks my dad, eyes wide and almost bouncing on her toes, as if I'm not present.

I choke on air and start coughing to cover it up. *If only she knew.* The upside is that comment just made it so much easier to sell the lie to them when I'm thousands of miles away.

"Stranger things have happened," my dad says in his deep baritone as he scrubs a hand over his trimmed beard. "But a word of advice, if you do happen to fall in love with this Latin lover—"

"Dad!"

"I googled him. What dad is going to let his daughter run off to a job and not research where and who she's going with?" He shrugs. "As I was saying, if things do happen to . . . *progress*, make sure he knows how to get his hands dirty. It's one thing to look smooth driving that car. It's another to know how to work under its hood."

My mom rolls her eyes and then smiles gently when she glances at the clock. "You need to get going."

"I know."

I'm not sure why, but when I hug them goodbye, I feel like it's for so much longer than a couple of months. It's almost as if I know everything is going to change, when there is no possible way I could ever know that.

Gravel crunching under tires tells me that my rideshare is here. We finish saying our goodbyes, and when I look up, I'm taken aback by the sight of Michael at the end of my driveway.

"I'm guessing he's not the rideshare," my dad says.

Fucking perfect.

"Um . . . I'll go talk to him while I wait for my driver," I say.

"Fine. Sure. We're going to head back to the house. Let you two have your privacy."

We exchange a few more hugs. My mom sheds a tear and my dad gets that gruff voice that says he needs to leave before tears burn in his eyes too. Within a minute, they're driving off in their utility vehicle toward their house as I make my way toward Michael.

He stands with his hands shoved in his pockets and his ass resting against the fender of his SUV. His blond hair is disheveled, and his jaw is clenched as he meets my eyes.

"For the record, I think this is shit," he says by way of greeting.

I was fine with how we left things last night. Him angry. Me feeling some weird sense of relief. I thought his anger had more to do with his bruised ego than us breaking up.

I look at him, my eyes squinting from the sunlight, and nod, not wanting to exacerbate this any more than it already is.

"You're trying to be someone you're not, Maddix."

"Or what if I'm trying to be the someone I want to be?" I counter. My night was spent doing a lot of reflecting. I didn't work two jobs to put myself through college just to snub an opportunity like this. Is my college degree in faking a relationship? Most definitely not, but would I be stupid to pass up the doors this charade might open for me and their exposure to different career and networking opportunities? Definitely.

"You could never be the woman on that stupid pinboard of yours. It's fantasy. *She's a fantasy.* Pipe dreams are just that. Unattainable and unrealistic. And the fact that you think you're better than everyone else because you're going to go chase yours is asinine. But don't worry, I'll still take you back when you realize your mistake. When you come to your senses and realize the girl you are belongs here. Not out there in the world." He chuckles like his comment is the wittiest thing in the world.

It's not. In fact, it shows his true colors. A whole rainbow full of them that I want no part of.

They make it so much easier to just nod at him as my rideshare pulls up. To deposit my luggage in the trunk without a glance his way before sliding into the backseat without another word.

Goodbye, Michael.

Ties have been cut. *You just made sure of that with your comments.*

With a deep breath, I glance over my shoulder one last time in the direction of my parents' house and then nod.

I'm ready to play the role.

It isn't until my driver pulls onto the main road that I finally exhale in relief and then inhale in anticipation of where this road is about to take me.

Nerves rattle with each minute that passes. Nerves that have my hands trembling as I scan the page of instructions that Kevin's assistant sent over to me. Not like I haven't already committed it to memory or anything.

Here's to an adventure, Maddix.

And to accepting what I've sacrificed to get there.

You've got this, Hart.

You've got this.

CHAPTER SEVEN

Maddix

I'M IN WAY OVER MY HEAD.

Like a million miles plus infinity over my head.

That's all I can think as I climb the last stair to the entrance of the private jet. I am astounded with all the finer things in a life that sure as hell isn't mine.

The interior of the jet is a light taupe with burled walnut paneling. Plush, oversized leather chairs face each other with a table in between. This same setup is repeated four more times over the length of the cabin. The interior is bright with running lights in the ceiling and the floor that only helps to brighten the sunshine coming in the numerous windows running its length.

It's luxurious and decadent in a way I only ever imagined, and I have to pinch myself to believe that I'm really going to be flying on this.

I can only imagine what my dad would say if he saw this setup.

Standing in the doorway, I'm dumbfounded and astounded, and truth be told, more than intimidated to walk inside. A stunning woman in a cashmere sweater and black slacks sees me. Her smile brightens momentarily and then her eyes narrow. "Hi. May I help you?" she asks cautiously.

Shit. Where is Cruz? Not like I'd find any comfort in seeing him as we've spent a whole five minutes alone together max, but at least I wouldn't feel like they think I'm about to hijack the jet.

"Yes. I'm Maddix. I'm here for—"

Laughter comes from the back section hidden by a partition of sorts. Laughter that I know to be Cruz's. The sound of it causes my shoulders to sag in relief, but at the same time, my heart jumps in anticipation of all this strange newness I'm embarking upon.

A sultry laugh follows Cruz's, and I must look like an idiot as I stare at the doorway, waiting for Cruz, ignoring the woman eyeing me.

"Cruz. I'm Cruz's . . ." *Girlfriend? Acquaintance? Plaything?*

Kevin's list of instructions flashes through my head. Be seen. Be affectionate. Sell the lie so the public and the board believes it. Sell the idea that Cruz is the doting boyfriend. Make him appear settled and successful.

Because that's going to be easy.

Especially when minute one on this journey, and a woman's hand is already resting possessively on his bicep.

Perfect.

I open my mouth to speak as Cruz enters the main cabin.

"Madds. You're here," Cruz says, flashing a heart-stopping grin.

Considering he left the meeting yesterday without looking my way, I'm definitely surprised at the warm greeting. At the nickname. At that smile of his. If my stomach wasn't already tied up in knots, that dazzling grin of his would do it.

Maybe he's accepted this whole idea when clearly, he was still fighting it yesterday.

Maybe this will be easier than I thought. We can act out this charade, convince the board he's reformed and be over with it sooner rather than later. Then, I'll be on my merry way.

But as for now, my head is swimming with thoughts as Cruz, Cashmere Sweater, and another woman who has emerged from the back behind Cruz all stand there and stare at me in expectation.

I lift my hand. "Yes. Yeah. That's me." Oh my God. I couldn't sound any more like an awkward teenager if I tried.

"Luggage?" Cruz asks as he takes a sip of the water bottle in his hand.

"The . . . whoever took it from me before I boarded," I say as Cashmere Sweater moves toward me and takes my carry-on from me, ushering me to my seat.

"I'm Mellie," she says. "I'll be assisting you on the flight today. And you're Maddix? Cruz's . . ."

"*What exactly are you, Madds?*" Cruz asks, amusement tinging his tone and those eyes of his glistening with humor, as he slides into one of the plush seats and motions for me to do the same.

I work a swallow, hating this feeling like I'm the butt of an inside joke that everyone knows but me.

"Give the poor girl a break," the woman whose hand was on Cruz says as she moves forward. She's even more gorgeous than Mellie with legs a mile long and sun-kissed skin that would make anyone jealous. She steps beside Cruz, her hand casually going to his shoulder—*again*—before leaning down and murmuring something in his ear.

They both chuckle and when he looks up at her, he also places his hand on hers. "Not today, Lola."

Her smile is as sultry as her laugh. "Why, Cruz Navarro, are you turning me down?"

Their eyes meet and he nods once. "In fact, I am."

"Ouch," she says, dramatically snatching her hand back from his shoulder, before taking a few steps toward the cockpit. She winks. "You'll be back."

His chuckle is loud and telling. You'll be back. Right. Sounds like this plane has seen a lot of miles . . . *in the mile high club*. A club I most definitely won't be joining. Especially given Legs A Mile Long Lola has clearly traversed with Cruz before. "Never say never, right?"

Guess I was wrong about him willingly selling this whole relationship thing. Saying shit like that tells me he most definitely isn't.

Wonderful.

"Hope not." Lola stops before me and holds out her hand. "Lola Macias. I'll be your captain today." *Captain?* "I promise to try and keep the turbulence to a minimum. Besides, this guy causes enough turbulence as it is when you're with him."

"But . . ." *I'm not with him.* I smile softly and shake her hand. "I've been warned."

"That you have. Us women need to stick together." She winks, glances back at Cruz, and just shakes her head. "We should be cleared and ready for takeoff shortly."

"Thank you." I watch her walk toward the cockpit and through the open door, see her take a seat before beginning to flip switches with confidence and authority.

"You can take a seat," Cruz says as Mellie busies herself near the back of the plane. "I promise, I don't bite."

"Oh yes. I should. Okay," I say, suddenly flustered now that it's just me and him and a whole hell of a lot of time on our hands before we land in . . . wherever it is we're going.

"Do you always answer in threes?"

"What? No. I don't think so." His grin widens as I realize I just proved him right. "Only when I'm nervous."

He lifts his eyebrows. "And I make you nervous?"

I shrug. "This whole thing does."

He tilts his head to the side, lips pursed, and eyes running up and down the length of me. They assess and scrutinize and make me aware of his calf resting so very close to mine beneath the table separating us. "Why?"

I snort. "For obvious reasons." I fasten the seatbelt over my lap and double-check its tightness. Anything to avoid the look in Cruz's eyes.

"I see," he murmurs as the jet begins to move.

Like a little kid, I look out the window at the runway and beyond as we taxi. I haven't flown much to begin with, let alone on a private jet, so I'm going to take this in.

But it's when I look back toward Cruz that I realize he has abandoned our conversation, and it's not because I was preoccupied with being enamored. Since we're facing each other—his back to the front of the plane, and me forward—I'm given a front-row view to the whitening of Cruz's knuckles as he grips the armchair. He closes his eyes and rests his head back.

At first, I think he's playing me. A Formula 1 driver who cheats death every time he straps in the car is afraid of flying? There's no way.

But apparently there is, because Cruz is most definitely apprehensive about taking off. His face pulls tight, his knuckles stay white, and his breathing is deep and even.

It's only after the plane levels off that his fingers let up and his eyes flutter open to meet mine again. We stare at each other without speaking as Mellie places a tray of fresh fruit and bottles of water between us.

"So, Madds. The only—"

"Maddix."

"*Madds.*" His grin is infuriating, especially when I know he's doing this to get a reaction out of me. Is it wrong though that as much as I hate when people call me that, a small part of me loves the nickname? It's almost as if in a world of all these people vying for his attention, I'm important enough for him to give a pet name to.

Get a grip, *Madds.*

"As I was saying"—he flashes another dazzling grin—"the only way this is going to work is if you talk to me, because I don't know you well enough to interpret that look you keep giving me . . . and that long sigh-thing you keep doing. So . . . you said I make you nervous *for obvious reasons*. What exactly are those reasons?"

I glance over my shoulder to where Mellie is busy in the back where I can assume there is a galley of some sort. "I don't know how we're going to pull this off," I whisper cautiously.

"You can talk in a normal voice. Everyone here is on my staff and has signed nondisclosure agreements."

"Kevin told me that no one can know the truth," I continue to whisper. "That I have to sell this like my job depends on it."

Cruz nods, his finger running over his bottom lip as he does so. "And does it?"

"It wasn't stated outright but . . . I can infer. Yes, it does."

"And is that why you said yes?" His voice is soft, probing, and I hate that I want to ramble about the events of the last twenty-four hours to him when I'm sure he doesn't care.

"Partly."

"Partly?" His eyes narrow. "What's the other part of the partly?"

I shrug, a tad flustered over being put on the spot. "I have my reasons."

"Ah, the cryptic response that means she's holding the real answer close to the vest because she's not quite sure she can trust me yet. Either that or she's so attracted to me she's embarrassed to let me know that she has posters of me on her walls and one as a screensaver on her phone."

I bark out a laugh. "You're serious with this shit?"

"Show me your screensaver then," he says.

"Absolutely not." I move my cell off the table and tuck it under my thigh.

A smile toys at the corners of his mouth. Playful is not what I expected from him and yet here we are with gazes locked and smiles warring.

"And yet you still don't think we're going to be able to pull this off. Why's that? I'm me. You're you. Clearly, we get along."

"It's been a whole hour."

"Good thing I have stamina."

I roll my eyes. "Whatever."

"Okay. Fine." He holds his hands up.

"My turn. You tell me. Why did you pick me?"

"Because I hate the color red. My rivals bathe in that damn color."

I snort and then realize he's dead serious. "You're not joking."

"Nope. I hate the color red."

"So if the folders had been blue . . .?"

"Not sure." He grins and then narrows his eyes. "Why won't this work?"

"I think we're two very different people who live in vastly different worlds. It feels like it might be a tough reality to sell."

"And yet opposites attract every day."

"True. But when is the last time you had a girlfriend, let alone a steady one?" I counter.

Cruz's laugh rings out. "The woman doesn't hold any punches. I like it."

"Your drinks," Mellie says as she slides what looks like a Negroni in front of Cruz and then a vodka cranberry in front of me.

What the—

My eyes whip up to hers and then to Cruz's. An absent "thank-you" falls from my lips but confusion reigns.

A smile plays at one corner of Cruz's mouth. "Since we're *together*, I took the time to search your social media to learn more about you. This"— he points to my cocktail—"seemed to be your drink of choice and so I took the liberty to make sure we had it on board for you."

Oh. *Ooohhh.* My eyes widen as I realize all the things he may have seen.

He nods to tell me my assumption is correct. "And yes, I saw good ol' Michael there too. Should I be jealous of my competition? I'm not used to having competition if I'm honest, so this is all new territory for me as well."

"Competition?" I practically snort. How could he ever think of someone like Michael as competition? It's not like Michael was a slouch in the looks department, I have to give him that, but on a scale of one to Cruz, he is about a three.

"What does he think about all of this? No doubt he has strong opinions." And the way Cruz says it, makes me uncertain if he's amused by this or serious.

"Hitting with the hard questions right off the bat, huh?" This was not how I expected this to go. I should feel raw from breaking up with a man I dated for a year and a half . . . but I don't. And that is . . . liberating in a sense.

"I think it's an important one."

"Michael and I broke up," I say softly.

"I see," he murmurs as he lifts his glass to his lips but doesn't avert his eyes from mine. They seek and search, but he doesn't ask the curious questions I can see weighing in his eyes. "So you broke up with your real boyfriend to be with your pretend boyfriend. Interesting."

"It's complicated."

"Oh, so you're not attracted to me, then."

"No. I mean yes. I mean, it's not that."

"Not exactly a boost to my ego, Madds." He pouts.

"You're infuriating."

"And you're newly single. Dare I say that I see the sowing of some of your wild oats on this adventure?"

"No. Not at all. I'm working."

He chuckles, and I swear to God, the sound vibrates through me and straight to every nerve ending. He's charming without trying. And he's hands down gorgeous even with his hair a mess and his jaw unshaven.

In all the chaos and, dare I say it, excitement last night, I spent hours poring over everything there is to know about Cruz Navarro. He was born into the family of racing legends. Of Formula 1 world champions. A Spaniard living the life of luxury and excess in Monaco with the majority of other drivers. He's partied with who's who of Hollywood and members of royalty. He's traveled the world several times over. Being promoted to Formula 1 with Team Gravitas at the age of twenty-two, he's come close to winning the elusive title two times in the past four years, but never actually clinching it.

The media paints a picture-perfect image of the Navarro family. One of affluence, pedigree, and expectation. Sergio Navarro, Cruz's grandfather, reached the pinnacle of the sport at age twenty-five. After that first world championship, he went on to win four more during his career. Then there was Dominic Navarro, Cruz's father. A man who was thought to be just as skilled and devastating on the track as his revered father, but never seemed to win a championship during his eight-year tenure as a driver. *A disappointment* was the description in one article that stuck in my head.

And now there is Cruz. The third in line to a Formula 1 dynasty with the weight of the world on his shoulders to reclaim the greatness with which his grandfather once dominated with. *Skilled. Technical. Cunning. Fearless.* All four words were used to describe him. All four a means to explain why he's placed second in the points championship twice already in his short tenure, and that the world championship is so close that everyone in his camp can all but taste it.

He's been slated to be the racer his father was supposed to become but never was.

Talk about pressure. About being under a microscope when an entire sport and its worldwide fan base watches your every move, waiting and wanting it for you.

Maybe that's why his antics have been documented for all to see. His indifference toward those transgressions shown in interviews. But his pull among the younger demographic is strong despite nonchalance—or maybe because of it—hence Genesee Capital's pursuit of him.

Cruz is the one thumbing his nose at the patriarchy despite benefitting *from* the Navarro patriarchy.

But as I sit here across from him and question what the next few weeks if not months will hold, I don't see any of those warring traits.

I'm a people-watcher. Always have been. And over the past twenty-four hours I've consumed endless clips, interviews, even Cruz's own social media posts, that show me that Cruz has a distinct *on* persona.

I'm also starting to believe there is an *off* persona that's rarely seen too.

It's the man in the break room having a panic attack. It's the talented driver continuously compared to his noteworthy family. I'm wondering if the seeming difference is possible defiance—a man unapologetically trying to be Cruz Navarro and no one else.

That man who is utterly devastating with his flashy smile and rumbling voice. It's no wonder women throw themselves at him.

His chuckle interrupts my thoughts. So does that slow crawl of a smile that does funny things to my insides, when it's stupid to even think whatever it's doing is real.

"One can work and sow oats at the same time. I won't tell your boss if you don't."

"You're not funny. *This is important*," I say to try and even the footing of the ground it feels like he's trying to tilt beneath my feet.

I straighten in my seat, not wanting to continue on this topic. This isn't a get-to-know-you session as I expected. And maybe I anticipated Cruz Navarro to be more aloof, more of a pain in my ass, when he's being neither.

"I live in *important*," he teases and motions to my drink. "Are you afraid to drink around me? Afraid I'll take advantage of you or is it more you might believe some of the rumors out there about me, and you're not sure if you want to or don't want to?"

"Rumors?"

"That's a lot of baggage to go through for a first date. Maybe we should start with something simple." He nudges my leg beneath the table when I'm already fully aware that his leg is positioned casually between mine. "Like—"

"Like rules and parameters. What you expect from me. What I expect from you. Kevin gave me a list of what—"

"Jesus. Can we not be so uptight on the first go-round here? Kevin is nowhere in sight. Therefore, his list doesn't matter. So tell me something, Madds—"

"Maddix," I huff.

"Hmm. You're strung so tight, it's going to be fun plucking your strings one by one until you come undone."

Our eyes meet, his flirt game in full effect. But is he flirting to prove a point or is he flirting because he really thinks there is chemistry here?

You shouldn't care, Madds.

Shit. Maddix.

He already has my head in circles.

"We should lay down our boundaries."

"Lay down?" He smirks.

I huff. "Discuss. Determine. Outline. That kind of thing."

"You know the Miss Priss thing is kind of a turn-on for me." He leans back and sinks his upper teeth into his lip. "Continue. By all means. I'll just sit here and watch."

"Look. I'm serious." He's infuriating. And adorable if a man that's as sexy as he is can also be adorable. "We need to—"

"What do you like to do for fun?"

"What?" I stare at him blankly.

"Fun. Let loose. Have a good time?" He lifts his eyebrows. "What is it that you like to do because your social media didn't really show me."

No doubt, my life is a bore compared to his. There is no jet-setting from one place to the next. There is no exotic travel or celebrity hob-knobbing. My life is one he would never understand in a million years. "I like to read."

"How fun," he says drolly.

"Don't knock it." I tap my knee against his.

"Oh, there's that fire again." He winks.

"And I like music."

"Okay. I can get with that. Who do you like? What bands? What artists?"

Knowing him, I'll say I like someone and he'll say he knows him personally or some shit like that. "Does it matter?"

"Considering we're supposed to be fucking each other, yes, it does matter."

I cough over my own breath. "Well. Um. Okay."

He shrugs and fights a smile. "Why sugarcoat it, right?"

"That's one way of putting it." I take my first sip of my drink and wonder why I haven't already downed it and ordered another one to soothe my nerves. "For the record, I doubt anyone on this jet buys that we're a couple."

"Why's that?"

"Because I look nothing like the women you date. Because you're the pie in the sky. Because this is just ludicrous."

"Do you sell yourself short often? Is this a normal thing you do? I've gotta say, Madds, we just met and I'm already finding that trait of yours rather annoying. That might have to go on the things we fight about list." He smacks his hands together and rubs them. "Do you fight dirty? I bet you do. I bet you throw the kitchen sink in there with it."

"No. I . . . don't."

"Because hesitating when you answer says otherwise." He rolls his eyes but his smile remains. "I need to know things."

"Things?"

"Mm-hmm. Like what are your turn offs? Your turn-ons?"

"For someone who was wholeheartedly against this twenty-four hours ago, you sure are embracing this. Why?"

"Maybe I've seen the error of my ways."

"Or maybe you're being bribed."

"The possibility of a billion dollars when all is said and done over the years is a pretty convincing bribe."

I choke on my sip. I had no idea. Absolutely no idea that was what was possibly at stake here. There weren't really any terms discussed at our meeting other than him having a girlfriend and appearing settled. No wonder the board is wanting him to chill and act like he's more than the playboy prince of Formula 1.

"You were in on the meeting but didn't know?" His eyes narrow as he studies me. "I take that choke as a no. Well, now you know. Michael is out. I'm in. And now we're stuck together for better or worse while I do the song and dance for your boss until the board is satisfied. So . . ." He clasps his hands in front of him like he means business. "That's where we're at."

"And no one is going to buy it."

"So you say, but my incentive is worth it. Let's hope like hell yours is too because I'm not the easiest fucker in the world to date . . ."

"Thanks for the warning."

"Did you find something different in your Google search of me?"

"I didn't . . . I—"

"Of course you did." He winks. "You're a smart woman who wanted to see what she'd agreed to. I clearly did the same." His smile is genuine when I'd expect placating. "So you like reading and music. What else? Let me guess. You help orphans in your spare time and raise money to save the whales too?"

"What?" I cough out a laugh.

"We've been in talks with Kevin for months. All of a sudden you show up at the meeting for the first time like a plant, so I figured you were Mother Teresa or someone saintly to try and make me look better."

"I wasn't in any of the three possible girlfriend folders Kevin had for you to pick from. You chose me. Not the other way around."

"Ouch. Hit me where it hurts. I can take it."

"And I'm not a saint."

"A sinner then?" He gets a devilish smirk and a gleam in his eye. "Right up my alley."

"Do you ever take anything seriously?"

"I take everything seriously. And with a grain of salt. It's called balance. Kind of like how some days I drink whiskey and others I drink water. You have to change positions every so often or else things get boring, right?" he asks, the innuendo front and center.

"Right. Sure. Sounds good. Easy for you to say when this whole conversation has been about you asking me questions."

"And?"

"And," I state, not certain what it is I need to say.

"*And* you can google me down to what kind of underwear I wear, my favorite food, my favorite vacation—even my goddamn height and weight. You have a question? Ask away. The floor is yours."

Our gazes hold for a beat. "Why don't you have an accent?" It's there one minute, gone the next. It doesn't make sense to me.

"I was sent to the best schools. The kind where diplomats and billionaires send their kids with the goal in mind to be able to fit in any part of the world. English was a privilege we were expected to speak flawlessly."

"And yet your family seems so proud of its heritage."

"We are. And you'll hear my accent in full force when talking to fellow Spaniards . . . but my grandfather grew up in a time when he was looked down upon, sometimes discriminated against because of his accent. He missed out on endorsement deals because he wasn't mainstream enough. He was looked over for interviews because his accent was so strong. He was determined for that to not happen to his children and their children. We were taught to own our accents with our family, in our country, but to sound worldly everywhere else." He angles his head to the side and stares at me. "Do you think Kevin would be interested in me for this deal if my accent was so thick that the global market couldn't understand me? No. He wouldn't. So something I hated as a kid has served me well as an adult."

"I get it. But I don't."

He nods subtly. "There is a lot about being a Navarro that doesn't make a whole hell of a lot of sense."

I study him. The concept's interesting and sad all at the same time, but I understand the why behind it. His grandfather gave him a gift that most would overlook due to pride.

"What else do you have for me, because if you dug deep enough you would have found that answer too?" He winks. "There is nothing secret nor sacred when you're in the public eye, Madds. You'll learn that soon enough."

He says that like people are going to care about me simply because I'm going to be seen with him. *They won't.*

"You have to have some things that are kept private," I say.

He tilts his head from side to side. "Privacy is a luxury I'm not afforded as a Navarro, but yes, there are a few things that aren't public knowledge. Things I intend to keep that way. Other than that, it seems I'm fair fucking game, so when I ask you questions, I want answers."

"And when I tell you this isn't going to work, I mean it."

"I'm thinking sowing some of those oats might do a whole hell of a lot of good on adding a bit of optimism into your life," he deadpans, which only serves to irritate me.

"This is getting us nowhere," I mutter in frustration, unbuckle my seatbelt, and head toward the restroom. A plane bathroom is a plane bathroom but even this one is just as luxurious as the rest of the jet.

I take a moment to try and regain my wits. This conversation has been rambling and amusing and, just when I think we're going to actually touch on a topic of importance and stay there, Cruz diverts with his humor and boyish grin. It's maddening at best and amusing at worst.

I look at myself in the mirror. At my blond hair with the slight wave to it. At my pale green eyes and thick dark lashes that have always been a joke in my house. How does a blonde have dark lashes? At my peaches and cream complexion and pink pout of a mouth.

Am I pretty? I'd like to think so, but I'm not winning any beauty contests and I sure as hell look the polar opposite from the women on Cruz's arm I saw in pictures last night.

Why do you keep fixating on this? Sell the lie. Even when you feel like he's out of your league, sell the lie. And enjoy this once-in-a-lifetime experience.

Isn't that what this comes down to? *Isn't that why you took this chance?* To have the experience? To network so I can jump a couple of steps up the corporate ladder and into some large branding firm in the next couple of years?

I draw in a deep breath and look at myself one last time. *Stop the doubt. Own the moment.* "There is no time like the present," I murmur.

But when I emerge from the restroom, Cruz is now in my seat. What game is he playing now?

Better than give him the reaction I bet he's going for, I decide to walk right past him and into his seat without saying a word. But I'm about a foot past him when his arms close around my waist and he pulls me into his lap.

I yelp in surprise as my ass hits one of his thighs and my legs spill out and over the opposite side of the chair. I'm sitting crossways on his lap and in that split second between surprise, it turns into awareness. An awareness of every hard, corded line of his body. The dents and the ridges pressed against me as he wraps his arms around me. The strength in his hands as he spreads one of them on one thigh and the other across the side of my torso.

But it's his face that has me hitching my breath. It's nearness to mine. The warmth of his breath on my lips. The spark of gold in his amber eyes. The hint of a smile that challenges me as his hand moves up my thigh to lock around my wrist and hold me in place.

"What—" The word sounds breathless and so I stop myself and clear my throat. "What are you doing?"

He tilts his head to the side, eyes never leaving mine as he clearly contemplates something. And as he contemplates, I am in complete and total awareness of every single part of our bodies that are touching.

"For the record, I don't have a type," he murmurs, his eyes flicking down to my lips and then back up.

"Great. Good to know." My words are clipped and my body is taut.

"Is it? Because you seem awfully tense." Amusement dances in his eyes.

"I'm fine," I state when I'm far from fine. My pulse is racing and my body is flush with heat. *This* isn't supposed to be happening. Me. Him. This sudden feeling of want when I don't even know this man.

Mellie walks toward the cockpit with refreshments in her hand for the pilot before placing fresh drinks in front of us.

I absolutely freeze as she wipes up the condensation because Cruz is holding me on his lap like this is an everyday occurrence.

"Mellie?" he asks as she starts to walk away.

"Yes?" she asks.

"Can you please give us some privacy for a bit?" he asks.

"Yes, Mr. Navarro," she says as she slides a door shut between the galley and the cabin space.

What the hell do we need privacy for?

Nerves rattle even more.

"We're going to have to work on that," he murmurs against my ear, causing goosebumps to chase over my skin.

"On what?"

"You not freezing up any time someone is near. If you're going to sell it, we have to sell it. The last thing I want to do is not seal this deal because you couldn't like me enough to show it."

Like him enough? The man is . . . Jesus, he's walking perfection. It's more the opposite. In this very short exchange, I'm slightly afraid I might end up liking him too much.

"I didn't freeze up."

"No?"

"No."

"You like me then?" he murmurs as he runs the tip of his nose down the line of my neck and yes, I freeze. The heat of his body against mine. The scent of his cologne. The feel of his hands on me.

The simplicity of seduction by suggestion and touch.

You can't be turned on, Maddix. You just broke up with Michael. The same Michael who I thought I had a pretty healthy sex life with. But when was the last time he made you feel like this? The butterflies in your stomach and ache at the center of your core? The tingle across your skin as you anticipate where he's going to touch next? As you wait and want?

How about never?

My pulse races. I'm embarrassed and worried that he'll be able to feel it with how hard it's beating. His face is so close to my neck.

I struggle to maintain even breathing. To not let him know I'm affected by any of this. Not the hardening of his cock under my ass. Not the subtle change in the rise and fall of his chest. Not the way he just darted his tongue out to lick his bottom lip.

He lifts a hand and runs the backs of his fingers down my cheek. My face instinctively turns into it. Into him. And I'm already mad at myself for it and for how he's making me feel, before his hand finishes running the length of my cheek.

He's right there. Inches from my lips. Those eyes and that mouth and . . . just everything.

"Maddix?" he murmurs.

"Hmm?" Is he going to kiss me? Why do I want him to kiss me?

"This is how we do it."

"Do what?" I ask, completely distracted by everything that is him.

"Pull this whole charade off."

I freeze, and this time it's for so much more than fear of Mellie seeing this isn't real. It's because I thought this was real—him desiring me—and now realize what an idiot I am for thinking that.

"Oh." It's a stuttered sound.

"See? I'm so good, even you believed it."

I extricate myself from his hold and take the seat opposite him, not thrilled about what just happened and pretending not to care or feel as stupid as I do.

This was all a game to him.

Just like it seems everything is.

CHAPTER EIGHT

Cruz

I T SEEMS A COLD SHOULDER IS A NORMAL STATE WITH HER.

Fucking perfect.

Or at least that's the state Maddix has been in since she fell asleep after my little demonstration and then woke up when we landed.

Is she that sensitive that she's pissed off over how her body reacted to me? She can deny it all she wants, but I heard the hitch of her breath. I felt the heat of her pussy on my thigh. I saw the parting of her mouth as my lips touched the shell of her ear when I spoke.

To say I wasn't affected would be a lie. I'm a guy. She's hot in that librarian, girl-next-door American way when I'm used to more of the exotic, sultry woman.

She's right. I do have my type. Have I veered from it in the past? Yes. Few and far between, but I have veered.

Would I veer for her?

The jury's out at this point. It would only serve to complicate matters that are already complicated, but fuck if it isn't fun toying with her.

Sofia's riot act she read me last night repeats through my head. The one and only person I confided in over this stupid, bullshit charade. *Take the experience for what it is. Use it to your advantage.* Use it as a *fuck you* to our dad. To prove him wrong. Use it as a means to an end.

And hell, if I happen to veer with Maddix, then *I veer.* No harm, no foul, right? Not that I'll be telling Sofia that. The last thing I need is my sister on my case about how I need to respect women more. I respect the hell out of women . . . in more ways than one.

If we're going to fake it, is it so bad if we enjoy it while we do?

But by Maddix's reaction earlier? I'm not sure what she'd think about that.

I don't know much about Maddix Hart other than what I found on her social media and the limited interaction we've had, but here's what I have perceived: she's by the book. She likes boxes and lines and for the coloring to be inside of them and not outside.

Her social media posts are curated to show the tidiness of her life and not the messiness. And messiness is where true character is. It's where people are made and validated. It's where they become their true selves.

There were pictures of Michael. Michael who loves American football and cold brews but who never looked overly enthusiastic about being in any picture with Madds. His smile was there but his eyes weren't.

I know that look. *I've given that look.* And then I promptly extricated myself from the situation so I no longer had it.

In addition to Michael, her social media had pictures of sunsets, days on the lake, and balloons with blurry people in the background—all from about thirty feet away—but nothing in your face. Nothing goofy and raw and unscripted. Life at a distance instead of living in the moment.

Cautious. Choreographed. Uninspired.

Was it Michael who held her back or does she do it to herself?

Either way, the guy's a prick for doing that to her or letting her do that to herself. Good riddance, *even* if he's a nice guy.

Because the woman has a backbone. It came out in glimpses each time I pushed one of her buttons, but not for long enough.

She's a mess of contradictions, and I'm curious how this will play out.

Will she get frustrated with me? She's structure and I'm chaos.

Will she want to fight all the time? She's black and white and I'm most definitely all shades of gray.

Will she prevent me from letting loose? She's rules and I'm anarchy.

Will she struggle with the lifestyle I lead? She's perfectly folded clothes in a dresser drawer, and I'm an open suitcase with everything thrown into it in complete disarray.

I study her from across the car. She's watching the town of Amsterdam through the window as our driver navigates its streets. Her pale hair falls in the slightest of waves down her back. Her features are delicate—button nose, pouty lips, high cheekbones. Her frame is petite but muscular and surprisingly strong if the tensing on my lap on the plane was any indication.

I bet there's a side to her that's a little wild. A side I can get to cut loose. I refuse to spend these next weeks or even months with the ball-and-chain babysitter girlfriend and not get to have any fun.

I get this whole thing needs time to play out, but I refuse to be a monk during that time. A monk? *Not. Fucking. Happening.*

"I can feel you staring at me," she says but doesn't turn my way, her mouth opening in a yawn due to the time difference.

"*And?* We're boyfriend and girlfriend. It seems like that's the least of the things I'd be doing to you to make your cheeks blush."

Her sigh fills the car and weighs heavy before she turns to face me. "Look, we got off on the wrong foot."

"We did? You helped me. That could be construed as the right foot, no?"

"So that's why you picked me over the supermodels? Because I was *nice* and helped you?" she asks, sarcasm tingeing her voice. "Because that does wonders for my self-esteem."

"Whatever inference you're making otherwise is on you, Madds." It's not my job to stroke egos. Not in the least.

"Great. Perfect. Apparently, we got off on the *right* foot then."

"Why are you mad?" I ask. "I picked you. Isn't that enough? And now that I have, and now that I know a bit about you, I think we're going to have a hell of a lot of fun sowing those wild oats of yours and getting you to let loose."

"That's not the purpose of me being here."

"What if I make it the purpose, huh?" I tilt my head and pout playfully. "Life is meant to be lived, Hart. It's meant to be taken by storm so that whatever is left in your wake is proof that you had a great time doing it."

"Sounds like a Hallmark card." She rolls her eyes.

"Yeah? So? Your job is to calm me down. Make me seem presentable and mature. What if my job is to push you out of your comfort zone? To make you see life through my eyes?"

"Sounds dangerous."

"Perfect. Danger is the code I live my life by."

"Look, I appreciate the pep talk here, but this is a lot of supposition for someone I only met thirty-six hours ago. You looked at my Instagram, saw my pictures, and clearly labeled me as boring. What if I like my life? What if it's what I want?"

The clench of her jaw says otherwise, but our stares hold as I wonder how much to push her. Then again, since when do I think about shit like that? My life is an endless cycle of lap times, track tests, weights and cardio, simulator training, the media, and nutrition. *Okay, and women and clubbing. Let's be real.*

But now it includes Maddix, and I'm still figuring out what the fuck that means.

"You wouldn't have said yes if you weren't curious otherwise. You could have said screw you to Kevin and walked. I'm sure there are a million other jobs like yours elsewhere. *But you didn't.* You could have called Michael over and gone to the rodeo or hoedown, or whatever it is you guys do in Texas, and laughed about what a prick I was and how you escaped being stuck with me. *But again, you didn't.*"

"That's not fair," she asserts, her spine a little stiffer. But her eyes tell the truth.

"You didn't because, deep down there's a small part of you wondering what it's like to live this life. One different than the one you see set out before you. And you want to know the truth before you settle for your life of complacency."

She grits her teeth. Doesn't seem to like that word—*complacency.*

"For the record, *Cruz*," she says, my name almost like a curse word. "I was biding my time. I wasn't complacent. I have goals I'm trying to achieve. A career in brand management I'm working toward and money I'm trying to save so I can eventually move to New York or Los Angeles and achieve it. So what might have looked boring to you was me laying the foundation for my goals."

There's that fire. There's that backbone. And that's why I chose her. She didn't know who I was, and yet she was both kind *and* assertive.

I nod slowly as her anger eats up the air in the car. Clearly, I touched a nerve.

"I picked you, Maddix, because you don't want anything from me. You weren't being selected by Kevin to play a role. You weren't trying to figure out how to segue this to an acting or modeling career. I picked you because you didn't know who I was, and you were still kind without demanding to know 'why' like every other fucking person in my life. And it doesn't hurt that you're easy on the eyes or that the expression on your face when Kevin slid the folders across the desk said you were horrified by his ask. Does that answer the question you were afraid to ask?" I lift my eyebrows and take in her lips shocked into an O and her eyes wide. "So . . . can we be done with this or what?"

My phone ringing tells me we are. Like my father couldn't be any more of a buzzkill than he already is.

I push the button to answer the call and put the phone to my ear but don't say a word.

"I see you're in Amsterdam. Good. Time to get back to the business of racing and not this bullshit you've been up to."

"Hello to you too, Papá," I say quietly. I should be surprised that he knows my whereabouts but no doubt he tracked the flight and knows it landed.

Just a different version of the ball and chain when it comes to him.

"You didn't stop home first."

My chuckle lacks all humor. "Says the man who says I wasn't welcome." I'm aware that Maddix can hear my side of the conversation. The last thing I want to do is to explain anything about my father right now.

"So how did the meeting end up? Is the deal signed and done or did you fuck that up already before it even began?"

I hesitate. Torn between hanging up and telling him to fuck off. Either will give too much away to Maddix.

"You fucked it up, didn't you?" he says, mistaking my hesitation for the worst possible thing. Par for the fucking course. "You couldn't even seal it. *As expected.*"

I clear my throat. "I have company," I say by means of explanation. "And all is fine on that front. Not a problem in sight, but thanks for your obvious concern about my business dealings."

"Company?" He snorts. "Just like you to bring someone from the States with you before you tire of them. Yeah. I saw the flight manifest. I know you brought one of the ladies—and I use that term loosely." He emits a sigh of frustration that seems to be the soundtrack to my life. "You still have a championship to win. You do not need her as a distraction."

"Again, thank you for your concern, but I can handle myself."

He will not know about Genesee or Revive or all the details until the deal is finalized, ink dried, and is something he can't try to influence or change. That is if I want to tell him. His curiosity is killing him and I love that it is.

"So you skipped coming home and are now in Amsterdam days before scheduled. No doubt that means more debauchery is in your sights."

"Yep. You got it. I have a schedule full of it. And oh, look at the time—I'm already late to the start of it."

And before he can say another word and ruin my mood more, I end the call and toss my phone on the seat beside me. When I look up, Maddix is studying me in the same way she did when we first met. With curiosity and compassion.

One thing I can tolerate.

The other I will not.

CHAPTER NINE

Maddix

"**S**O YOU DON'T HAVE TO CHECK IN ANYWHERE?" I ASK AS I FOLLOW behind Cruz.

"Team hotel. They've already checked in for me. Key is digital." He raises his phone as if to show me the imaginary key stored on it. "That way I can bypass all that."

I have to double step to keep up with his pace, his legs eating up the space. "Good. Great." My brain is foggy from the time difference, and I'm still trying to process everything that Cruz Navarro is.

His judgments.

His opinions.

His declarations.

It's like I've been tasked to fake date a man who suddenly has made it his mission to make me a wild child like he is.

And I'm the furthest thing from a wild child.

What I am is exhausted and overstimulated and desperate for some peace and quiet. As I hurry behind him, all I can think about is falling face first into a comfortable bed—after I strip the comforter off, of course—some black-out shades, and much-needed sleep.

"Here we go," Cruz says as he opens the door to the room at the very end of the hallway.

I walk past the luggage, which has already been delivered, and my eyes widen to epic proportions as I take in the oversized suite. All I've ever heard about European hotels is that they are small and cramped compared to

American ones, so I'm astounded to find the space bright and airy with a killer view of downtown Amsterdam.

A king-sized bed fills up the main wall. Its bedding looks more luxurious than anything I've ever slept in before. I run my fingers across the desk in the corner as I step toward the windows to get a look of the city I merely caught glimpses of on the way here.

But it's in the split second in between falling more in love with the view and the door clicking shut that my brain registers the *we* in Cruz's statement.

"What do you mean, *we?*" I ask, eyes narrowed, and turn just in time to see him moving the luggage from the floor to the walk-in closet. *Since when does a hotel have walk-in closets?*

"Just what I said. *We,*" he calls over his shoulder. "You okay if I put your bag here?"

"Wait. Hold up. I mean . . ." I stalk to the closet, my mind grasping what's happening here but not wanting to believe it.

"There you go with your responding in threes again." He scrubs a hand through his hair and when he looks over at me, it's sticking up at all different angles. It makes him look like something you want to snuggle into. That's the last thing I want to do, considering what's dawning on me.

"Why are you in my room?" I ask.

"Madds, we can't exactly fake being a couple if you're in one room and I'm in another."

"Yes, we can."

"That's cute. You do realize my every move is watched every second of every day. Fans know how I take my coffee. They know my drink of choice. They even comment on what fucking socks I'm wearing. So believe me, it'd be noticed if my girlfriend and I were not sleeping in the same room."

"You're being—"

"Right on the money?" He flashes that smile of his at me. "Of course, I am. I live this life every day."

All of my googling last night? Those pictures came from somewhere. The paparazzi that follow him around. The media's fascination with him.

Sure, I wasn't given a lot of time to wrap my head around this situation, but I'm intelligent enough to conclude that Cruz Navarro's life is anything but private.

But I'm sure we could somehow fly under the radar and not stay in the same room.

"We could get adjoining rooms. No one would know—"

"Except for the hotel staff who could easily be paid off to tip something to the media." He lifts his eyebrows. "Keep them coming and I'll keep explaining away how anything and everything is possible when it comes to our fans."

"This is . . . *impossible*," I say as I shake my head in frustration and walk away from him, needing some space.

"It's not that big of a deal." He follows me.

"*But it is*. I barely know you and now I'm forced to share a room *and* bathroom with you? I mean, it's one thing to pretend. It's another to . . . *live together*."

"You're just realizing this?"

"No, it's just . . . it's *a lot*."

"It is. You're right. Again, it's not my choice but then again it seems I don't have one. I do this or I lose the deal." Cruz chuckles and studies me. "How did you think this was going to go?"

"I guess I should have assumed but, I mean . . . I don't jump straight into bed with men I just meet."

"We're not technically jumping. It would be more like sliding beneath the covers."

"Aren't you full of jokes," I say wryly.

He holds a hand up. "Wait. Are you telling me you've never had a one-night stand, Maddix?"

His question flusters me when it shouldn't. I've never been ashamed of that thought before and, suddenly faced by a man who clearly has, I feel juvenile. Naive. Goody two-shoes.

I swallow over the lump in my throat. "No."

His grin widens as he smacks his hands together and rubs them. "New goal in our quest to sow those wild oats."

"While I'm supposed to be dating you. Because that's smart," I say sarcastically and determine that'll be the only way I can get out of his absurd idea. "We can't sleep in separate hotel rooms, but I can sleep with a different man."

Why is this man so determined to get me to step outside my comfort zone? We've only just met.

"I'll find a way." He winks and then yawns as he motions toward the bed I want to sink into. "Time for bed."

"Can't wait," I mutter as I stare out at the city beyond with its lights twinkling under a darkened sky. It's nearly six and the city looks so peaceful.

I never expected to get the chance to go to a place like this. Maybe later in life when I'd saved enough money and felt comfortable, but not now. Not like this. And not in a situation where it's for someone else's benefit.

But you can make it to your benefit, Maddix.

"Look, it's been a long day—," he says. "Why don't we sleep on it and figure shit out later once we have clearer heads. I have some time before I'm technically required to be at the track."

The conversation from the car comes back to me. The slight snippets I overheard through the receiver. His dad's words about getting into trouble because he had too much time on his hands.

The look on Cruz's face. Part disgust. Part irritation. A lot of sadness.

There's a motion in the window's reflection that pulls me from my thoughts and back on Cruz. And his now very shirtless torso.

"What are you doing?" I whip around to face him.

Mistake. *Big* mistake.

I mean, from sitting on his lap, I knew he was hard and sculpted and had dents in the muscles at his hips where he has no business having dents—but to see it, him, like this. It's just not fair.

And the large suite suddenly feels very cramped.

He did it to win this argument. Or to put a stop to it. There is no way in hell a man who looks like that—tanned and toned and utter perfection—doesn't know he's going to get a reaction when he does *that*.

His slow crawl of a grin says as much, but he bats his lashes like the perfect picture of innocence.

"I'm going to bed. It's the easiest way to get rid of the jet lag. Sleep through the night." He runs a hand through his hair, and it sets off a chain reaction of muscles contracting that should be illegal. "Wake up refreshed and all is good."

"You're *not* sleeping in the bed."

He looks around the room and holds his hands up. "Where exactly do you expect me to sleep?"

"We could ask for a rollaway bed."

"That would be in the press faster than you can blink. I can see the headlines now. *Big fight between Cruz Navarro and his new lover. Cruz can't satisfy his girlfriend, she asks for a separate bed.* Should I go on?"

"A gentleman would offer to sleep on the floor."

"Firstly, if I were a gentleman in any sense of that word, we wouldn't be in this predicament in the first place. And secondly, me getting a good night's rest is part of my job. It's in my contract."

I snort. "By the pictures I've seen of you, it doesn't seem you follow that caveat much so why follow the first one?"

He hisses and pounds a fist to his chest. "I'm wounded. But I'm also flattered. You just admitted you were looking me up."

"I don't want you to be flattered. I want you to find a different bed. Some things should be sacred, right?"

"What are you afraid of? That you snore? That you talk in your sleep and you're going to spill your deep, dark secrets about how you secretly want me? I mean—"

"Jesus," I cough out.

"*What*? They're valid points but not ones I'm concerned with."

"Can't it be nothing more than giving a girl some damn privacy?" I ask and turn back toward the view beyond.

"This hotel has a killer rooftop view. If you want privacy, that's where I go."

"The roof?" I ask, perplexed.

"Yep. We have access because this is the penthouse."

"Please don't tell me you're telling me to go sleep on the roof."

"I'm not saying shit." He holds his hands up. "Just telling you a place where you can find that privacy if you need it."

He's missing the point. "That doesn't help our current situation."

"Again, this wasn't my doing so we have to make do with what we have. And what we have . . . is one bed and a whole lot of time that we're now forced to be together." He moves toward me and puts his hands on my shoulders and squeezes. "We sure waste a lot of time doing this back-and-forth thing. We need to be more efficient at communicating."

"You're maddening."

"I know." He grins. I can see it in the reflection of the window. "So here's the thing. I've seen you in a bikini on your socials. And I'm not complaining by any means, but there wasn't a whole hell of a lot of fabric going on there. I assure you that whatever it is you sleep in, it'll cover more than that bikini did."

I open my mouth and then close it. *Touché.*

"That is unless you sleep naked. In that case, I'll definitely be seeing more. But hey, you are in Europe now, where breasts are just breasts and not a big deal like you make them out to be in the States. But if that's the case,

I'll have to ask you to cover up then because that would just be plain cruel to me if we're on the *you can look but not touch* plan."

His playful tone puts a smile on my lips. He seems to be a master at manipulation. At twisting a narrative to make you want to cave. It's not a bad thing. It's not even a devious thing. It's just not something I'm used to.

"Yes." I say the word rather forcefully. "That is exactly the plan we're on."

"Only time will tell," he flirts.

"Hate to disappoint you, but I don't sleep naked."

"Well, I do, so see? Both of us will have to make adjustments. I'll have to wear bottoms and you'll have to get used to me in our bed."

"This isn't happening," I say more out of principle because *this is so happening*. I know it. He knows it. This whole conversation is for argument's sake.

"But it is. It's going to be quite the adventure, you and me. So many firsts for both of us." He squeezes my shoulders again before taking a step back and moving toward the bed. "I can already feel the fights coming. The glares from across the room. The gritted teeth when I annoy the fuck out of you. The *where do you want to eat* since we don't know each other's preferences. I mean, talk about a crash course in fake dating." He shakes his head, his grin widening. "Just promise me one really public fight. Those always sell well."

"Only if they get to record you groveling for me to take you back," I reply. "Everyone loves a good grovel."

"I don't grovel."

I laugh. "We'll see about that," I say but it's interrupted by a ridiculously dramatic yawn on my part.

Cruz just quirks a brow as if to say, *I told you so.*

"Fine," I huff, but head to the only place I can have any type of privacy— the bathroom. I take my time washing the day's travel off me before moving back into the room and making a show of getting ready for bed. Organizing my things on the little table on my side of the room. Hanging my clothes up so they don't wrinkle. Checking my phone because it was easier than making eye contact with him. And then finally unable to postpone the inevitable any longer, crawling into bed without saying another word to him. His chuckle every few seconds in response to something I do or a response I don't give a question he asks me, only serves to fuel my obstinance.

I'm staging my own private protest despite being all too well aware of the man who is lying next to me.

"Aren't you even going to say good night?" he asks to which I grunt. His sleepy laugh fills the room as I turn on my side so that my back is to him. He emits another playful chuckle that feels like it's feathering over my skin. As if I weren't already aware of his presence.

I struggle to fall asleep, despite Cruz's slow, even breathing.

My mind replays the events of the craziest few days of my life.

My brain tries to wrap itself around the idea that Cruz Navarro is in fact, in the bed beside me.

Three days ago, I didn't even know who the man was. I had a boyfriend—albeit a loose interpretation of the term—a job I was content with for the time being, and a stable, normal life. Now? Now, I'm loosely responsible for a billion-dollar deal between F1's playboy prince—the tabloids' term, not mine—and a global company, whose ladder just became way more possible to climb.

How is this my life?

And the sinfully handsome man beside me?

He's a rung on that ladder, Maddix. Out of your league. A means to an end.

At least I know my heart will be safe.

CHAPTER TEN

Maddix

"WE NEED TO STAGE OUR SOCIAL MEDIA ACCOUNTS."

"What?" I glance over to Cruz as he opens the door to the hotel for me. We walk outside and I'm hit with a rush of fresh air and sound. But it's not like sounds in Texas with Jake Brakes and angry horns. It's bike bells and accented hellos. Soft voices, quiet streets, and birds tweeting.

"Our social media. We need to explore—the city, the countryside, the landmarks—and take some pictures together so that we can sell this. Then we'll do a photo dump where we act like we like each other."

"Gee. Thanks," I say but then falter when he stops at a car parked on the curb. It's a top-of-the-line sports car with sleek lines, a sexy profile, and easily worth more than everything I own added up together. And of course, Cruz steps forward to open the passenger door for me. *Because why wouldn't this be his?* "What . . . where did you get this?"

You need to stop looking at all these things with your jaw dropped, Maddix. This is his life of luxury. He's used to it. Your reaction only makes you look like a country bumpkin.

"Per contract, drivers are required to drive the cars off the track that we do on the track. The team transports and delivers them for us. This one was delivered last night for me."

Questions, *so many questions*, float through my mind about the extravagance of this sport, and I've only been part of it for a few days. No doubt, those questions will double and quadruple as the days wear on.

"Oh. Okay." I slide into the passenger seat and remain silent, only to jump a little as the engine fires to life and rumbles through my body.

I steal glances at him as he drives. I'm torn between the view around me, the man beside me, and the endless thoughts over what it was like to wake up beside a rumpled, sleep-tousled Cruz. I've never found pillow creases and bedhead sexy but then again, I've never woken up beside him.

I may have feigned that I was still asleep when he rose from the bed and stood in his shorts, staring at the world outside our hotel room, but that doesn't mean I didn't sneak a peek or two. And I can't deny that those peeks may have had me thinking thoughts I clearly shouldn't be thinking.

It's delirium that had thoughts about what those strong hands would feel like on my body. Delirium and a dose of pure Cruz Navarro sex appeal. That's all it was. That's all the weird flutter in my stomach still is. Write it off, Maddix. Move on.

He drives, seemingly oblivious to my thoughts. I don't ask where we're going and he doesn't offer. Rather, I revel in not having to think about anything. I simply sink into the rich leather seats and take in the world Cruz is showing me.

First stop of the day is lunch on the canals in Jordaan.

"I rarely get to explore when we travel," he says, taking a sip of water and glancing over his shoulder at someone laughing on the other side of the outside patio where we're sitting. He slinks a little lower in his seat and adjusts the brim of his baseball hat a tad. He's yet to be recognized, and his quick glances around make me think he's hoping it stays that way.

"No?"

"No." He takes a bite of food and looks at me while he chews, almost as if he's contemplating how much he's going to tell me. "Typically we fly in, spend a week in whatever city's on the schedule, but it's all business, all the time. Even when we're going to sponsor dinners or laughing with our crew, we know that every minute of every day we're being watched by the public, by our team, and by the people who pay the teams' bills. So this is . . ." He motions absently. "Different. *Nice*."

"And here you thought being stuck with me was going to be miserable," I tease.

"You're right. I did," he says unapologetically. "But . . ."

"But we're in the early stages yet." I chuckle. "It's okay to reserve judgment for later."

"Are you talking about you or me here?"

"How about both?"

He taps his water glass against mine. "Deal."

After lunch, we head to Vondelpark and walk around.

"For a country with this many bikes, you'd think they wouldn't be big into Formula 1," I say as a steady stream of bikes and their riders move down the pathway in front of us.

"Meaning?"

"Meaning cars and gas and racing don't seem to be a part of their culture and yet, clearly it is, because we're here," I say as I lift my phone to snap a picture of a tree-lined path.

"Never thought of it that way," he says as another bike bell rings and we move out of the way of a horde of bikes making their way down the path. "Hey, Madds?"

"Cruz." I go to scold him for the nickname until I notice he's holding his phone up for a selfie.

"We need documentation of our togetherness, no?" He steps in beside me and puts a hand on my waist to pull me closer.

"Yes. Sure." The heat of his hand on my back flusters me. Thoughts of yesterday on his lap and waking up this morning beside him only make that heat more prevalent.

And when he leans in so his face is right beside mine, our reflections in the camera looking back at me, I can't help but stutter a breath. We are opposite in every way but look incredible together.

He clicks a few pictures, and I swear it's only after he steps away, his hand leaving my back, that I feel like I can breathe again.

After Vondelpark, we head out of the city, driving endlessly through fields of flowers, a never-ending sea of color.

Cruz allows me to be absurdly giddy over every windmill I see, stopping every time I ask him to so I can snap a quick picture. He may roll his eyes and give a quick shake of his head at each of my squeals, but not once does he tell me I'm being ridiculous or to stop like I know Michael would have.

He lets me be me, when it kind of feels like I'd forgotten how to be that.

Our conversations—when we have them—consist of superficial topics. Tidbits he knows about the country. Its history I look up on my phone until we lose service. An anecdote here and there about different times he's raced here.

At other times we fall silent. The quiet is easy between us. Comfortable when it probably shouldn't be. But it is. We don't have to work at conversation. We either have it, or we don't. And it seems that either way, we're fine.

We get lost on some backroads, or at least he says we do, but I secretly think it's on purpose so he can keep driving at top speeds and not have to work at being not recognized.

"I need to stretch my legs," he says, pulling over beside a field of dahlias. They blanket the field to the right of us in every imaginable color.

"*Really?*" I ask.

"Don't sound so excited." He laughs.

"No. I am. Very." I jump out of the car and run down a narrow path in the field of flowers. I hold my hands out and spin. "Dahlias are my absolute favorite!"

The sun feels good on my face and for the first time since we started this . . . adventure, if you will, I feel a little bit more like me. Simple. Unapologetic. Happy.

I keep my arms up with my spin on slow until I stop and stumble a bit. When my world stops spinning and Cruz comes into view, he's standing about ten feet away from me with an odd look on his face. Part amusement. Part . . . what I swear might be *jealousy?*

That emotion seems strange and out of place, but it's gone as soon as I see it. It's replaced with a warm smile as he walks toward me, plucks a bright pink dahlia, and tucks it behind my ear.

"There. It fits you," he murmurs, his fingers lingering on the strand of hair that fell out from behind my ear when he put the stem there.

"It fits me?"

"Mm-hmm. Carefree."

Carefree? That's not a word I think anyone has ever used to describe me. But before I can question it or him, he holds out his phone and takes several selfies of us—all of which I, no doubt, will hate.

"We need a nickname," he states.

"A what?" I ask as I take in and try to memorize every inch of landscape around us. The flowers. The blue sky. The fluffy white clouds. The silhouette of a large windmill off in the distance.

"A nickname. You know, like all power couples have."

How is it that Cruz continues to surprise me? Like, what man thinks of something like that?

And how freaking hilarious that he does?

"Excuse me a second." I hold my finger up and grin at him. "It was only days ago that I thought you were going to flip a table over Kevin's ultimatum. And now you're asking for us to have a nickname. What exactly changed?"

"Cruddix? Nah." He chuckles. "That's not going to work. The Dix only works on a girl's name. What about . . . Madcruz?" He makes a ridiculous face. "Even worse."

"You're not answering my question."

"And you're not naming us."

"My question first. Then . . . I'll help."

He sighs and looks at me. For a brief second, I think he's going to ignore my request but then he says, "I figure the more we embrace this, the sooner I can ink the deal. Then the quicker we can both get back to our own lives . . . and our own sex lives."

Should've guessed this had something to do with sex. He's a guy, right? "Wow. Okay. It must be a rough, lonely life if not having sex for a few days is this much of an incentive for you." Sarcasm drips from my tone.

"It's a rough job, but somebody has to do it." He huffs on his knuckles and shines them on his chest. It earns him the death glare from me. "*Relax.* The media makes me out to be way worse than I am. Besides, just because I'm out partying doesn't mean I fuck every girl I meet. I do have standards," he teases.

"Classy."

"You asked." A smile toys at the corners of his mouth.

"I did not."

"You did without asking in that way that women do. And for the record, I have a clean bill of health."

"The fact that you even have to utter that proves my point." *What is this conversation?*

"I don't have to utter shit, Hart. But from what I've gathered so far, you're a girl who likes her t's crossed and i's dotted and everything to be in its proper place. No doubt you were wondering since we're sharing a bed together. Now, you don't have to."

"I can't believe we're having this conversation."

"And I can't believe we're not important enough to you to pick a name for us." His boyish grin is in full effect as he flashes it my way.

Everything about him is a juxtaposition right now. His dark hair and bronzed skin in the middle of a field of vibrant colors.

"For what it's worth, I think you're being ridiculous."

"And I think you need to step into the role a bit more and have some fun with it."

Our gazes hold, that smile of his winning me over.

"Fine. Sure. Okay. We'll figure a name out for us. But . . . we might need some time to come up with a good one because the two you just offered up are horrible."

"Creativity is not my strong suit. It's supposed to be yours if I'm not mistaken." He narrows his eyes at me. "Hey. Wait. Are you saying yes simply because you think I'm going to forget?"

"No. I'm saying yes, but we need to come up with something way better than *Cruddix*."

"Deal." He holds his hand out and I shake it, ignoring the sudden heat his touch brings.

"Deal."

CHAPTER ELEVEN

Maddix

OUR RIDE BACK TO THE CITY IS FILLED WITH MUCH THE SAME. Me pointing out things while he explains the little he knows about the city and its customs. The sun begins to set, the sky deepening in its colors in this alluring city.

"I told you, I rarely get free time in a city, so we're taking advantage of it," Cruz says as he eats a poffertjes, a miniature, fluffy Dutch pancake with icing, from a street vendor.

"Why do I not like the sound of that?" I tease and avert my eyes from the couple across the pathway who is staring at us.

For the most part, we've escaped recognition most of the day. Either that or people here are just damn polite and Cruz's penchant for driving through the countryside has kept us out of the public eye.

Either way, I'm all for it because it's rather unnerving when people are staring at you but pretending not to stare at you. It's an awkward dance of do you smile and acknowledge that they see the person you're with or do you avert your eyes and possibly come off like an asshole?

"You get used to it," he murmurs before taking another mouthful.

"Used to what?"

"People looking. People squinting their eyes as if it's going to help them realize that it's really you. The nudges. The people walking back and forth several times in a row. The people obscuring their phones to take a picture and the ones blatant about it. You just get used to it."

"How? It's weird. It's—"

"Not every city is like this. The people here are pretty chill. Other places not so much where the people are pushy and in your face. Enjoy this while we can."

"Other places as in America?"

"As in a lot of places. This is a sport where people grow up rooting for the team their grandfathers loved. For some it's a pride over heritage thing. For others it's a car thing. And for even more it's a popularity thing. Everyone has their reasons why they love their team and their driver. Regardless, Formula 1 is the one constant in their life when everything else seems to continually change."

"Oh."

He turns to look at me. "You really don't know much about the sport, do you?"

I shake my head. "Were you under the impression I did?"

"No." He smiles. "And you really didn't know who I was in the hallway?"

"Nope. Not a clue."

"Huh."

My cell phone ringing startles me. When I glance down to see Tessa's name on it, I wince. My best friend of ten years. The peanut butter to my jelly. The one person I confide in about everything.

And yet, I haven't said a word to her about this. Shit. Between the traveling, zero privacy to have a real conversation, and good old-fashioned jet lag, I haven't had the time to talk to her.

That's a lie and I know it. I could have texted her, I could have said I was going abroad for work—but that would mean I'd be lying to her.

Now I'm going to have to face the consequences on top of lying.

I motion to Cruz that I'm taking the call and step away from him, the phone to my ear. "Tess. Hi."

"Why do you sound guilty?" she asks immediately.

"I'm not guilty. I'm—"

"Where the hell are you, Maddix?"

"It's a long story. I haven't had time to call." I glance over my shoulder. Cruz is happily devouring his food with his hat pulled down low over his brow, blending in with the crowd like a tourist.

"Amsterdam, perhaps?"

"Why would you say that?" I ask, the words coming out slowly.

"There are pictures. *On the Internet*. Someone who looks exactly like my best friend but can't possibly be my best friend because if she were having some hot, torrid love affair with a smoldering Formula 1 driver who could melt my computer screen, then she would have called me at the first hint of it. She *wouldn't* let me find out from Landon holding out his phone to me and saying, '*that girl looks exactly like Maddix, doesn't she?*' and me knowing that it is in fact you."

"What do you mean there are pictures on the Internet?" I ask, disbelief woven in every fiber of the words.

"You didn't answer me. Where are you?"

"Like I said, it's a long story."

"So it's true? The pictures? Amsterdam? Cruz fucking Navarro? What the hell, Maddix? I go away on my honeymoon, and you run off with a fuck-hot man and don't tell me?"

"I'm here for work. With Cruz. It's . . . complicated."

"No shit. Why don't you tell me something I don't know?"

I sigh and then just like I did to my parents, I lie by omission to my best friend. "It's not what you think. Really. It's a work thing that turned into a *this* thing that I really don't have time to explain right now."

"You dumped Michael." There is zero judgment in her tone, and I'm grateful for that.

"It was going nowhere." Simpler is better.

"Couldn't agree more. In fact, I'm kind of happy about that turn of events. What I'm not happy about is learning that my best friend is halfway around the world with some superstar, and I only found out because Landon follows F1," she says referring to her new husband.

"Like I said, I'll explain when I can. It's . . . if you think this is all making your head spin then you should be standing in my shoes."

Silence greets me and I wait patiently for her to swallow down the hurt over my lack of willing transparency. "Maddix?" Her voice is soft. Concerned. When I don't answer, she does what I thought she'd do. I can all but see her nodding as she tries to process all of this. "Okay." The word sounds like a way to reinforce her resolve. "Just . . . are you okay? Say the word and I'll be there if you're not."

My smile is automatic and my chest constricts. "I'm okay. Everything is good." I swallow over the ball of emotion in my throat.

"So he didn't abduct you against your will for some hot, kinky sex? You're not tied up to a bed and he let one hand out so you could answer my call?"

"That's exactly what it is." I smile.

"That's what I thought." Relief floods her voice but her curiosity remains. "I'm a phone call and a flight away."

"I know. I'll explain it all to you when I can. I promise."

"You sure?"

"I'm sure."

"Okay. I'm trusting you."

We end our call and I stare at my phone for a second, guilt eating at me that I just lied to yet another person. And as soon as that epiphany comes and goes, comes the revelation that there are pictures of me on the Internet. *Linked with Cruz.*

How?

"Madds? You okay? You look like you've seen a ghost?" Cruz asks as he approaches.

"That was my friend. She . . . she asked me if I was here with you."

"And what's the big deal with that?" he asks, like I'm not getting it.

"I didn't tell her where I was. No one has. She saw me or us or—" I pick up my phone and instantly search for Cruz Navarro and Maddix Hart. A gasp falls from my mouth when within seconds, article after article populates with a split-screen image of me and Cruz. The picture of me is from my company headshot posted on the Genesee Capital website. His is in his race suit. "*How?*" I ask as I see Cruz hold up his own phone and start scrolling.

"Well, I guess I should have warned PR about this whole situation." He chuckles and then sighs as if this is some kind of joke.

"How can you act so casual about this?" I stare at him dumbfounded. "Like, I don't understand. I don't—"

"Baptism by fire." He puts a hand on my shoulder to quiet me.

"And that's supposed to make me feel better?"

"No. It's unnerving and invasive. I know that more than anyone." He squeezes my shoulder. "I find you to be a highly intelligent woman, Madds, but were you that naive to think your world wasn't about to be turned upside down by agreeing to *date* me?"

"Yes. No. I mean, how does anyone even know who I am? It's not like I have a name tag on. It's not like someone posted a picture about me, and I'm a celebrity so they know who I am. It's not like we've posted any pictures yet. I don't understand. How could they identify me?"

"Did you give your ID to the hotel staff for anything?" he asks, his voice calm, the playful tone gone now as he senses my panic.

"No."

"Did you leave anything in the hotel room with your name on it?"

"I mean . . . my luggage tag. My business cards." The comment comes out in a whisper as I realize he was right about hotel staff snooping and talking.

"And you thought I was crazy for telling you someone would sell our information."

I stare at him, hearing the mocking in his tone, and blink blankly before drawing in a deep breath. I can do this. I can stop overreacting. I can manage with—I look down at my email and see two hundred and thirty new emails—*wow*. Guess that's what it means when you are linked to someone as high-profile as Cruz.

People suddenly seem to notice you.

"I'm fine. I can handle it. I just . . . I guess I didn't realize how people would react. That anyone else other than your inner circle would care."

"I tried to tell you."

"You did. And I heard you but . . . I'm just me and you're *you*"—I shove my hands out toward him to emphasize the disparity between us—"so I thought the focus would remain on you. Stupid on my part."

His shrug does wonders for my self-confidence. "It's logical to be upset. I do know what I'm talking about when it comes to this though."

"Yes, I am naive, Cruz. Does that make you feel better to keep pointing it out?" I bite the words out, not sure where the unfounded anger at him is coming from.

But I know. It's because I feel vulnerable, judged, and like my privacy has been invaded.

This came with the territory. He's one hundred percent right about my naivety. And yet his being right doesn't make me feel any better.

"I'm sorry. Truly. I wasn't trying to rub your face in it. It's something I rarely say so please know I mean it."

I nod and clear my throat.

Cruz stares at me, his expression softening before he puts an arm around me and pulls me against his side. He presses a kiss to the top of my head and leaves his lips there, his breath heating my scalp, as he says, "I got you into this mess, Madds. I'll try to shield you from it as much as possible but even I'm not that much of a miracle worker."

And as much as the idea appeals to me—him shielding me—I know I can't let him. I know this is what I agreed to do. I now realize why Kevin had originally selected actresses to play the part. Somebody who wants the limelight and their name out there. Not me.

"No. I said it's fine."

"Says every woman ever when she's nowhere near fine. In fact, usually that means you're pissed. So be pissed. Be angry. You didn't ask for this and yet here you are." He meets my gaze, but I can see the regret in his eyes. There's the slightest glimpse of the man from the break room that first day. The off-Cruz. The real Cruz.

God, was that only days ago? It feels like a lifetime since then.

"Here's the deal," he says, leaving his hand on my arm but turning so we face each other. "We take our own steps in announcing us. In posting about us. Right now everything out there is assumption. But if we post ourselves then we steal any and all thunder. That allows us to control the narrative as much as possible."

"Yeah, okay. Agreed." Control the narrative that already feels like it's spinning out of control.

At least on my side of the world it is.

"You sure?" He leans down so our gazes are level and lifts his eyebrows.

"It's not like I can be anything other than, right?"

He presses a brotherly kiss to my forehead. "I'll take care of you, Madds." He moves an arm around my shoulder and steers us toward where we left the car. "Let's head back to the hotel. We can figure out which photos to post and take some control back."

Minutes later, we're in the car. I'm still processing—part shaming myself for being so naive, but also acknowledging that Cruz wasn't a total dick about it.

Once in our room, we scroll through our photos of the day and decide what to post. A few images but no captions. Let the photos speak for themselves.

And then with a deep breath, we both publish our complementary posts and become Instagram official.

Tessa will be pissed over this. No doubt her texts will be coming fast and furious later. But this is my job. It's what I have to do. When I'm finally able to explain it all to her, I know she'll forgive me.

Of course, by the time night falls, when we head out to eat dinner, word has spread. If the paparazzi following us to the restaurant is any indication, the news about us has hit.

Cameras blind us as we leave the restaurant and get in the car. The term fishbowl suddenly feels very real when it used to be something I thought was said for dramatics.

"It's okay," Cruz says, reaching out and squeezing my knee in reassurance. He leaves his hand there for effect, no doubt since cameras continue to flash through the heavily tinted windows of the town car we had drive us here.

I exhale a slow, steady breath as a response.

"Talk to me, Madds. What is it that's the most troubling about all of this for you? If I could fix one thing, what would it be?"

I turn to look at Cruz in the darkened light of the car. As we move through the city, shadows move over his face, but his eyes are steadfast on me.

His question surprises me. It's not something I expect to come out of Cruz Navarro's mouth. He's labeled as selfish and self-centered. As not caring for what others think. But his question, his offer, says he's anything but that.

Maybe the label he's often branded is wrong. Or maybe I just feel so alone in all this, he's the only one I have to turn to. The only person I can be honest with. And that's an extremely humbling thought.

"I have no control over any of this. What they post about me. What they say about me. What they assume about me." The admission is hard, but true.

"All we can control is this. Is us. Is being stuck together, right?" His grin is fast and wicked when it flashes over his face. "I know just what you need right now. Do you trust me?"

Lord help me.

"Yes."

CHAPTER TWELVE

Cruz

YOU'RE OUT OF YOUR MIND IF THAT'S WHAT YOU THINK *I* NEED RIGHT *now*.

Maddix's words ring through my ears, but by the looks of her out on the dance floor right now—hips swaying, hands flung up, head thrown back, eyes closed—letting loose a little seems like just what the doctor ordered.

Good thing I persisted when she resisted.

The bass bumps a wicked beat as the techno music vibrates through my body. A little alcohol, some loud music, and a dark room with a crowd to get lost in always seems to do it for me when I need a break.

Seems Maddix and I might have that in common.

Call me a bastard, but it's what I need right now, so whether she wanted it or not, this is where we were heading.

I tip my glass up and meet the eye of the brunette across the bar who has been giving come fuck-me eyes all night.

Doesn't she know I'm trying to be on my best behavior? Doesn't she know I have a "girlfriend" now? Because fuck if it doesn't seem like the whole world found out in a matter of hours.

Look away, Navarro. Look away.

God, how I don't want to, but I grit my teeth and do just that. Eyes back on Maddix. On the sway of her hips and the way her body moves to the rhythm. But no matter how much I see her in front of me like this now,

I'm reminded of her expression from earlier. The shocked eyes and utter vulnerability. Shit that makes me uncomfortable.

Again, why I needed to come here and get lost for a bit.

I thought Kevin had prepped her for what to expect. Nope. He threw her to the wolves for the sake of a business deal he's going to look like a fucking hero if he closes.

Why do I care?

Because I brought this upon her. I selected her. I rebelled so that no one else could make the choice for me and in doing so . . . here we are.

And now . . . fuck if I want to have this on my conscience, but again . . . here we are.

Let's just hope Maddix and her family don't have any skeletons in their closets because if they do, her life is about to be more real than she'll ever know when the paparazzi dig anything and everything up about her.

Fuck me.

Just another damn thing to have to consider in regards to her when I usually only have to think about myself.

"Hey," I say as someone reaches out to take the drink from my hand and then stutter a smile when I meet the eyes from the brunette who'd been eyeing me.

Her smile is slow and seductive, and she's even more gorgeous up close as she tips my glass to her lips and takes a sip.

"I figured one of us needs to make a move," she says in her subtle accent. "So I'm making it."

I grit my teeth and fist my hand, the temptation at my fingertips to do what I'd normally do. Order some bottle service. Go get lost on one of the couches in the VIP section. Have a little fun with her.

Don't do it.

I look up and over her shoulder and find Maddix looking at me. Her grin is goofy as she waves at me.

Would she even notice if I snuck out for a little bit? *Most likely not.*

I groan. Sinking into the woman in front of me? It owns my mind. It's all I want. All I can think about. She smells phenomenal. Her tits are pushed up and on display. Tempting me.

Yeah. Let's get this on.

I'm about to pull her into me, accept what she's so blatantly offering, when I spot Maddix again. Dancing freely . . . like she did amongst the dahlias earlier.

Fuck me.

She wouldn't notice if I took this woman and fucked her.

But other people? *Most definitely.*

"Sorry," I say with a tight smile as my body fights my own betrayal. As I force myself to physically take a step back. "I'm here with someone. My date. Uh, keep the drink though."

Her laugh is sultry and just below the beat of the music. "I don't mind if you don't." She trails her finger down my chest. Everything about her spells trouble, and hell if I don't want to jump feet first into it.

"She would though." I lift my chin in the direction of the dance floor and Maddix.

"Here," the brunette says and slips a hotel room key into my back pocket. "The number's written on it. I'd love to give you a proper welcome to my country, *Mr. Navarro.*"

I lean into her, my lips near her ear. *Walk away. Walk the fuck away.* So I do one better. I push her away to remove the temptation. "It takes a lot more than that to impress me. What's the fun if there's no chase? But thanks."

A sneer replaces her smile. She can be offended all she wants but . . . oh well. And as she stomps away, I pull up the post I made on my socials earlier. Photos from today of Maddix in the flower fields. Of us in the park. Of her looking out the window of the car and the wind blowing in her hair.

Playing the press who always plays me and paints me in the worst light.

Yep, I am the asshole who doesn't care as I move on from one woman to the next, but for some reason, I care about Maddix. And now because of all this bullshit, I have to abstain from giving in to the urge to use this hotel room key. From another woman.

Because of this deal. This fucking necessary evil.

All she did was give you an office to hide in and a bottle of water. You don't owe her your firstborn or anything.

And yet . . . I feel bad.

"Navarro."

I look up to see Maddix walking toward me. A grin is plastered on her face and the tension in her shoulders when we walked in here two hours ago has gone away.

"Having fun?" I ask.

"Cruzy-Cruzy-Cruz," she coos.

"I take that as a yes." I chuckle and lift my finger to the bartender for another drink.

"Thank you." The words are slurred, but it's the sigh of satisfaction as she leans against the bar top beside me that gets me.

"For?"

"For knowing I needed this." She hooks her arm through mine. "For knowing I needed to forget for a bit." She rests her head on my shoulder and the subtle scent of her shampoo hits my nose. "For letting me sow my wild oats." She tilts her head up so those green eyes of hers meet mine. They are a complicated mess of emotions, and I'm not certain I like how they make me feel.

Happy. Sad. Regretful. All pertaining to the fact that I put her here. In this position.

It's done. It's over with. Move the fuck on, Cruz. You being a pussy over this doesn't change shit.

"Is that what we're doing, Madds? Sowing our oats?"

"We are." She giggles and the action has her breasts rubbing against my arm. "Or I am. You're so done and sowed I think you've probably sprouted a garden."

"God, let's hope not," I say but laugh. She's an adorable drunk.

"So yeah, I'm sowing and for now, I don't give a shit what anyone else thinks about it."

"Agreed."

She stumbles a bit and falls against me to hold tighter and right herself. "Whoopsie." But when she looks up this time, her face is closer to mine. Her lips are right there. Her tits are brushing against my chest.

Christ.

I've been with her nonstop for what feels like forever, so why do I suddenly notice her perfume? Why are there flecks of dark green in the light green of her eyes that I never noticed before? Why are her lips the perfect color of pink, and why do I wonder if they'd get redder if they were kissed?

The music fades away and fuck if I don't want it to.

She's fucking adorable like this. Sexy. Beautiful in so much more than the girl-next-door way I had her pegged for that first day.

And right before I make a decision that could fuck up this platonic thing we've got going, Maddix throws her head back and laughs. She pushes away from me, throws her hands in the air, and emits a little whelp as she shimmies her way back out to the dance floor.

We're on the *you can look but not touch* plan.

She keeps moving like that and that plan is going to be out the fucking window.

Her eyes meet mine again. A slow, seductive smile crawls across her bee-stung lips as her hips move to the beat.

Definitely out the window.

"You two together?" a guy asks as he walks up beside me.

"No. Yes. It's complicated," I say in clear Maddix Hart fashion.

He laughs. "Then I take it that she's fair game."

"I think you should rethink that supposition," I say.

But I have no claim on her. None whatsoever. And I don't even want to. Or don't even want her. She's just here. A pawn in Kevin's ridiculous game and a means to an end for me.

Keep thinking that. It'll get you far.

And yet when the guy who asked me circles around her more times than I care to count . . . when his hands slide up her torso and he tries to grind against her, it's time to go.

For my sake. For the gig's sake—can't have any press seeing my girlfriend grinding against someone else. For the need to avoid creating more media attention when my fist meets this guy's face.

No closing down the club tonight.

Looks like I'm having all kinds of firsts.

And all of them are because of Maddix.

~

"You decent?" I ask as I stride out of the bathroom and into the suite.

"Nope. Nude it is," she teases, her voice dreamy but playful.

"Must be my lucky night. I'm sleeping naked too," I say.

"Cruz." Her eyes fly open and then she gives me a dubious look.

"I made you look though."

"It seems I'm always looking," she murmurs as she sinks her head back down onto the pillow. *What does that mean?* Her yawn is in slow motion, her eyelids heavier with each breath. "So tired."

"Get some sleep. The race week unofficially starts tomorrow."

"Hmm."

She doesn't move as I slip into bed next to her. Whereas last night she kept her back to me, tonight she's on her side, facing me. I take in the long sweep of her lashes, her flawless skin, and the way her pale hair lays across the white linens.

"You saved me," she murmurs. "From the handsy man. And the weird one. And definitely the creepy one. You saved me."

I reach out to brush hair off her forehead but think better of it. No. That's not what this is. No physical. No emotional. Just pretend. "Don't believe the lie we're selling, Madds. I'm not a white knight and you sure as fuck don't need saving like a princess."

She giggles and it falls off into a sigh. "Nope. I'm the queen and before this is done, they'll all bow down to me. Even you."

Dream the fuck on, Madds. I don't bow down to anyone.

And yet my smile stays fixed in place.

CHAPTER THIRTEEN

Cruz

FINGERS.

They tighten around my cock.

They stroke me up and down with the perfect amount of pressure before reaching down to cradle my balls.

Lips.

They brush against mine.

They're soft and the gentle warmth of her tongue presses against the seam of my lips as she seeks access.

I grant it. *Christ, how I grant it.*

A low groan rumbles through me as I reach out and pull her toward me. One hand tangles in her hair as she shifts and sits astride me and the other palms her lower back. Both tighten when she sits down and the heat of her pussy hits just above the lowered waistband of my shorts.

She's wet.

So fucking wet through the fabric of her panties that my skin dampens from it.

I can smell her arousal. Feel it. Want it coating my fingers and cock. Want to taste it on my own fucking lips.

She reaches out and takes one of my hands and presses it over her breast, arching her back so that it fits perfectly. Her pebbled nipples and her stuttered sighs own me.

"Cruz." It's the softest of moans that we swallow in our kiss.

I'm yanked from the dream. Immediately regretting waking up to a cold reality I won't be able to satisfy only to realize . . . *this isn't a dream.*

Far fucking from it.

And the details of it—the tickle of the ends of her hair on my chest. The taste of her on my tongue. The slickness of her arousal as she slides her hips against mine and grinds . . . it's so much fucking better now that I'm awake.

Her lips. They're the right amount of finesse and demand. Of greed. Of need.

I'm a goddamn fucking goner and we haven't even started yet.

Thoughts try to break through the haze of lust. Rational ones. Necessary ones. But hell if the weight of her body on mine doesn't cloud those out.

Everything about me is at war. My conscience and my libido. My head and my heart. My cock and my sensibility.

I'm so goddamn hard, so fucking turned on, that there is only one thing I want to focus on—*Maddix.* Being in her. Fucking her. Coming with her.

"Madds," I murmur against her lips, my hands moving to her biceps and holding her firmly there.

A protest falls from her as she tries to struggle out of my grip. "No. Stop. Don't talk." Her lips find mine and I willingly let them staunch my protest. Her hands roam and fingernails scratch up my bare chest while my cock begs—*fucking begs*—for me to shut the hell up.

Every part of me took note of the way she moved on the dance floor. Every part fought the urge to kiss her when she pressed against me at the bar. And now all I want to do is act on it when I damn well shouldn't.

She's not the kind of woman you can fuck and walk away from. *Literally.* I can't. She can't.

And that's terrifying but not enough to stop my tongue from licking against hers.

Be honorable. Fucking try.

"You're drunk," I say.

"So are you." She fights my hold and, in the process, writhes her hips over me. Damp heat with her ass pressing against my hard-on.

Lord, have mercy.

"This isn't a good idea." *Oh, how it's the most perfect fucking idea ever.*

"Does it look like I care?" she counters and then licks her tongue up the line of my throat.

She's Maddix.

She's not supposed to be sexy.

She's not supposed to be goddamn desirable.

She's supposed to be a safe bet. A voice of reason to my chaos. The opposite of temptation.

Not adding to it.

But here we are.

"You're going to regret this in the morning." My voice is strained. So is my restraint. *Remind me of that after you're buried balls deep in her, and you've come.*

"My regret. My problem."

"But it's not . . ." Why am I choosing this moment to be honorable? *Of all the times in my life.* I shake my head to try and think straight. "Maddix. I can't take advantage of you like this. You're clearly drunk."

A slow, seductive smile crawls over her lips as she leans down and whispers in my ear. "Then fuck me till I'm sober so I can make the right decisions." Then she laughs, and every part of me is desperate for her.

It's the freest sound I've heard from her and when I look up, my breath catches in my fucking throat. She's bathed in moonlight. Her skin. Her perfect fucking tits that are pressed against the white fabric of the thinnest tank top known to man. Her chest rises and falls, her lips are swollen and pouting, and her eyes are begging me for this.

Fuck me till I'm sober.

Her name is a groan on my lips. The last ties on my restraint fraying with every touch of her lips to my skin and the fisting of my hands at my sides.

"I feel out of control. My life. People's judgments of me. What happens tomorrow. Let me feel like I'm controlling something." She flicks her tongue over my nipple.

Control me. By all fucking means.

Her eyes look up to meet mine, her grin seductive. "Pretty please."

"I'm not the right guy for this. For you. I . . . I'm drunk too. I'm too . . ." My excuses are lame and fall flat.

I'm far from drunk. I'm stone-cold sober and so fucking desperate to not stop what she's doing.

She reaches back and grabs my cock with one hand. I groan involuntarily and my eyes roll back in my head. "You're drunk? Doesn't seem to matter in this department." She scrapes her fingernails over me and my cock jerks in response. She chuckles. "Stop thinking, Cruz. Start acting."

"I'm trying to be respectful." The minute the words are out, I groan as she grinds her ass against me again.

"I'm not in the mood to be respected." She pulls her tank top off, and her hair falls to sit above the dusty pink of her nipples. They're even more fucking perfect than I thought they were. "I'm sowing my oats, Cruz. Isn't that what you said I needed to do? Sow them? So it can either be you or it can be someone else, but I'm going to fucking sow them tonight."

"This isn't fair." I scrub a hand through my hair as my other one grabs on to her hip.

She laughs. "Life isn't fair. Isn't that why we're both here? Both stuck with each other?" Then she edges backwards, her pussy sliding over my bare cock and, fucking hell, my hips jerk in response.

"Christ," I grit out.

"You have by the time I roll this condom on you to decide." She holds up a condom between her two fingers.

She's not fucking playing and thank fucking God for that because I don't have enough sense right now to think straight.

She giggles again. The sound tells me she's still drunk, but hell if she doesn't falter rolling the condom onto me. "What'll it be, Mr. Navarro?" she asks, breathless. "My pussy or your hand for relief? I know which one would feel better."

From one heartbeat to the next I have her on her back. I'm mad. At myself for trying to be respectable and failing. At her for tempting me when she shouldn't. For me fucking caving and wanting everything about her way more than I should.

So fine.

We'll do this.

We'll fuck out our anger, our lack of control over this situation, our goddamn desire, and get it out of our systems.

Just this once.

Just this time.

Our lips meet in a savage union of desire where I shut out all thoughts of right or wrong—especially at how this is going to be so fucked up in the morning. And I just get lost in her.

Her skin. Her taste. Her goddamn hunger.

We shift so that I'm on my knees between her thighs. Our hands roam clumsily, laughs falling out between rapturous moans. And when I sink into her, I almost come on the spot.

She's so fucking tight. So fucking wet. So fucking everything, that I dig my fingers into her hips to quiet her movement so I can last.

Because on a normal day, that's not a fucking problem. But with a shit ton of alcohol and what feels like a few days of foreplay mixed in, holding out is the worst form of pleasure-pain known to man.

"Relax," I murmur as I strum a thumb over her clit, trying to give her something to soften her more. "You've got to relax, Madds, so I can fit as much of my cock in you as possible."

Her legs spread wider. That's her response. A mewled moan and glassy eyes on me saying she trusts me—a trust I don't fucking deserve—before trying to give me more of her by widening her thighs.

Her arousal glistens in the muted light. It coats my cock like a candy I want to lick. That I want to savor.

"You're gorgeous." I don't know where that fucking came from. But it's there and I cover it up by leaning forward and pressing my lips to hers.

I don't say shit like that.

Not during sex. Not like this.

But my lips meet hers and swallow her gasp from the action pushing me even farther into her. I slide a hand down to her ass to hold her there, and I begin to move.

Slow at first. Gentle. Trying to let her get used to my size. To the stretch and burn mixed with the pleasure. She throws her head back, exposing her throat. I run my stubbled chin over the sensitive skin there and she tenses all around me in response, milking my cock with the contraction.

It's a stuttered groan on my part. A need to draw this out and rush to the finish at the same time.

My head dizzies. My pulse races. My balls draw tight.

And then I begin to move. Thrust after thrust, I piston into her. A grind of the hips. A pull back out so I hit her clit.

We do this dance. Over and over. Her body moving in tune with mine until the pressure builds and the pleasure grows. All I can see is the bounce of her tits as I slam my hips against hers. My name falls from her lips.

"Touch yourself," I tell her. Fuck if I need to be turned on any more, but I'm not complaining.

An intoxicated Maddix Hart is an uninhibited one, and hell if it isn't sexy to watch her teeth sink into her bottom lip as she rubs her fingers back and forth over her clit.

She's a goddamn siren, and I'm about to crash on her rocks as she moans out—her body tensing and thighs tightening against my hips. Her pussy pulses all around me, wave after wave as I slow my strokes so she can sink into her orgasm.

But the minute her breath hitches again, I'm a goddamn goner. My hands grip and hips hit over and over and over. *The sound of slick skin. The scent of sex. The feel of her wet heat gripping me.*

I cry out when I come. My vision goes white.

Then black.

And when I open my eyes before I collapse and roll off her, all I see is Maddix.

Gorgeous. Uninhibited. Unexpected.

Maddix.

CHAPTER FOURTEEN

Maddix

I'M NAKED.

That much is apparent when I stir awake, the sun beaming in the windows and the cool of the sheets sliding over my bare breasts.

My head is pounding—the sunlight's not helping—and there is a deliciously sweet soreness between my thighs.

Maddix . . . what happ—

Shit.

Awareness hits.

Double shit.

I slide a look beside me and lose my breath for a second. Cruz Navarro is lying beside me in all of his naked glory. Every sculpted line. Every firm, defined muscle. His incredible cock, thick and heavy against his inner thigh.

Did we?

How did I have sex with Cruz Navarro and not remember it?

We did though, right?

Panic strikes. Panic mixed with snapshots of last night.

Good snapshots. Incredible snapshots. Ones that I'm going to struggle looking at him and remembering and not wanting to act on.

Cruz Navarro is . . . Jesus. He's like a walking wet dream and lives up to the notion. His skill. *His cock.* His lips. His . . . everything.

I shift gently and try to *unremember* and know it's futile. There is no forgetting last night. Even through the haze of a hangover, there is no forgetting.

Cue the panic.

What do we do now? I don't have casual sex. I've never had it . . . and yet we just did. *I just did.*

You're going to regret this in the morning.

This isn't a good idea.

You're drunk. We're drunk.

He resisted and I persisted.

Oh my God. I took advantage of Cruz. I refused to take no for an answer. I pulled a Cruz Navarro on Cruz Navarro.

I bury my face in my hands and try to process every way imaginable this could have gone and *this* wasn't it.

In all the scenarios that ran through my head the first night I found out there was only one bed, it was me rejecting him. It was me frustrated with him being a guy, with him disrespecting my boundaries. With him being him and wanting casual sex for the sake of casual sex.

Who the hell is this woman I've become in a few short days?

And what am I supposed to do now? How am I supposed to face him when this . . . shouldn't have happened?

I sneak another glance his way, at all of him, and ignore the sweet ache that begins in my body.

Cruz Navarro is the player-est of players. He dates women a couple of times and then moves on.

He can't move on from me.

We're stuck in this . . . situation. And now I've slept with him and don't know how to fix it.

⤝

When I get out of the shower, he's no longer in bed.

In fact, he's nowhere in the entire damn hotel room.

That's good, right? That means I have more time to figure out how to handle this.

But wait. He's nowhere in the damn hotel room. That means he's silently freaking out about this too. Is he?

No. He most definitely is not.

This is a normal thing for him. Casual sex. Sex without strings. Fucking your pretend girlfriend until she comes so hard she sees stars, and then being gone when she wakes up because you regard what happened as being nothing more than just sex. As her being easily replaceable with the next person wait-ing eagerly in line.

But I'm not and that's the problem.

I'm stuck here.

We're stuck together.

And now . . . now we've screwed this all up.

By the time I hear the door click shut at my back, I've already worked myself up into a frenzy. I have ten speeches rehearsed—why this shouldn't have happened, why it can't happen again, why it was a huge mistake—and all of them are basically allowing me to save face.

And none of them come out when our eyes meet.

"Please tell me what I think happened didn't happen."

"Well, shit, Madds. Way to knock a man's ego down a peg right off the bat." He chuckles but stays near the door of the hotel room, arms crossed over his chest, and shoulder against the wall.

He's keeping his distance. He's letting me know there will be no warm fuzzies after last night. That there is nothing more to it than a physical act, a release. He couldn't be more obvious about it if he tried.

I should be thrilled by that. That's what I want. Then why does it hurt a little bit too?

"That's not what I meant. It's just . . . we were drunk."

"Very."

"And I don't remember much." *I remember everything.*

"That makes two of us." He tilts his head to the side and studies me. I'm not sure why the intensity of it disarms me, but it does. It's almost as if he's trying to see something in my expression but what it is, I don't know.

"It wasn't a big deal," I say.

"Some fumbling in the dark. I think there was a bonked head or two. Some laughter. A condom. And . . . *you know.*"

"I know." I shift on my feet, hating this awkwardness and wishing he'd take the lead on this. "It's just that . . . that isn't who I am. The casual sex thing. I don't just sleep with someone to sleep with someone and . . ."

"Usually there are feelings involved. Emotions. Meaning behind it. I get it." He holds his hands up, face stoic. "No need to explain or apologize."

"Right." Then why is there a lump in my throat that feels like rejection? Why does my body ache in places it shouldn't ache for a man I'm still getting to know but still want all the same?

Why am I looking at you and remembering every single second, despite the amount of alcohol I consumed, and hating that it meant nothing to you?

"It happens to the best of us." He shrugs, wearing indifference like a suit. "No harm. No foul. Fun had. Oats sowed. Now back to business like it never happened."

But it did happen. So much happened that I . . . "Cruz," I say it softly, and I'm not sure if it's a question or a statement.

We stare at each other across the short distance, the hood of his sweatshirt on so that his eyes are shadowed.

Are you still thinking about it like I am?

Do you still smell me on your skin like I do you?

Do you—

"Good, now that that's covered, I've got to get showered and to the track. The team's all here now."

Without another word—or another look my way—he gets ready for work.

And I sit at the desk, staring at my blinking cursor. I did this to myself. I initiated sex. I persisted when he tried to reason with me.

I know he said there'd be regrets.

"No harm. No foul. Fun had. Oats sowed."

So why do I feel so . . . used?

CHAPTER FIFTEEN

Maddix

THEY'RE STARING. HEADS TURNING SUBTLY AS WE WALK PAST TO GET a first glimpse of me—Cruz Navarro's *Instagram official* girlfriend—while casually trying to pretend like they're not.

The chatter quiets as they look and then suddenly starts up abruptly when they realize that they've stopped talking.

"Aren't you glad I'm so good-looking that everyone is staring at me?" Cruz murmurs, amusement in his tone. His attempt at humor eases my nerves but not by much. He nudges me. "Relax, Madds. We've got this."

"You've got this," I correct.

"And since I have you, then *we've* got this."

The weight of Cruz's hand in mine, our fingers laced, is what I focus on. This is the first time we've touched like this since . . . *the other night*, and fortunately for me, there is so much distraction around us that I'm not thinking of what that palm felt like sliding over my breast.

At least not the whole time.

Maybe for the first few seconds I did, but it was quickly replaced by the unabashed scrutiny of everyone around us as we make the long stroll through the gates and into the paddock.

The paddock is a mini city in and of itself. A stretch of real estate at the track occupied by each team and the portable buildings they erect. These buildings serve as the teams' home bases during race week. My neck cranes as I walk past each one, marveling at the fact that these get built for a race and then torn down and transported to the next soon after the checkered flag is waved.

It's only official race people allowed in here, a pass to the paddock is like the holy grail, and yet as professional as everyone here is, I still see phones being angled our way. I still sense that pictures are being taken.

And it's unnerving.

People are on the go everywhere around us. Race teams come in and out of their selected places and cross the walkway to the garages where the race cars are housed, and the crews work on them. People with press passes around their necks mill about with their cameras in their hands or their camera crews standing beside them. People—celebrities I'm assuming by the entourage of people crowded around them—hang back with their favorite team gear on. Or rather whichever team gave them the pass to be in this area.

It's a coordinated dance that I learned from watching qualifying can either look like a flash mob rushing in to take its places or a synchronized swim team that knows exactly what the other person is going to do next.

Kind of like me and Cruz. After a week of virtually living together, we've created our own rhythm of sorts. For the most part, it's giving each other a wide berth of privacy while we do our own thing.

For a while I struggled with that. We had sex. How can everything be back to normal . . . or even weirder, how can there be more distance between us than before?

I had to put my hurt feelings aside. I had to tell myself that Cruz creating distance between us was a necessity for this to work and in the end, probably better for me, a woman who is suddenly thinking about sex way more than she ever has in her entire life.

That's not a bad thing.

It's just not an opportune thing when you think you're growing a secret crush on a man you shouldn't have one on and who clearly isn't one to crush back on anyone for an extended period of time.

But with race weekend upon us, we must get back to the business of being a couple again for the show of it.

It rings different this time around though. More forced. More scripted.

Or at least I thought it would, but walking in here together, making this visual statement, makes me realize we're okay. *This* is okay. And that I need to stop overthinking fucking everything.

"You still good?" Cruz asks and lifts a hand to wave to someone across the way.

"Yep," I say and look over at him. "Is this weird for you?"

"So fucking weird," he says and flashes a grin as we reach Gravitas Racing's paddock. Its exterior is a bright white with a splash of orange throughout to match the color and schematics of Cruz's car—or livery, as I've learned it's called in my *Welcome to Formula 1* crash course. A lesson of sorts that was put on by Cruz's public relations minder, Amandine.

"Why though?" I ask.

He stops and tugs my hand when I keep walking. Even through his sunglasses, I can see his eyes narrow, puzzled. "You do realize you're the first woman I've ever brought into the paddock with me, right?"

"I—what?" I ask more out of reflex than anything, startled by his admission. I know he's never had a *real* girlfriend, but surely, he's brought a woman to the track with him before. *Right?*

"I made a rule a long time ago to never mix business with pleasure. Never."

My smile is stuttered in response. Then I murmur, "Well, if you want to be technical, the rule's not really broken. This is one hundred percent business."

Our gazes hold, and I'm confused by what I see in his eyes but that I can't exactly decipher. And before I can, Amandine appears out of nowhere.

"Hi," she says with enough enthusiasm for the entire race team. She's the perfect definition of the saying *dynamite comes in small packages*. From what I witnessed yesterday, she's fiery when she needs to be, not afraid of putting Cruz or the press in their place. She's coaxing at other times. And gentle at others.

She was my everything all rolled into one yesterday when I was brought into the paddock through a private entrance. My tour guide. My teacher. My protector. My go-to. Our decision for me to stay out of public view yesterday during qualifying was a joint one. Cruz wanted to concentrate without distraction on securing a good spot on the starting grid and I agreed, willing to keep as much of my anonymity that was still left for one more day.

At the time, a part of me was assuming he wanted to hang on to his solo status publicly as long as possible. Posting pictures on Instagram is one thing, but showing up with a woman on his arm to a race takes things to a whole other level.

But after his admission, maybe his promise to himself was what he was trying to hold on to. Maybe that's what him saying it was better if I stay out of sight yesterday was all about.

And now today, that promise he's made himself for the last four or five years is broken.

"Good morning, Cruz. How are you feeling today?" Amandine asks, her smile big and her eyes alive.

"Like it's race day," Cruz teases, placing his hand on the small of my back, something I'm still getting used to the feel of.

"Well, starting in P4 makes any race day a good day, right?" she asks.

"Unless you're starting in the first three spots ahead of P4."

"Grumpy," she counters.

"Always." He pauses and looks at me, his smile softening. "I have to get to work. Are you okay?"

I nod. "Go do your thing. Don't worry about me."

"Okay. I'll see you in a while then."

We stand in awkward silence for a few beats—almost as if it can be inferred by anyone watching that he doesn't want to kiss me due to lack of privacy, when I know it's because this is all a farce.

Sure, we keep posting pictures of our first adventures around Amsterdam to keep up pretenses. The endless calls from my family about what in the hell is going on that I've had to fend off say it's working. But deliberate affection for one another other than our one private slip is a line we've yet to cross publicly.

"Sounds good," I say, to which he takes a step back before turning and then jogging the few feet across the path to the garage.

"Well, that was awkward," Amandine says and laughs. "You can bring a horse to water and all that."

My smile is tight, not one hundred percent certain what she's implying so I just leave it be.

"Are you wishing you'd gotten this out of the way yesterday?" Amandine asks as she directs me into the hospitality suite.

"What, the *public walk of curiosity?*" I ask and chuckle.

"It's better than the walk of shame." She grins, unknowing that I felt like I walked that for a whole day after we slept together.

"There's always that." I smile and then shrug. "I think staying incognito yesterday was for the best. As it is, I had enough of the crew giving me double takes. The last thing he needed was to get shit from other drivers."

"You think?"

"The perpetual bachelor bringing his date to the track? Come on."

She holds her hands up and laughs. "True. True."

"Besides, Cruz needed to work without distraction, and I could observe up in the box in anonymity without anyone knowing I was here." I follow her into one of the office spaces in the suite where I had set up my computer and worked some of yesterday during the downtime.

"Well today is going to be even crazier, and now that everyone knows you're here, expect the cameras to pan in on you and get your reaction to everything."

"That's . . . wonderful," I say with all of the enthusiasm of getting my teeth pulled.

"Cruz Navarro dating a camera-shy woman? Now that's a first." Once the words are out, she pauses and hangs her head for a beat. When her eyes meet mine, there's regret woven in them. "That was a shitty thing to say. I didn't mean for it to come out like that. I'm just not used to—"

"It's okay," I say and laugh. "It's no secret that we both had pasts before this . . . and his was a little more documented or should I say *spirited* than most."

"Whew." She pretends to wipe her hand on her forehead. "Crisis averted." Another day of Amandine's humor? I welcome it. She's a new friend I've found in this very strange landscape.

I spend the next few hours taking everything about *race day*, as everyone calls it, in. The intensity on the faces of the crew. The constant movement of the Gravitas staff around anything and everything Cruz or their other driver, Nico Schilling, need.

I stay in the background and take everything in from a distance, not wanting to disturb Cruz's usual race day routine. My concentrated effort is to exist in this space, to be present for everyone to see I'm there, but to not be a single thought in Cruz's head.

It's a fascinating process, though—the semantics of race day. From catered meals with customized nutrition to carry them through a race and the scorching temperatures inside their cockpits to the reaction drills with tennis balls meant to help sharpen his reaction times on the steering wheel. Steering column? That correct terminology wasn't covered in my F1 crash course of terms. No doubt I'll mess other ones up as well.

I make myself part of the race day hustle and bustle and when Cruz retires to his private driver's room—a place Amandine has informed me is where the driver's go for either a quick nap, to meditate, or whatever it is they do to find the quiet they need to focus before heading out to the track for the start—I decide to brave the world outside of the Gravitas bubble.

Make yourself seen. Weren't those Kevin's reiterated orders via text this morning before we even left the hotel?

At least I can say I'm trying.

On my venture around the grounds, I note that each team has their own cadence of sorts. There is a pomp and circumstance to it all. A choreography to who does what in the garages.

The crews go through checks so practiced they could probably do them in their sleep and yet they do them anyway, anticipating everything that could happen other than routine.

There are so many different people doing their jobs but one thing is certain, the energy is palpable. Like the track has its own electricity to it that keeps getting charged with each and every minute we get closer to the start of the race—or *lights out*, as I learned from Amandine.

But as race time pulls near, I find myself being drawn back toward the Gravitas circle. Toward its paddock location. Then, escorted by Amandine into the garage area.

When Cruz walks in with his fire suit on with it unzipped down to the waist and its arms hanging loosely at his hips, my breath hitches.

Sure, I've seen the pictures of him. The promo shots. The podium celebrations. But when he walks into the garage, partially suited up with his headphones in, his expression intense and focused, there's a mesmerizing air about him I've yet to experience.

He's in control. Calculating. Dedicated. And a little cocky.

He's gorgeous.

He looks up from where he's talking to Otis, his race engineer, about something, and we inadvertently lock eyes across the space.

Something happens in that moment. I don't know what it is, but my heart starts racing and my body heats. I'm suddenly struggling to breathe.

And by the way his Adam's apple bobs beneath the neck of his long-sleeved Nomex shirt, I swear he senses something's different.

He gives me the slightest of nods before moving to his car and pointing at something like the moment never happened.

Maybe it didn't.

Maybe I'm making shit up.

Maybe I'm just fascinated by the excitement of all of this and am reading into things.

Regardless, my pulse is still pounding and it's nearly impossible to tear my eyes away from him, even briefly.

You're being ridiculous, Hart. Utterly ridiculous.

And as the minutes tick away to race start, I'm beginning to believe myself more and more. That the sudden awareness of everything about Cruz was simply because we were the only two people in a crowded room who know the truth about our secret.

I'm getting good at convincing myself there's nothing there.

People come in and out of the garage like it's Grand Central Terminal. Camera crews for the telecast of the race. Camera crews for a streaming platform that's making a series about the sport and its drivers. Media personalities and journalists.

It's no wonder Cruz protects his ability to tune out so fiercely because there is no way I'd be able to focus and concentrate in this environment.

The tension slowly ramps up in the garage. It's expectation mixed with anticipation and a steady dose of knowing what needs to be done and hoping everything goes smoothly.

At least, that's from my newly educated opinion of it all.

"Do you want ears?" Amandine asks.

"Do I want what?" I laugh but then stop when I turn to see her holding out a headset to me so that I can presumably listen to radio communications during the race.

"Really?" I ask.

"Um, yeah," she says like I'm being ridiculous. "We can't have you not knowing what's going on."

"Oh. Wow. Thank you." I smile as I put the headset around my neck like everyone else around here has it. At certain times I seem to remember the role I'm here to play and other times, I'm so enamored and overwhelmed by the sheer enormity of this whole operation that I forget why I'm here.

"Sure. So what's going to happen next is that Cruz will be getting suited the rest of the way up. Then he'll get in the car and be strapped in. Then about forty minutes out from start, they'll fire the engine and Cruz will drive the car around the track for a flying lap. Just to make sure all is well with the car. He'll get to the end of pit lane where the crew will meet him and use what we call wheelie boards to bring the car to its correct starting spot on the grid. At that point, Cruz will get back out of the car while the crew keeps the tires warm and does last-minute checks. While they do that, Cruz typically puts his music back on and tunes out everything around him. Then, well . . . you know the rest. He'll get back in the car and—"

"And the next time I see you, I'll have won the race."

I jump at the sound of Cruz's voice, my smile as automatic as the jumping of my heart. "Hi." It's the most ridiculous thing to say, but it's the first thing that comes out of my mouth when I meet his eyes and feel his hand slide to my lower back.

"Fancy meeting you here," he says with a shy grin that defies every ounce of intensity emanating off his body. Amandine steps back in my periphery to give us our privacy. "They've got you set up like one of the crew, huh?"

"Do I look official?" I ask.

"Very," he says, his eyes on mine as the muscle in his jaw works. "So I have to get back. Get in the car. Go around the track a few times."

"No big deal. Just another day," I tease.

"Right. No big deal."

The awkwardness is back, which is weird because it actually feels completely normal to be here.

Clearly it doesn't for him.

"Okay. Good luck out there. I'll be right here to congratulate you when you win."

"And if I don't?" he asks, the question throwing me.

"Then I'll still be here to congratulate you. From what I've read, there are a million other people who would kill to be in your shoes, so just being here is pretty fucking incredible."

His eyes widen briefly, a disbelieving look follows, before he utters a half laugh—almost as if he doesn't believe me. He takes a step away and then stops momentarily before turning back toward me. Our eyes meet briefly before he steps into me, his hand reaching up to cup the side of my face a heartbeat before his lips brush ever so gently against mine.

I swear anyone in the vicinity would be able to hear my hitched breath.

It's deafening in my own ears, but it's drowned out by the rush of sensations rushing through me.

Surprise. Desire. Want. Disbelief.

And as soon as the kiss happens, it's over. "I like you being here," he murmurs and is already turning on his heel before I can process any of it.

"Cruz." His name is a syllable full of those four emotions.

He stops and turns to look at me, eyes swimming with what I think is confusion and an expression still stoic before he pulls his balaclava over his head and strides toward the other side of the garage.

My eyes track him, my body flush and pulse racing once again with the warmth of his kiss still on my lips and the chills he created still dancing over my skin.

My thoughts are as scrambled as my hormones. The overthinking from the past few days seems ridiculous. He just showed me that there might have been more to us, that—

The movement to my right snaps me out of it. The camera crew about ten feet away, the lens focused on me, that is now slowly moving in to where Cruz now stands.

I hang my head momentarily.

You're an idiot, Maddix.

Did you really, for a second, think that was a real kiss? That it wasn't for show? That Cruz isn't doing exactly what was asked of him in looking stable and calmed down?

That's why the confusion was so heavy in his eyes. Why he went to walk away and then turned back to me to kiss me like a normal couple would do. He saw the camera. He's playing the game.

And yet knowing all of this does nothing to abate the ache that simple kiss stirred back up. But what is hitting my heart is that torn look in Cruz's eyes. I'd like to think it has to do with me. I'm naive, but not enough to know what that just cost Cruz to do that.

"Ready?" Amandine says, as if she can sense the moment having passed.

"Yes. Sure." I clear my throat and refuse to give a third response like Cruz says I do. Just as I refuse to allow myself to be hurt about the superficiality of that kiss.

It wasn't real.

So not real.

Yet . . . it felt so real on the heels of the other night.

And why am I suddenly worried about his safety during the race? What's up with that?

"This way," Amandine says, motioning me toward the staircase that leads to the observation room above the garage for Gravitas employees. It's where I spent most of my day yesterday during qualifying, but something tells me to look to my right.

I'm met with a steely stare from a man standing on the opposite side of the garage. His hair is salt and pepper in color and his lips are in a hard, un-forgiving line. His arms are crossed over his chest and his shoulders are stiff.

If it weren't for the harsh, derisive expression on his face, I imagine the man would be considered classically handsome.

Dominic Navarro. He has to be by the mere resemblance alone.

And clearly, he is judging me. That is not up for debate.

Wouldn't you judge me if you were in his shoes? His son's new girlfriend when he's never had one? A woman in the pits no less?

I offer a smile in return. It's tentative but kind.

But he doesn't reciprocate.

Not at all.

Instead, he gives a disgusting shake of his head and then walks away.

CHAPTER SIXTEEN

Cruz

THE CAR IS QUICKER THAN SHIT.

It's dialed in more than it's been all season, and I can sense it.

"Good sector time, Cruz. Point three seconds faster than your fastest lap and ten seconds from Cavanaugh," Otis says into my ear regarding the leader.

A fucking tight race. No room for error.

"Place?"

"Still P4. Top three remain unchanged."

Fuck. I can be fast all I want but if I can't move up the grid, I'm not doing my job. But it's been an uneventful race if the lineup hasn't changed. No crashes. No overtakes. No fucking nothing.

In the back of the field, yes. But not what's stretched out before me.

"Bide your time. Something's bound to change."

"How far?" I ask, my voice vibrating with the G's as I come out of the corner on the backstretch and engage the throttle for the fastest part of the course.

He knows what I'm asking. How far ahead of me is Rossi? What time do I have to make up or him to lose so that I can gain a position?

"One point two."

"Permission to push?" I ask, knowing they have way more information than I do about the car's telemetry.

That and they know that Rossi and Evans, the Apex team, has been struggling as of late. During last season, a podium without an Apex driver was an anomaly. This season? It's a struggle for them to finish in the top five.

"Hold," Otis says. No doubt he's conferring with our team principal on a decision that's best for the team collective.

When I hit the next straight, Rossi's car is in my sight. His engine hasn't been the strongest near the ass-end of races. I can reel him in. I know I can.

I push a bit more while I'm in limbo waiting for an answer.

Seconds ticking by as I wait. Precious fucking tenths of seconds.

He doesn't want to speak to you. I'm sorry, Cruz.

The bitter taste of rejection hits me now out of all moments. My call to mi abuelo. The silence as his caretaker went to ask him. The crushing blow when she uttered those words.

Clear your head, Cross.

Clear your fucking head.

"Go ahead and push."

"I need DRS," I say more to myself than to Otis. We all know I need it. I just need to pull within range.

"Ten-four. Yes. Okay."

Three answers. The thought has a smile flickering seconds before the G's pull it tight again.

The engine whines its distinctive sound as I push it harder, faster, trying to get within DRS range when the caution lights flash on the light tree at the edge of the course.

"In the back of the field," Otis explains where the caution has occurred.

"Everyone okay?" I ask as I slow the car down and weave back and forth on the track to keep the tires warm.

"Ten-four. Bustos and Costa touched tires. Just cleaning up debris," Otis says in his uncanny calm voice that could narrate a nature documentary.

"Box?" I ask when I don't want to. I have fresh tires, but it's not worth risking a grid position.

"Tires?"

"Still have traction," I explain. There's not enough time left in the race to make up for a lost grid place. And even though I'm not content with a P4, it's still better than P5. "Nico?"

"P7."

It'd be a strong finish for us. It would be better if I were on the podium though.

I stretch my fingers out as I pull up right behind Rossi, the caution on the track allowing me to close the gap.

Just like almost everyone on this circuit, we've raced against each other our whole lives. In karting as kids. Up the ranks as teens into Formula 4. Then Formula 3 and Formula 2. And now.

We know each other's signature moves. Our tendencies. We know who dives right off the line and who favors their left. There are patterns we've studied. Memorized. Become part of the way we drive.

And that pertains to everyone on the grid . . . everyone *except* for Oliver Rossi. He's a loose cannon who's unpredictable and who has made his reputation off being just that. A guy who has more talent than his own good and who doesn't have any fucks to give.

He's dangerous in the best kind of way, and right now I have to figure out which fucking way he's going to favor so I can go the opposite when the green flag drops.

"Right," Otis says, knowing exactly what I'm thinking. We've done this enough times that it's like we share the same brain.

"He's going left," I say.

"Your call, but the track is clear. Caution will be lifted when you hit the start/finish."

"Ten-four."

And just as I say the words, the pace on the track picks up as we all begin to jockey for the best positioning possible.

I weave back and forth to keep my tires sticky and when we turn the corner on the last straight, we all pick up speed.

My body presses deeper into the seat with each and every kilometer per hour the speed increases to. We hit the line and we're at full throttle within seconds. The first corner coming. We all bunch up as we let up some before hammering back down again.

I go to the right of Rossi as he feigns left before cutting back just as quickly.

"Fuck!" I shout as we make contact.

Tires rub.

Our front wings touch.

My brakes lock up as I prevent disaster. As I avoid the wall.

I fight the steering wheel. The car.

It's a mere second but by the time I have the car straightened out and the ability to accelerate back, Rossi is out in front of me and Evans is pushing his nose to midrange on my car.

I fight him off. Try to squeeze more out of the motor to push past him and leave him at my rear.

I shout as I do, as I succeed.

Because P4 is still better than P5.

But that's all I'm able to hold on to. All I'm able to gain.

And when I come down the grandstands straight to the roar of the crowd and the blur of color from fans waving their flags and signs of their favorite driver, I'm nowhere near fucking satisfied with my performance.

With my finish.

With my incorrect call on Rossi.

I could do better.

So much fucking better.

"Great job, man," Otis says in my ear. "You know how these races go. No movement, no mistakes, makes it hard to advance. The four of you ran a flawless race. No complaints on our end."

I grimace. I was far from flawless. "Great job, team. Pit times were incredible. You executed flawlessly. This one's on me, guys."

There's more chatter but I tune it out as I make my way around the track and back to pit row.

And when I pull into the garage and climb out of the car, I accept the high fives and the pats on my back from my team, but it's all for shit.

Because I may be in the shadow of the garage, but the man standing in the corner with his arms folded, lips pursed, and whose eyes I know are locked on me from behind his sunglasses looms so much darker.

Fuck.

Just fuck.

I do all my normal post-race requirements. Weigh in for the FIA. A quick shower out of my fire suit that's soaked from the heat. Interviews that Amandine stands beside me through. Debriefing with my team.

All the while I can feel the two edges of what feels like my very small universe pulling at me. Maddix, and this ridiculous deal I made on one side. My dad, and his iron fist wrapped in disappointment on the other.

A tentative smile versus a deriding grit of teeth.

Fuck. Might as well get the worst of it over first.

"Papá."

He narrows his brows and holds my stare. No doubt everyone around us is watching, waiting to see the proud father pat his son on the back. The show for everyone to take part in and report to others on. "A word, please."

It's not a question. And by the way he's striding toward one of the private rooms in the Gravitas hospitality suite, he's assuming I'll follow.

For my own sake and privacy, I do, but tension sets in my shoulders with each and every step I take. I smile at the staff who congratulates me on the way while internally rehearsing the speech he's about to give me.

Same shit, same words, different race. More derision.

The second I shut the door behind me, I hold my hands up, grin sarcastic, and a fuck you lift of my eyebrows. "Save it. I know the speech by heart. *I made the wrong choice on the lead off with Rossi after the caution. I was too timid. My reaction times were too slow. I'm an embarrassment to the Navarro name. I wasn't living up to my potential.*" I shrug. "How about you surprise me and throw in there *a great job, hijo, you kicked ass today?* How much would that kill you to say that, huh?"

"You're distracted and it showed."

"We're back to that, are we? Yes." I flash a grin. "*You* being here distracts me. How did you know?"

He hisses out a frustrated sigh.

To anyone looking in, I would come off as a spoiled, disrespectful asshole. But they don't know the hell I go through. The standards I'm held to. The restoration of the Navarro status.

"Even with today's . . . *error*, the math works for you. If you finish where you need to place in the remainder of the races without any unforeseen . . . *instances*, then the championship could be yours."

So in other words, live up to the perfection you expect but that you couldn't deliver yourself.

"This is racing, Papá. I can only control what I can control. Everything beyond that is out of my hands. Perfection is impossible. One race maybe, but the remainder of the season? You know that better than anyone."

"You should expect that out of yourself."

"I fucking do. Every minute of every goddamn day I'm fully aware of the perfection expected of me so for once . . . just back the fuck off and leave me be."

His tsk grates on my nerves. The clasping of his hands in front of him is his telltale sign that he's settling in for the long haul here, when all I want is to get the fuck out of here.

"A good start would be you getting rid of her."

"What?" Talk about whiplash. Here I think he's talking about my drinking and partying—something I've paused—and instead, he's talking about Maddix? "What the hell are you talking about?"

"The American. You can't date her. She's not acceptable."

Not acceptable?

I chuckle but it has zero amusement. "Since when do you think you can tell me who I can or can't date?"

Probably about the same time he thought he could prevent me from seeing mi abuelo.

His chuckle crawls over my skin. "Isla. Bianca. Penelope." He ticks off each name on his fingers. His eyebrows raise as mine narrow. "They weren't good for you either, and I took measures to mitigate that." His smile is placating as my temper fires.

There's no fucking way he . . . whatever he did to steer them away.

His chuckle says he did. "Funny how you think they're there for you when it's the status they're after. They took the first sum I offered and a promise of who knows what else to steer clear from you proves it."

"You're serious, aren't you?"

"I am, yes." Matter of fact. Cold as ice.

I shrug to piss him off. "Thanks for doing me the favor. I was done with them anyway. Our . . . affairs had run their course, so . . . thank you."

He grits his teeth. He wants to know he got to me with that admission. My response says I refuse to bite.

"Nice to see we're on the same page." He shoves his hands in his pockets and rocks on his heels, lips pursed and eyes unrelenting.

Where's he going with this?

I nod to wait him out, because we are most definitely not on the same page.

"You brought one of your . . . *whores* to work with you," he says, disgust as evident in his body language as his voice. Every muscle in my body tenses. *This is what you brought on her, Cruz.* A label she doesn't deserve. "What are you going to do next, write affirmations of love to her on your helmet?"

"What's it to you? You should know by now that your disapproval begs me to bring her to every race from here on out." Funny how in the whole weird situation, disapproval from my father is the last thing I expected. "You asked me to stop partying and shaming our name. I did what you asked. Shocking, I know. I found a girl to settle down with and surprise, surprise, you're still not happy." His grimace makes me grin. "Did you ever stop to think that maybe you're the problem?"

The tendons in his neck tense. *Ah, you don't like that, do you, Papá?*

"She's not Spanish."

"And?"

"And by the way she dresses, she clearly doesn't have any sense of who she's dating—and please know I use the term loosely. Or, how it'll reflect on the family. She *does not* have the pedigree fitting of a Navarro."

Fuck. You.

"The pedigree?" I shake my head ever so slowly as my jaw clenches and hands fist. My body is exhausted, but my temper is ablaze.

Who's not good enough for whom?

"The last thing you need to do is stick your cock in her and get her pregnant."

My anger turns to rage. Normally his words roll off my back but, Jesus fucking Christ. "If you had any clue about the women *I've stuck my cock into*, you'd die."

His jaw works as he glares at me. No doubt crudeness is okay for him, but not for me.

"Hijo, you're walking a perilously thin line when it comes to what is and isn't acceptable in this family."

I snort. "What is the threat? That I'm going to be kicked out? It's not like you can take my last name away or the blood running through me."

"No, but I can cut you out of every goddamn thing that is Navarro." His eyes are as ruthless as his tone. Both have my heart clenching in my chest. Aching.

"You can keep your money, Papá. Clearly, I've made my own." I hold my hands out to the side to say look at where we are.

"Money doesn't make the man, Cruz. Blood does. The last name does. The heritage does."

"You say that like it's a threat when I'm the one you're counting on to prove to el patriarca that you're worthy of that last name you swing like a sword. Must suck being a grown man and needing your son to do the job you couldn't to make him proud of you. It sounds like your shortcomings, not mine."

He nods, his lips pursed and his eyes blazing with fury. "I don't need my son to make my father proud of me." *Yes, you do.* "But I need my son to not embarrass me or him or this goddamn name you were blessed with. That is something I won't tolerate."

"Or else what?"

His smile is devious as it turns up the corners of his lips. "I have more clout in this industry than you know, Cruz. You think you got this ride on your own accord? You don't think I pulled strings to get you here? To keep you here?" he asks.

He's full of shit. First, I earned my ride myself. *Then why do memories tickle the recesses of my mind that make me doubt myself?* Second, he won't bite the hand that's feeding him the much-needed approval he craves from my grandfather. *But his spite is so strong maybe he would.*

"You don't pull my strings. No one does."

"As usual—and as expected—you are disrespectful and shortsighted. She's not good enough for a Navarro, plain and simple. *Take care of the problem or I will.*"

CHAPTER SEVENTEEN

Maddix

"P4 IS GREAT, RIGHT? WHY DID HE LOOK LIKE HE JUST TOOK LAST place?"

Amandine slides a look my way, almost as if to say I clearly don't know my boyfriend well enough and isn't sure if she wants to break the bad news to me. "P4 *is* incredible. It's in the points. A lot of teams would kill to place fourth, but Gravitas is a top-tier team. We're supposed to place on the podium." She pauses momentarily. "Cruz is harder on himself than any critic out there could ever be. Every race. Every lap. The man has more talent and instinct in his little pinkie than most of the drivers out there, but he never seems to see it as good enough. And even when he finishes in first place, there is something he thinks he could have done better."

I'm hearing her words, but am having a hard time squaring that description with the man I've come to know in the short time I've been here.

He comes off as a man who takes everything with a grain of salt. His fame. His life. And I incorrectly thought *this*—his racing.

But how can he be upset? The race was . . . exhilarating. Exciting. Nerve-wracking. Each lap was a thrill ride full of oohs and aahs and crossed fingers and tensed muscles as I willed him from my seat in the media box to go faster and, at the same time, not crash.

I'm exhausted from the adrenaline of watching so I can't imagine how he must feel.

"He's a perfectionist in every sense of the word when it comes to racing. I mean . . . he *is* a Navarro."

"Well, then I guess now wouldn't be a good time to tell him it was an incredible race," I say playfully and smile, trying to make up for my blatant error.

Amandine laughs. "No. Probably not. But"—she cranes her head back and forth—"he is probably about done if you want to go find him."

"I would. Thank you."

"I saw him head that way." She points. "Probably in his driver suite."

"Thank you. For everything this weekend," I say and squeeze her hand. "I'm sure you're probably glad to be rid of me and my endless questions."

"It was my pleasure. See you next race?"

"Um, yes. Sure." I'm taken aback by the question. "Depends on my schedule."

"Hopefully it works out so that you can be here. It's been fun."

"It has."

I move down the hallway toward the back of the complex. The staff is slowly packing their things up, because if my F1 crash course was correct, this whole place will be deconstructed and on the move within the next forty-eight hours.

I'm preoccupied thinking of the enormity of it all when I hear Cruz's voice. It's the first time I've heard him speak in his native tongue. His accent is thick and beautiful.

And angry.

My years of Spanish in high school, living in Texas, and a high school job where I had to practice speaking it, pay off right now. I can actually understand what is being said between the two.

"You don't pull my strings. No one does."

I take a step forward, thinking the conversation isn't a big deal, but falter when I peer into the partially open door in front of me. Cruz's back is to me and the man I now know to be his dad, Dominic Navarro, is facing my direction. There is a closed door at his back so I highly doubt by the tones of their voice and the expression on his dad's face that they realize this door is open and that others can hear their argument.

Dominic's nostrils flare as he crosses his arms over his chest. "She's not good enough for a Navarro, plain and simple. *Take care of the problem or I will.*"

It doesn't take a genius to figure out who or what he's talking about. Before I have a chance to wrap my head around the words, the meaning, and the sting of hurt they cause, the next comment staggers me even more.

"You're a pathetic excuse for a Navarro, Cruz."

He thinks his son is pathetic? Is this a joke?

Those words would crush me if my father said them to me. How is this the same man who I witnessed bragging about his son over the past few hours? Who I saw stride through the garage with his distinguished legacy surrounding him like an aura, and his son's team emblem on the right front of his polo shirt.

Cruz's shoulders sag and I don't need to see his face to know that devastation is etched in its lines. How can it not be?

I move and accidentally draw the attention of the older Navarro because, when I look back at him, our eyes meet briefly. Within seconds and before Cruz even turns to notice, Dominic strides across the space, eyes full of irritation meeting mine briefly, before shutting the door with a resounding thud.

At a loss for words and with a heavy heart, all I can manage is to stare at the closed door for a few moments.

Did that really happen?

Yes.

Yes, it did.

Tears burn in my eyes and shame I shouldn't feel, but do, washes through me. There is a part of me that wants to open the door and march in there and ask Dominic Navarro who the hell he thinks he is. There is another part of me that knows I'm way out of my element here, way out of my league in terms of pecking order. And then there is the tiny part of me that wonders if Cruz agrees with his dad.

If he feels the same about me.

The lump in my throat grows bigger and the urgent need to get the hell out of there takes over.

I should be livid, furious, trying to extricate the feelings of shame that initially washed over me—and I am, all of those things—but just as I'm about to scurry away, it hits me.

Cruz.

He's the one dealing with this abuse. And yes, it is abuse.

Why does he put up with it?

Why doesn't he tell his dad to go to hell?

He's the one those words hurt more than me. He's the one I'm worried about and want to reach out and hug.

Dominic Navarro is no one to me. Sure his words stung, and no doubt his unabashed rejection will hit me full force when the shock wears off and the exhaustion hits, but again, in the scheme of things, he's not relevant.

But I have a feeling he's everything to Cruz.

Completely uncomfortable and at a loss over what to do, I head back to the room where I've kept my stuff for the day. My one and only thought is to get the hell out of here. Dominic is the last person I want to come face-to-face with, especially in such close quarters.

I pick up my laptop and belongings and shove them into my tote bag. Never in my life have my parents spoken to me like that. Not when I won. Not when I failed. Not even when I went against their wishes and tried to spread my wings and prove my independence from them.

They let me try and fail. They let me try and succeed. They let me grow and learn. And in each and every instance, they stood beside me cheering me on. Or they stood behind me so I knew they were there, knowing they wanted me to see I could do it on my own.

They never belittled or scolded. They never said *I told you so* when they had every right to.

I can't imagine how I'd have felt if they spoke words similar to Dominic Navarro's to me. I'd be crushed. Devastated.

"She's not good enough for a Navarro, plain and simple. Take care of the problem or I will."

His words hit me again and I pause as I look around the small space. There is clearly so much more than meets the eye to Cruz and what motivates him.

Or holds him back.

The deep rumble of Dominic's voice floats down the hall. It's light and carefree—fake as fuck—to whomever he's speaking with, but I can't shake the tone of it minutes ago from my head.

I need fresh air. I need space. I just need away from this world that suddenly feels claustrophobic. Suddenly frantic, I move toward the back exit of the building, open the door, and then my feet falter. Cruz is just outside the door. His hands are braced on the wall, and his head is hanging down. His eyes are closed as he draws in slow, even breaths.

The flashback of the first time we met hits me. Back then I felt I knew what to do and how to offer help to him. This time around? Now that I know him better? I hesitate from a feeling of helplessness like I've never known.

"Cruz," I say softly, but when I reach out to put my hand on his shoulder, he yanks his body away from my touch and spins on me.

"Don't. Please," he says as we stand face-to-face, eyes warring and uncertainty swirling. Every emotion imaginable emanates off him—hurt, grief, anger—but it's the isolation lurking in the depths of his eyes that guts me. "Just . . . fucking don't." Each syllable is pained.

I lower my hand slowly and will him to feel the compassion in my eyes. A compassion from the looks of it he's not used to receiving. "What do you need from me?" I ask, choosing my words carefully.

His jaw works. "Nothing. I'm fine." He swallows forcefully. "I'll have a team car get you back to the hotel."

"Cruz. Will you at least talk to me? Tell me—"

"There's nothing to talk about," he says gruffly, his shoulders squaring and his resolve back front and center.

"You're not going back with me?"

"You don't want me around you right now. No one does." He spits the words out like he believes them, and that's almost worse than the hurt in his eyes.

"We can go take a drive. We can—"

"I don't need to be babied, Hart. Not by you. Not by anyone." His jaw clenches as if he's restraining himself from saying so much more. "Just . . . go."

Our eyes hold, words exchanged without speaking. He needs space. I need to give it to him. And yet every part of me struggles with letting this man I barely know, go.

"I said, go," he repeats. "Please."

The break in his voice kills me.

"Okay. Sure."

And of course, Dominic Navarro is casually chatting it up and laughing with the race engineer as I make my way out of the Gravitas paddock's footprint.

Being the cordial, welcoming person I saw all day—except for when he spoke to his son.

Our gazes lock, but this time I don't look away first. This time I glare right back at him before giving the slightest shake of my head and then head for the exit.

Asshole.

The paddock is still a buzzing city, allowing me to get lost in its hustle as I make my way toward the turnstile. I'm hoping the post-race chaos will allow me to blend in with everyone, but the sudden shouts of my name the minute I'm at the edges of its confines, tell me I was wrong.

Maddix, how did you and Cruz meet?

Is it serious between you two?

Rumor is that you're engaged. Is that true?

The questions hit me one after another, rapid-fire like bullets. I'm flustered and disarmed. I'm at a loss for how to wade through the sea of people and get to the team driver waiting for me.

Right as the fluster turns to panic, a man dressed in a Gravitas uniform appears and ushers me away from the madness and to his waiting car. I don't breathe a sigh of relief until the car is rolling out of the parking lot.

I'm leaving Zandvoort so differently than I'd expected. Cruz likes to call me naive. I like to call myself optimistic. But for some reason, I had envisioned Cruz and I leaving together, ready to celebrate a great race, before packing up and moving on to wherever is next.

Instead, I'm alone. Confused. And questioning whether this will turn out how Kevin wants it to.

I have a feeling there's much more at play here for Cruz than Kevin ever knew.

CHAPTER EIGHTEEN

Maddix

CLAUSTROPHOBIA IS SETTING IN.

The kind I can't escape by walking outside of the hotel, because fans have since discovered that this is home to the entire Gravitas team and have camped out waiting for Nico and Cruz to return. One last glimpse of their idols before they move on to the next city on the circuit.

No doubt their social media posts when the racers do see them will be flattering. Unlike the images of me circulating around the Internet. My hair wild and my eyes wide as I try to push through the crowd to the team car. The ones I've seen so far capture me looking exhausted, irritated, and like a complete and total bitch.

Granted, I can be all three of those, but that's the last image I want out there in the public.

The captions and comments beneath the posts I've studied only serve to reinforce Dominic's shitty comments about me earlier. My lack of pedigree. My shortcomings for being Cruz's potential girlfriend.

And truth be told, the more I stare out the window as I sit here and wait for Cruz to respond to my texts, the more space I let all this noise eat up until I'm antsy and starting to feed into my own insecurities that rival the criticism. In a fishbowl, things can only keep going around and around until that's all you see and hear.

Until you feel smothered.

The roof.

I don't know why I didn't think of it before. Cruz's comment about it being where he goes when he needs a break. But it hits me now and within minutes, I'm in the elevator and shortly thereafter, pushing the heavy exterior door open.

Relief hits me immediately, knowing I can be out here and not be seen. That I can move without a photo being taken or have an expression without it being misinterpreted.

Freedom.

I've only been doing this whole public life thing for a short time, but to be able to be outside without eyes on me provides the oddest sense of relief that I previously wouldn't have needed.

I take in the exterior patio of sorts. It's bathed in darkness on this moonless night. There is patio furniture up here, from what I can see of it anyway as the lattice cover casts an even darker shadow over its far recesses.

I move to the edge of it—the glass partition that keeps the wind from the patio and keeps its occupants from falling. The breeze is gentle as the faint sounds of the city at night travel up to meet me.

"Don't jump."

But I do just that. I *jump* at Cruz's voice and spin around to see him just beneath the cover. It's his white sneakers and the glint of the glass bottle in his hand that allow me to find him. "Jesus. You scared me."

"Took you long enough to find me." He chuckles and the slur in it is all I need to hear to know he's escaping too.

I have a feeling he's escaping much more than me though.

"You're drunk."

"Ding, ding, ding, we have a winner." He steps toward me as he lifts his hands up. "How'd you guess? Was it the bottle? The slurred words? Or are you just such a fucking genius that you can't figure out what I'm upset about?"

"Don't be a jerk."

"A jerk? I'm a happy drunk, Madds. So long as I can drink more."

"Here I was texting you, worrying about you . . . getting frantic with each and every minute you don't respond and—"

"I'm a big boy. No one asked you to worry about me."

"And you're up here getting plastered this whole time," I say, ignoring his flippant comment so I don't get even more pissed.

Because he's right. He didn't ask to be cared about or worried over . . . and yet I did. *I am.*

"Would you rather I had done it in public because I have no problem with that? In fact, I'm pretty damn good at it, but I have a feeling that good ol' Kevy-Kev might have a problem with that. So see"—he flashes a goofy grin—"I can show growth. I can take direction. I can be a good pet."

"I have a feeling this has nothing to do with Kevin."

He takes a sip straight from the bottle and hisses at the burn. At least he isn't so drunk he's immune to it. "Good for you. I'm glad you have feelings."

Ah, so that's how we're going to play this.

"You left me alone in a strange country to go get drunk."

"Last I checked, I'm not your fucking babysitter."

"Great. Perfect. Not a babysitter, *and an asshole.*"

"Never claimed to be any different." He leans against a pole that holds the lattice up. There's challenge in his eyes. A need for a fight.

"You didn't answer my texts. I was worried."

"Again, I didn't ask for your worry. I'm not obligated to do shit." He shakes his head. "Oh. Wait. *My bad.* I guess that's what a boyfriend would do. Guess that just serves to prove I'm not relationship material."

"Or it just proves that I'm not of the right pedigree to warrant a response."

"Ah. Tú hablas español?" he says evenly. *You speak Spanish.*

"Enough that I got the gist of what was being said, yes."

Our eyes hold. "And you didn't think that was pertinent enough to tell me over the past few days?"

"Would it have mattered?" I counter. "Would that have upped my level of pedigree?"

The muscle pulses in Cruz's jaw as my pettiness shines through. *Fuck.* The comment about pedigree wasn't supposed to become words on my lips. But it just did and it's been said, and I can't take it back. Whatever is bugging Cruz clearly isn't about me . . . and yet I just made it to be because yes, I'm hurt. Yes, I'm human. Yes, I'm not immune to being disregarded.

And yes, I didn't hear him say a single word to stand up for me.

I think that's what stings more than anything.

"Forget I said anything," I say. "They're just words."

Cruz just stares at me with an intensity and a million words loaded in those eyes of his that I have a feeling he'll never say.

"Welcome to Club Navarro," he exclaims, arms out and sarcasm dripping.

"What the hell does that mean?"

He angles his head to the side and reaches out, cupping the side of my cheek. It's a completely unexpected action that has me holding my breath and pushing my heart back under lock and key.

Kiss me.

It's the stupidest, most selfish thought and yet it repeats over and over.

I'm not supposed to want him. He's a player who has already played me in a sense, and yet there's a vulnerability to him right now that makes me see the man I believe he can be. The man I genuinely like. The man I get glimpses of every now and again.

And now I'm just talking crazy. It must be the cloud of night or the emotions of the day, but Cruz Navarro has already dealt his cards when it comes to me, and that hand was a bust.

His Adam's apple bobs and a soft smile ghosts his lips as his thumb brushes over my bottom lip.

The moment feels right and wrong and everything in between.

My body thrums with a need I don't think I've ever felt before. A knowledge of what he feels like. What he tastes like. How he can make my body feel.

"Cruz." His name is a whisper on my lips. A single word laced with the confusion and desire rioting within my body.

There is so much in his eyes that I can't decipher but want to. And just as I think he might soften, might let me in, might replace the pad of his thumb with the softness of his lips, he drops his hand and abruptly takes a step away, turning so his back is to me.

He clears his throat. Rejection eats at the ache still simmering inside me. "For what it's worth, my dad's disappointed in me and taking it out on the one thing he thinks he can control—*you*. He can't."

And yet the sting remains. From him. From his dad. From this whole damn night.

This isn't about you, Maddix.

"I don't understand. What in the world does he have to be disappointed about? You're one of the top drivers in the world. A success in so many ways. I'd say that's pretty damn impressive."

"Humph." It's the only response he gives as he glances back at me, regret swimming in his eyes before moving even farther away from me and to the edge of the patio. He's a striking silhouette, haunting almost, with the city's lights beyond and him bathed in darkness. There's a sadness to him I'm not used to. A withdrawal.

"I'm here if you want to talk about it," I say softly.

"Rooftops are my thing." I barely get my chuckle of confusion out before he continues changing the subject. "The higher the better."

"Should I be worried about that preference?" I try to add some levity.

"Sometimes you just need a minute, you know? Where you can go and just . . . *be*."

"I get that." I murmur the words more to let him know I'm listening, but I'm almost afraid to speak because he's finally talking. I don't want him to pull back into himself.

"You live your life under constant scrutiny, sometimes you need the distance to reset your shit."

"I thought you enjoyed the limelight. The attention."

He takes his time answering. I get the sense he's not one hundred percent certain he knows how to. "If that's what you want to call it. It doesn't unnerve me if that's what you're implying."

"You grew up with it. You probably don't think twice about it."

"I grew up a Navarro where I didn't have a choice. That and I don't give a fuck."

"What does that mean?"

"The I don't give a fuck part?" He looks my way with a grin that's much more melancholic than anything.

"The Navarro part."

"My family is everything. It's who I am. It's the talent I've been given and the chances it's afforded me. My grandfather—mi patriarca—is the only person I've ever idolized. He's the only man I've ever wanted to emulate. I have my father to thank for that. And him to hate for it too."

"What does—"

"Look, I face more scrutiny before I drink my morning cup of coffee, so who cares if cameras catch me drinking or having a good time?" he says, almost as if he just slipped with that little admission and is trying to cover it back up. "Why would it faze me if they write about the women I date or the exploits I have? That's a drop in the bucket to the pressure I put on myself."

I don't even know how to respond to that. Here I am freaking out about my name being tied to his, when he lives under the magnifying glass every second of every day.

"I'm sorry." It's all I can think to say, but he just laughs it off and moves back beneath the lattice. The sounds of alcohol sloshing in the bottle as he lifts it to his lips follow soon thereafter.

"I don't want your pity, Hart. What I do want though is some peace and quiet. Alone."

"Are you sure that's a good idea—"

"It's time for you to go back to the room and let my bottle be my company. It doesn't ask questions and it doesn't make me feel obligated to answer them."

"Cruz . . ."

"Just give me this. For tonight. I'll be okay. Just need to work through some of that shit I was talking about." He takes a drink. "Tomorrow, we head home to Monaco."

I move toward him and we stare at each other through the darkness. It pains me to walk away, to give him what he asks for, but I also don't have the slightest clue what to do or say to him.

The articles I read about a tight-knit, impenetrable Navarro clan? I'm beginning to think they're as bogus as this relationship we have.

What I saw today was brutal repudiation . . . and it's clearly not the first time if Cruz has a built-in coping mechanism.

What worries me the most though?

Like with all things knitted, they have the ability to unravel.

CHAPTER NINETEEN

Cruz

SHE SLEEPS.

I don't slide under the covers into the bed beside her. I don't dare fucking tempt myself with everything she is when I'd give anything to get lost in her right now. When the alcohol is dulling my sensibility and restraint.

Hasn't that been the fucking problem since the other night?

God, has it only been a few nights? It feels like for-fucking-ever since I took one for the team—allowed her to save face—by acting like the sex we had didn't rock my fucking world. Like I wasn't standing there watching her turn every shade of red because she was embarrassed by what we did.

She said it was a mistake.

She blamed the alcohol and said it can't happen again.

She begged me to understand that she's not that kind of girl.

That it was just sex.

How many times have I told myself the same since then? Tried to convince myself? And why have I thought about it way more than I should?

"You're distracted and it showed . . . A good start would be you getting rid of her."

I have to hand it to the fucker. He was right about that one thing.

It's been absolute goddamn torture. Watching her lips as she talks to me. Seeing the curve of her ass in those tiny sleep shorts she wears. Sliding into bed, knowing she's within reach, remembering just how damn good she is.

I've kept my distance. Tried to as much as one possibly can when you're essentially living with someone. Filled my head with the cold, hard truth.

She'll never be mine. I'll *never* deserve her. And quite frankly, *she deserves much better than me.* She deserves a man who can tell her the things she needs to hear. Who can treat her how she deserves to be treated. Not one who can't commit for shit because of the life he lives and the abandonment issues he has.

Gotta love those Mamá and Papá issues.

But isn't that what is causing all the confusion?

Since when do I, Cruz Navarro, ever care about shit like that? I care about the next orgasm. About not getting bored with the woman of the moment. With the good time to be had by all.

I don't worry about feelings. I let my cock do the thinking when it comes to women. And I let the alcohol lead the way to the party.

So why do I care about it this time around? Why is Madds different?

She shifts in her sleep. Murmurs. And I swear she says my name. My cock twitches and balls ache.

We spend so much time together. *I've never been around one woman this long. Ever.* That has to be *the why* behind all of this.

And yet I can't look away. Her soft lips. Her dark lashes. Her fucking perfume.

Fuck, man.

I need another drink. I hold up the bottle and sigh. It's fucking empty.

Then is the only reason the room's spinning because of the woman in front of me?

I rest my head back against the chair.

You're distracted and it showed.

A good start would be you getting rid of her.

Fuck. That. Fuck. Him.

I might be distracted, Papá, but I'm not getting rid of her.

Your comment, your order, just made fucking sure of that.

CHAPTER TWENTY

Cruz

"A RE WE READY TO . . ." I LET MY VOICE TRAIL OFF AS I SHUT THE
door to the hotel room when I hear Maddix's voice from the open
door on the balcony.

"I'm fine. It's not a big deal." She pauses, but I'm not that much of an asshole that from her tone, I don't know something is wrong. "It's just words,
Mom." A sigh. "Yes. Words *and* pictures. It's not like I wasn't aware of that,
but thanks."

I set the coffee I brought her down and hang back, clearly walking in on
a conversation. One I'm more than curious about.

"I told you. I'm fine. We're fine." Maddix moves now so that I can see
her. She's in one of those tight pair of black leggings that hug her ass and a
tank top that no doubt does the same for her tits.

Fucking hell. Yeah. Not gonna lie. Those are my favorite outfits of hers.

"I don't care if Michael's calling you. I'm not obligated to pick up the
phone when he calls. Neither are you. From the looks of it, he's one of the
anonymous sources so . . . *no*, I don't owe him anything." She falls silent,
her head hanging down as she nods. *What the fuck did Michael do?* "I wasn't
lying to you, Mom. Things just . . . they just kind of happened between us.
Quickly. And now . . . *now all of this.*" She makes a noncommittal sound to
whatever her mother says. "I guess it's par for the course. It's just a course
I'm not exactly used to."

I look around the hotel room. Maddix's bags are already packed and sitting beside mine. She's collected the half-empty water bottles we left around

and has them piled in the recycle bin beside the desk where her laptop is open. The comforter is pulled up on the bed, and all of the bath towels are in one pile on the floor.

The ever-efficient Maddix Hart, ladies and gentlemen, is ready for checkout.

"I promise. Yes." She looks over her shoulder and sees me and hesitates. "Look. I have to go. We're heading to the airport. Yes. Monaco." Another murmured sound. "Please don't worry. I said, I promise. Love you too."

She moves into the room, her face a mask of indifference when she speaks. "You're here." The words are as stiff as her posture.

Apparently, I'm the asshole. This is beginning to become a regular thing, and I'm not a fucking fan of it.

"I am." I hold the coffee up—my apology of sorts—and move toward her as she eyes me. "For you."

"Did you even come to bed?"

Does it fucking matter? That's my instinctual response. My distaste for being controlled.

And then through the steel in her eyes, I see a break. I see a hint of worry before her guard goes back up.

Fuck. She really was worried. Last night wasn't just for show. Look who's the asshole . . . *again*.

"Couldn't sleep." I glance over to the chair I sat in, fighting every urge until I had to gain more space before I did something we'd both regret. *Again*. "So I walked for hours. Got us coffee."

She looks down at hers, but still doesn't take a sip. "Just like that. You can drink like you did and"—she snaps her fingers—"you're perfectly fine?"

"I've had a lot of practice."

"This isn't fucking funny, Cruz."

"What? The race was over. My job was done. I get a mulligan. A day to cut loose. You going to bust my balls or what because I have enough people doing that?"

"You don't get it." Her voice softens momentarily, and I immediately straighten my shoulders. None of that shit.

"I'm perfectly capable of taking care of myself."

"I was worried about you. All night on a roof while you were drunk."

A strange feeling hits my chest. One that is as foreign as me sleeping in the same bed with one woman for six nights in a row.

"So that's why you're mad? Because I worried you?"

"No." She sighs heavily, goes to pick up her coffee, and then sets it back down without drinking it, almost out of principle. Kind of like a refusal to accept my olive branch of an apology.

"Then why? Because I put too much sugar in your coffee? Clue me in here, Madds, because there's only room for one of us to be moody in this fouple situation, and I hate to break it to you but that's going to be me."

"Fouple?"

Well, at least I got confusion to replace her anger for a second.

"Fake couple." I offer a grin. It usually wins her over, but when I meet her eyes again, I don't think it moved the needle whatsoever.

Jesus. Whatever I said to her last night must have been bad if she's still holding on to her anger.

What was it though, because from where I'm sitting, I remember almost every damn thing.

"Not even a crack of a smile on that, Hart? Damn. Tough crowd."

"You don't get it, do you?"

"Get what? Why you woke up so bitter? No, I don't. We've survived living together this far without any monumental issues." I tap my cup against hers still sitting on the desk. "Yay. Go team." I pump a fist in the air. "Well, unless you call *this* an issue. I mean is this our first fight as a fouple? Should we take a selfie to document it for all to see since apparently, we have to document everything?"

"No. You don't get to do this."

And this, folks, is why I don't have a girlfriend. We fuck. I leave. And none of this inane back-and-forth conversation that makes no fucking sense.

Just spit it out and let's be done already. *Christ.*

"Do what?"

"Make light of this. Try and joke your way out of things. You don't get to be how you were last night and then be like this this morning." Her teeth grit. "Stop looking at me like that."

"Like what?"

She motions to me. "Like that."

"I can't help it if you're sexy when you're angry."

By the scowl on her face, I probably shouldn't have said that.

"Cruz. Stop it. It's not just you in this, and you keep seeming to forget that."

"So we *are* having our first fight, then. Okay. Gotcha. Because me need-ing space and you giving it to me seems like a really stupid thing to fight over. Especially when we have the jet on the runway, a new place to go, and a flight plan filed to get us there."

"Classic fucking Cruz. Let's just brush it under the rug, shall we? You seem to be really good at that. At getting to say your piece and being selfish enough to think that no one else deserves to say theirs. Well, I'm here and am every part of this fucked-up plan as you are so respect the fact that my voice fucking matters too."

I stand there holding her stare at a loss for words. What the actual fuck? And yes, in *Classic fucking Cruz* fashion, I'm going to react like the selfish, sarcastic asshole that I am.

"I wasn't aware you knew me enough to know what I do or don't brush under the rug, but by all means." I motion my hands like the floor is hers. "Please practice your psychology degree on me."

"Now you're just being an asshole."

"Bingo. You just figured that one out?"

"Do you ever think about anyone else besides yourself?" Tears suddenly well in her eyes and cause panic to take hold of me. I'm not good with tears. Never have been. Thank fuck she blinks them away.

"Is there something you're not telling me, Madds?" My voice is softer this time. Probing. "Something I should know?"

She swallows audibly and I brace myself for the floodgates to open. Ones for the life of me I wish could stay padlocked closed.

"I'm getting calls left and right. From my mom. From Kevin. Am I all right? Are we all right?" Her voice escalates with each and every syllable. "Do my job. Do it better. Every fucking person picking me apart. Every—every-thing. And then there's the—" She throws her hand out like that's supposed to explain everything, and now I'm just more fucking confused.

"Maddix." I round the table, stand behind her and put a hand on her shoulder. "What's going on? I can't fix it if I don't know what to fix."

"It's not fixable. Don't you see that?"

But it's then that I do see it. What she was motioning at. The screen of her laptop. The images. The headlines. The hurtful fucking words. The petty bullshit.

My dad's words come rushing back to me. The ones I now know she overheard. The ones I have learned to brush off, to disregard, to let eat at me until I drink enough for them not to—but fucking hell. I skim them again. Add his words combined with these headlines and . . . *just fuck.*

Texas Rags to F1 Riches. Sleeping her way to the top.

The Navarro's Case for Charity Taken Too Far.

What Does Cruz Navarro Know That We Don't?

Each headline is demeaning. Each one a slight to Maddix in some way. Every one I click on has an unflattering picture of her, courtesy of paparazzi taking a ration of photos and using the one that fits their narrative best.

I lean over and click the last one. *Trouble in Paradise: She can't give him what he needs.* This is the image being repeated over and over. The one being manipulated to fit the story. It's when she reached out to me yesterday after the race. When she tried to comfort me, and I yanked my arm back from her.

I didn't want to be touched. To be soothed. It's the last thing I deserved from her. All she's been is kind to me and my asshole father denigrates her like he does everyone else.

That's what I know to be true, but by the looks of the articles, the media interpreted it as a fight. As me being furious with her. As Madds asking for too much and me being sick of giving it to her.

Cruelty.

Each and every goddamn article is cutting. The anonymous comments below from the keyboard warriors are even worse. I shouldn't care. Lies and rumors and all the bullshit come with this career, come with the limelight . . . and yet, one look at Maddix and I can see the toll it's already taken on her.

"It's all bullshit, Maddix. You know it and I know it."

"Is that supposed to make it easier? My parents are seeing that and wondering what the hell is going on. They're worried sick about me, threatening to hop on flights here that they can't afford. Kevin has called me, telling me I'm not doing my job well enough because it looks like we're about to break up."

Fucking Kevin. Her parents' concern? That's well founded and expected. But her boss? The only thing he cares about is his income.

I was the one pushing her away and *he* blames her? She's a fucking stranger to me and he knows that. What a prick.

And then I recall her phone call.

"I don't care if Michael's calling you. I'm not obligated to pick up the phone when he calls. Neither are you. From the looks of it, he's one of the anonymous sources so . . . no, I don't owe him anything."

"And Michael?"

Her wince hits me in the weirdest of ways. Is it because I wonder if she still cares about him when she shouldn't or is it because he did something to hurt her?

Both piss me off.

Her shrug confirms one of the two and I'm not sure which one. "Some articles quote him but . . . I don't know if he'd really do something like that."

"It's amazing what money makes people do." He'd sell the story for money. *No doubt.* He let her walk away without a fight after all. "So that's it? That's why you're upset?"

By the look on her face, that was the wrong way to phrase that.

"Why I'm upset?" The evenness in her voice is almost ten times harder to listen to than if she were screaming at me. "You threw me to the wolves yesterday. This situation is for you so you get your billion-dollar deal. It's not for me. I'm in *your* world, *your* fishbowl, for *you* and *your* benefit, and when you told me to leave the grounds without you yesterday, you left me to fend for myself with the media. Look at me." She throws her hand at the computer. "I'm far from helpless, but this is your realm. This is where you were supposed to step in and tell me how to handle it. Instead, I look like a total bitch in these photos. I was flustered and overwhelmed with the flashes and the questions and everyone staring and now that person—that crazy-looking woman in the photos—is who's splashed everywhere. That's what people know me as. Who they assume me to be."

Fucking hell. I scrub a hand over my unshaven jaw knowing there's not a goddamn thing in the world I can do to fix this. I can't even take all of those shitty pictures back.

"I have hundreds of messages and requests and disgusting comments on my socials from *your* fans." She works a swallow and thank God she pauses, because the break in her voice is a gut punch. "I have thick skin. I can handle a lot. But it still hurts. It still fucks up your head."

"I'm sorry, Madds. I am. There's nothing I can say or do or—"

"If that's what you think then that's half the problem, isn't it," she says, shutting her laptop, shoving it in her carry-on. "Do better. Think about someone else besides yourself." And with those parting words, she heads out the hotel room door.

She leaves the coffee untouched. A subtle dig. A reminder that she's done way nicer things for me, and I've treated her much the same way.

Abandoned.

Fuck.

Her silent treatment remains. Through the car ride to the airport. Through preflight check. Through the small talk she makes with the flight crew but not with me. *Thank fuck Lola doesn't choose today to showcase the fact that we've fooled around.*

From behind my sunglasses, I watch Maddix work on emails in silence, her expression changing with each and every word she types.

One is to Kevin. That one I saw when she set her laptop down to go to the restroom. A reassurance that all was fine and she was doing her job to the letter as he'd outlined. A subtle *fuck you* for putting me in this position if ever I read one.

She responds to texts. Some with a soft smile. Some with a bittersweet grimace. Others with downright hurt in her eyes.

She takes the time ignoring me to catch up or check in with those in her life. A life I guess I never considered she up and left for this. To help me make a fortune while she gets what in return? To be raked over the fucking coals? To be demeaned by the public and belittled by my father?

Did I stand up for her? Did I tell him to go to hell?

The problem? I don't fucking remember. I'm so used to brushing off whatever the fuck he says that I can't fucking recall.

And then when she finishes her correspondence, rather than have a conversation with me, she sleeps. The slow, even rise of her chest. The lock of hair that falls over her cheek. The way she moves every few minutes as her head slips down to an uncomfortable position before it jerks back up as she tries to get into a more comfortable one.

I can't look away. I try. I have emails to answer. I have texts to respond to. I have a life to check in with, and yet the one thing that holds my interest is sitting across from me.

Just like earlier this morning. But the difference between last night and right now is one thing: fucking guilt.

It's a useless emotion I never feel and yet here I am, sitting here fucking feeling it when it comes to Madds. *Again.*

This shit has got to stop. And stop quick.

I see women. I fuck women. We walk away. I don't worry about what the press prints about them because they want the words to be printed. They want the notoriety that comes with being with me.

But not Maddix.

Fuck, man.

Her head slips again and her whole body jerks in correction.

I react without thinking. I rise from my seat and move to the opposite side of the table to sit beside her.

She mumbles when I put my arm around her. She resists momentarily when I position her head on my chest.

Then she settles down and her breathing falls off again.

But I sit there for a long time with the scent of her shampoo on my nose, the tickle of her hair on my cheek, and the warmth of her body beside mine.

What the hell am I doing?

CHAPTER TWENTY-ONE

Maddix

> **Dad:** Baby girl. Pressure only turns stones into diamonds. Sparkle and shine.

TWO THINGS SURPRISED ME WHEN WE LANDED IN MONACO.

The text from my dad, a man of few words and even fewer texts. But those eleven words greeted me when I woke up and brought relieved tears in my eyes.

The second was waking up to feeling an arm around me and a heart beating beneath my cheek. It took me a few moments to realize where I was and who I was partially lying on. And for a brief moment, I allowed myself to sink into the feeling. His warmth. His steady heartbeat. The feeling of comfort. His slow, even breathing as he slept.

It was something I didn't realize I needed, didn't realize he could even give me, but he did without me knowing it and that goes a long way with me.

And right before the plane landed, when he thought I was still asleep, he slipped out from beside me, tucked the blanket back around me, and moved back to his seat as if it never happened.

It was his apology. This morning's cup of coffee but on a much bigger scale.

And why does his gesture seem more significant than anything Michael ever did for me?

Because it's out of character. Because he did it and it wasn't for show. In fact, he did it never thinking I knew it happened. *And it was something I really needed.* That means a lot to me.

Slow down, Madds. He was nice after you read him the riot act. Do not read into it.

Sitting here beside him as he drives the winding roads through the hills from the airport in Nice to Monaco, I focus on that.

On the soft side to Cruz Navarro. A side he clearly chooses to hide from the world. A side I like and hope to see again.

But all of these thoughts get muddied with the virtual chaos around us. The call from my mom. The articles online. The stomach-churning press about me.

I can't do a single thing about it though. What's out in the world can't be taken back. All I can do is take a deep breath, relax, and try to appreciate my surroundings as much as possible.

My new home away from home.

"This is stunning," I murmur, as we make the descent into Monaco. From afar, the city looks tiny in size but gigantic in stature. A harbor bobs at its center with gigantic yachts in row upon row. Sports cars of every make and model drive around us and beside us. The hotels and buildings are lavish in their exterior and stature. I've never felt like I've stepped onto a movie set until now.

There is an air about this place. An opulence. A feeling that everywhere you look, money isn't an object and whoever is in the luxury sports car passing us is off to jet-set to some exotic location.

Wait. Isn't that what I just did and isn't that like the car I'm in?

Pinch me.

"I can't believe people actually live here," I murmur, aware I sound like a kid and not really caring that I do. This is a bucket list city for so many, and I get to stay here. *For now.*

That doesn't erase the chaos and cruelty of the media, but it does help a bit.

Cruz chuckles and pats my thigh. "People actually do."

But when the pat is done, he leaves it there, oblivious to the weird things the heat of his hand does to my body. I stare at it. At his fingers that could easily slide their way and touch me like he did the other night. Pleasure me. Undo me.

I shift in my seat, needing to ease the ache, and when he glances at me, I simply pretend I'm looking ahead.

Does he think about it? Ever? Because I remember it all too well.

And just as the thought passes through my mind, he spreads his hand even wider on my thigh and then squeezes before lifting it and pointing to the large casino we're passing, much like he has some of the other landmarks.

"Another place I'll take you to while you're here."

But just as quickly as we see it, it's in our rearview mirror as we begin to move toward a residential neighborhood.

"Cruz?"

"Hmm?" he responds absently.

"I thought I was staying at a hotel. Back there. In town somewhere." I look over my shoulder and down to the hub of the city.

"I cancelled the reservation."

"You *what?* Why?"

"It isn't necessary."

"But it is. I mean, we're dating. Dating does not mean living together."

I yelp as he swerves the car abruptly to the side of the road, right before a sign declaring the Fontvieille district. "You're free to go back to Austin for a few days, but then we'll have to start this process all over again. We could play the whole distance makes the heart grow fonder thing, if need be. But you can't go to a hotel here. Do you know what that would look like considering everything that has transpired over the past twenty-four hours? I mean you want to throw fuel on their fire, be my guest."

I look out the window toward the ocean sparkling beyond. There is no right answer in this situation. But my gut tells me he's right. If a non-fight can be extrapolated into all of this online drama and speculation, then God forbid we stay in different places in Monaco.

"I have a guest room. Two actually. You can stay as far away from me as possible if that's what you prefer. I'm rarely home as it is. When I am, I'm on the simulator training for the next race or working out so . . . I'll be out of your hair. Besides, I have to fly to Spain in a few days. Make a trip there and back before the next race. That'll give you time to yourself."

"Fine. Thank you." My words are a whisper of consent, my sudden longing for home strong. It's ridiculous and silly but I think it's just the emotions of the past few days hitting me all at once.

Comfort. Being able to head over to my parents' house and sit at the kitchen counter eating some of my mom's home-cooked food while getting her advice.

I can't exactly do that when I'm lying to her.

Within minutes, we pull into the district and then into a garage of an unassuming structure. It has modern architecture—sleek lines and a minimalist exterior—in this town that feels old world.

Tension still radiates between us but it hits differently now, and I'm not sure why. We sit in the quiet of the car for a few moments as Cruz grips the steering wheel.

"*THIS* is the only place I can protect you, Madds," he whispers. "It may not be what you want. Hell, you're no doubt sick of me, but this is the environment I can control and protect you from the wolves."

And with that declaration, he climbs out of the car and has my door open for me before I grab hold of my purse on the floor. "Thank you."

A short elevator ride later and I walk into his penthouse. It's open and airy with windows on every wall allowing in incredible views of the Mediterranean. The interior is minimalistic modern. Light woods and neutral colors mixed with creams and whites. It should be cold but somehow with the aqua of the sea beyond, it isn't.

The condo is a stately great room, with a chef's kitchen on one side, a living space on another, and then a hallway leading to the back with the bedrooms and office. There is a balcony that runs the length of the wall complete with a workout section, a hot tub, and a television and patio furniture.

I stand in the middle of it, taking it all in, as Cruz makes an effort to disappear and give me the space we haven't had over the past week or so. This is home. That's clear.

"*THIS is the only place I can protect you, Madds,*" he whispers. "*It may not be what you want. Hell, you're no doubt sick of me, but this is the environment I can control and protect you from the wolves.*" He *wants* to protect me, which seems like a major step forward from indifference.

And strangely, I feel a modicum of peace. I may be completely out of my depth, but for the first time since this whole thing started, I don't feel so . . . desolate.

CHAPTER TWENTY-TWO

Maddix

"SO THIS IS ALL PRETEND. ALL OF IT." TESSA'S EYES ARE WIDE, HER
face in shock, as she looks at me through the computer screen.
I nod and breathe a little easier now that I've confided in
someone.

"I sure as fuck hope your boss is paying you a crap ton of money to one,
put up with some spoiled playboy who's no doubt probably fighting this every
step of the way, and two, for having to deal with all of these absolutely shallow headlines and horrible comments people are posting about you."

"Gee, way to make a girl feel better."

"You know what I mean."

"I do. It's definitely been an adventure of sorts." I chuckle and then sigh.
"But honestly, Cruz is pretty chill."

"Who wouldn't be for a cool billion, right?" she asks.

"Yep," I murmur and glance around the condo where he's everywhere
in theory but nowhere physically. He left yesterday to head to Spain for forty-eight hours. Some family something or other he needed to attend before
we hit the road for the next race on the circuit.

It's weird without him here. You'd think I'd be sick of him after being
stuck at the hip for almost two weeks, that I'd be reveling in the solitude I
typically crave, but I find myself waiting for him to make a smart-ass comment about anything. Or to have him walk in and ask what movie we're
watching at night.

"Yep. Right," she says, her eyes narrowing at me. "And you're putting up with all of this bullshit for . . ."

"A raise and a promotion."

"*And for him,*" she says.

"Well, yes. It's for him. We're doing all of this to prove to the board that he can be a trustworthy spokesperson and partner they don't need to worry about."

"That's not what I meant."

"Tess? If you're trying to make a point, just get to the point."

A slow smile crawls onto her lips at the same time a soft breeze comes in through the open windows. "You like him, don't you?"

I fidget at the question. There are so many facets to the man. He's arrogant, cynical, sarcastic, and brash, but he's also thoughtful. Allowing me to sleep on his shoulder but hiding the fact, bringing me here to his home rather than leaving me in a hotel. *Do I like him?* "Yeah. Sure. He's . . . Cruz."

She bursts into laughter. "As I said, you *like him, like him.*"

I chuckle nervously. "You're being ridiculous. We're playing pretend."

"And sometimes pretend becomes reality," she counters. "Unless of course that reality—like a horizontal one perhaps—has already happened."

I roll my eyes and blow out a dramatic sigh, hoping the flushing of my cheeks isn't noticeable. "Whatever."

"You're in a pressure cooker turned on the highest setting. The whole world looking in at you, pushing you together, creating a bubble around the two of you that only you understand. It's a far from normal situation—like far, far from normal—so it's no wonder if you like him since you've been pushed together."

"Tess, it's not like that."

"So you haven't slept with him then?"

My hesitation is all she needs to point at me and shout, "Ha! I knew it."

"I didn't say a word." I feign innocence despite knowing that of all the people in the world, she'd be my number one cheerleader on this.

But I hesitate because what do I tell her? Yes, we slept together, but then he just moved right along as per what I can assume is his typical MO?

I mean . . .

"You didn't have to say a word. You only ignore me when you feel like you've done something wrong, and you were ignoring me." I go to open my mouth and then shut it as her grin widens and her eyes light up. "So . . .

please tell me Cruz Navarro lives up to his playboy status. Was he everything Michael wasn't in the best of ways and then some?"

I stare at her, blinking, as a slow smile crawls onto my lips. "We were drinking."

"Good. That means inhibitions were thrown out the window. And?"

"And I may have been the one to initiate it."

She throws her arms up and shouts, "Woo-hoo," like I just scored a touchdown.

"Tess. I was drunk—"

"So?"

"And he tried to say I was going to regret it in the morning and—"

"Did you? Do you? Talk to me so I can live vicariously through you."

I hang my head for a beat and relive the highlight reel. "No. Not in the sense that we did it because, damn, Tess, the man . . . he knows how to make a woman come."

Her grin is iconic. "After Missionary Mike, that's saying something."

I snort. "Hey . . ."

"Don't defend him. Nice guys finish last and he wasn't really that nice to begin with. He was the rut you got stuck in, and Cruz is the hill you mount to get out of said rut. So"—she clasps her hands and sets them on the table in front of her with authority—"why am I sensing a good time was had by all but hasn't been had again?"

"Because I freaked out. When I woke up, he was nowhere to be found and—"

"And you backpedaled your way out of it, didn't you? You took the blame. You said it was a one-time thing. You said it was a mistake that can't happen again."

"How do you know all of that?"

"Because I know my best friend and that's what she'd do."

I nod and chuckle a little. "Yeah, well, you're right." Then I sigh. "I don't do that, Tess. I don't just sleep with someone just to sleep with someone."

"If you're looking for me to judge you for it, you're going to be waiting a long-ass time. So what if you slept with the man? I sure as hell would. It's normal. You're normal. You just came out of a relationship that didn't light your fire. It's perfectly fine to want to get burned by that man's flames."

"Well, *that man's flames* were nowhere to be found the next morning. And when we tried to talk about it—"

"You mean when you played it down and tried to write it off as being a one-time thing versus something perfectly normal that most people do at least once in their lives?"

Jesus. She's right, isn't she?

"Well, he acted like it wasn't a big deal. We had sex. We had fun. We cleared the air over it. And . . . then we went on our way."

Her grin is full force now. "And you're just taking him at his non-words that he wouldn't do it again?"

"Of course I am. It's awkward enough talking about it the first time. And for him, this is probably an every week or two occurrence."

"Uh-huh." She draws the syllables out. "So you're saying that you wouldn't do it again with him or that you're not catching feelings for him or . . ."

"It's only been weeks since Michael and I broke up."

"And your point is what, because that didn't answer either of my questions?"

"Because the question is irrelevant. Cruz isn't like that. No doubt he looks at me and—"

"Wants more."

"Bullshit."

"Has he been avoiding you? Does he pick fights with you? Keep you at a distance?"

"So what if he does? I'm majorly cramping his playboy lifestyle. Plus, he has to be sick of me and doesn't want to give me ideas that he wants more."

"Girl, that kiss he gave you on camera? You're telling me that was just for show?"

"One hundred percent." I relive the wave of euphoria I had when his lips touched mine and then the pang of disappointment when I realized the cameras were there. "Kevin was on us to make our *relationship* known. The cameras were there. Believe me, by the look on Cruz's face, it was the last thing he wanted to do."

"A man doesn't cup a woman's face if he doesn't want her. He gives her a peck on the lips. A kiss to the cheek. He does not step up to her and cup her face before slowly going in for the cinematic kiss."

"You are so full of shit."

"Watch the replay. It's all over social media played to the sounds of women's hearts breaking."

I have watched it. Many times. Each time reliving the feeling of his hands on me. But I never looked at it in the way that Tessa did. I never saw it in that light.

"But you don't like him. Don't want him," she deadpans. "Says the woman who bit her bottom lip when she stared after him in the garage."

"I did not." Oh, shit. Did I?

"It's your tell. The thing you do when you are crushing hard on a guy. I saw it plain as day. So did however many millions who watched it."

"I do not have a tell." *I so* do.

She smirks and that look on her face tells me I'm screwed and that she's right and has the receipts to back it up. "You don't? Watch the replay."

Fuck.

"You're making my point for me. It was all for show. For the cameras. That kiss was to sell the lie. I promise, I'm not into him. He's not into me. We had sex. It was fun. Now we're all business."

"That's a lot of explanation for someone trying to convince herself there's no spark there when, sweetheart, you two were smoldering."

"Tess. This is me we're talking about here. A Texas girl who wants to pay off her student loans and work her way up to vice president of branding at some top firm somewhere. I am not Cruz Navarro material. What happened was a blip in the matrix."

"The same blip in the matrix that forced you two together when you never would have met otherwise."

"You're talking nonsense."

"Maybe, but I'm still left wondering why you're fighting this so hard." She throws her hands up. "It's me here. The one you go to for everything, and I'm sitting here watching you try to convince yourself you're not into the man when it's clear as fucking day you are. You wouldn't be arguing otherwise. It's okay to admit you *want* to fuck him again. It's even okay to admit you kind of have feelings for him—hell, you're living with the man, it would be impossible not to. But the question you need to be asking yourself is why do you think you don't deserve either of those things?"

Deserve those things? Like the hardening of my nipples every time he touches my lower back? Or the slow simmering ache in my lower belly every time he leans in to whisper in my ear, his breath tickling my cheek? Or is she talking about the butterflies that hit me when sometimes I look up and he's staring at me from across the room?

Reading into everything is second nature to me. I've written all that off as a *me* thing. As the result of wanting to be touched like a woman—the way Cruz touched me—versus like a stuffed animal you're kind of bored with but take out and play with every once in a while. And maybe I didn't realize the difference until the night we had sex.

"I do deserve them. You're right. But at the same time . . . this whole charade will be over in a few months. Then we'll be back to our regularly scheduled programs." *And where will that leave me?*

"Meaning he'll be richer and you actually think after a few months of jet-setting and living the high life in Monaco that you're going to be able to come back here and live the same life you were and be content with it?" She looks at me like I've lost my mind. "I sure as hell hope not."

"What are you saying, Tess?"

"I'm saying live a little. You're getting a chance at a life and a situation most would kill for. Fuck the haters. Ignore the outside noise and the jealous comments. Own who you are. Flaunt it. You're the girl from Texas who snagged the playboy prince of F1. Go out. Make some headlines for all the wrong reasons. In all the years I've known you, I've never known you to be shy or hesitant, and this whole situation has made you that." She shakes her head. "Reclaim that shit back."

I start to disagree with her, but then stop myself. She's right. This self-doubt thing isn't me. I'm here because I made my case to Kevin and got in on the meeting. It's why I graduated from college cum laude, working diligently and never shying away from the hard stuff. It's how I got my job at a top equity firm when there were what felt like a million other candidates more qualified from prestigious schools.

Walking away from something is not in my nature, so why am I letting myself question that about myself now?

Was it Michael? Did I lose belief in myself somewhere along the way during our time together? The old me would have kicked him to the curb ages ago.

Why in the world did I let anyone take anything from me, let alone my confidence? *What do I have to lose?*

Reclaim that shit back, Maddix.

Is this all I needed to find my footing? Not my mom's coddling but the no-nonsense facts from my best friend?

"It's way easier said than done," I murmur.

"What is? Being the badass you are or realizing that part of that reclamation you need to do is fucking your pretend boyfriend?"

I spit out my drink of water. It sprays all over the floor beside the table. "Tessa." I cough the syllables out.

"What?" She bats her lashes. "I only speak the truth."

"Truth or not, that's not . . . that would just complicate matters."

"The way I see it, they're already pretty fucking complicated." She shrugs. "*Why the hell would you not?* No one is talking about a deep-seated relationship here. Cruz clearly isn't that kind of guy. Besides, you need Cruz's expertise to help get you out of the *Missionary Mike trauma.*"

I burst out laughing. Can always leave it to Tessa to add some humor and honesty to every situation.

"See? I'm right." She straightens her shoulders.

"I am neither confirming nor denying anything."

"Look, Maddix, you're being put through the wringer with all this public bullshit. If you have to endure it, then make it fucking worth it. And orgasms are worth it."

"You're forgetting one major thing though."

"What's that?"

"It takes two and Cruz hasn't made a move since."

"Then you make one. You had no problem before, right?"

"There was a lot of alcohol," I say.

"One"—she holds her finger up—"the garage kiss. Damn thing was so simple, so hot, it turned me on. And two, you're living together. I have no doubt he's gotten off to thoughts of you already."

"Um." My cheeks pale because maybe . . . I just might have done the same. But lucky for me the connection isn't clear enough for her to catch that.

"That's a compliment. Take it accordingly."

"But—"

"He's interested. Believe me, he's interested."

"It will make one hell of an awkward few months with each other if he isn't."

"Are you forgetting the man has already seen you come? Has already been inside of you? I mean . . . at what point are you going to realize you're past the realm of embarrassment now?"

"I have no words right now. None." My cheeks are as pink as the paint on my toenails.

"There's always risk with a reward and, I hate to break it to you, sis, but Cruz Navarro is one hell of a reward," she says boldly. And I know for a fact she has me all riled up and believing in this theory, but that the minute our connection ends, I'll be at a loss about what to do next. And as if we share the same brain, she asks, "When does he come back from his trip?"

"Tomorrow afternoon."

"Okay. So here's what you need to do. Go buy the hottest bikini you can find. Wear it around the house. See his reaction to it."

"This isn't high school."

"No. It's most definitely not high school and thank fuck for that." She laughs. "Beat the man at his own game. What do you have to lose? He's a player. You're newly single. Girl, enjoy the ride while you can. What's the worst that's going to happen? He sees you and walks right past? If so, you have your answer. But what if he does a double take and Mr. Smooth struggles to find words? Then . . . you have a different answer."

"I think you've lost your marbles."

"And yet you're considering it."

I don't respond. Can't. Because I am considering it. Every bone in my body is wanting it, wanting him. Hasn't it always wanted him even when I questioned if I liked him?

This is so wrong in so many ways and yet why does the fantasy of being with him feel so right?

"You said this was a temporary situation, Maddix. Well, so is lust."

CHAPTER TWENTY-THREE

Cruz

"OH, LOOK, THE PRIZED SON HAS ARRIVED."

I roll my eyes at my sister, Sofia, as she lifts the sangria to her lips. "Prized? If that were the case then Papá wouldn't have looked like he was going to lose his shit when he saw me walk in here."

"You sure know how to make an entrance. I'll give you that."

My father told me I wasn't welcome to the monthly family dinner. That mi patriarca still didn't want to see me. That there wouldn't be a place setting for me when there always has been.

I definitely poked the bear in Amsterdam but fuck that and fuck him.

And by the look on mi patriarca's face when he saw me walk into the villa, I made the right decision to come.

Now to try and get some alone time with him without my father hovering and trying to manage our relationship without him as intermediary.

I shrug and glance at my sister. "Last I checked, this is my family too. Since when do I care if he approves of me?"

Her eyes soften and her smile is sad. "I'm sorry, Cruz."

"Don't be." My voice is gruff. I hate the pressure in my chest that this kind of shit brings up. "Is it no wonder Mamá lives a different life away from here?"

"Maybe that's why his grip on this family is so tight."

And maybe you're making excuses because you don't get the brunt of it.

But I don't voice the words. Can't. She's the only person in this family I have to hold on to other than our grandfather who has zero expectations of me. Our mother is good for showing up, taking some pictures, and leaving some lipstick marks on our cheeks before heading back to her fantasyland that my father affords her. If he pays for her abandonment, it saves him and the Navarro name from something it has never had stain it before—divorce.

"Mmm," I murmur, my lack of response my dissent.

"He does love you, you know. He talks about you to everyone like you are the second coming of Christ, while I'm just the spare over here." Her words sound like mine most days—truthful tinged with a little hurt.

But isn't her observation the whole of it? So long as he can put me on a pedestal and show my shine off to everyone else, then he's happy. Then it makes him look good to have sired the heir who will restore the nostalgia of mi patriarca's era. It's his way of staying relevant. Of being relevant to a hard man who loves him but he fell short of living up to.

But when, God forbid, I step out of the Navarro line, one that's about as fine as a knife's edge, then I'm a disgrace.

I'm shaming him and his quest for approval. And with that comes an underlying animosity that I've never quite been able to understand.

"He's good at putting on the show, I'll give him that," I say.

"He's just not good with emotion. Never has been."

"Well, maybe he should figure it out before he loses the only legacy he has left—us." I chuckle but it's empty. "At least he's not using el patriarca as a pawn with you."

"I know." It's barely a whisper as she nods. Being a male in the Navarro family comes with added strings and expectations. Strings that strangle and expectations that cripple.

She smiles softly and then reaches out to squeeze my hand. "I know it's hard on you and I'm here for you. Always."

I nod but look away because there's not much more to say. Especially when I look over to where the monthly Navarro family dinner is being set. A long, narrow table with thirty-two place settings is set up. It's positioned beneath a trellis rich with vines, and with the view of the rolling fields of our family land stretched out into the horizon.

It looks like the setting for a picture-perfect family. Yet I stand here and bristle with everything that is and everything that isn't.

Tradition. That is what the Navarro family was built on. What our reputation has been founded on. That and discipline. Well, at least when it comes to the men.

I open my mouth to say more but then see my grandfather being wheeled out onto the cobblestone patio by his nurse. His shock of white hair is styled to perfection and his custom-tailored shirt is impeccable as always. You'd never know that his eighty-nine-year-old body is failing him with how he presents himself.

He is the patriarch of this family in every sense of the word and the minute his wheels hit the patio, everyone's attention shifts to vie for his attention.

But I'm the prized grandson, the one walking in his footsteps, and so make the most of the opportunity and approach him before anyone else can. My father will have to watch his step with how he handles that with so many eyes on us.

I'm sure I'll piss off someone for greeting him out of pecking order.

"Patriarca," I say and lean forward and kiss both of his cheeks.

He smells of sandalwood and mint. I'm immediately transported back to my youth when I'd sit on his lap, his fire suit itchy against my bare legs, and shop being talked around me. Tires and pit stops and swear words that made my eyes bulge and my lips twitch into a devilish smile. Other memories include the rough callouses on his palm as he'd hold my hand and we'd watch my dad race. My dad fail to finish near the top. And then the string of curse words that would follow.

"Cruz." His voice is thready, but his dark brown eyes hold so much love as he reaches up with shaky hands and cups both sides of my cheeks. "You came."

This. *Him*. He's the only one who makes my heart feel anything.

"Always. For you, always," I respond reflexively while wondering why I'm getting this reaction when I was told he didn't want to see me.

"You're racing strong. Your championship will come soon enough. We can all see it." His smile showcases his trademark gap in his front teeth as he pats my cheek again. He shrugs ever so slightly. "It's what us Navarros do."

"I know."

"Don't question your instincts. Keep working as you are. You'll only get better as everyone else plateaus. This is in your blood."

"Yes, sir."

He stares at me for a beat and for a few moments, the world around us carries on but it seems like it stops for him. He gets a distant look in his eyes and he goes somewhere else. It's been happening more and more lately. And just when I glance up to his nurse with worry, he speaks.

"Is she here?" he asks, confusing me momentarily. "The American?"

Maddix. How does he know about her?

"No. This is for our family."

Our eyes hold and he gives me the subtlest of nods. I swear to God he sees right through me and knows the whole thing with Maddix is a ruse.

"In time, perhaps."

"Yes, sir."

"She makes you smile." When my eyes narrow, he lifts a crooked finger toward his nurse. "She shows me pictures of you."

"She does. Yes." I clear my throat. This is the only time I hate this lie—here. Now. To my grandfather. But my discord is softened by the fact that he's right, she does make me smile. That is not a lie.

"Good. Good." He pats my hand. "She's not Spanish."

My smile is tight. The reins of my heritage held tightly. "It's nothing serious."

He nods. His actions may show age, but his eyes are now very astute. "Your father became distracted. He lost his edge. He ruined his entire career over a woman who . . . wasn't worthy of our name."

My shoulders square at the mention of my mother. She's not a favorite around here, but she's still my mother regardless of how much I agree with him. I meet his eyes but don't speak. It's not my place to. He is who he is and if there is anyone in this world I respect, who I don't mouth off to, it's him.

And not just because he's my grandfather, but more so because he's the only man in my life who has looked at me with love in his eyes.

I'm not immune. I'm the one he thinks will reclaim our name. But at the same time, it's more. It's love. It's adoration. It's everything I wished my father would look at me with but doesn't.

Tough love is one thing. Bitterness that your son is better than you a completely different thing.

"Come closer," he whispers, and I lean forward so that my ear is near his lips. "Very proud of you."

My throat closes up. The praise I yearn to hear, he gives me. Our eyes meet again, and I nod because words escape me.

"Papá." And there he is, like fucking clockwork, the pecking order now corrected. My dad waltzes across the space, a glass of whiskey in hand for el patriarca, and an irritated glance my way.

Yes. I got to him before you could get here and listen. Before you could try and steal my own thunder for yourself.

"Dom," he says, reaching a hand out to squeeze my father's and accept the whiskey he places in the other.

There are five generations of Navarros here tonight for our family dinner. And yet the three of us standing here are the only ones capable at this time of carrying on the family name. Every other male here is through marriage.

You'd think that would count for something but, by the way my dad takes my grandfather's wheelchair and pushes it away from where I stand, it's clear I'm still the outcast for one reason or another.

Once my grandfather is settled at his designated place at the center of the table with the oldest generations closest to him and the youngest ones toward the ends, my father moves back toward me.

"Glad to see you came to your senses and moved on from *the American*," he says by way of greeting as he hands me a fresh glass of wine. I don't respond, don't have to because he's so used to carrying on conversations with me by himself, he just keeps going.

"I wasn't aware you were going to be here," he says, "but it's perfect that you are."

That's an unexpected turn of events.

"It is?"

"I took the leisure of calling Esmerelda and inviting her tonight. Lucky for us she happened to be home this evening." He motions to a stunning woman lingering on the edges of the patio with my cousins. She's curvy with classic Spanish looks—dark hair, dark eyes, and light brown skin. Her smile is wide and her gaze is suddenly on me as if she knew he was about to introduce her into the equation.

She smiles and I return the same as is polite.

She's been a family friend for years. Always there, always hinted at as the perfect and almost equal companion to me.

It's only fitting that he uses her to drive the point home right now. How he no doubt had her waiting in the wings just in case I showed up.

Would I fuck her? She's gorgeous enough, *yes*. Would I actually refrain? As a fuck you to him, *definitely*.

But Esmerelda is all show. Just window dressing trying to catch her claws in anything with money to fulfill her lavish tastes.

Sounds like someone else. *My mother.*

"Of course, you invited her. I'm assuming her pedigree is worthy of the Navarro name?"

"It is. Yes."

"It better be, considering you've been fucking her aunt for months." I lift my eyebrows as I bring my drink to my lips and murmur, "Since you're making it a thing that we judge who we stick our cocks into, right?"

His jaw works as he stares at me. *Grit those teeth any harder they just might crack.* "That's completely inappropriate and disrespectful to your mother."

I chuckle loudly and draw the attention of some of our family. The drink goes down a little smoother this time. *Leave it to him not to see the hypocrisy here.* "And fucking a woman who isn't your wife is the epitome of respect, no?" I say as I swirl the liquid in my glass. "The irony that you're concerned with me being disrespectful to your lover when you're the same to mine, and you've never even met her."

"I don't have to meet her to know she's not right for you."

"Just like I don't have to fuck Esmerelda to know her aunt's a gold digger leading you around by the balls." I shake my head and step in a little closer. "You stand here on your pedestal thinking you're better than I am. I have the same blood running through my veins too, old man. I'm your legacy. Push too hard and I just might fuck it up to spite you."

"I'm not someone to fuck with," he grits out.

"Then don't tempt me." I take a step back and meet his eyes. "Give my best to Esmerelda. I have a girlfriend. The one you need to leave the fuck alone."

I stride away toward the table, hating the emotions bellowing through me. *Hate* for the man who raised me. *Love* for the man who nurtured me.

"Is she here? The American?" He wanted her to be here . . .

"Very proud of you." He loves me. My family is as rich in knowledge and love as they are in love for each other. It's a legacy I'm proud of. Amazing to be part of it.

Except for one man, whose hypocrisy and narcissism knows no bounds.

So why the fuck do I still *want* to please him?

CHAPTER TWENTY-FOUR

Cruz

DINNER IS FULL OF SMALL TALK. OF INSIDE JOKES THAT CAN ONLY BE understood by one another. Of a lot of wine and even more food.

I came here needing this. The connection. My family. And when the dessert is done and the sun has set, leaving the sky awash with color, I sit with my feet up, another glass of wine in my hand, and Sofia beside me in much the same posture.

"I met up with Lennox when I was in London," she says about my agent who she's become friends with.

"Nothing good ever comes out of that for me," I groan, thinking of the last time they met up and Sofia spilled details on my personal life.

"Hey, she's good enough to kick ass for you, she's good enough to be a friend to me," she teases. "Besides, she's awesome."

"She is." *Where is she going with this?*

"So, we were talking, and she shared the details about this whole situation you've got going now since you're a guy and never tell me the good stuff."

"Which situation would that be?"

"The one where you have a pretend girlfriend?"

"Remind me why I told you?" I groan and rest my head back. But I know why I did, because I was livid about it that first night and had to confide in someone. And besides Lennox, she's the only one I could have.

"Maddix was your choice?" There is confusion laced in her voice. "Why didn't you tell me she was a real person with a real life and not some actress paid to play the part?"

"Because it's not important."

"Clearly she was, or you wouldn't have plucked her out of obscurity and thrown her into all this mess with you."

"I'm well aware of what I did." *What's the point, Sof? Because you never ask without having a reason.*

"Tell me about her," Sofia says softly, her eyes straight ahead, but the question that has been lingering in them all night finally spoken aloud.

And there it is, folks.

"Not sure what you mean."

"You're so full of shit. You know exactly what I mean." She takes a sip. "Tell me about the woman you came here tonight to make a statement for."

"What?" I cough the word out. She's fucking crazy.

"You're here when normally you wouldn't give a rat's ass. You're here to stick it to Papá. I mean this whole dating thing is a farce between you two and yet you're using it as a fuck you to him."

"You're wrong."

"I'm right." Her grin reminds me of when we were little and she'd threaten to tell Papá I had done something wrong unless I caved to her demands. "You gave Esmerelda the cold shoulder when normally you're at least cordial to her. You made sure to be with el patriarca every chance you got to rub it in Papá's face. And you entertained questions about Maddix from everyone when normally you'd change the subject. So yeah, there was a reason for you showing up here and it wasn't because you wanted some homestyle cooking. It was because you wanted to use this whole charade to your advantage. Wanted to use Maddix yet again."

"Hmm," I say as I take a sip of wine and opt for that to be my only response. Is that what I'm doing? Using Maddix yet again for my own selfish needs?

"Cruz?" I can feel the weight of her stare but ignore her. "This is all a farce, right? You two aren't sleeping . . ." Her eyes meet mine and they widen slowly as she reads whatever she sees in mine. "Oh my God, you two *are*." She swats at me. Hard. "Eres un cabrón." *Yep, I'm an asshole.*

"Hey." I hold my hands up in surrender. "I didn't say shit."

"And here I thought I was going to like the hell out of her for putting up with you and being smart enough not to fall for your disgusting, bachelor bullshit. Ugh." When I look her way, she has the look on her face when I used to try and convince her that earthworms were cool.

"Hey. No bad-mouthing Madds. There's enough of that around here."

"Madds? A nickname *and* he's sticking up for her?" She raises her eyebrows. "*But nothing is going on.*" She snorts.

I stare at her as I figure out what to say. "We're not . . . she's not like that. Far fucking from it." I chortle out a laugh riddled with the frustration I feel every time I see Maddix and know I can't fucking have her. Mad at myself for feeling the need to defend her when . . . what am I defending her from? From my own reputation tainting her? From my sister painting her in an unfavorable light?

Does it fucking matter? Maddix doesn't want me. She made that clear with her whole *this is a mistake* bullshit.

Bullshit. That's exactly what it is though. I catch her staring at me. I feel her body soften when I touch her lower back. I see her nipples harden when I accidentally brush against her.

Sofia goes to open her mouth and then shuts it. Instead she angles her head to the side and simply studies me long and hard. A slow smile paints her lips. "*No. Fucking. Way.*"

"What are you talking about?"

"You like her, don't you?" Her eyes grow wide.

"I respect her."

"She's gorgeous." *She's breathtaking.*

"Of course she is." *Because that's what's expected of me.*

"That's not an answer, Cruz."

"Back off, Sof." Maddix is more than just gorgeous. She's smart, sexy, funny, thoughtful. Everything a guy like me doesn't deserve, and yet I still find myself wanting her. Yep. I'm the selfish bastard benefitting from all this while she's hurting because of it. *And yet, I still want her.*

"*And* protective." She smirks.

"She's real. The realest person I've met in a long time. You're right. She left a life behind for all this. She agreed to keep her job and get a raise. To try and better herself. I mean . . . I heard her on the phone fighting about deferring her student loan payments, and here I am living in the lap of luxury, never knowing anything different. So just leave her alone, because she's already gotten enough shit from the media and online trolls and Papá."

"So you've finally met a woman that you see as a person rather than just a sheet warmer to occupy your bed one night at a time?"

I slide her a dubious look. "I'm not sure what you're trying to get at."

"It's okay to like someone, Cruz. It's even more okay to want to defend them. And shock of all shocks, it's okay to want something more from a woman than just sex. Companionship. Friendship. Support. *Love*."

I blow out a breath. "It's not like that."

"Whatever you say." She holds up her hands.

"It's not."

"You're just living with a woman who could have easily stayed in a hotel, you show up here tonight to all but defend her honor, and you're not bragging about any exploits with her like you normally would, but . . . it's not like that."

It's not.

It isn't.

She's crazy.

"Let it rest, Sofia."

"Not every woman is like Mamá, you know?"

My hands tighten into fists, and I drain the last of my drink. And yet that is the constant comparison, isn't it?

"Glad I found you two together."

And the hits just keep on coming.

"Dad," Sofia says.

I sigh and opt to stare at the sunset. At the dark silhouette it casts of the mountains and the orange of the sky.

What is Maddix doing right now? Is she working? Is she curled up in a ball on the balcony with the breeze in her hair and her nose in a book like she enjoys doing? Is she standing in front of the open pantry trying to figure out what to eat but doesn't have me there to ask what each thing is—some of the items foreign to her—so she can decide?

"Yes, Cruz?" my dad asks, forcing me to participate in this conversation.

"Yes, what?"

"The Prince of Monaco has invited the Navarros to the charity gala again this year. I'd like you and Sofia to represent the family. El patriarca is too ill, and I have other business to attend to, but you two will go."

"Other business?" I probe.

"That's what I said."

"Mamá can't go this year?" I ask, my eyes boring into his. The charity gala is exactly what my mother loves. Glitz. Glamour. To fly in on the jet, to show off the body good money has bought her, and then leave the second all the cameras are gone.

"No." Steel is in his eyes when they meet mine. So his wife won't go with him this year, huh? Can't have that stain on the Navarro name now, can we? We can have affairs that we think are hidden but that everyone knows about, but your own damn wife can't stand you enough to show up.

"*The* Dominic Navarro is going to pass up the opportunity to have the limelight?" Sarcasm drips off my every word. "You live for that shit. For the chance to be the prized son."

He grits his jaw. His disdain owns his every feature. "You and Sofia will attend."

"Ah, so the prized children get the *privilege*," I toy with him.

"I expect you both to represent our family appropriately. You will not make a scene. You will be seen with who needs to be seen with. You will converse with the prince. You will be Navarros."

"Might be weird if we go as each other's dates, but, whatever," Sofia says with a shrug and another full pour of wine in her glass.

"You will go together," he repeats with no room for interpretation, but there is a flicker of a smile at the corners of my sister's mouth.

Well, well, well. Look at that.

Seems rebellion might just run in the family.

CHAPTER TWENTY-FIVE

Maddix

KNOW HE'S THERE.

I heard the key in the lock. I heard the front door slam.

And I heard the falter in his footsteps when he saw me.

But I keep my eyes closed for a few more seconds to bolster my courage so I can go through with this. So that I can seduce Cruz Navarro.

While a shot of liquid courage would do wonders about now, I wanted to let this play out with a completely clear head. Something I didn't have the first time.

And now, I'm slightly regretting that decision.

"Madds?" His voice is a hoarse syllable of sound. *Perfect.*

Time to reclaim that shit.

I flutter my eyes open and pretend to be startled. "Oh. Hi."

The look on Cruz's face is priceless. Jaw lax. Eyes wide. And his fingers twitch like he's itching to touch.

He works a swallow and then scrapes his eyes up my body until they meet mine. "Hi." It's a throaty syllable.

I know exactly what I look like right now. Every damn thing about this moment has been thought of and planned out.

The white bikini that covers just enough skin but leaves plenty to the imagination. The gold belly chain that shines in the sunlight. My freshly painted fingers and toes that match the red on my lips.

Because while we may have felt each other's skin in the dark, it's a whole different thing seeing all this skin on display in the daylight. Or at least that's what I'm counting on because I never realized how much I still wanted more of Cruz Navarro until this moment. Until he's standing before me with his nostrils flaring and by the growing bulge in his pants, in obvious need of relief.

And this time, I'm playing this game to win.

"How was your flight?" I ask as I use my spray bottle and casually mist cold water over my skin. I might accidentally spray a bit too much on the bra cups of my bikini, knowing the fabric liner is thin and so just a hint of the pink of my nipples will be visible because of it.

"*Christ.*" He scrubs a hand through his hair and shifts on his feet. "I mean . . . good. It was good."

"And your family . . . event, was it?"

"Event. Yes. A dinner. It's monthly. Done. Over with." His eyes roam again as his tongue darts out to lick his lips. "What have you been up to?"

I make a show of swinging my legs over the side of my chair and then standing up. A slow bend over with my ass toward him to position my sandals so I can slip them on when I could have just used my feet. "I went into town. Wanted to celebrate so I went shopping to buy myself a little something."

A glance over my shoulder tells me he's taking in my ass. Perfect.

"Shopping for what?"

"A new bikini." I turn and hold my hands out. "What do you think? Cute, huh?"

Another rough swallow. "Cute isn't exactly how I'd describe it."

My throaty laugh is my answer.

"What exactly are we celebrating?"

"*We* are not celebrating anything." I'm toying with him. "I am celebrating putting the finishing pieces on a market analysis I've been doing for months for Kevin. For coming to the realization that I wasted eighteen very good months of my life with Michael, a guy who was nice, but who didn't give me that sweet ache every time I looked at him. And for making a new friend and having a dinner date with them later tonight."

He eyes me with a mix of curiosity and lust. I know which one I want to win in this personal battle he's waging.

"You're going out? What happened to you not wanting to deal with the press? What changed all of that?"

I shrug nonchalantly and then reposition my belly chain, drawing his eyes to linger there. "My best friend, Tessa, gave me a pep talk, and I realized while this might be miserable for you, having me be your shadow, it's a chance of a lifetime for me. That I need to embrace it for what it is and take the hits that come with it as the trade-off."

"Miserable is one way to put it," he murmurs, thinking I don't hear it. By the desire glazing his eyes, I know he means misery in the best way possible.

I'm pretty sure I've got my answer. He wants me as much as I want him.

Now it's time to go in for the kill.

"What was that?" I ask, feigning innocence.

He clears his throat. "I said I like this self-assured version of you, Maddix."

"I do too." I give a curt nod and stretch my arms over my head, drawing his eyes back to my body. Not that they strayed very far to begin with. "She's kind of a badass." I laugh and stroll past him and into the house.

"Are we done here?"

"You can follow me if you want. I need to go touch up my makeup for my evening."

His footsteps follow me. "Where did you meet this new friend of yours?"

"In town. When I was shopping. The bikini was their idea."

He grunts as I move to the fridge and pull out a bottle of sparkling water, making a big deal over trying to unscrew the top. "Let me," he offers as I step toward him. So close I can see his pulse thundering in his jugular.

"Thank you."

"No problem." He hands it to me. "Where are you going to dinner?"

"On his yacht. You think this bikini is appropriate attire? I've never been on a yacht before."

His jaw clenches and his eyebrows raise as he tries to keep his cool. "It's not a good time of year to go on yachts," he says.

I bite back my laugh as I turn and accidentally rub my breast against his arm. "Oh, I'm sorry." I wipe imaginary lotion off his bicep. "I didn't mean to get suntan oil on you."

"It's fine." He jerks back a step like I've jolted him with electricity.

"I wasn't aware there was a good or bad time to go on yachts. I mean, you're making me think there might be jellyfish in the water while I was over here wondering how I'm going to keep this top on when I jump off the top deck and hit the water."

"Maddix." My name is a stern two syllables of frustration.

"Yeah?" I meet his eyes, the face of innocence. "Did I do something wrong, Cruz?"

The sexual tension is so damn thick you could cut it with a knife. But I stand there, eyes wide and lips lax, baiting him.

I was certain I would have chickened out by now. I'm the furthest thing from the seductive siren . . . and yet there is an empowerment in this. In owning my sexuality and using it blatantly and unapologetically to get a man's attention. In using it to try and get what I want.

I've never been shy. But I've also never actively pursued a man. Maybe because I never found the right man to pursue.

I'm here for the next however long, and during that time, I can be whoever I want to be. Isn't that the epiphany I came to this morning while staring at myself in the mirror after I had shaved and moisturized every damn inch of my body in preparation for this?

"No." His hands clench. "Nothing wrong. Just trying to . . . it's nothing."

"Okay. You scared me for a second." My smile is soft and then I startle just as I go to walk past him. "I need to get ready. I don't want to be late. Thanks for—"

"Who's your new friend? The one who helped you pick out your bikini and is having you on their yacht?"

"I think he's a friend of yours actually. Said he knew you wouldn't mind him stealing me away for the evening."

"Name?" he demands as a smirk he can't see plays on my lips.

"Rossi? Another driver. Or do I call you guys racers—"

But before I can even get the rest of my taunting comment out, Cruz has his hand on my bicep and yanks me solidly against his chest. His lips are on mine in a flash.

The kiss is a torrent of hunger. Of desire. Of fulfilling wants that have been building minute by minute, hour by hour, day by fucking day.

It's perfection.

Our tongues meet and lick against one another's as my body screams for his touch. For any kind of connection with him because this is what I've been wanting. What I've been craving.

His hips pin me to the counter as his lips unleash sensation after sensation, taunting me with his taste and tempting me with his skill.

His hand fists in my hair and I mewl in protest when he pulls on it to break the kiss. His eyes own mine as he looks at me. His breath panting against my lips, his cock pressing against my lower belly.

"Cruz—"

"*That.* That is all I've wanted to do every second of every day since I was last inside you." He kisses me senselessly again until my body is melting against his. "For the record? I lied. I remember every goddamn minute of that night. It's been torture wanting you. So you can say it was a mistake. You can claim you don't want me again, but fuck that, Madds." He gives another delectable kiss. "Because you do and I'm not believing your bullshit this time around. There will be no yachts. No dates with friends. Because I'm here and this time I'm taking what I want."

CHAPTER TWENTY-SIX

Maddix

I LEAN BACK AND MEET HIS EYES AS HIS HAND TIGHTENS IN THE HAIR at the base of my neck. My smile is slow and victorious. The words I'm about to utter only said to ensure there is no turning back. "Then take it."

His feral growl reverberates off the walls of the room as our lips meet again. Where the kiss before was hungry, this one is laden with desperation from weeks of pent-up sexual tension.

Of wanting and wondering.

Of wanting and remembering just how damn good we can make each other feel.

Of wanting and knowing we're about to sate the shared need that's strung tighter than a bow string about to snap.

He picks me up so that my legs wrap around his waist and carries me as we laugh and kiss and then kiss some more on the way to his bed. The second he sets my feet down, we're stripping off our clothes as fast as we can, our lips only breaking apart when his shirt passes over his head.

He pulls the strings of my bikini as my hands find his cock. He's hard and thick and my body already aches from the want of having him.

"You're so goddamn gorgeous, Madds," he says in the one stuttered moment where he steps back and takes me in.

I could say the same of him. The defined abs. The strong thighs. His beautiful cock. His arrogant smirk on lips I could kiss all day if allowed.

Our lips meet again. This time a bit gentler but still with the same overwhelming desire. He pushes me to sit on the edge of the bed, as he leans over to not break the kiss.

"Lay back. Let me look at you," he murmurs. "Last time was in the dark. Last time I didn't get to see all of you. This time I'm not missing the chance . . . and *fuck*." He groans the last word out, an audible aphrodisiac as he reaches down and starts stroking his cock.

I watch him, my bottom lip between my teeth, and my body strumming with need.

"You're gorgeous," I murmur and I swear he blushes. But there is no time to think through the thought because all I can see is him. All I want is him.

"You want this, don't you?" he asks as he makes a show of stroking it. How does he have this much restraint when we've had weeks of foreplay?

But I already started this game, and I intend to play it to its fullest.

"You want this, don't you?" I mimic as I lie back on the bed and slide my fingers over my breasts, pinching my nipples ever so slightly as I go. Then lower them farther—oh so slowly—down my abdomen while I spread my thighs.

His gasp is audible and fuck if it doesn't turn me on even more. My fingers part my slickness as he watches with an intensity that is part turn-on part chill-inducing. I dip my first finger into me, wet it with my own arousal, and then slide it back up to circle my clit.

I begin to tease myself. To taunt him. To pleasure myself until I can feel the sheet beneath me soak with desire.

"You're not getting this cock until your goddamn good and ready. So make yourself ready. Just like that. I want to watch. I want my balls to hurt I want you so bad. So play away, Madds. With yourself. With your games. You want to seduce me? Baby, I'm goddamn good and seduced."

His words? They incite. They arouse. They are an added element I didn't know I needed or wanted. So I play it up. The moan . . . as I dip my fingers into me. The arch of my back . . . as I add friction to my clit. The jiggle of my breasts . . . as I absorb the pleasure I'm giving myself at his expense.

And all without uttering a damn word.

"You're a cocktease," Cruz murmurs as I hear the rip of foil. I open my eyes to see him rolling the condom over his cock, but his eyes are one hundred percent on my fingers between my parted thighs.

"I'm just making sure you don't back out of this deal. I'm already too far invested to have to finish this myself," I tease.

"Oh, I'm invested all right." He grabs me behind my knees and slides my ass to the edge of the bed so that his cock rests right on top of where my fingers are playing. He grabs my hand and lifts it to his lips, making a show of sucking on one of my fingers. His hum and the heat of his mouth are like a mainline right back to where my fingers just were. And as if on cue, Cruz takes his other hand and lines the crest of his cock at my entrance.

"Just because it's been weeks since I last had you, it doesn't make the want any less. I'm going to fuck you, Maddix. You're going to take every goddamn inch of me, and I'm going to fuck you until my cock is soaked and my balls are dripping with proof of what I do to you. The only words I want on your lips are *Cruz* and *more*. Understood?"

"Yes."

He quirks a brow. "Already breaking rules?" He pats my pussy with force and the jolt to the nerves is an unexpected turn-on. "Should we try that again?"

I smile. It's a slow seductive crawl of curve to my lips. "More."

"There's my girl." This time he pats me more gently, but I arch my hips up, desperate for the friction of his touch, not just my own. "After you come, after I get to watch this sweet pussy of yours beg for more, then I'll get mine. Understood?"

Jesus. Did I miss this the last time around? The dominance? The dirty talk? The possessiveness? And holy hell does that add another whole element to Cruz Navarro that could bring any woman to her knees.

And not just to be down there worshipping his cock.

Sure I might have needed the alcohol to initiate that first time between us, but I have a feeling I missed a whole hell of a lot because it was dulled.

And if the sensations he brought on me then were dulled, I can't imagine the explosions of color I'm going to be seeing momentarily.

"I can handle you," I say, my smile strained with need.

"Oh, I know you can and you will."

"More," I taunt again.

His grin is wicked but it's his eyes that try to hold mine before they slowly roll back in his head as he pushes into me ever so slowly that own me. It's so quiet you can hear a pin drop in the room as he allows my body to stretch and accommodate every glorious, thick inch of him.

His guttural groan fills the room as his fingers dig into my hips in restraint. It's a heady feeling knowing and seeing what I do to him. That his desire for me—not just the sex—seems to be as strong as mine is for him.

"Tell me when, baby, because it's the best fucking torture being buried this deep in you."

I reach forward and scratch my fingers down his abdomen, his body tensing with the motion, causing his cock to jerk deep inside me.

I moan. I can't help it. It feels so damn good, so damn full, so damn right. And that moan is consent to Cruz to do anything he wants, because there is no way I'm walking away from this feeling right now.

No fucking way.

"Madds." My name is a swear word of pleasure as he begins to move. Slowly at first. Diligently. Strategically. "Keep touching yourself," he murmurs. "Show me what you like. What you want. How to touch you."

Each sentence ending is punctuated by a forceful drive back in so that he bottoms out within me and hits every desperate nerve ending craving his touch.

I lift my hips to give him better access. "*More.*" My fingers add pressure to my clit as he gives me delicious pleasure elsewhere. "*More.*" Over and over again. "*More.*" In. Out. Grind. Repeat.

The first time, I knew the pleasure, I recognized his skill, but again, the alcohol dulled it. But this time I'm on high alert. My senses. My nerve endings. Every goddamn place he touches lights with fire. A smolder of a burn that intensifies with each pass of his cock.

He leans forward, driving even deeper, and kisses me. Our tongues mingle. Our pants are shared. Our bodies working to a fever pitch.

"That's it, Madds. I can feel you tightening. Can feel you dripping. Can . . . there it is. Come for me. Come on my fucking cock for me."

I cry his name out, or God, as the orgasm consumes all sense of reason and faculty. It's a freight train of desire that derails and wrecks my every nerve perfectly. Currents shoot through me. From my lower belly out to my fingers and toes and then back again, hitting me even harder the second time around.

I'm lost to reason.

To my surroundings.

To everything but the feelings inside me and the man still braced above me.

And then with the sexiest groan I've ever heard—one that personifies restraint snapping in the best fucking way possible—Cruz rises to his knees and drives back into me.

Over and over.

Harder and harder.

Faster and faster.

Until it's my name on his lips. Until it's my body that he claims. Until it's his orgasm that I give him.

And I don't think he's ever looked sexier.

CHAPTER TWENTY-SEVEN

Cruz

I STAND IN THE SHOWER, WATER POURING DOWN MY BACK, AND MY COCK already growing hard again. Already wanting Maddix again.

Where the hell did that insatiable need come from and why the fuck was I fighting it for what feels like so goddamn long?

Normally I'd stroke myself. Give in to the need to come again so I could last even longer for her next time . . . but fuck if I'm going to be satisfied with my hand when I have goddamn perfection in the other room.

With a groan and the knowledge that the next time with her can't come soon enough, I turn the shower off, scrub a towel through my hair, and pull on a pair of sweatpants.

But fuck if my cock doesn't fly half-mast again the minute I walk out into the great room to see Maddix standing in my T-shirt, pouring us both a glass of wine.

How can I be turned on and want to sit down and just talk to her all at the same time?

"What?" she asks. Those green eyes look over toward me as I stand in the doorway, shoulder against the wall, hands shoved in the pockets of my sweats, and my feet bare.

"Nothing." I shake my head and move toward her. "Thanks."

"Of course." She moves toward the couch and takes a seat. I catch the slightest of winces.

"You okay?"

She nods, her eyes averting from mine. "Just a little sore." A smile turns up the corners of her lips as her eyes find mine. "And I'm not com-plaining about it."

My flash of a grin is automatic. Nothing says a job done right better than the sweet ache of sex afterwards. "I'll go easy on you next time."

"Please. Don't." Her cheeks flush in embarrassment—it's endearing—as she curls her legs against her chest and pulls my shirt over them and down to her ankles as she sips her wine. I can't take my eyes off her. One, because my shirt doesn't reach all the way to the couch and so every time she shifts, it shows me the curve of her ass and the hint of her bare pussy simply sitting there as a temptation to take again.

I sit on the arm of the couch opposite her and she offers me a shy smile. *Jesus*, it hits me right in the solar plexus. Her hair is mussed from my hands, and her lips are bare but pink from kissing me. How did I leave here a few days ago uncertain how this would all play out and return to this? To her? To what just happened? To my world being thoroughly rocked?

Thank you, Tessa.

"When you find your footing, Madds, you really find your footing. Watch out world." She covers her face with her hand as her cheeks heat. "Nope. You don't get to get all shy on me." I take a sip. "You just played me like a fiddle. Right into your hands. You seduced me and I'm fucking glad you did."

"I've got more in me where that came from."

"Thank. Fucking. God. For. That."

Maddix Hart *before* was beautiful. Beguiling. Sexy. This Maddix, with her *fuck the world* attitude, is a goddamn stunning knockout.

"I believe that is a compliment."

"It is. A huge one." I shift and sit on the cushion, unable to take my eyes off her or get the feel of her wrapped around me out of my head.

Is this what it feels like when you have to wait for something? Because if it is, fucking hell, the intensity makes it well worth it.

"Tell me something, Cruz," she asks above the rim of her wineglass.

"What's that?"

"Why haven't you had a girlfriend?"

"Jesus." I cough the word out and laugh. "Let's not jump that far ahead of ourselves, huh?"

"I'm not talking about me." She rolls her eyes, but why do her words hit me wrong? "It's just . . . from the outside looking in, you either get bored quickly—which is worrisome since we're stuck together for the time being—or you have a serious commitment issue that you've yet to address."

Shit. That footing I just said she found? She's really digging in.

But it's Sofia's words that come back to me with a vengeance right now. I shove them and the feeling they cause all the way down.

"People are rarely what they seem." It's a chickenshit answer but my place still smells like the sex we just had, and the last thing I want is to ruin the high of that.

"Maybe it's because you never stick around long enough to find out."

"And maybe you stick around too long because you're afraid to just go for it. Change isn't always bad."

Her grimace tells me it was a direct hit. A punch to deflect the ones she could easily hit me with if she keeps going in this direction. But unlike me, she takes the hit and nods. "It isn't. I figured that out over the past few days and am trying to fix that."

"Well, all that fixing better not have anything to do with Oliver Rossi. Ever."

She lifts an eyebrow, no doubt noting my deliberate change of topic. "Is that so?" Her smile taunts.

"That is most definitely so." There's amusement in her eyes. And then it hits me. "There was no Rossi. No date on a boat. Was there?"

Her smile widens and she stands and moves toward me. "Whatever would give you that idea?" she says coyly as she sets her glass down on the table.

"Fucking hell. You did play me, didn't you?"

She steps forward and trails a finger down my bare chest. "I can neither confirm nor deny, but I can tell you, we ended up right where we needed to be."

Me in you. Yeah. No fucking complaints there.

I reach for her hips, for the globes of her ass, and pull her toward me so that she has no choice but to straddle me. "You're a wolf in sheep's clothing, Madds."

I lean forward and kiss her. Lick between the seam of her lips and dig my fingers into the flesh at her hips.

"Watch out. I just might bite."

"Pretty please?"

"I like you jealous," she purrs against my lips before kissing her way down my shoulder. "I like you sweaty." She flicks her tongue over the disc of my nipple and sucks, her eyes looking up at me as she slides back on my knees so that her thighs are spread wide. I can see the pink of her pussy. "I think you're sexy as hell in your fire suit before the race." She moves off my lap, her knees hitting the floor between my feet. "And completely fuckable after when your hair is wet and your muscles are tense." She leans back and pulls my shirt over her head. Her nipples are pink and the little marks on her breasts from where I sucked too hard—turn me the fuck on.

I marked her as mine. Why does that give me such a sense of satisfaction?

"Madds." It's the sound of a desperate man. *Please tell me you're going to do what I think you're going to do.*

Her laugh is throaty as she takes both hands to pull my sweats down when I lift my ass up. My cock springs free. It's hard as a rock and pre-cum is already glistening at its tip.

"And I especially like you like this. Desperate. Wanting. Your eyes dark. Your cock hard." She leans forward and licks the drop off. "I want to taste you, Cruz. I want to feel you hit the back of my throat. I want to hear my name on your lips. *I want you at my mercy.*"

Have me, Madds. Fucking take me.

And when she places my cock between her soft lips, when the first slide down goes to the back of her throat, when she hollows out her cheeks and sucks hard, my eyes roll back in my head. *I'm a fucking goner.*

"Maddix." It's the softest groan and the closest thing I'll ever give to submission.

I fist my hand in her hair and pull back on it ever so slightly so she's forced to look at me as she takes me again. So I can see her accept even more of me in that sinful mouth of hers. So I can tense my ass and fight the urge to fuck her mouth when she gags on me but keeps trying to go farther.

Those lust-filled eyes still hold mine.

Over and over.

Hand over fist. Lick after suck.

And when I can't fight it any longer, when the pleasure is so intense it borders on painful, when my place is filled with my encouraging praise and the slick sounds of her mouth fucking me, the coil snaps. Detonates.

Ignites. And I spill everything I have down the back of her throat until she swallows every goddamn drop.

Until she has me one hundred percent at her complete mercy.

Fucking hell.

This woman. I've gone toe-to-toe with my father for her. I've tried to be a bigger person for her. I've even gotten jealous over her.

What the fuck is happening?

CHAPTER TWENTY-EIGHT

Cruz

"THIS IS . . ." SHE TURNS AROUND AND SLOWLY TAKES IN THE
Marché aux Fleurs Cours Saleya. "Incredible."

The famed flower market in the heart of Nice runs the length
of the promenade. It's a long corridor with restaurants on both sides and
stands, one after another, lining its center. The vendors sell handmade soaps,
dried fruits, tourist trinkets, fresh-cut flowers, pastries, and other various
wares. The outdoor market is busy with both locals and tourists and the
ocean breeze cools down the cobblestone courtyard.

"It is." I nod, my baseball hat pulled low over my head in the hopes of
blending in with the crowd rather than becoming a spectacle in it. "I thought
you might like it."

"But you were supposed to go out with your friends today. What happened to that?"

A day on the Riviera with the boys. Sun. Alcohol. The sea. The bro-code.

I had said yes. It was just what I needed weeks ago when it was planned.

It was just what I needed until it wasn't. Until I looked across the room
to see Maddix tapping away on her keyboard, her hair pulled up, and a pen-
cil between her lips as she concentrated on whatever it was she was doing,
cooped up in my place.

Isn't that where she always is? Here? For me and my benefit? Taking this
like a champ when I know it's turned her world upside down?

Her brow furrowed. She shifted in her chair so that the strap of her
tank top fell.

And without asking her, I texted the boys and backed out. And I'm staring at the definitive reason why in her flowy skirt, tight top, and wild eyes.

"I was, but I also promised when I brought you here that I'd show you around. That we'd explore. We're exploring, Madds."

She glances over to me from where she's smelling soaps, her smile whimsical. Appreciative. "Thank you."

Those two words and the way she says them have a lump forming in my throat as I nod and stand with my hands clasped in front of me, a bag of trinkets she bought for her family in my hands like the doting boyfriend that I'm not, and watch her. She's like a little kid. Each booth, her face lights up with whatever new items she sees. She touches. She smells. She tries to converse with the shop owner and compliment them on whatever it is they're selling.

She's kind.

Isn't that why she's standing here in the first place? Because she was kind to me before she even knew who I was?

And now . . . now that we're a fake couple who lives together and sleeps together, what do I think of her?

"Look!" she squeals and then drops to her knees to get face kisses from the kiosk owner's French bulldog. She gives the brindle-colored dog belly rubs as her smile and happiness light up her entire face.

There's something about the moment that pulls me back to those first few days with her. To how she looked at everything so fresh-faced and full of wonder. The private jet. The waitstaff. Amsterdam and all its wonders.

Maddix made me rethink things. I didn't realize it then, but I do now. I've lived this life of privilege for so long that none of these things feel like luxury. Rather, they're just the way things have always been. I've taken them for granted. And being with her, watching her experience each new thing after another, the wonderment of it all, has given me a newfound perspective. Has afforded me the opportunity to watch her discover new things that I've always had.

At first that was why I enjoyed spending time with her. Her reactions were cute and so very different than the women I normally dated. It didn't hurt that she was gorgeous, intelligent, and just a little stubborn, but just like the givens in my life, I took that for granted too.

But now, watching Maddix with a puppy in the middle of the market, I realize *this* is exactly why I wanted to be with her today. She gives me a different perspective. She allows me to be me without expecting more. She makes me smile and consider things I never really considered before.

Fuck if I know how to feel about any of it.

And I'm enjoying every ridiculously boring minute of it.

"Oh my God, these look like heaven," she coos over a case of fresh pastries and holds a hand to her stomach.

"Hungry?" I ask and look at my watch. How have we been here for three hours already?

"Starving."

I hold my hand out to her. "I know just the place."

She glances down at it, and then a soft smile graces her lips as she takes it. Yes, we're sleeping together. Yes, we're pretending to be a bit more. And yes, those lines are beginning to blur when I've never allowed anything to blur before.

I shove the thought away and busy myself playing tour guide through the twisting alleys of Vieux Nice—*old nice*. The pathways are so narrow you can stretch your arms out and touch both walls. We pass several patisseries and boulangeries, stop and admire art in the narrow doorway of a studio. She takes photo after photo of the idyllic and picturesque streets with their worn cobblestone and history etched in the buildings around them.

"Here we are," I say as we enter a large plaza with a church on one side, a fountain in the middle, and then an Italian restaurant complete with red checkered tablecloths.

Maddix's face lights up as we're seated in the outdoor patio, her eyes constantly scanning and taking in and falling in love over and over with each and every nuance and detail of the area.

"What?" I ask when her eyes find mine.

"Each time I think I've seen the coolest thing ever on this trip, it's topped by the next thing I see or place you take me." She takes a sip of her wine. "There is so much history here. So much tradition. It's just so damn cool." Her smile makes me smile. "Thank you for hanging out with me today."

"I've enjoyed it."

"You're so full of shit." She taps her feet against mine beneath the table. "You looked bored to death watching me shop at the market, but I appreciate your patience and letting me soak it all in."

"I . . . I was bored, but you know, I still enjoyed it." I rest my hand on her thigh, needing that connection with her and growing confused as to why.

If Maddix has to think twice about it, she sure doesn't show it as she smiles at a bunch of school kids loading up on ice cream on the other side of the square.

"Do you come here often?" she asks.

"The flower market? The restaurant? Nice?"

"Any of it?" She laughs. "If I lived here, I don't think I'd ever get sick of exploring. Monaco. France. Your home country. Everywhere."

"I've done my fair share of traveling, yes."

"No. Not like that," she says and reaches out to put her hand on top of mine on her thigh and squeezes. "Not for work. Not for racing. How often do you just get in the car like we did today, like we did in Amsterdam, and let the sun shine on your face and just enjoy your surroundings?"

I open my mouth and then close it, grateful for the first time ever over a crying baby to our left. But even after the mother has quieted the little boy and our salads are served, the question still lingers in the air.

"Rarely," I finally admit. Come to think of it, I've played more than I have in ages and that's solely because of the woman beside me.

"Why not?" Her head tilts to the side as she takes me in.

"Because it's the Navarro way."

Her eyes hold mine and she nods ever so slightly. "One of these days, you're going to give me a real answer to one of my questions instead of using your family as a reason for everything you don't want to answer."

"I don't use it as an excuse."

"Yes, you do," she challenges, a smile toying at the corners of her mouth.

"My family has a complicated dynamic."

"Tell me about it," she says and I start to refute her but she cuts me off. "I want to know, Cruz. Not to run and sell it to the tabloids, but because I want to understand you better."

Words like that usually make a man like me suffocate, but for some reason they have me breathing easier. And yet . . . I hold back. "Like I told you before, it's all online. Look it up."

"So you'll let me in your bed, in your world, but you won't let me know you better."

"That's not fair."

"It doesn't have to be fair to be true."

My sigh is exasperated. So is the way I look around the square. She gives me time to come to grips with this, with her . . . but after a few seconds, I answer her. "For as long as I can remember, the only focus I've ever had, ever been allowed to have, is to reclaim my family's place in the sport. To bring back the nostalgia and prestige my grandfather had in Formula 1 and his father had in motorsports in general."

"Why was it not your father's job?"

My chuckle lacks amusement. "He had the heart but not the skill."

"And that's your fault?" Our eyes meet and I can see the cogs turning in that astute head of hers. I don't know the whole of what she overheard in the suite that day, but I have a feeling she heard enough to put two and two together and realize it doesn't equal five.

And this is why I keep people at arm's length. For them not to see how I'm treated—because God forbid, we don't sully the Navarro name. For them not to realize the way I allow my father to speak to me, to treat me, to pressure me, because it's embarrassing enough coming to grips with it myself.

Why does a strong, secure man put up with it?

Because when it comes down to it, I am a Navarro. I am proud of that fact. Of who I am. And as long as I can remember, being a Navarro was more important than breathing.

But the older I get, the more the air I breathe feels more and more toxic.

"Not my fault, no," I murmur, staring at the dark red of my wine. "But I'm the one who can reclaim the glory he lost from mi patriarca when he failed to live up to his potential. I am the golden son who can restore his pride."

"That doesn't make sense to me."

Me either.

"Enough about this." I wave a hand in indifference, suddenly closing down. I shared too much. Said too much.

"No. It matters." She links her fingers through mine and holds tight when I try to pull away. "You matter."

I hate the weird constriction of my chest. The sudden heat crawling up my neck.

"It's not a big deal."

"It is though." Her words are barely audible and only serve to heighten those feelings. I'm saved by our pizza being delivered. By a small chat with the waiter. By serving her a piece of it.

I take a bite but when I look up, she's staring at me and not eating.

"Look, it's just pressure. That's all it is." I want to change the topic. Maybe she didn't hear more than my father's cruel words about her. Maybe I'm telling her too much. "The Navarro familial drive, our family dynamic . . . it's fucked up in so many ways. So me not talking about it is my way of protecting you from it." And my way of not looking like a spineless sack of shit to outsiders who don't understand what it's like in the Navarro bubble.

"Well, maybe one day you'll trust me enough to tell me."

"I do trust you." And isn't that part of it? The trust? It scares the shit out of me that I do. That I want to explain to her about my father's bitter jealousy and my mother's abandonment. Of my grandfather I admire and his tough love that I respect. Of my sister being the only one who understands me and even then, she doesn't exactly. "This is more than I've ever given anyone of myself."

Maddix leans over and presses the tenderest kiss to my cheek, letting her lips linger for a beat. "For what it's worth, Cruz, I trust you too." She leans back, her smile soft. "Thank you for today. For this. For being my friend in all of this when you could resent me for this whole thing."

Never.

The word dances through my head but dies on my tongue.

Resent her for this?

How, when for the first time ever, someone has made me look forward to days that aren't race days?

CHAPTER TWENTY-NINE

Maddix

HANDS.

I feel them sliding over my skin.

Lips.

Lazy kisses down my shoulder. The slip of the sheet and the cool air of the bedroom. A lazy circle of tongue around my nipple.

"Cruz," I murmur, my eyes fluttering open in the early dawn light. All I see are shadows. All I feel are sensations.

The denim of his jeans scraping over my thighs. The pressure of his fingertips as they push my thighs apart.

"Shh," he murmurs against my stomach.

A glance at the clock has me stilling. Five in the morning. He has a flight to catch. In ten minutes. Monza is waiting.

"You have to go."

"I know." I can feel his lips curl up in a smile against the top of my mound.

"Like really have to go." My words hold little urgency as his fingers part me and slide through the slickness already waiting for him.

"There's unexpected traffic on the way to the airport." A kiss to my clit. "Road closures." A slide of his tongue with the perfect pressure. "Animals crossing."

My laugh turns into a moan as he dips his tongue into me.

"I can fuck you with my tongue, Madds, or I can get in the elevator and leave. Your choice."

"And this is why I'm not coming with you right away."

He chuckles against my skin as his tongue draws lazy circles around my clit. "Coming is the name of the game."

He flicks it back and forth with expert pressure and finesse. With the actions he knows drives me feral. He tempts and taunts, and my struggle to have him not be late for his flight gives way to the pleasure taking over every nerve of my body.

My gasp fills the room and its early morning light. My fingers thread through his hair as he pleasures me. As he undoes me. As he reminds me just how adept he is at this. Not like it's been very long since he did it last. What? Three days? I couldn't get Michael to go down on me once every few months yet Cruz acts like it's a necessity to his health to make me come this way.

What woman complains about that?

"I love the way you fucking taste," he murmurs, the heat of his breath against my most intimate flesh.

"Cruz." His name is a guttural moan as my fingers grip his hair tighter.

"I love when you say it like that." A lick. "Desperate." A suck. "Breathless." A delve of his tongue into me that has my hips bucking up so he can probe deeper and hit where I want him to hit. "Greedy."

My body tenses as my core liquefies.

"This makes me so fucking hard. Smelling you. Tasting you. Having you come on my tongue."

I moan as he adds his fingers to the mix.

I grip the sheets as his tongue works me over. As I buck my hips. As the center of my universe tilts off its axis and crashes back down with stars behind my closed eyes. My body's a mess of sensations and nerves.

"That's my girl." He continues the slow thrust of his fingers in and out of me to draw out every ounce of pleasure from my orgasm before he crawls back up my body.

I expect to feel the scratch of his jeans as he pushes them down. To hear the rip of foil from the condom. To let me pleasure him.

But instead he leans forward and kisses me with unexpected gentleness. I taste myself on his tongue as his hand comes up to frame the side of my face.

"See you in a few days, Madds," he murmurs before pushing off me and standing.

"Cruz?" *Let me reciprocate. Let me feel you inside of me.* I start to sit up and he leans over and kisses me one more time.

"After the race. Leave me hungry for it." He leans back and the smile lights up his eyes. "I like to leave my woman satisfied and wanting more."

And if ever there was a Cruz Navarro comment, that was it.

But as he walks out the door, it doesn't bug me like it might have when this first started. Rather it has me hugging my pillow and smiling.

Leave me hungry for it.

Doesn't he know that's a permanent state for me when it comes to him?

CHAPTER THIRTY

Maddix

"YOU NEVER GET USED TO IT."

I glance over to the woman standing beside me. I was so engrossed in the race that I didn't notice her walk up. My smile is stuttered when our eyes meet. There are so many people here that I never know who is press or staff or a guest of Gravitas.

And I've learned that each one of those groups needs to be handled differently.

She's stunning with her dark hair and light eyes framed by thick lashes. She's statuesque in posture and if I didn't know better, there's a gracefulness to her that makes me think of a dancer.

"Never get used to which part?" I ask, curiosity piqued.

She smiles, the motion softening the sharpness of her features. She looks familiar, like I should know her, but I can't place her. "The exhilaration. The rumbling in your chest. The whine of the engines. You hear it when you close your eyes at night to sleep."

"This is my second race so I'm learning."

"I know." Her smile widens as I stand a little taller, desperate to move my eyes back to the monitor so I can watch Cruz fly around the track, but at the same time needing to know who this woman is. "I've been around it my whole life. My grandfather. My father. *My brother.*" She lifts her chin to the monitor as they show Cruz's car, and now I know exactly who she is.

If she wanted my undivided attention, she now has it.

"Sofia, right?" I ask.

"Ah, so he does talk about me." She holds her hand out to me. "Nice to meet you, Maddix."

So Dominic Navarro can talk shit about me, can mean mug me across a garage, but he doesn't have the balls to meet me face-to-face. He sends his daughter in for the recon.

I shouldn't have expected any more from him.

I look at her hand for a moment before reaching out to shake it. "Nice to meet you too."

She's not good enough for a Navarro, plain and simple. Take care of the problem or I will.

The chip on my shoulder weighs heavy as Dominic's words repeat in my head. I look toward the left of the straight, waiting for the few seconds I get to see Cruz.

"And your thoughts?"

I wait for the pocket of cars he's in the midst of to zoom by before turning my entire body to face her. I narrow my eyes and stare right back since it's clear I'm being assessed. "About what? Racing? Your brother? If I'm good enough for the Navarro name? What I plan to get out of this whole relationship? How many of those things are you here to evaluate and report back to whoever sent you?"

We wage a visual war and the slow curl of a smile on her lips surprises me. "I knew I liked you."

"I'm sorry, *what*—"

She holds her hands up. "I'm not my father, Maddix. I assure you, I'm one hundred percent *Team Cruz.*"

My only response is to purse my lips and stare.

"Take me at my word. Don't take me at my word. No skin off my back." She shrugs, unoffended, and for the first time I notice that her body language is identical to Cruz's. The tilt of her head. The crooked smile. The subtle arch of one eyebrow. "Just know that I'm fully aware of the situation the two of you are . . . engaged in, and I approve."

That comment could mean two things. The fake dating or the sleeping together, and I'm not sure which one to respond to.

A wave of sound comes from the grandstands. I whip back to watch the monitor and see one of the Moretti cars barely kiss the wall out of a turn before gunning to pass Cavanaugh on the back straight.

I watch a few more seconds, my breath held and my heart pounding, knowing that after he chases down Cavanaugh, he'll have a go for Cruz.

"C'mon," I murmur to myself as if my lone word will grant him any luck at all.

"Monza has always been good to him. For him," she says, referring to the track and pulling my attention back to her. "And it seems quite surprisingly, so are you."

Her words take me by surprise and this time when I face her, she simply lifts her eyebrows and gives a hint of a nod and a knowing smile, despite continuing to look at the monitor.

"I'm not quite sure how to respond to that," I say, letting my guard down ever so slightly as I'm desperate for some female companionship. *Um, you've known her a whole five minutes and you're already believing her?* Maybe you ought to run this by Cruz first before you're anything but cordial to her, considering the gem his father seems to be.

"You don't have to respond. I've been looking for you all weekend though. Where have you been hiding?"

"I had . . . work. I had to come in early this morning."

She nods and I feel like she can see straight through my lie.

It's not work that has kept me away. It's Cruz's contractual obligation to get a set amount of sleep during race weeks that has. And since keeping our hands off each other has served to be quite the problem, sleeping when the two of us are near each other only comes after a round (or two) of toe-curling, sweat-inducing, orgasm-giving activity.

That doesn't guarantee great sleep.

And Cruz may not be by the book on anything else in his life, but he sure as hell is when it comes to his job.

So rather than spend the entire race week at Monza with him, I opted to fly in early this morning to avoid being a distraction. *Even though being his distraction is unbelievably awesome.*

"You know, sometimes distractions are a good thing."

I open my mouth and then close it. My cheeks heat, but I don't fight my smile.

She crosses her arms over her chest and gives a quick look around, as if to check and see who's near, before looking back at me. "I'm not a fan of the women he normally dates. Shallow. Opportunistic. You, on the other hand . . . it seems you are loyal to him. Protective. Private. I like that for my brother. From what he tells me, you challenge him, and being challenged is good. It makes you a better person. I know you two have only been 'together' for a short time, but I've already started to see a different side to my brother. A better side. And I like that."

I glance over my shoulder and then back to her when I see no one's near us. "You do know I'm just doing my job, right?" At least that's what I keep telling myself. "In a few months he'll have the deal signed, and we'll both go back to our separate corners of the earth."

She chews her tongue and fights a smile. "Whatever you say."

"What does that mean?"

"You two are just way more alike than I expected you to be."

I eye her, torn between watching the race and the significance of this conversation—because there most definitely is one. I'm just not sure what it is yet.

She's not who I expected upon first meeting her. I assumed she'd be in Dominic's corner, not her brother's. And the fact that she clearly isn't, makes me like her instantaneously. But I have a feeling if I'd met her under different circumstances, I'd have taken to her and her no-nonsense nature just as quickly.

Like her brother, there is just something about her that pulls you in.

Don't get attached, Maddix. To him. To her. To this family. To this situation. This whole thing is temporary.

"Good thing or it might be a miserable few months."

She steps closer, leans her elbow on the ledge that is our barrier between us and looking down on pit row. It's the perfect birds-eye view when Cruz comes in to pit—or box as they call it for some odd reason. The speed with which they do it is incredible.

I mimic her posture, relieved that this conversation seems to be over but still uncertain why I feel I'm missing something.

Maybe it's a sibling thing and since I don't have one, I don't understand what it is.

"He likes rooftops," she says out of the blue.

A part of me wants to tell her I know this. Another part wants to keep that knowledge to myself.

"It's where he goes when he's stressed or needs a break from life, from being a Navarro."

"I know," I say softly.

"To him, the only male heir, being a Navarro is so much more than just

188 | K. BROMBERG

the name. It's the upholding of a legacy. The continuation of a line he loves as much as he hates and some days could not give a shit less altogether."

"Isn't that how we all feel about family some days?"

"Perhaps." Sofia waves at one of the crew members down below before continuing. "Let me guess. You have a mother and father. Happily married. Always been there for you. Tight-knit. That kind of thing." I look at her. "It's not a knock," she says. "I'm just trying to make you understand what he comes from. Why he might be how he is."

"Okay." I draw the word out, my eyes moving between watching the race on the monitor and figuring her out.

"Cruz used to talk to himself when we were kids. A lot. For the longest time we thought he had an imaginary friend named Cross. My dad abhorred it. Forbade him from talking to whoever this *Cross* was because only weak kids did that." She sighs and gives a slow shake of her head. "What none of us knew until he was older was that it was just Cruz talking to himself. He wanted to be Cross—his name in English. The kid who wasn't a Navarro. Who had no expectations on his shoulders. Who could be a normal kid and not the next second coming of Formula 1. The kid whose mother loved him instead of resented him for being just like his father."

"Sofia." Her name sounds like heartbreak when I say it. There's no other way to describe it as I watch the grown man battle it out on the course while thinking of this little boy who wanted to be nothing other than a kid with a different name.

She reaches out and puts her hand on my forearm. "Find the Cross be-hind the Cruz. He's the good man. He's the one he hides from the world. When you see him, you'll know the man I love. The one I'm proud to call my brother. All of this"—she motions to the grandstands and the pomp and circumstance—"it's just window dressing for the kid underneath who is scared to death no one is going to love him if he doesn't perform and live up to ridiculous expectations."

I blink away the tears that well in my eyes. "Why are you telling me this?"

Her smile is as soft as her words are cryptic. "You know why."

"I don't. I need . . ."

"It's clear you matter to him. If you haven't seen it yet, you might start wanting to look a little harder." She pats my arm and takes a step back. "I'm glad to finally have met you. Now I'll let you be." She points to the screen.

"This is typically about when the race starts to get interesting, and there's a podium spot calling my brother's name."

When she walks away, I stare after her with my head swimming with new information, new insight. I can't wrap my head around it.

"Find the Cross behind the Cruz. He's the good man. He's the one he hides from the world. When you see him, you'll know the man I love."

But there's a slight problem. If I find Cross, I have a feeling my heart might find he's the man I can love too. That's something I can't consider . . . *not when there's no way he'll want my heart in return.*

CHAPTER THIRTY-ONE

Cruz

THE CAR VIBRATES AS I PUSH IT AS HARD AS I CAN.

"You're good. Push. Push. Push," Otis says in my ear as I chase down Evans. He's quicker than shit in the straights. Whatever issue they were having with his engine before the break has clearly been fixed.

"Two to go."

"Ten-four," I say as the G's pull tight on me into the turn. "McElroy?"

"One point two back."

One point two seconds behind me. I have to keep him there. He hits one second and he'll gain DRS capability, and regardless of the dirty air he's getting off my car, he'll be able to make a run for it.

"That sector was your fastest yet. Grim is P4."

My teammate Schilling is after McElroy. That means he can't help me fend him off and buy time.

"One to go."

I drive fast and tight and come out of turns with inches to spare between my tires and the walls. I can see Evans in front of me. My sector time might be fast but there is no goddamn way I can close that gap in one lap.

I need to hold on to second.

Preserve it.

"And that's P2, Cruz. Well done. Great race."

"Fuck, yeah." I pump my fist and shout as euphoria washes over me. We've had race after race where things haven't gone our way. One bad mishap after another at the start of a race making the next sixty laps a crash course—pun intended—in trying to recover.

I've been placing well, but it's been a battle.

This time it was smooth and that's a welcome change.

Champagne stings my eyes and my suit sticks to my body. My cheeks hurt from smiling. My head dizzies with the euphoria of a podium and the points earned to keep us in second place on the overall leader board.

I walk off the stage with trophy in hand and all I see is Maddix. She's standing in the midst of all the chaos with her Gravitas racing shirt on, her smile bright, and a press pass around her neck.

"Woo-hoo!" She throws her arms up in excitement.

Without thought, I do the one thing I've wanted to do since I got out of the car. I walk over to her, hug her so that when I stand straight her feet leave the ground, and then kiss her soundly on the lips.

It's brief—there are people all around us. Professionals. Press. Other teams. And what was once all for show, doesn't feel like it anymore.

And it's something I'd rather keep private.

So I keep the kiss brief, but fuck it grounds me. And when I put her feet back on the ground, she doesn't let go. She leans into my ear.

"I'm proud of you."

Four simple words spoken by a woman who isn't supposed to mean anything to me—and yet her words pack an unexpected punch.

When I look at her, eyes narrowed, all she does is blink away tears and lift her hand to my cheek.

Her smile is full of hope and excitement and something else, but I'll fucking take all of it.

"Go do what you need to do," she says and steps back, giving me clear sight of Sofia standing there.

Oh shit. The two of them together? *Alone?* That's fucking trouble.

But I'll take the trouble. I'll take my sister being here. And I'll definitely take the hug she squeezes me with before I move to recovery.

"Thanks for coming," I say as I catch sight of Amandine leading Maddix away.

"Monza is always lucky for us Navarros. Glad to see some things haven't changed."

"Me too."

"Great race." I look over to the voice and accept a handshake from Spencer Riggs. Longtime friend and competitor from way back in our karting days till now.

"Thanks, man." I place a hand on his shoulder and squeeze. "You too. You had a hard fight today."

"Next time." He shrugs.

"There's always next time," I say as he moves on to his own PR setup that no doubt I need to get to myself.

Sofia and I watch Riggs walk off before her silence has me turning to face her and her hands on her hips. "What?" I ask.

"I like her."

"Everybody likes her." Well, except for Papá but he doesn't count. She continues to stare at me with lips pursed and a ghost of a smile. "I swear to God, Sof, please tell me you didn't say something to send her running off."

"Considering she was waiting for you at the finish line, I think you have your answer . . . but we did talk, yes."

"Why don't I like the sound of that?"

My sister catches sight of something over my shoulder and she stands taller. "Introduce me," Sofia says under her breath.

"To who—nope, absolutely not," I say when I turn to see Rossi making eyes at my sister.

What is it with this fucking guy?

"C'mon. He's hot. You're getting to play around, why can't I?"

"Because he's trouble."

"Perfect. I like trouble." She grins at me but, thank God, when I look back, Rossi is gone.

"You should probably get in the ice bath with me if you're that hot and bothered. That will cool you off," I say as she begins to walk with me.

"Says the man who can't have Maddix here before a race because he can't keep his hands off her. Pot, meet kettle."

"Whatever." I wave a hand at her.

"You know what? Maybe I do need to get in that ice bath with you. I think I'm coming down with something." She fake coughs. "I need to make sure it gets worse."

I glance over at my sister and her shit-eating grin and know exactly where she's going with this.

"You're fucking awesome."

"I know. Now reward me with that introduction."

I push her playfully. "Over my dead body."

CHAPTER THIRTY-TWO

Maddix

"I DON'T UNDERSTAND." I LOOK AT CRUZ WHERE HE STANDS IN MY doorway, towel wrapped around his waist, and rivulets of water running down the plane of his chest.

I don't think I've ever wanted to be a drop of water more.

"There's not much to understand. The prince has a charity gala every year. I was invited. Pretty self-explanatory."

"But . . ." *Me? At a palace?*

He chuckles and moves toward me. He takes my face in his hands and looks into my eyes. "Is it so bad I want you to be my date? Just you, Madds." He lifts his eyebrows up to reinforce the words. "That I want to share this with you and only you?"

My heart quickens in my chest. I know they're just words. But damn do they make my pulse quicken.

"*But Cruz* . . ." Panic replaces the feeling of glee and skitters up my spine. "You're telling me I'm going to the palace. One where a real live prince lives and that I'll be meeting him too."

"Him and others, yes." He says it so nonchalantly. I'm extremely grateful he's not making fun of me for sounding so awestruck.

"And others. *Of course.* As in others I'll probably faint at the first sight of because they are actors and actresses—a different sort of royalty in their own right." I roll my eyes. "You dropped this on me without any warning. This is crazy. I mean. When? How? I need—"

"You're adorable when you're flustered." He leans in and brushes a kiss to my lips. Gentle and soft. That turns into our tongues dancing against one another's in a quiet sigh of a kiss that is so tender you can feel the goosebumps chase over your skin.

I want to sink into him. The feel of him. The warmth of him. The everything of him.

It's so easy to. He makes it that way.

When the kiss ends, he rests his forehead against mine, keeping his hands on my face, and I can feel his lips turn up into a smile against mine. "If we don't stop here, my towel might fall off and you'll have to take advantage of me."

Will the wanting him ever stop? The need for him? The turning to look at him only to get that twist in the pit of my stomach that starts the ache all over again?

"That's a task I'm pretty sure I can handle," I say and cup him through his towel.

He moans into my mouth and I take the invitation to slip my tongue between his lips again. I kiss him as I snake my way beneath the towel to where he's already hard and ready beneath.

The doorbell has us both groaning. "They can come back later."

His laugh rumbles through me. "As much as I wholeheartedly agree with that line of thinking, this interruption is on me."

I step back, his cock still in my hand. "What do you mean?"

"Go answer the door. It's for you. I'm not exactly suitable for door answering right now." He grins as he looks down at his cock.

"Wasted opportunities make me so sad." I pretend pout.

"I promise I'll make this one up to you later." He presses a chaste kiss to my lips and then pats my ass. "Now go."

I all but float to the front door. *How is this my life?* I'm in Monaco. I have an incredibly sexy man who can't keep his hands off me. My job is going well—Kevin's feedback of my market analysis was high praise and surprise at my thoroughness and attention to detail. Then again, it's always been there, I just haven't always reported to him, like I am right now. Regardless, his praise of my actual work, and of this pretend work, has had me on cloud nine the past two days. I mean—

"Hi?" I say cautiously when I see a team of people all dressed in black facing me.

"Hi," the man standing in front says. His shorn hair is bleached platinum blond, a ration of rings decorates his fingers, and he has eyeliner around his pale blue eyes. He holds his hand out for me to shake. "I'm Jacque and we are your glam squad for tonight."

"Tonight?" I ask.

"Oh yeah," Cruz says over my shoulder. "Did I forget to tell you the gala was tonight?"

"What?" I whip my head toward him and his smirk as he stands in the middle of his condo in a pair of track pants, shirtless, and hair still wet. The crew of people move in without me saying another word.

Cruz shrugs. "I figured the more time I gave you to freak out, the more you'd freak out. So . . . I thought a surprise attack would be the best bet."

My grin is one of disbelief. "You are . . ." I shake my head.

"Handsome. Incredible. The fucking best. I mean, I'll take any of those and a bunch more but some of them"—he winks—"might make our company blush." He walks past me and brushes a kiss to my lips. "Have fun."

"Where are you going?"

"I'll work in the simulator for a bit. Have some paperwork Kevin sent over about Revive to look at. A nap?"

I stare at his ass as he cruises down the hallway toward the extra bedroom, and I repeat the question of the day—or rather of the last five weeks—*how is this my life?*

CHAPTER THIRTY-THREE

Maddix

THIS IS A FAIRY TALE WHEN I'VE NEVER BELIEVED IN THEM.

The fairy godmother wand—the crew of makeup artists, manicurists, hairstylists, and stylists—that came in and got me ready today.

The dress. It's champagne in color and has delicate beading that's both sufficiently formal for the event but not so formal I feel stuffy and out of place.

The jewels. The ones Cruz got on loan from his jeweler, which arrived with armed guards, and that have a value worth more than my rent . . . *for a decade.*

My date. Cruz knows how to wear a tuxedo. He's devastating in every sense of the word with his dark features and broad shoulders. He looks like he was born to attend events like this.

To our chariot. Who knows how expensive the car we arrive in is, but its doors swing up and the engine purrs instead of rumbles.

To the venue. A freaking palace. One that a real prince and princess live in. One that has been there for centuries and through different reigns. One with gardens we're standing amongst in the moonlit night on the coast of the Mediterranean.

To the people milling all around us. It's affluence on steroids. I've never seen more diamonds and designer clothes and people I think I know but can't place before.

I won't allow myself to believe this is just for show for Cruz. Me being here. Me being on his arm. I know it probably is, but I don't want to think about that tonight. Tonight, I want to get lost in the fairy-tale world we've stepped into and not think about tomorrows or fouples or the fact that when I look at Cruz or feel his touch, I feel my heart slipping.

I study his profile as he looks around, smiling at those he needs to smile at and nodding at others. We've done the mingle rounds and are finally having a moment to ourselves.

"Did I really just meet a real prince?" I ask Cruz who chuckles.

"You did." He nods, his eyes finding mine.

"He seemed so normal. I mean . . . And he knew you by name, Cruz. What person is known by the Prince of Monaco?"

Tessa is going to die. Simply die.

"The family he was born into isn't his fault. He's a normal guy with a fancy last name and ridiculous expectations put on his shoulders," he says, and I can't help but wonder if he's talking about the prince or himself.

Cruz's hand is steady on my lower back as he lifts a flute of champagne off a tray and hands it to me.

"You look absolutely stunning," he murmurs in my ear, causing goosebumps. "It was definitely worth the fight to get the extra ticket for you to be here."

"What?" I ask, fingers going back up to toy with the necklace and make sure it's still in place.

"Tickets to this are limited. Extremely selective." His smile is shy and his eyes glance across the room momentarily. "I had to petition for an extra one because this night wouldn't be the same without you—my gorgeous, stunning date—here at my side." He kisses the curve of my shoulder. "You being here made the night perfect."

His words have my smile widening and my chest tightening. He seems so genuinely happy right now. This is the Cross that Sofia was talking about. The one I could easily fall for.

"There's nowhere else I'd rather be." If it sounds clichéd, it is. But it's also so very true.

"I can think of a few others," he whispers as his eyes scrape up and down the length of me. He leans forward. "And all I can think about is getting you out of this dress and fucking you with just the jewels and heels on."

My body warms with that slow, sweet burn that it seems only he can create within me.

"I don't know if I'm going to be able to wait that long." I turn and slide my hand on the inside of his jacket and skim my nails up and down his rib-cage. I love his quick hiss of a breath and the tensing of his hand on my back.

"Well, we've met the prince. We've done the mingling. Now we just have to wait for them to announce the silent auction is about to end and we can slip out."

"Did you know they brought undergarments for this dress? Lace bust-ier. Satin garters to go with the thigh-highs. Too bad I forgot to wear the matching panties that goes with it."

His nostrils flare and the muscle in his jaw pulses. "You're a cocktease."

"Never want to leave an opportunity wasted and"—I lean in toward his ear and whisper—"you never know when those opportunities might arise."

"I've got something rising all right," he mutters, his eyes heavy with de-sire, boring into mine.

"Ladies and gentlemen," the emcee says directing everyone's attention toward him. "We'll get tonight's festivities started shortly. Please make sure you have your drink in hand, your wallets ready, and get your last bids in at the auction tables. Silent bidding will end in twenty minutes, and we all know how you like to outbid each other in the waning moments."

I can only imagine what those final moments would be like. I walked through the items up for bid and choked at the starting bids. I don't think anything was less than one hundred thousand euros.

"This way," Cruz says with a tilt of his head.

"But all of the auction items are that way."

His grin is lightning fast. "Exactly." He links his fingers with mine and leads me toward the back of the party area. I glance over my shoulder ner-vously. There's no way that he's going to, that we're going to . . .

"Where are we going?"

His chuckle falls through the darkness, and that's all the answer I need as to where we're going. The walk is short. Down a corridor. Into a darkened part of the palace that Cruz obviously gets clearance to by the nod of the se-curity guard as he grips my hand tighter.

"Cruz," I whisper because for some reason I feel like whispering is nec-essary right now.

"Shh," he says as he pushes open a door, looks inside, and then grins when he tugs me along with him. "The Navarros donated to have this room refurbished. I have access any time I want."

"We're going to get caught. I can see the headlines now—"

"Perfect. I love headlines." He laughs.

I get a quick glance around—it's the history of sports in Monaco—at least I think it is by the pictures lining the walls and the trophies housed in glass cases—but my glimpse is short-lived because within seconds, Cruz has my back against the now locked door and his lips are on mine.

The kiss is the epitome of desperation. Lips and teeth and tongue as his hands slide down my sides to fit between the door and cup my ass.

He tastes like the whiskey he was drinking and like a drug I can't get enough of.

"It shouldn't hurt this much to want you," he groans into my mouth as my hands fumble with his trousers, fingers scraping over his already hard cock. "But Christ, all I've done all night is look at you and fight the urge to fuck you on every surface out there."

His words are gasoline thrown on a fire.

On embers that seem to constantly be smoldering.

On a woman burning just as hot for him as it seems he is for me.

"I need you," I whisper into his mouth. Our hands switch positions, each of us taking care of our own clothes now. "I want you."

We move in hurried motions. My hands inch my elaborate gown up over my hips. Cruz frees his cock from his pants.

But it's when he looks up from his cock in his hand to see me standing there, dress around my hips, garters attached to stockings and no panties, that his feral groan reverberates around the room.

It's one heartbeat to the next that his lips are back on me. That his fingers are sliding through the slickness between my thighs and tucking into me. That my gasp fills the room the same time I take his cock, which is thick and heavy in my hand.

It's hard to concentrate—to remember to stroke him instead of just gripping him tighter—as his fingers manipulate and sensations swamp me. My head leans back against the door, and my mouth falls open as I moan at his touch.

"You're fucking addicting," he says as he takes me in. And I'm sure I make quite the sight—legs spread, body shaking, my arousal soaking his fingers. He leans forward and tugs my bottom lip with his teeth. "This mouth. This mind. This body. This pussy. The whole goddamn package." He slips his tongue between my lips. "You look so goddamn gorgeous just like this, right now, that I don't want to mess you up."

He puts his hand on the small of my back and pulls me against him. My body craves the connection. The feel of his cock hard against my lower belly. The warmth of his breath on my lips. The scent of what he does to me clinging to the air.

"Hold your dress with one hand," he orders and waits till I collect the fabric and hold the bunch of it at my waist. "Good. Just like that." His praise is like a feather over my skin. My core aches. "Now turn around and put the other hand against the door."

I do as he says, using the urging of his hand on my waist to guide me until my back is to his front. And it's then that he slides his hand slowly up my body—over my abdomen, across my breasts—until his hand firmly spans my neck. The heat of his breath hits my ears as his other hand caresses my bare ass.

"We don't have much time. As soon as the auction is over, people will get to roam these halls. I'm desperate for you." He slides the head of his cock up and down my slit, his own groan causing the coil in my stomach to tighten. "Have been all night, but I'm about to make a mess of you, and I can't have that on your dress now, can I?" He chuckles and my nipples harden.

"Cruz." It's a plea.

"Can you take what I'm about to give you and stay quiet?"

"Yes." Breathless.

"Because I need you gripping my cock. Coating my cock. Coming on my cock. Do you understand?"

"Mm-hmm."

I yelp when his teeth nip my shoulder. "I need words, Madds. Yes, Cruz, fuck me with your hard cock. Yes, Cruz, give me every goddamn inch. Yes, Cruz, make a mess of me. Yes, Cruz, fuck me so hard that when I leave this room, all I can think about is being fucked again."

His words . . . they're like lightning in a dark sky—energized and electrifying. "Yes." It's hard to swallow over the desire and need that's building. "Please."

He pushes his way into me oh, so slowly. The testing of his restraint demonstrated by the tightening of his fingers on the column of my throat and the hiss of his breath.

"Fucking hell," he groans out as he seats himself fully into me. The delicious burn of him fitting into me, stretching me is still present even after all this time.

A mewl is in my throat when his free hand grips the side of my hip and holds tight as he begins to move into me. Out of me till just the tip remains. Then back in again.

He's the guilty pleasure I never knew existed and now wonder how I'll ever live without. It's his words. It's his actions. It's the feel of his cock teasing each and every nerve within. It's the grip of his hands on my skin that say I'm his. That he's mine. That he's controlling every ounce of pleasure until there is no control left.

Just bliss.

Just him.

Just us.

Just the way we seemingly fit perfect together.

I'm completely aware that the only reason I'm afforded the time for these thoughts to hit me is because Cruz is being selfless. He's taking this as slowly as he can—to give my body the time it needs to build my own orgasm—when I know he could push himself to the brink and be done without caring about me . . . as I'd grown accustomed to with my ex.

But I need him. Want him. Want to feel his desperation surge. His restraint snap.

I wiggle my ass against him, drawing a groan. "Yes, Cruz," I utter, knowing his hand can feel the vibration of my words. "Make a mess of me."

His chuckle has me tightening around him and the weight of his hand on my throat like a necklace growing heavier. "You sure? Once I—"

"Fuck me. Now. Hard. Deep. Just . . . *now*."

And before I can even finish the word, Cruz slaps his pelvis against my ass, driving himself as deep as he can inside me until he bottoms out.

It's heaven when he's in me and hell when he pulls out. But he does it over and over, an onslaught of sensations I can't imagine never knowing again.

Desire.

Bliss.

Undeniable pleasure.

He fucks me hard. Hips pistoning, hands tightening, and his own feral groan rumbling somewhere deep within.

My vision goes white. My body's a mess of contradictions as my orgasm slams into me. Sure, I was expecting it, felt it building brick by brick, but I've never been so fucking turned on before in my life, and I can only surmise that is why.

Because it has nothing to do with the feelings rioting through me. The ones that have fluttered about every time our eyes have met tonight. The ones that just took fucking flight right along with that orgasm.

"Maddix." It's the sexist groan I've ever heard as Cruz comes. His hips jerk. His fingers tense. His forehead rests, landing in the middle of my neck as his ragged breathing fills the room around us. Our bodies are connected in every way possible—our hearts frantic, our breaths coming out in pants, our muscles pliant.

"Mine," he murmurs and then presses his lips to the skin of my shoulder while my heart stumbles over that single syllable. "*Just fucking mine.*"

CHAPTER THIRTY-FOUR

Cruz

MADDIX LAUGHS AT SOMETHING SOMEONE SAYS AND IT'S IMPOSSIBLE to look away. Even standing in a circle with the who's who of Hollywood, it's Madds who holds my attention.

How the fuck can she not when what happened in the trophy room earlier owns my goddamn mind? *How can it not?*

Just fucking mine.

Temporarily though, right? And why does that thought not hit as easily as it used to?

I distract myself knowing the scent of her arousal is still on my hand.

I like it that way.

She's the only high I've ever chased that's stronger than the track, and I'm not sure what to do about that. Is it only because she comes without expectations? Or is it because she's Maddix? A woman I've watched in a short time step into her own in so many fucking ways that it makes her even hotter?

"You lucked out with that one," Zane Phillips, entrepreneurial Australian billionaire, says with a nudge. "I looked at my now wife that way. Still do."

I chuckle and hold my drink up. "Let's not get ahead of ourselves now."

He shrugs. "One minute it's one-night stands and moving on to the next woman as fast as you can. The next thing it's staring at that one woman at parties and wondering how the fuck you fell so damn hard for her."

I snort. "I'll remember that," I say and then promptly look away from her to sell the lie.

Zane throws his head back and laughs. "You're so fucked, Navarro. So fucking fucked."

It's when I glance back toward Maddix though that I freeze, and then I'm on the move in a heartbeat. "Mamá?" I call out as Maddix looks over to me with wide eyes over this strange woman who is hugging her.

"Well, look at you. Perfect in every way just like I knew you'd be."

"Mamá," I say again. My throat feels like it's beginning to close up.

She turns to face me, her hand still clasping Maddix's as Maddix's eyes dart back and forth in uncertainty. "Cariño," she says holding her arm, bejeweled bangles clanking, out like I'm supposed to run into it.

And there she is. Genevieve Navarro. My mother. Owner of what looks like yet another facelift. Keeper of my dad's heart and equally responsible party for his misery. Culprit of my abandonment issues and oblivious to the harm she's done. Woman in a dream world, in a pretend life.

"I thought you were unable to make it tonight," I say, avoiding her hug and stepping up to tuck Maddix underneath my arm and away from her.

Don't touch what's not yours, Mamá. That includes me.

"Oh, you know how it goes." She flickers her fingers as if time and place is irrelevant. "I was on the way from Ibiza to the Seychelles and figured I'd stop here and see you, *hijo.*"

Bullshit. *You stopped here because there were cameras and money. It had nothing to do with me. Never has. Everything else in life that gives you status is more important than us.*

"You'll be staying then?" I ask unenthusiastically.

Her smile falters as the truth fights to make it through. Of course not. Once the sparkle and limelight is gone, so is she. "Oh, Cruzie, you know how it is."

"*Don't* call me that," I grit out between clenched teeth.

She laughs and rolls her eyes, turning her attention to Maddix, avoiding giving me an answer. So that means no, she won't be staying in town longer than the next few hours.

Which I'm glad for. I don't want to see her.

So why can't she just fucking say no for once? Be truthful. Just fucking once.

"So this is the lovely Maddix?" She stares blatantly, and I can tell Maddix is caught between her manners and my obvious disdain for my mother.

"It's a pleasure to meet you," she says.

"Oh, you're sure to piss him off, aren't you?" She turns to me as she chuckles. I know she's referencing my father, but confusion blankets Maddix's face. "Dominic always had to have a say in everything you do, and you bringing her here is your way of sticking it to him."

"Eso es sufficiente," I warn. *That's enough.*

"Why? You don't want her to know the truth?"

"Truth?" Maddix tries to pull away from me but I hold her tight.

"She was just telling me how you got her a ticket to be here tonight. Funny though as that's total bullshit," she says in Spanish, oblivious to the fact that Maddix understands her. Her smile is benign, but I can see her need to hurt me, to hurt my father, beneath it. Aren't I always the pawn in their selfish game? "There were two tickets. I know because your father asked me to attend. When I said I couldn't, he gave them to you and Sofia. And then Sofia fakes being sick so you can bring your newest plaything simply as a means to piss off poor ol' Dominic. Like father like son, using women as pawns in their game."

Maddix tenses beside me as I wince at my mother's fucking words. She knows exactly what my mother is saying. I don't have to look beside me to know Maddix is staring at me with those big green eyes loaded with question and confusion.

"That's not the case," I state for damage control.

"Yes, it is," my mamá continues, ignorant to anything and everything unless it benefits her. "Your sister said so herself. I couldn't find her in this mess of a crowd so I called her to ask where she was."

Fuck. Shut the hell up.

"You do like to dangle your toys in front of your father's face, knowing he can't touch them." She makes the comment like a student eager to let the teacher know she understands the backstory.

Maddix steps out of my reach and when I try to keep my hand on her back, she steps even farther away. "It was a pleasure meeting you, Mrs. Navarro, but I have to run to the ladies' room," she says in flawless Spanish.

My mother's eyes widen as she chuckles. *Yes. She heard and understood every goddamn word you said.*

I sneer at my mother as Maddix starts to walk away. "Maddix?" I call after her.

She turns to look at me, tears welling in her eyes. "Petition to get an extra one, huh?" Her eyebrows narrow. "More like, *use me*." She doesn't say another word before walking away. My chest aches with the need to go after her but—

"Well, she's a sensitive one, isn't she? Not gonna last much longer in your world if she can't handle—"

"That's enough. Got it? That's fucking enough," I snap.

"What did I do?" She bats her lashes.

"The same thing you always do. Every goddamn time." I take a few steps away, looking at this woman who I used to think hung the moon. She was unconventional and exciting and free-spirited and so very different from my father. Only to be crushed when I was old enough to realize the whirlwind trips into town—to spoil us rotten and treat us like adults when we were kids—were simply a means to assuage her guilt for leaving us behind because she was too selfish to be a mother. "I love you, Mamá, but right now I kind of hate you."

"Hijo," she calls out as I start to walk away.

My chest aches. The dread is like a weight in my stomach. Is that how this whole thing started out weeks ago? Me using Maddix to stick it to my papá? I'm not proud of it, but yes, it was.

But then I came home. Then the white bikini happened. Then ... whatever this is between us happened. And I did want her here tonight. To share the evening with. To spoil her with. To make the memory with.

I'm proud to have her on my arm and not just as a fuck you to my papá. I'm proud to have her on my arm because she's her. Because we're whatever we are. And because when I think of this evening, she's the reason it has been fucking incredible.

Until now.

"Stay. Chat."

"No," I say to my mother, my voice low, my back to her. "I need to go fix what you just broke. Again. And I'm getting fucking sick of having to do that over and over again."

I can't find Madds anywhere. Not at the main party in the palace gardens. Not inside in the great hall where people mill about drinking cocktails. Not out front where guests have veered off near a catwalk of sorts to take in the sparkling lights of the world's smallest and wealthiest country.

I head toward the valets. "Hi. Have you—"

"Mr. Navarro. Great race in Monza," the eager valet says.

"Thank you. Um ... have you seen my date by chance?" I ask, feeling like a teenager looking for his girlfriend at a high school dance. "She wasn't feeling well, and I wasn't sure if she left or not while I was engaged in an important conversation."

A lie to save face while my insides twist.

"Your date? Blond hair? Light-colored dress?" a second valet asks as he walks up and I nod. "I had a car drive her home. She's not far ahead of you. Shall I get your car for you?"

"Please." He can't get it fast enough.

The streets are busy with tourists milling about. Tonight's gala has been advertised to the public as a place to watch for the stars so people are lining the streets, and I have to be more than cautious as I ascend into the hills of foot traffic.

I'm home within minutes but a weird panic hits when I open the front door and Maddix isn't there. *Fuck.*

"Where are you, Madds?" I say into the emptiness.

The minute the idea hits me, I'm back in the hallway and running up the stairwell to the roof. I fling the door open with a desperation. *I need to make things right.*

It's a makeshift outdoor space with a few chairs and a built-in pergola. There are some hanging plants that the heiress on the third floor takes care of, and a fire pit that the socialite from the fifth had delivered years ago. It's nothing fancy but it serves its purpose on nights when I feel cooped up in my place.

Relief surges when I see her standing there. Her back's to me and the ocean's beyond. Loose strands of her hair blow in the breeze coming off the water. Her feet are bare, heels on the ground beside her.

She takes my breath away.

Fuck. Just fuck.

How did she creep past my defenses? Why am I not mad about it?

"Madds."

"Don't, Cruz. Just don't," she says, her voice nasally. She's crying. Even worse.

I'm that much of an asshole that I made my pretend girlfriend, who is now my . . . whatever we are, cry. It sucks.

"I should have told you," I say softly. Why lie? It's the truth.

"Here I thought tonight was because . . . it doesn't matter." She shrugs the words off that my mind fills in for her.

Real.

Official.

Because I wanted to see you like this in my element.

Because I wanted to show you off as mine.

"It does matter." I reach out to touch her, but she steps back to avoid it. It's like a knife in the heart when, for the longest time, I swore I didn't have one.

When her eyes meet mine, the tears in them glisten and twist the knife a little harder. "You lied to me. I wasn't invited tonight. I wasn't even supposed to be there."

"You're wrong. I wanted you there."

"You wanted me there as a *fuck you* to your dad. For trying to control you. For telling you who to date. How to race. How to live. For whatever it is that I don't understand."

"He doesn't control me," I state.

"It doesn't matter if he does or he doesn't, you used me as a pawn tonight and didn't have the courtesy to tell me. You made me think it was me you wanted there when all you really wanted was a prop to put the screws to him."

"Maddix." My voice is an apology in and of itself, but I know it's not going to be enough.

She holds her hands up for me to stop. "It doesn't matter, right? None of this does. Soon enough, the board will meet again, and you'll be approved to move forward with the deal. Then you'll be rid of me and your dad will get his way." Her smile is as strained as her words.

But it's her words that have a lump forming in my throat. "I'll never let him get his way. That's what tonight was about. I went about it the wrong way. I should have told you. I should have—"

"You're right. You should have. You don't think I would have supported the idea? That I wouldn't help you?" Her head angles to the side and for the briefest of moments, I'm not sure which hurt her more—me lying to her or me not confiding in her. The fact of the matter is, I'm not used to having anyone to share anything with. Apart from Sofia, I tell little to anyone. And prior to Maddix, I trained, raced, fucked, partied, slept, and thought only about myself.

I never let anyone in. Never let anyone know the real me, and I was fine with it that way.

Then came Madds and her patience and her fire and her selflessness. Then came a woman I suddenly valued more than I thought was possible.

I trust her.

And I fucked up by wronging her tonight.

"I'm sorry. You're right." I shrug. "It's as simple as that. I can't take it back. I can't do it over again. I'm sorry." This time when I reach out to run a hand down her arm, she doesn't shrug it off.

"I'm sorry too. I overreacted. I shouldn't have left, I shouldn't have . . . I don't know, but my feelings were hurt, and I didn't know what to do. I'm surrounded in a world where everything is familiar to you and foreign to me. I felt alone and betrayed and . . . a little lost."

"You have me."

"Maybe someday you'll let me in, Cruz. Maybe someday you'll let someone in, because I promise it eases the burden."

"I have let you in," I say evenly.

Her eyes are sad as she nods. "You let me in until you get uncomfortable. But it's when you get uncomfortable that you see the real person. The real you."

"Cross," I murmur to myself knowing she has no fucking clue what I'm talking about. And rather than asking, she stands there and simply stares at me. I can push her even farther away right now or I can do something I've never done before.

I can hold on a bit tighter.

"C'mere." I pull her into me and wrap my arms around her. Her hair tickles the bottom of my chin and her heart beats against mine. She fits perfectly there and the thought is like a gut punch. *She fits perfectly.* "I'm sorry."

The words are hard to get out. And not because they're an apology. It's because they are sincere. And it's because *she fits perfectly.*

"I know you are." She rests her cheek against my chest. "I mean, I could have really lived up to that lack of pedigree thing tonight if you'd have just told me. Thigh-high pink boots. Leopard-print bodycon dress. Hair teased out. You want to make a statement, I mean . . . I'm your girl."

She looks up at me, her chin on my chest, and the sadness cleared from her eyes. Thank fuck for that. "He would die. Absolutely die." I lean down and press a kiss to her lips. And I'd love every goddamn second of it.

She kisses me back tenderly. I never knew how relieved I'd be to be kissed like this. Simple. Without urgency. To just kiss.

We make our way downstairs. Into the condo. We change out of our clothes. We agree to a nightcap. I leave her on one of the chairs on the balcony to pour us a glass of wine, but when I come back out, she's sound asleep.

Her hair is still pinned up, the fifty carats in diamonds we have to return in the morning still sparkle around her neck and on her ears, and my faded Gravitas racing shirt is the only clothing besides a pair of boy shorts peeking out beneath its hem.

I scrub a hand through my hair. "How the fuck did we get here, Madds, huh?"

I cradle my arm behind her shoulders and then lift her up. Her arms immediately go around my neck. "Cruz?" she murmurs.

"Shh. I'll take you to bed." But rather than turning into the first door on the right where her bed is, I keep walking down the hallway to mine.

Don't ask me why because I don't know. In all the time we've spent together, here in Monaco, we've never slept in each other's beds. It's been sex and then back to our respective rooms. A barrier of sorts for one reason or another.

But tonight, I don't feel like being alone just yet.

I lay her on the bed and after I brush my teeth, I slide in beside her.

We've done this before—the sleep in the same bed thing—so it isn't a big deal. But never like this. Never with her head on my chest, her hand on my heart, and her thigh draped over my own. Not with the scent of her perfume in my nose and the warmth of her breath on my skin.

I close my eyes.

I try to sleep.

But all I keep thinking about is how she ran away from me tonight. Although it was brief, that feeling was so familiar.

"When are you coming home, Mamá?"

"Oh, Cruzie baby. I'll just be gone a day or two."

"That's what you said last time. It was weeks. You missed my kart race. You missed—"

"That's the best part about being an adult, hijo. You get to come and go as you please. You get to make your own rules. I get to go and then come back to you and Sofia."

"You promised me you weren't going to go away again."

"No, I said I'd go away but that I'd always come back. There's a difference." She kisses my cheek. *"This time will be short. I promise. I'll be back before you can blink."*

But it wasn't short. It never was. She missed my birthday but came back for Sofia's.

That's when I stopped believing in her words.

That's when I stopped trusting my mamá.

That's when I stopped believing I was worth coming back for.

Maddix left tonight, but she came back. This time. No doubt I'll hurt her one day—probably soon—and that time she won't come back.

That's why you guard your heart, Cross. It's safer. It's better.

It's all you have.

CHAPTER THIRTY-FIVE

Maddix

"YOU SAID YOU'D NEVER BEEN ON A YACHT SO . . ." CRUZ STANDS on the dock with one hand on the gangplank railing and the other motioning for me to walk about the massive boat beside him. It's titanium gray with a sleek hull and black accents. I don't even dare question how large it is because it looks massive and expensive and—

"Oh my God. Is this yours?" I ask, the epiphany dawning on me in the most ridiculous of ways.

"It's the family's." He lifts his eyebrows. "What? Rossi's is better?"

I burst out laughing. "Definitely." He swats my ass, and I yelp as I climb aboard.

If I thought the jet was extravagant, the yacht puts it to shame infinitely. Cruz lets me explore while he talks to the captain about boat things. I have very limited knowledge about boats, but I know enough to conclude that every bell and whistle is on this damn thing.

"Is it to your satisfaction, ma'am?" Cruz asks playfully when I find him on the back upper deck, hands braced on the rail, and surveying the wake of the boat as we make our way out of the harbor.

"It's beautiful." I wince. "Is that the right terminology?"

"Do you think I care?" He pulls me into him and kisses me softly.

This still feels like part of the Cruz apology tour. Something that is completely unnecessary but, at the same time, is totally welcome. And not because of the material things—the hundred dahlias delivered, the second Vespa he bought so I could explore Monaco on my own while he was off training or weightlifting or whatever it is that he spends hours doing to hone his body into the perfection that it is. But because I get time with him.

Time that I'm beginning to realize is ticking away toward a date—a board vote—when this whole thing between us might be over.

"You're too quiet."

"I was just thinking."

"About?"

"About all of these changes that have happened. About how much I miss my parents. About how Kevin praised my market analysis I did and said it was one the most detailed and informative he's ever seen. About what my life was like weeks ago and what it is now."

"That's a lot of thinking."

"It is." I slide my hand down and link my fingers with his. "And I was wondering if you were okay."

His fingers flinch in mine. "Of course, I am."

I nod and tread carefully. "You saw your mom for less than ten minutes the other night." I shift on my feet, staring at his profile while he looks straight ahead. "It was contentious to say the least. I didn't know if—"

"I'm fine." I've known him long enough to know the smile he flashes my way is insincere. It's the one he uses when he poses for pictures with fans. "Not a big deal at all."

"I just wanted—"

"Have you ever been on a Jet Ski?" he asks, topic clearly changed.

"No. Never."

"Seriously?"

"Dead serious." I look at the water, and our distance from the land, and then back to him. "Do we need to worry about sharks?"

He throws his head back and laughs. "You're looking at one of the top drivers in the world. Do you think I'm going to throw you off?"

"You being a good driver didn't address the shark issue."

He puts a hand on my ass and pats and playfully nips my shoulder. "Last I remember, you don't mind when I bite."

"Little different."

But all thoughts of sharks go by the wayside as Cruz convinces me to climb on the back of the Jet Ski with him. I hold on tight, arms wrapped around his waist, as he races across the top of the water. The swell is calm today, but the Jet Ski still slaps the water, my hair whipping behind me, and my thighs squeezing tight against his as our life vests bump against each other's.

It's an adrenaline rush like I've never felt before. Fast. A little on the edge of out of control. Addictive.

It's a mere glimpse of what he must experience under the ridiculously high horsepower of his Formula 1 car, but it's enough that I can understand it now. The draw to racing. The thrill of the speed and the draw to the recklessness.

Cruz eases up on the throttle and my hands fall onto his thighs. He turns his head so that I can hear his voice. "Your turn to drive."

"Um . . . but how?"

And before I can say another word, he bails off the Jet Ski and jumps in the water with a *whoop*.

His name falls from my lips but when he resurfaces and does that thing guys do where they shake their head, water spraying, and their hair sticks every which way, I just stare. How can I not? The man is absolutely gorgeous.

"What about sharks?" I ask.

"I'm too salty." He winks and then swims over to the Jet Ski, boosts himself up, and then onto the back of it. The whole thing rocks violently and I hold on to the handlebar tightly.

He scoots up behind me on the seat, the cold water on his skin and vest now on me, and his strong thighs cage mine in. But it's his cock nestled perfectly against my ass that has my attention.

Most definitely.

"Well, this turned out in my favor, now, didn't it?" He chuckles. "First, you need to put this around your wrist. It's the kill switch in case you fall off so the ski doesn't keep going." He helps me put it on and then he ghosts my arms with his so that his hands are on the handles too.

"Press here," he says, and the ski starts to propel forward. I yelp involuntarily and freeze but then after a bit, I get the hang of it.

It's simple really, and I love the feeling of the wind on my face without having to see around his life jacket.

"Take us out to where that bird is," he says, pointing.

I veer to where he's directing, and he drops his hands down off the handlebars and onto my thighs.

He slides them up. Then back. And then one slides beneath the fabric of my bikini bottoms. "Cruz," I gasp, realizing that the width of the seat I'm straddling provides him perfect access to between my thighs.

"Stop," I moan, clearly not meaning it.

"Drive, Madds. Steady on the throttle." He rubs a finger gently over my clit. "You keep letting up."

Another stutter on the throttle when he dips his fingers into me to wet them before going back to work on adding friction to my clit.

"Drive," he commands, and I try to focus on two things at once. One of them is definitely winning out.

"This is—"

"Being a driver is about learning how to drive under duress." His fingers dip back into me as the heel of his hand connects with the hub of nerves. "With distraction all around you." He leans down and laces an open-mouth kiss on my neck, his tongue licking there as his fingers keep working me over.

In. Out. Slide over my clit. A little more friction till I tense up and then back into me again.

"It's always hot. Something is always bothering you." He tugs on my earlobe and the sensation is like a mainline to my core where his fingers are now slick with my arousal. "Having to focus on anything but the pressure building in your body from outside sources."

I ease on the throttle as my body burns so hot I can't focus. I definitely shouldn't be driving right now. My head falls back against his shoulder as my body begins the weird dichotomy of soaring and falling at the same time.

"Why aren't we moving?" he asks as I buck my hips into his hand, my own hands tightening on the handles for leverage.

"I can't concentrate." I moan the breathless syllables out. His chuckle against my skin only heightening my hyperawareness of him.

"Come for me, Madds. Gush for me." He shifts so that his rock-hard shaft is against my lower back as his fingers work me over.

Again and again.

Until my body tenses.

And the orgasm washes over me.

CHAPTER THIRTY-SIX

Maddix

"SO WE'LL GET TO SEE YOU?" MY MOM'S VOICE RISES IN PITCH WITH each and every word. I can imagine her standing in the kitchen, her dog, Bo, asleep at her feet, and where she's practically bouncing up and down in excitement.

"You will. We're coming for the race in Austin."

"You know it wouldn't kill you to stop on home any other time." She chuckles but I know that sound. The one that says she has tears in her eyes and is trying not to show it. "I'm kind of missing my girl and am not particularly fond of Kevin sending you away on this work trip and of Cruz for keeping you there."

"He's not keeping me anywhere, Mom. You say that like I'm a hostage."

"Well . . . people have weird kinks these days. You never know—"

"Say no more. I'll make sure he brings his whole portable BDSM chamber with him when we come home."

Silence. My words are met with it. Then she bursts out in laughter. "Fine. Point made. Although I would like to hear about my daughter's adventures with her new beau herself instead of seeing them on her social media pages."

"Beau? Who says that anymore?"

"I've been on a historical romance reading binge. Go with it."

Leave it to my mom to insert historical romance in her everyday life. It doesn't hurt that I love her madly for it.

"But things are good? He's good to you? Beyond the diamonds at palaces and fancy dresses? He's really good to you?"

My smile is automatic. The past few weeks with Cruz have been . . . incredible. We've hiked the hills of Monaco. We've gambled in the Monte Carlo casino—my kisses on his dice the good luck he needed to win several thousand dollars that he in turn donated to charity.

We've challenged each other at game after game of checkers until our stubborn streaks resulted in us knocking the board to the floor and having sex on the table where the board had been. We've watched movies and made meals that tasted so horrible we had no choice but to order out.

And we've laughed. God, how we've laughed. In bed. Walking hand in hand through the town. Across the room as I worked and he studied his opponents' latest moves.

I left for this adventure thinking the memories I'd be making would be solo. Me out exploring as we pretended to date. But it seems that I can't think of a single memory I've made over the last two months that doesn't involve Cruz. Not one. My phone is full of pictures of them.

And many of those images are for my own use. For my memory bank, not to be posted to perpetuate this farce that doesn't feel like a farce anymore.

Is he good to me?

"Yes." I know she can't see the smile, but I can't help that it's there. "He is. I promise."

"Okay. Good. That's all your dad and I need to know."

"Mom." My voice breaks and it's for so many reasons that I can't quantify them.

Because I miss her desperately.

Because I know that going home is only going to be temporary. I want too much now to stay.

Because hearing her voice, the feelings it evokes, hurts. *Cruz has never had that comfort. Ever.*

"That didn't sound so sure, kiddo."

"I miss you. That's all."

"Well good, because I was beginning to think you were forgetting about us around here."

CHAPTER THIRTY-SEVEN

Cruz

"**A**RE YOU FEELING OKAY OVER THERE?" A BRITISH ACCENT ASKS TO my right.

I look up to see Riggs walking toward me in the paddock. His fire suit is unzipped, its arms hanging down around his waist, and he has an ice vest on his chest to keep him cool in between testing runs.

"Is that a trick question?"

He snorts. "You tell me. You're the one who went from the playboy prince of F1—"

"Fuck off." I hold my middle finger up to emphasize my words.

"To looking pussy-whipped with a capital P." He rests his hips on the barrier beside me, his grin wide so I know he's joking, but his eyes say he really wants to know.

"Says the man who's marrying his team owner's daughter."

He holds a finger up. "If you want to get technical, she'll be the team owner sooner rather than later," he says, referring to his fiancée.

"So then you slept your way to the top. How very Riggs of you," I joke.

"Nah, pretty sure that's under your title. The playboy—"

"You know how much I hate that fucking nickname. Can we just not?"

He chuckles and looks out at all of the chaos around us. It's testing day. Teams mill about. They mingle with competitors in a way they won't after today when qualifying starts and competition kicks in.

"So what gives?" he asks.

"About?"

"Maddix? Is that her name?"

"It is." I nod and lift a hand to wave to Halloran who is walking by.

"So . . .? You a changed man, or what, because we all have whiplash so bad, trying to figure out what's going on."

"We?" I ask with a laugh.

"Yes, *we*," an Australian accent says to my other side. Lachlan Evans. He's on the larger side, physically, for a driver, and he's intense, keeps to himself, and rarely gets involved in any shit around here. Every so often he's a sounding board for me to bounce things off. And . . . he just might be one of the only drivers here who has an inkling about the pressure I endure. In our F2 days, we were on the same team. "What's up, man?" He clasps my hand in his and smiles.

"Nothing. You?" I ask.

"Same ol', same ol'." He glances around. "What were we talking about?"

"His woman," Riggs says.

"She's not my woman," I say.

"You're so full of shit, you stink, Navarro." Evans laughs. "Other than Riggs here, whose woman has to be here because it's her job to be, I don't think anyone else has their *female companion*—"

"Much better," I assert at the term.

"—with them every race." He shrugs. "So from where I stand, you're either head over heels or dick-gripped by this new chick."

I start to refute him but remember the ruse. The pretend fouple we are. And then wonder if we're even pretending anymore. How can we be, when I wake up to a race morning alarm clock of her lips wrapped around my cock, *for good luck*—in her words.

Or how I search for her in every crowd, almost as if I'm so used to her being here that I now need her to be.

She's my good luck charm.

Or is that my lame excuse to justify why I want her here? Why kissing her before I get in the car or getting out of the car after the last lap and finding her has become my thing?

It's like when she's around I'm a better version of myself—less bitter about my papá, more sure of my own place, more secure with who I am and what I've accomplished—and fuck if it isn't freeing.

She approves of me. She likes me. She is with me for who I am.

"I mean"—Riggs whistles—"I never thought I'd see the day hell froze over, but I'm thinking it just might be."

"You're such an asshole." I laugh but know I felt much the same way a few months ago. Before Maddix. And now we're in the *After Maddix* phase, and I'm not one hundred percent sure how I feel about it.

Scratch that. I know. I just am afraid to admit.

"Been called worse by better," Lachlan says and grins. "And she gave me a blow job so . . ."

"So you didn't mind the name-calling," Riggs jokes.

"She can call me whatever she wants," Lachlan says.

We all bust out laughing and when I look up, I see my papá standing across the garage.

I wasn't aware he was coming to Suzuka for the race.

The phone call after the gala was expected and just as demanding and harsh as I figured it would be. The podium I stood on in Singapore, and his complete lack of acknowledgement over it, even more so.

"*You defied my wishes.*"

"*I was a good boy just like you asked.*"

"*You took the American trash with you to the palace. She ran off like an undisciplined child. People talked. We looked like fools.*" I had a retort on my tongue, but his next words sobered that. "*I have warned you what I will do.*"

And that? The unknown, the myriad of things my father is capable of, is what's fucking scary.

He locks eyes with me and nods ever so slightly before turning on his heel and walking away. He barely kept his demeanor in check, but I could see the burning hostility in his expression. I caught the slightest smirk as he walked away. Fuck do I want to know what that's all about.

I must stare after him without thinking because Lach nudges me. "You good, mate?"

"Yeah. Sure." I return to the conversation. To the light-heartedness. To the ribbing. "All is good."

Lachlan eyes me for a beat, silent concern in his eyes, before he nods. "Good. Now, why don't I explain to you how I'm going to kick both of your arses on Sunday."

Both Riggs and I lift our middle fingers at him.

"I mean, if you're offering," he says with a smirk and shrug before walking away.

CHAPTER THIRTY-EIGHT

Maddix

MY HEART THUNDERS IN MY THROAT AS CRUZ BATTLES BUSTOS DOWN the back straight. Suzuka is a technical track—at least that's what he told me—and is difficult to race.

He gets his nose in front and then Bustos pulls up even again. The wheel-to-wheel racing is both exhilarating and nerve-wracking.

It's like I want to watch and can't watch all at the same time.

"You've got this," Otis says in my ears over the race comms.

"I'm struggling with power," Cruz says. From what Cruz has explained to me—and it took a while to understand—the "dirty air" from riding behind Bustos will affect his car's handling.

"Your input is good. Keep pushing."

"Understood," Cruz says, his voice strained with concentration and the G's on his body.

They fight valiantly. Bustos skillfully blocks Cruz on the turns as he tries to get past him. It's a cat and mouse game for two laps before Cruz swerves out from behind Bustos on the start/finish straight and flies past him with the assistance of DRS. The crowd in the grandstands roars at getting to see the action that up close and personal.

And the breath I feel like I've been holding for an hour finally eeks out of my chest.

"P3," Otis says about Cruz's place.

"Let's keep reeling them in. Car is strong."

"You've got this."

I can't sit. I move about the booth. From one side to the next. I shift my posture. My arms. Anything and everything as if the movement will help Cruz get the upper hand and gain another spot. And then another.

He so desperately deserves a win.

When I lean down to grab my water, I notice Dominic Navarro at the back of the hospitality booth. His eyes are laser focused on me, scrutinizing me, and the scowl that accompanies it is no doubt for me too. The man typically stays in the garage during the race. He's an imposing presence there. A presence it seems everyone reveres by the way they kowtow to him in sirs and an immediate berth of space.

But I've yet to see him here. In the booth.

I've yet to engage with him.

But this time I don't avert my eyes. I meet him stare for stare and lift my eyebrows, willing the confrontation.

The more I've gotten to know Cruz, the angrier I've become at his father. At his unfair treatment of his son. At his disrespect and demeaning ways.

I'm sick of walking around here, avoiding him. Intimidated by him. Worried about what he thinks of me.

I don't matter in this game . . . but Cruz does.

I move my headset to my neck, a somewhat invitation to engage in this impending conversation.

"Miss Hart," he states from where he stands and I notice that conveniently, everyone has moved to the other vantage point to watch the race so that we are left in privacy.

"Mr. Navarro." The muscle pulses in his jaw as he folds his arms over his chest. "You must be pleased to see he's doing well. Fighting his way up the pack. Another great race after a podium last week."

"He had a poor quali," he says, referring to Cruz qualifying with a P8 starting position.

"And now he's in P3."

"By the skin of his teeth. His lines aren't clean and he's almost kissed the wall several times. He should have already gotten Bustos. Far from perfect."

"So far he's on the podium," I say, wondering why I feel the need to defend Cruz from the harsh criticism.

"He should have started from a better position. He's distracted."

"Distracted? Hmm. Happy seems to be a better term for it, but"—I shrug flippantly—"who am I to judge that?"

I turn to watch the monitors directed where cars are battling on the course. It's been an exhilarating race that no doubt will come down to an infinitesimal driver error. But at speeds of two hundred plus miles per hour, the tiniest of mistakes can be a disaster for not only the driver who makes it but everyone around him.

Relieved that this conversation seems to be over, I'm just about to slip my headset back on when Dominic speaks again.

"I don't like what you're doing to him."

"Doing to him?" I turn to face him. "What's that? *Loving him unconditionally?* Not putting pressure on him to be anything but himself? Letting him know he's good enough just how he is?" I put my hands on my hips and square off with him and his clear distaste for me. "I'm sorry, Mr. Navarro, but most people would be thrilled with that for their son. You, on the other hand . . . I don't know what it is that you want from me."

"Loving him unconditionally?" he says. I have never seen such hatred directed at me before. "You have no clue what you're talking about. His family loves him unconditionally. *Not you.* We know what he needs. I know what he needs. And no, it's not you."

Do I love him unconditionally? Did I just say that out loud? Or am I flustered and so desperate to make this man see how incredible his son is that I'll say anything to drive the point home?

But does it matter? Will a rude fucker like Dominic Navarro hear anything other than what he wants to hear?

"You don't know the first thing about what your son wants or needs." There I go again trying to defend Cruz.

His sneer is one of disgust. His tone even more so. "He's distracted. He's doing uncharacteristic things like blowing off sponsorship events." *He is? Is that true?* His tone is clipped and posture stiff. "The very fact that you are here, in the pits, race after race, is demonstration in and of itself."

"I'm here because he wants me to be here," I assert.

"You're here because you want something from him. You should bow out now, save yourself the embarrassment, because you definitely won't be getting whatever you want."

This man is a piece of fucking work. But just as I think that, just as I'm considering fighting back and hitting below the belt with anything and everything just so I can land a punch, I notice a camera pointed our way. And as hard as it is to swallow down the fight in me, I refuse to be used as more clickbait.

So I throw my shoulders back and hold my head high, placing a genial smile on my face.

"I was always taught to be respectful, Mr. Navarro, so I'm going to walk away now. The last thing I want to do is lower my *non-pedigreed standards* and break them for you." I take a few steps back.

"And I was always taught to do whatever it takes to protect my family."

Even if that means losing them, huh?

"For a family you covet publicly, you do a damn good job of sabotaging privately. I just hope that when you finally acknowledge it, your kids afford you the same grace you never gave them."

I move my headphones onto my head and walk out of the hospitality area and down to the garage.

Love him unconditionally.

Again, did I really just say that?

But isn't that what I'm doing? Loving him?

This wasn't supposed to happen.

Shit.

I'm in love with Cruz Navarro.

CHAPTER THIRTY-NINE

Maddix

HOLD MY PASS UP TO THE SCANNER OF THE TURNSTILE AND RED LIGHTS flash. With a nervous chuckle, I hold the pass up again and get the same result. I glance over to the guard standing at his post, preventing anyone who doesn't have a pass from getting into the paddock, before trying again.

Same result.

"Excuse me. Sir?" I ask to the guard. He adjusts his keffiyeh and moves toward me.

"Can I help you?"

"My pass. It isn't working."

He glances at it and motions for me to try it again. A red light flashes.

"It's no longer valid," he says with a tight smile and a nod before starting to move away.

"But it is. It worked yesterday. I'm with Gravitas. I'm Cruz Navarro's girlfriend. I have to get in there." Panic claws its way up my throat for some reason.

"I'm sorry, miss. I'm not allowed to let anyone through who doesn't have a valid pass."

I stare at him dumbfounded and then immediately pull my phone out and start firing off texts. One to Cruz, which I know he won't see since he's in the zone. Another to Amandine, hoping she'll see this and come help me. And another to her assistant.

I stand at the gates waiting for a response. People jostle my shoulders as they jockey to get in line, and I stare at my screen waiting for a response.

Here I am in Qatar. Alone. No one is answering my calls. And no doubt Cruz is in there looking for me.

CHAPTER FORTY

Cruz

I HAVE MY EYES CLOSED, MY MUSIC IN MY EARS, AND VISUALIZE EVERY curve of the track I'm about to take on. I had a good qualifying run yesterday and will be starting at P2—an improvement from my P8 in Qatar. But the start here is tricky and prone to accidents, and I need to steer clear of that.

It's a visualization technique I learned years ago. It's partially from all the sim training and partially from experience, but it helps me know the curves and angles of the course.

A touch on the shoulder has me jolting to the present. My smile is on the ready to see Maddix, but it fades when I come face-to-face with my father and Esmerelda.

What the . . .

"Cruz." Esmerelda steps into me, her tits rubbing against my chest as she slides her hands up my biceps and then leans in and presses a kiss to my cheek—a little too close to my lips.

I step back like I've been jolted by lightning, but not before I hear the click of a camera. I look up to see an Associated Press photographer snapping pictures of the two of us.

Fuck. I remove her hand from my arm and glare at my father.

"What?" Esmerelda bats her lashes and smiles seductively, making sure to turn so that her face is toward the camera. She has always loved the limelight. "I just wanted to wish you the best of luck. Buena suerte, Cruz." Her words are breathless. Seductive. And have no place in my garage.

I look from her to my father and then back again.

"What are you doing here?" I ask her but the words are meant for my father. Why is *she* here?

"I thought you could use some love from home. A little . . . reprieve to jolt your system and remind you of what is important."

"I'm more than aware what's important and what's at stake." I search the garage, looking for a head of blond hair and a pair of green eyes.

Where is Maddix?

"She's not here," my father said. "Just like the rest of them, she was easily paid off. Easy to walk away from you when you needed her the most."

Fuck you.

The words are on my tongue. The most vulnerable of my spots hit.

"What did you do?" I ask.

A ghost of a smile frames his lips. "Have you ever known me *not* to follow through on my recommendations?" he asks. *Recommendations?* He means threats. *Asshole.*

"Amandine?" I call out as she walks by, my eyes surveying every inch of space in the garage.

"Yeah?" She stops and looks up from her clipboard.

"Have you seen Maddix?"

"No. Not at all. Why?"

My father's smirk returns and the sight of it has a pit dropping into my stomach. "You should be focused on the race at hand. Not the woman who is a distraction. *Verdad?*"

"It's time," Otis says, pulling me out of this fucked-up and frantic headspace.

"Yes. Okay." I glare at my father and Esmerelda, no doubt a pawn in this game. Just like I made Maddix become.

You can't think of that now. You have to focus now. You have to work.

"Amandine?" I call again.

She's at my side in seconds and I have a hand on her shoulder, guiding her away from the crowd in the garage as a crew member hands me my helmet. "What's wrong?"

"I need you to find Maddix. Something is wrong. She's not here when she's supposed to be here. My father . . ."—I glance over my shoulder—"something happened, and that must be why she's not here."

"Okay. Sure. He uh . . . he was sorting through the paddock passes yesterday. Maybe things were accidentally mixed up? I don't know. Let me go grab my phone. I'll figure it out."

"Yes. Thanks." Would he actually fucking do that?

He would.

"Cruz?"

I look over to Amandine. "I'm taking care of this. Clear your head. Go to work."

"Okay." My smile is forced, my head already fucked with.

I give one last glance to my father before I slip my helmet on. It's a glare. A threat. Fucking with me is . . . *whatever*. But fucking with my woman? That's where I draw the line.

And then I force myself to compartmentalize. To shut it out. To worry about the track and the race at hand.

But I search the crowd one last time before I climb in the car.

She's here.

She didn't walk away.

CHAPTER FORTY-ONE

Cruz

ELATION.

The highest fucking high.

Euphoria.

Relief.

My body vibrates with the thrill of pulling off a fucking victory. Everything went in our favor. Bustos losing traction after hitting the curb and spinning off into the gravel. Gaining DRS to overtake Finnegan on the back straight with two laps to go to take the lead.

It doesn't hurt that I raced like a fucking madman with an anger and fire in my belly over what my father did. What he thought was okay to do. And the confusion over the fact that it spurred me on to a victory. *He's going to claim it was because Maddix was nowhere in sight.*

The goddamn fucking cocksucker. I just won and he's going to think it's because of him.

The checkered flag waved but my eyes were so damn blurry from the tears burning in them I didn't actually see it.

I pull into the P1 marker, my nose cone inches from it and am unbuckling and climbing out of my car to stand on its top.

I raise my arms in victory as my team roars around me. Not that I can hear them because the grandstands is still cheering too.

When I jump down, my crew is there to greet me. I hug as many as I can as I unbuckle and remove my helmet. It's a great day for Gravitas with a P1 and P4 for us.

Celebrations all around.

But when I turn from my team, there's only one person I'm looking for. The one I trusted Amandine to find when I couldn't. For her to protect when I couldn't. I needed her to make sure Maddix was here for me . . . when I needed her most.

There's only one person I want right now.

One woman I need to celebrate with.

My dad stands there with his hand outstretched to shake mine and a partial smile on his lips. Esmerelda stands beside him, smiling, and expectation in her expression. No doubt my dad snowed her into why she was here today too.

Fuck. Him.

Fuck him if he thinks I'll give him a goddamn inch right now.

I move toward him, meet his eyes. "Vete a la mierda," I mutter. *Go to hell.* My only greeting before I walk right on past.

Maddix stands there with tears in her eyes, an unstoppable grin on her lips, and jumps into my arms the minute I'm close enough. Her legs wrap around my waist as she grabs me in the tightest hug ever.

"You did it," she whispers in my ear and despite the crowd still roaring around us, I can hear every word.

I did do it.

I won, when it's been so fucking long since I have.

"Madds?" I say when I lean back and meet her eyes. "Where were you?"

"We'll talk about it later. Celebrate this win. Your win." She grins. "You did it."

"I did. Fuck him."

And before she can respond or react or ask questions, my lips are on hers in a soul-crushing kiss. It's far from a peck on the lips and, with all of the cameras all around, will be posted on every site imaginable for days to come.

And every time my dad sees it, he'll get another fuck you.

And every time I see it, I'll be reminded of what matters most. This. Right here. Right now. This woman. This moment.

Her eyes are wild with excitement when the kiss ends, and she lowers her feet to the ground. "I'm beginning to think you're my good luck charm, Madds."

"That's a label I'll claim any day." She kisses me again. "Go celebrate with your team."

CHAPTER FORTY-TWO

Maddix

T HIS CITY.

I don't know why I love it so much with its constant noise and graf-fitied walls, but I do. It's the skyscraper-filled skyline and the sparkling of the Hudson. It's the feeling of opportunity just around the next corner and the nonstop bustle of the people in its streets trying to grasp it.

I love this town. Its people. Its attitude.

The funny thing is, I thought this place was everything before. I still do. But after the past few months, I realize that my opinion was based solely off how small my world was. Now my eyes are open much wider and that per-spective has been skewed.

"So the board is happy?" I ask, my cell to my ear, and my eyes glued to the world beyond the wall of windows of the twentieth floor.

"The general consensus is yes. They're pleased that Cruz has kept the promises he made and publicly looks more responsible. His social media is more you and racing than anything else. The photo with the Esmerelda woman did cause a little discomfort. Like maybe he can only behave for—"

"There was nothing to the photos," I assert. "Just an old family friend wishing him luck in the garage."

Her smug smile had disturbed me when I finally made my way into the garage. She'd been standing beside Dominic, which had caused me to won-der if being locked out hadn't quite been the "accident" it had looked to be.

Would his father really do something like that? That was where my mind went eventually.

"It was one hundred percent my father interfering."

"Why? Why would he bother, Cruz? I mean, it doesn't make sense."

"I've known her for years, and there has never been anything between us. Never will be. He told me that he'd paid you to leave me."

"You didn't believe that, did you? When I saw her, I couldn't help wonder if you wanted her . . . She's the type of woman you want—"

"Wanted. Past tense." He leans in and brushes his lips over mine. "You're everything I want now."

"Won't your dad keep persisting? The media had a field day with that image of her kissing your cheek."

Cruz grabs my hand in his and sits down on the chair in front of me so I have no choice but to see the intensity in his eyes. "One, he'll always keep pushing. Nothing is going to stop that, but the fact that the video of me kissing you like that is all over the goddamn world and will be synonymous with my victory forever, just might temper him a bit. A kind of fuck with me and find out." A kiss to the palm of my hand. "And two, the media's field day with the Esmerelda photo is drowned out by our kiss. But it also goes to show you how they'll paint a picture to fit their narrative when there is no story to begin with. That is something you already know."

"I know. It doesn't make it any easier."

"Madds. You stood up to my dad in Suzuka. You threatened and challenged him enough that he brought Esmerelda to Doha to try and intimidate you. Neither worked. You're not scared of him, you know how the media misrepresents things for clicks, so why believe the rumors the media printed?"

He has a point. A very good point. I stare at our hands intertwined and nod. He's right. I know he is. But it still was . . . traumatizing in a sense to feel shut out of the paddock, then being manipulated by first his dad and then the press.

"And can I just tell you I'd have given anything to see his face when you confronted him? No one does. They walk on eggshells around him. So the fact that you did makes me lo . . . love your grit."

Was he going to say love? I get goosebumps. Does Cruz love me?

The unspoken words hang in the air as panic flickers through Cruz's eyes. I rescue him by leaning forward and pressing my lips to his. "We do make a good team."

"We do. I told you, you're my good luck charm."

"You sure about that?" Kevin asks.

"I am. Cruz is with me twenty-four seven. The woman is desperate for media coverage and used the moment to further her modeling career. Tell the board not to worry."

"If you say so. I mean, I get he's not squeaky clean, but he's been washed with a nice window dressing and that seems enough for them. I just don't want that image ruined."

My spine stiffens at the comment. At the implication that Cruz wasn't good enough how he was before.

And there's irony in that.

In the fact that I sat in that conference room three plus months ago and found Cruz to be an asshole who I didn't like. And now I'm sitting here speaking to my boss and wanting to defend Cruz for his actions.

"For what it's worth, I've seen nothing but Cruz being an upstanding guy."

Kevin makes a noncommittal sound, almost as if he's not sure if he buys my sales pitch. "I have to say, Maddix, I'm impressed with your hard work on this. It's an unconventional ask on my part and you handled it beautifully. In fact, it turned out even better than I thought. The big F1 driver plucking a Texas girl up out of obscurity who he met at a business meeting. I mean, that's wholesome. Again, I'm impressed. I was more than certain you were going to leave within a week and then run home with your tail between your legs because it was too much. You showed resilience."

I bristle at that. At his lack of faith. At his ability to think so little of me and yet have no problem throwing me into a situation like this with a man he really didn't know for the sake of his business venture. Is this a man I really want to work for long-term if he thinks of me this way?

What if Cruz was an absolute prick? What if things had turned out the polar opposite?

I took the job. I didn't really question things yet accepted the terms. But for some reason, and maybe it's because he's bad-mouthing Cruz, this is hitting me all wrong right now.

Oblivious to my train of thought, he keeps talking. "Not only did you step up to the plate in this regard, but you also did an incredible comparative on the energy drink market that gave me a different vantage point to look at. A different set of eyes. I was impressed and wondered why I hadn't noticed your work before."

"Because there are people in middle management competing for your attention just as much as I was, and therefore why show you something that would rival their work?" I say without really thinking about it.

Silence eats up the distance and I wonder if I've overstepped. I sink my teeth into my lower lip and wait to see what he says.

"There's a reason I asked you to attend the meeting today, Maddix. And your work is one of them."

"Thank you," I say cautiously.

"Don't thank me yet. The management at Revive are workhorses. You might be in New York for a few days, but they'll probably make it feel like a week by the time you leave."

"I'm grateful for the opportunity."

"Make the best of it."

"I will."

"Just think, you'll most likely be done with all this Cruz nonsense after the Austin race. The board will have voted, the ink on the signatures will be dry, and you can figure out a creative way to publicly break things off with him."

"Okay." I swear to God the word catches in my throat.

In fact, this whole trip has felt this way. Especially being called to these New York meetings as a Genesee representative at the same time as race week in Mexico.

It's like I'm so very excited to be here, to get to work in this city I love, but know I'm missing out on all the new experiences of being there too.

And more than anything, I already miss Cruz.

Ridiculous, I know. We've been together almost every single day for over three months and so I should welcome this time for myself. This time to be able to breathe without Formula 1 *everything* being in my face . . . but weirdly, it has become a part of my life now. My temporary life, but my life nonetheless.

Sofia was right.

"The rumbling in your chest. The whine of the engines. You hear it when you close your eyes at night to sleep."

It's become so much a part of me.

I pick up my phone and fire off a text.

> **Me:** Don't get in too much trouble while I'm gone. And kick ass on the track.

"Miss Hart, are you ready to get started?"

I look up at the man waltzing into the room in a no-nonsense manner and the three women walking in behind him. If New York had a type, they are the personification of it. Brusque. Cosmopolitan. Efficient.

"Yes. I'm excited to get started."

"Great. After Kevin's glowing commendations, we have high expectations of you."

CHAPTER FORTY-THREE

Cruz

"CHRIST, NAVARRO. QUIT BEING SUCH A BUZZKILL AND GET YOUR ass out here. The race is done and over with. The hard work is over. The interviews have been given. The autographs have been signed. Now is the time to go and have the fun we bust our asses to enjoy."

I look at Halloran and Grimaldi—the most unlikely pairing of friends on the circuit—and shake my head. "I'm gonna pass. I've got—"

"Wait. What?" Grimaldi asks, smile snarky and eyes wide. "You're turning down the offer to go out and let off some steam? You feeling okay?"

Halloran props his elbow on Grimaldi's shoulder and just tsks in disappointment. "Your woman is gone. Are you telling me she has a chain around your ankle so fucking tight that you can't go out on your own? I mean, what the fuck, man? You're shaming the rest of us right now."

"It's not like that. It's been a long fucking weekend. I'm tired. I'm coming down with something—"

"Yeah, it's called being pussy-whipped," Grim says.

"No, it's called I'm tired."

"We're so sorry that placing P2 and keeping your hopes of a championship alive is so taxing you can't go out for a drink or two." Halloran narrows his eyes and studies me.

Taking the edge off does sound nice.

That singular thought leads to the trendy club in the upscale part of town. The inside is neon lights, dark shadows, and vibrating bass from the dance floor two stories below. Numerous people linger just on the edge of the VIP ropes where we all sit with drinks in hand amidst the few women that Halloran invited to sit with us.

Buzzed but disconnected.

That's how I feel about all of this. The atmosphere. The bottle service. The flash. The women.

Didn't this used to be my preference of poison? The way to get lost in the noise?

"Hey, Navarro? Live a little, will you?" Grimaldi says and then tilts his chin to the woman sidling up beside me.

She's gorgeous in all the ways I typically like—the curves, the hair, the fashion—and yet my smile is a half-ass attempt when I greet her with a simple nod.

"A drink?" she asks.

"Yeah. Sure," I say, annoyed more than anything.

"Thank you." She rests her hand on my thigh and runs it up a little higher.

"You're welcome." I put my hand on hers and move it off my leg.

"C'mon." She pouts with those red-stained lips of hers. Lips that would give any man lascivious thoughts. "Party boy like you? Why don't we get out of here and I can show you around the town . . . or do other things?" Her hand moves back.

I grip her wrist and lean into her so she can hear me. "Why don't we keep our hands to ourselves before you get embarrassed for the rejection I'm about to give you?" I stand up, my fingers still around her wrist. "Have a good night. Enjoy the drink."

⟩⟨

"Madds." The syllable is slurred and followed by a chuckle.

"Cruz? You okay? It's . . . I don't even know what time it is here or there for that matter."

"I'm on the rooftop." With my bottle. With my eyes closed and the stars in the sky spinning around me. Without her.

"What are we contemplating?"

"All the ways I've fucked up." Another chuckle to cover the ache that has been in my chest all night.

"Cruz?"

"Nothing. Never mind. I'm good," I say.

"What do you mean?" Panic? Concern? Annoyance? Whatever it is, it vibrates through her voice.

"It's fine. I'm fine. Goodnight, Madds."

I miss you.

I need you.

I lo . . .

I lift the bottle to match the burn in my chest that those words cause.

It's too dangerous. *Even if it's true.*

After her optimistic texts about her meeting, I know it won't be long before she leaves me.

So I won't say the words. I can't. I'll hold them in and shove them deep down. *That way, it won't hurt so much when she disappears from my life too.*

CHAPTER FORTY-FOUR

Maddix

T HE MINUTE CRUZ PUTS THE CAR IN PARK, I JUMP OUT AND RUN TO
where my mom is standing with her arms open waiting for me.

"Mom," I cry as I cross the distance and then am wrapped in the
arms of the woman who has been my rock. She smells of vanilla and spice—
the scents of every memory I've ever had—and I just hold on to her as the
tears well and fall.

And I don't care that they do.

"Goodness. Look at you. Sunkissed and . . . happy." She holds my arms
out as I grin goofily at her before she pulls me against her again and soaks
me in.

"Maddster." It's my dad's gruff voice that has me shifting and hugging
him. His strong arms wrap around me, picking me up off my feet in a bear
hug for the ages.

We all begin talking at once. Months' worth of conversation reduced
down into a few minutes of speed talking and gesticulation and touching
each other's arms constantly to reassure ourselves that we're really together.

But it's when my dad stiffens that I realize I forgot about one very important thing. I turn to look in the same direction as my dad. Cruz is standing against the team-provided sports car, his hands are in his pockets, and
he's simply watching us from behind his sunglasses.

My smile widens if that's possible.

I told myself that this wasn't a big deal—Cruz meeting my parents. That
it was just the continuation of the charade, a natural progression of things,

but I suddenly have butterflies in my stomach knowing the two most important men in my life are about to meet.

And I know for a fact that Cruz's job and status won't have any sway with my father. How he treats me will be the deciding factor.

"Mom. Dad. This is Cruz Navarro. Cruz, this is Gavin and Clarissa Hart."

They shake hands, and I breathe a sigh of relief as the four of us fall into easy conversation. The topics are all superficial—Cruz asking about the property we're on, my mom asking him whether he enjoys coming to America or not, my dad uttering few words as he silently judges—but there is an unexpected ease. No doubt, a huge part is because Cruz is so practiced meeting strangers and making them feel comfortable in a short amount of time.

We move into the house and then out onto the back patio. "A drink anyone?" my dad asks. His litmus test for everyone is their drink of choice.

"Normally I'd say yes to whatever beer you have on hand," Cruz says, earning some raised brows by my father. No doubt he expected something swankier. "But it's race week so none for me. Thank you though." He puts a hand on the small of my back, which by the look exchanged between my parents, doesn't go unnoticed. "What'll you have, Madds?"

"You know what? I'll help," I say to my dad and rise from my seat.

I know that Cruz can one hundred percent handle my mother. It's my father, whose sliding glances communicate distrust, that I need to placate.

"Oh. Uh. Okay." Cruz shifts in his seat and smiles at my mom, but not before casting a strangled glance my way.

My footsteps falter as the thought crosses my mind. Cruz Navarro has never been taken home to anyone's parents before.

At least there's one first I get to claim . . . even if it's pretend.

My dad's hulking figure stands at the refrigerator door staring at the items inside, but he never reaches for anything.

"Dad?"

He shuts the fridge, crosses his arms over his chest, and leans his ass against the counter. "I don't like him."

"What?" I ask, partially laughing in disbelief and in worry. "You can't possibly—you just met him."

He nods definitively. "And yet I don't like him."

"Shh," I say and glance over my shoulder, as panic has my heart racing and my hands trembling. "You never said anything like that about Michael. Ever."

He nods, those green eyes that match mine staring at me. "Michael is nice. Was nice. He treated you well. But, fuck, kiddo, I never had that feeling I was being threatened by him."

I bark out a laugh. "That's the most absurd thing I've ever heard. Why would you be threatened by Cruz?"

His smile softens but the intensity in his eyes holds. "Because you love him."

His words hit me like a fist to the stomach . . . then reaches up and tightens its fingers around my heart.

I blink several times over, unsure what to say or how to respond. Gavin Hart doesn't say shit like that. Ever.

"You can deny it all you want, but it's written all over your face. It's how you look at him. It's the confidence you have now . . . confidence that no doubt you've always had but that somehow, he helped you find and own. Things that I should have done for you as a father, but clearly didn't, because he did. So no, I don't like him."

"You just met him," I say again.

"I'm aware, but I already know." He shrugs.

"I don't even know what to say."

"There's nothing to say. I'm just trying to figure out how exactly to strangle the guy if he ever hurts you . . . because I already like him when I don't want to, and I have a feeling if he goes missing and gets buried under an oak tree out here, his absence might be noticed."

His slow crawl of a smile tells me all I need to know. He loves me. He's trying to figure out if he approves of Cruz while feeling like he's letting his baby go.

And all three of those things fill up my cup that already seems to be running over. I am so lucky. I have known this quality of love my entire life. Affirming. Unconditional. Adoring. It's how I wish I could love Cruz too. It's the kind of love he deserves to know exists. To experience.

He grabs our drinks and as we walk out, he hooks an arm around my neck and pulls my head over so he can press a kiss to the top of my head.

CHAPTER FORTY-FIVE

Cruz

"**T**HIS IS MY ROOFTOP," MADDIX SAYS SOFTLY.

We're lying on our backs in a field of long grass, the breeze swaying all around us, as we look up at the stars in the sky above. The rustle of the trees surrounds us and crickets or some weird beetles chirp.

Our stomachs are full of some smoked brisket and all things barbecue, and her parents have turned in for the night.

But the time difference and jet lag has us up. It had Maddix grabbing my hand and telling me she wanted to show me something.

This place.

This endless field.

The view of the sky above.

All of the outside noise gone so that it's just us.

This is her rooftop.

"The field or the sky?" I ask.

"Maybe all of it. I feel like I'm the only one in the world here. Just the stars and the sky. It's like I feel so small that all of the trivial stuff doesn't matter, and I'm forced to see the bigger picture."

"I can see that." I put one arm behind my head as a cushion. The stars are so bright compared to how they're drowned out back home with all the lights. "Is that why we're out here? You stressed about something?"

I can feel her shrug. "Just lots to think about with all the changes coming my way."

"Like?"

Her sigh is soft but full of concern. "The head of Revive, Brian . . . he was dropping hints while I was in New York about me going to work for them. Nothing outright, but enough that I got the picture."

Excitement hits. Dread follows soon after. Her texts hinted to as much and maybe I've just been choosing to put my head in the sand on that. "That's . . . incredible. Right? Isn't that what you wanted?"

She's slow to respond. "Yeah. I guess. It seems I don't know what I want right now."

"That's your dream. Go chase it." The words taste bitter on my tongue because if she's chasing that then she's not with me and if she's not with me . . . fuck. It seems that's yet one more thing I keep brushing under the rug.

She falls quiet and I'd give anything to know what she's thinking. Does the idea of her in New York and me everywhere else feel like a ball of lead in her gut? Because it sure as fuck does me and I don't know what the hell to do about it.

I mean . . . is this what *it* feels like? The wanting to be with someone. The worrying when you're not. *The looking forward to what's next? Because if that's the case . . . what the actual fuck, Cruz?*

You don't do this. You don't want this.

And yet . . . *here you fucking are.*

"Say something," she murmurs and rests her chin on my shoulder. "When you're quiet I don't know what you're thinking."

"Well, that's kind of how it works," I tease to which she knocks her thigh against mine.

There is a peacefulness here. Yes, much like my rooftops but different. Or maybe it's just having Maddix beside me that's the difference. The calming effect.

I sigh and give her what she asks for. "He doesn't like me." Not sure why that's my first thought, but it is.

And her chuckle tells me she knows exactly who I'm referring to. Her father. "He does. He just . . . one day if you have girls, you'll understand. No one is ever good enough for your daughter even when they overwhelmingly are."

"Humph." I link my fingers with hers but don't respond other than make the sound. Kids have never really crossed my mind. Not with my career. Not with my family history. Not with the unspoken expectation that I'll carry on the Navarro name.

"I know a thing or two about parental disapproval." I laugh. "And the way your dad studies me in silence? I mean, textbook case of disapproval."

She laughs. "The bright side? This will probably be the only time in your life you have to see him, so I appreciate you doing this. Offering to stay here before the race week starts. Knowing you are going to be scrutinized and judged and everything in between when in the end it's all for show."

That's true. It is. So why do those words feel like an elephant foot on my chest and more importantly, why do I want Gavin to like me? Why does it matter?

"There's no need to thank me. You've dealt with plenty when it comes to my family, so I am definitely in your debt," I say.

Maddix Hart stood up to Dominic Navarro without batting an eye. Pretty fucking impressive. Not to mention the funny way it made me feel inside.

"Well, when it comes to my family, the vote is being held on Monday. You'll have won the board over and then for all intents and purposes, you're going to finally be rid of me cramping your style. That should make you happy enough."

"Will you stop?" I say and roll over on top of her, slanting my lips over hers. My hand threads through her hair between the nape of her neck and the blanket, and my thigh hooks over her body. But my lips taste and tease and tempt with a tenderness that even surprises me. I look down at her. Those expressive eyes. That beautiful face. *She's incredible.* "I'm sick of hearing about when this is over. Just stop, okay?" I kiss her again, this time a little deeper. A little longer. "Let's just enjoy this. The night. The now. This race. I don't want to talk about the after."

"But we never talk about any of it. Ever." Her voice breaks, and her eyes hold mine as her fingertips trail up and down my spine.

God. This woman. She deserves the goddamn world. A world I don't have to give her.

"I told you before that I've given more of myself to you than to anyone else I've ever met before. And I keep trying to give more when it's the hardest thing in the world for me." I lean my forehead to hers, the admission immediately causing panic to ricochet through me, even though I know those words are one hundred percent accurate. "I sat on a rooftop and drank alone in Mexico for God's sake because it wasn't the same without you there. Because in the bar, women were hitting on me and I had zero interest in them."

"Poor baby," she teases.

"You don't get it. It's not about that. It's about . . ."

It's about the fact that that's when I realized I was in love with you.

Every time the thought crosses my mind, it's like I can't breathe. It's like I've been force-fed oxygen through a ventilator for so long and now that I'm unhooked from it, I'm learning what real air tastes like and feels like for the first time.

"Cruz." She reaches up and cups the side of my face, but I can't look at her yet. I can't let her see everything because that *everything* is terrifying to me. And it's terrifying for reasons she clearly doesn't understand. Not after watching her with her mother and father all day.

Her parents and her have an unspoken connection I've never experienced. They could complete each other's sentences when sitting beside each other. They could look across the room and have a whole conversation without saying a word. There was an unwavering respect between them and a clear adoration.

It hit me several times—a pang—that I've never been a part of something like that—not even with my own parents . . .

"That has to be enough for you for now." I brush my lips to hers. "To feel it. To think it. To get used to it. But I can't ever promise what tomorrow brings. That's not . . . me."

But deep down, I know it's not enough for her.

It shouldn't be.

"You are enough," she murmurs and lifts her head so our lips meet. "This is enough."

"Maddix."

"No. Don't take the words back." Another kiss. A coax of her lips. "Show me with actions."

The kiss continues as we find each other in the moonlight.

It's soft sips of lips and quiet sighs of bliss.

It's the spread of her thighs and the murmured words of please.

It's the feeling of her gripping me as I push into her and the scrape of her nails on my ass as she begs me to fill her as full as possible.

It's the knowing each other's bodies so well now that we react without asking. We know without guiding. We please without urging.

It's making love when we can't utter the words.

When *I* can't utter the words.

When I use the actions to tell her I've fallen in love with her. Because she'll never hear the words.

I'll send her away before she can do the same to me.

CHAPTER FORTY-SIX

Maddix

SLEEP ELUDES ME, THE JET LAG FIERCE.

My heart is full from having him here with my family. In my space. In my home. But truth be told, I wondered if it would be weird coming back home. So much has changed about me over the past few months that I wasn't sure how I'd feel. I'm comfortable. I'm happy.

But I also know this town is too small for me now.

I was given the chance to spread my wings and moving back here permanently would be like clipping them.

But it's more than that. It's the unknown about the man breathing steadily beside me. I study him. The rise and fall of his bare chest. The line of his jaw. The curl of his lashes. His dark hair falling over his forehead. The fact that he's in my bed, surrounded by my things that makes him so very real.

It's the words my dad said earlier.

It's the ones Cruz couldn't say.

And it's the ones that his sister said.

Find the Cross behind the Cruz. He's the good man. He's the one he hides from the world. When you see him, you'll know the man I love. The one I'm proud to call my brother.

Cruz shifts and when he murmurs my name, my heart swells and squeezes and aches simultaneously.

I love him.

What that love is going to net me, I have no idea, but I do—and I'm sick of telling myself otherwise.

Wanting to capture this moment, this memory, this acknowledgement for my own personal memories, I reach for my cell that's on my nightstand and take a picture of Cruz.

I go to put my phone back but since I can't sleep, I decide to scroll through social media. I laugh at how much the platform shows me Cruz's posts since almost all of ours are joint now. It's like the algorithm knows I like him and keeps showing me pictures of him.

Wanting a walk down memory lane of the past few months, needing something to tell me this is all real—as real as Cruz sleeping beside me—I navigate to his page. My smile is automatic as the slide show of our relationship unfolds.

But I find myself pausing when I see some of the photos he posted. Ones I never knew he took of me. They're candid and real. Ones of me with my head thrown back and laughing. Others with my expression serious as I look at something in contemplation. Then there are some at the various race tracks, with me in the midst of his chaos.

Not a single one had I known he'd taken.

The odd thing is when I look at these photos, I see myself, but I see something equally as important. I see how Cruz sees me. I see me through his eyes.

And I'm touched and moved beyond words.

Their perspective is one of reverence. Adoration. Love.

My throat closes up and a single tear slides down my cheek. I'm not sure why seeing these makes me sad, but it does.

Is it because I know this is coming to an end?

Is it because I feel stronger for Cruz than he does me?

That's the crux of it. I don't. Tonight—in the field . . . these pictures . . . I know he feels the same way.

The question is, will he allow himself to feel? *To trust?*

They say love conquers all, but it's a hard fucking hill to climb when you're battling the giant who's guarded it your whole life.

CHAPTER FORTY-SEVEN

Cruz

E VERYWHERE I LOOK, THERE ARE HARTS. OR RELATIVES OF HARTS by one connection or another. Or friends of Harts they claim as family.

And food. My God, this family knows how to put out a spread of food that could feed a whole country.

It's not a long table in the family orchard complete with expensive wines and place settings as befits royalty. It's plastic tables placed sporadically and loaded with every kind of food imaginable. There are no formal servers or courses. It's dessert first for some. It's the main meal first for others. It's just alcohol for a few.

The laughter. It's a constant. Kids giggling and adults barking out and a few of the older people with a deep rumble that you can hear from any place in the yard.

The ease. There is an ease to this family. To their comradery. To their ribbing each other. To their difference of opinions that start out with raised voices and then end with laughter and pats on the back.

And then there is Maddix.

Christ, when she walked out in the yellow sundress with straps tied at the shoulders, a fresh face of lip gloss and mascara, and her hair piled on top of her head, she took my breath away. I've seen her in the glitz and the glamour of my life—she's learned to adapt and be a part of that—but it's the simplicity of this that knocked my feet out from under me.

I study her from my spot under a shady tree. She's sitting cross-legged on the grass with three little girls hanging all over her. They can't be older than four years old, but they are enamored with her and she with them. She looks over to her mom every so often and they share an exchange that's always followed by a smile or laughter.

She blows raspberries on little bellies and pretends to kiss the baby doll of another little girl. Her expressions are animated, and her smiles are bright.

Christ. I press a hand to my sternum where pressure stirs. Pressure seeing her like this has caused. I don't understand it and yet I can't look the fuck away.

She glances over my way, and when her eyes meet mine and her whole smile brightens, I swear to God, it tugs on the base of my balls and pretty much every other part of me.

"So, I hear you're into racing."

I glance over to the woman speaking to me. Her hair is dark and teased, her lipstick is dark pink, and her head is tilted to the side as she assesses me.

"Something like that," I say and hold my hand out. "Cruz."

She shakes it. "Aunt Becky." Her smile widens, and she glances around before looking back at me. "So I'm thinking you should just say yes now and save me all the explaining."

I laugh. "That's a trap if ever I've heard one."

"Damn. Did Sandy already get to you?"

I'm lost. "No. She didn't." I glance around. "Who's Sandy?"

She claps her hands and all but bounces on her toes. "Perfect. Then you'll be on Team Becky."

"Is Team Becky a winning team?" I ask.

"It is now, sugar." She hooks her arm through mine. "Let's go. The races are going to start soon."

I've raced a lot of things in my life. RC Cars. Bicycles. Karts. The gamut of Formula cars. But never, *never*, have I raced ride-on lawnmowers.

Yet here I am, a John Deere beneath me, my foot on the accelerator, and the whole mess of Harts screaming from the sidelines as I pull ahead of the other three lawnmowers on either side of me.

This is most definitely not the type of horsepower I'm used to. Not even close. But hell if it's not the same adrenaline rush as I cross the makeshift finish line first and throw my hands in the air in victory.

Maddix rushes over to me, wraps her arms around my neck, and plants a huge kiss on my lips. One I'm desperate to take deeper with her body against mine and my hands on the thin cotton of her dress, but know I can't.

No doubt Big Gavin is glaring at me from somewhere in this yard right now.

"You did it," she says as she leans back and looks at me, her grin goofy and eyes alive. She takes one of my hands and thrusts it in the air before she shouts, "Hart Games Champion!"

All I can do is laugh at the ridiculousness of this before pulling her backwards on my lap on the lawnmower and wrapping my arms around her waist. "This is insane. You're crazy," I say.

"Yep." She turns and plants a kiss on my cheek. "And that's why you love me."

She bounces up to go and hug a cousin or an aunt—or I don't know the fuck who—but I'm left staring after her, responding to her comment.

"It is why," I whisper. "One hundred percent why."

The feeling stays with me long after the victory celebration has worn off—a paper crown and checkered flag-draped teddy bear as the trophy—until I walk into the garage attached to the house to take a bag of garbage out.

I startle when I'm halfway across the space and see Gavin standing there, his hands braced on the front of an old Ford pickup, his head dipped down. He looks over to me and nods.

"Sir." It's all I say because I may have been intermingled with his family all day, but he sure as hell kept his distance from me.

He stares at me, lips pursed, eyes still judging. "God, I love my family but there is only so much crazy a man can take in a day."

I chuckle but don't respond.

"It's okay to agree. I won't hold it against you. They're all mine, and I find it overwhelming, so you must have your eyes crossed trying to remember who Aunt Becky is from Aunt Frankie."

I smile. "It is a lot. But it's not a bad thing. The love here . . . Christ, it's a love fest."

His smile widens as he looks back at the engine before nodding. "It is."

I put the garbage in the bin and then walk a few steps toward him, a sense that this conversation isn't over yet. Nor do I want it to be. "Sir?"

"She's my little girl," he says, and my feet quiet at the raw honesty in his voice. "She's . . ."

"Incredible? Beautiful? Intelligent?" I nod. "Yes, she is. She's also confident and sure of herself and her decisions. You should be proud of the daughter you raised."

"Oh, I am. I guess I'm not getting this whole thing. How it happened so fast. How the two of you are going to make it work. How you're not going to hurt her."

"Honestly? I don't know." Isn't that what I'm struggling with? All those same things? "We're opposite and yet we fit." I move beside him and look at the engine he's tinkering with. "What are you working on here?"

"Nothing. Everything. A problem I'll invent to fix so that I can take a break. Marriage and family . . . they're the best things in the world, they made me the man I am—but a man definitely needs a break now and again."

I bark out a laugh. I knew I liked him. "Then I guess I can't offer to help."

"Nope. Not unless you want to break something so you can fix it." He looks over to me, those green eyes of his locked on mine. "Same applies to Maddix. Don't break her just to say you fixed her."

I work a swallow. What must it be like to have a dad love you like this? To want to protect you. "Maddix can fix herself just fine."

He nods, his lips in a straight line as his hands grip the front of the car. "I like you, Cruz. I do. But I need you to promise me something."

"Yes, sir."

"You're a good man if the past few days are any indication. And if you don't love her, you're going to make whatever reason you break up with her about you. Not her. You live two very different lives and should this . . . run its course, be the man I think you are and take the blame yourself. Take it because you care about her. Take it because you know she's worth it."

His words stay with me long after the last empty beer bottle has been picked up and the strings of lights that zigzag the backyard have been turned off.

"Thank you for today," Maddix murmurs as she drifts off to sleep, a soft smile on her lips and my heart in her fucking hands.

She owns my heart. Believes in me.

And somehow her father does too even though I don't deserve that either.

"You're a good man if the past few days are any indication. And if you don't love her, you're going to make whatever reason you break up with her about you. Not her."

I will do everything I can to protect her heart, Gavin. Especially letting her go . . . even if it kills me in the process.

CHAPTER FORTY-EIGHT

Maddix

"**T**HIS IS ABSOLUTE INSANITY AND FUCKING INCREDIBLE ALL AT the same time," Tessa says as she spins around and takes the whole of the hospitality suite in, her pass on her lanyard swinging with her.

"It is, isn't it?"

I've gotten used to this—spoiled by it all really—but I still have a *pinch me* moment with each and every race I go to.

That I'm here.

That I'm here with Cruz Navarro.

That I'm in love with him.

I study him down below, standing just outside of the garage. The drivers' parade is over, the crew is checking last-minute items on the car, and Cruz is getting race ready as he talks with Otis.

"There something you want to tell me?" Tessa asks quietly as she steps up beside me.

"Not that I know of," I say just as Cruz looks up to me and gives a soft smile that has me sighing in the best way.

"Oh, because now's about the time you tell me that the fake turned to real."

"What do you mean? I told you we were sleeping together," I whisper. "That we were having fun."

"Yeah, but you never told me you had fallen for him."

I open my mouth to refute her, but then close it and nod before I have the courage to meet her eyes. "You're right. I have. But . . . there's no future for us. He has this crazy life and I have . . ."

"You have what? A life you're figuring out? A life that keeps adjusting? A life that you just realized you thought you wanted but aren't one hundred percent sure of anymore?"

"All of the above." Tears well in my eyes as I shrug and try to find my voice around them. "I love him, Tess."

"Have you told him?"

I shake my head. "I can't. If I do . . . I'm afraid what his reaction will be."

"Does he love you?"

I look back down at him. I know every mannerism. I can even assume what he's saying right now by them. "Yes. But . . . it's complicated."

"Okay. Why?"

"Because this is who I am. Someone who wears her heart on her sleeve and sees love as a good thing. And he's him. A man who guards everything and has only ever had love hurt him."

She nods in my periphery. "I could give you all the cliché advice in the world, but I can't fix anything. All I can tell you is that whatever happens, you need to put you first. You've been living in his world so it's easy to get caught up in it now . . . but five years from now, would that be enough?"

"We're not talking five years from now. We're talking right now."

"And yet the way you two look at each other says we're talking about a whole hell of a lot more."

"Maddix. This is incredible," my dad's voice booms as Amandine finishes their tour of the paddock and brings them back to the suite. "I mean . . ."

"I know. It's indescribable," I say as he and my mom walk up beside me and practically hang over the ledge as they gawk at anything and everything.

Tessa gives me one last knowing glance before she shifts out of the way to take a back seat for my parents. But it's when she moves that I see Dominic Navarro standing at the complete opposite end of the room. His arms are crossed over his chest in his usual pose as he surveys the team below.

I glance down to see where he's looking just in time to notice Cruz glancing up at him. Their eyes hold briefly, acrimoniously, before he shifts toward where I stand. My parents wave frantically at Cruz and yell out his name like excited kids. He just laughs and waves back.

"Good luck," my mom yells.

"Kick ass," my dad adds. My cheeks heat and eyes roll as some of the team looks our way.

But I catch the look on Cruz's face. His grin. The relaxing of his shoulders.

There is blanket acceptance from my parents. And blatant dissatisfaction from his dad. The unspoken absence of his mom.

What is he thinking as he watches us?

Is he wondering what it's like to have this kind of family? This kind of support? Is he jealous? Does he wish he had this too?

Talk about a tale of two worlds.

Of two lives.

Of all the reasons why we're incompatible.

CHAPTER FORTY-NINE

Maddix

"MADDIX?"

"Kevin? Hi." My voice is breathless. My mind's scrambled as I try to process the voice in my ear and the grin on Cruz's face as he slides beneath the sheets and looks up at me from between my thighs.

I glare at him and mouth the word *No* while I try and push at his head. His response is to slide his tongue over my clit at the same time he pushes two fingers into me.

"Oh," I bark the word out, without thinking.

"Am I interrupting something?" Kevin asks.

"No. Nothing." Cruz moves his fingers as his tongue circles and licks and tempts. My body reacts—hips thrusting into his face. "Just . . . finishing exercising is all."

Cruz blows on me. Then sucks.

"Good for you. Nothing like a good early morning workout."

"Not at all." I writhe and suppress a moan as he hooks his fingers and teases the bundle of nerves I have inside.

"The point of my call."

Concentrate, Maddix. Fucking . . . ohhhh, God, that feels good. And by the amusement in Cruz's eyes, he's finding this hilariously funny. Fingering me, licking me, trying to make me come while on the phone with our so-called matchmaker. "Yes? The point."

"The board voted in favor of going forward with the deal."

"Oh." Another croaked sound as Cruz presses a finger against the tight rim of muscles on my ass. My whole body jolts at the sensation. It's new and different and not intruding but enough to tease the overabundance of nerves there. "Great. That's"—Jesus, that feels incredible—"great."

"Should I tell Cruz or would you like to do the honors?"

My body aches with need. With greed. With the want for release but the need to suppress it right now.

"I can tell him." I fist a hand in Cruz's hair, making him chuckle against me so the vibration sends off another surge of shockwaves through me.

"Perfect. He wasn't answering when I just called."

"He's out." Or rather eating me out but we don't need to get specific.

"I'm thinking you keep up with this whole thing until he signs the paperwork. Maybe a few weeks after so it's not so obvious."

"Sounds good." And good isn't even in the same realm as what Cruz is doing to me.

"Oh, and Revive is asking about permission to recruit you. Give a think on that. I've got someone coming into my office right now." *That makes two of us.* "We'll talk later on it."

I end the call and drop the cell where it is.

"Cruz," I moan.

"That ache?" he murmurs and then dips his tongue into my core. "That burn?" A slide of his tongue back up so that his eyes meet mine and my arousal glistens all around his chin and mouth. "That's how I feel every minute of every goddamn day since meeting you."

He sucks on my clit, and I squirm as my body coils so tight I fear how violent the snap will be. He plunges three fingers into me.

"Come for me, Madds."

A lick.

A suck.

"Come on my tongue."

A quickening of his fingers fucking me.

"I want your taste seared into my memory."

Another circle over my clit.

And then my world explodes.

CHAPTER FIFTY

Cruz

"**F**INALLY. YOU'RE DONE. IT'S DONE," LENNOX SAYS. "I'M EXTREMELY impressed with your fortitude on this. It doesn't hurt that Maddix seems to be a total sweetheart . . . but you are one hundred percent done. Now you can sit back and reap the rewards of your patience to the tune of a lot of fucking money."

I snort. How should I feel right now? Especially after the bomb Kevin dropped on me during our discussion.

"The half-assed reaction is worrying me. Everything okay over there?" she asks.

"Good. Fine."

"Uh-huh. Sounds like it."

"I just have a lot on my mind," I reply

"Like? Care to share? Do I need to fly over there and pull it out of you myself?"

"Nah. I'm good."

She pauses, the line completely silent. "Personal or professional?"

"Thanks, Lennox."

I end the call and sink back into my chair, my finger on my lips and my eyes on the woman in front of me.

Maddix's back is to me. It's bare from the drape of the dress she's wearing. It comes down her shoulders and pools just above her ass, so I get a glimpse of her delicate shoulders. She is fastening a gold hoop to her ears, but her eyes meet mine in the reflection of the mirror she's getting ready in front of.

"What?" she asks.

You lied to me.

"Nothing." I force a smile, my chest constricting.

"You sure?" She turns around to face me.

Jesus. Does she have any clue what she does to me? Any clue?

"I'm sure." I rise from my seat. "You look stunning." Every part of me wants to move to kiss her neck, but I fight the urge and stay where I am.

"I'm nervous." She presses a hand to her stomach, oblivious to what I know.

"I apologize. Again. I told Sofia that I didn't want anything for my birthday. She planned it anyway."

"I'm glad she did." Maddix steps up to me on her toes and brushes a kiss to my lips. "I want to celebrate you."

I fight the urge to pull her against me and just hold on. I feel myself shutting down. I feel the brick wall being built second by second, layer by layer as I stare at her.

Sure Kevin called. Kevin said the deal was sealed. But not once did Maddix and I discuss what that meant for us. I had to head out to a meeting and when I came back, she greeted me in the doorway in what she called some celebratory lingerie. Little talking was done unless you count each of us groaning the other's name.

There was no room for conversation.

Just congratulations sex. Silly banter over great slogans for Revive that we both agreed we could drink right then so we could go a few more rounds.

But she didn't press for more from me. With me. Not then and not since. She didn't press for answers to the questions she'd asked me in Austin. The ones about *what's next* for us.

We're both well aware that it would look better if we continued the charade a little longer. It's only logical. *But for how fucking long?*

And why wasn't she honest with me?

She rests a hand on my cheek and looks into my eyes. "Everything okay?"

I nod. "Yeah."

"Lennox didn't surprise you with anything, did she?"

"No." *Only Kevin.*

"Congratulations on the deal being done."

"Thank you for doing this so I could get the deal done."

She nods and tilts her head to the side, eyes narrowing at me. "You sure you're okay?"

"Yes." I give in to the need and pull her against me. The feel of my hand on her bare back. The scent of her perfume. The need coursing through me that never seems to be sated when it comes to her. I kiss the side of her head and give myself a few more moments like this. A few more seconds where I can pretend that she's not going to leave and that she didn't think it was important enough to tell me. "Everything is fine."

CHAPTER FIFTY-ONE

Maddix

TALK ABOUT THROWING A GIRL INTO THE NAVARRO FIRE.

When Cruz said Sofia was throwing him a birthday dinner, the last person I expected to see there was Dominic Navarro. And I definitely didn't expect to be standing before el patriarca, his wise eyes staring into mine, and an amused smile gracing his weathered but still handsome face.

"I can't tell you how nice it was to finally get to meet you," he says, his accent thick, his eyes scrutinizing. "And while you're not Spanish, it seems you make mi nieto a very happy man, so I just might be able to overlook that."

My smile widens. I take zero offense to his words and actually find them and him quite endearing.

"At least I speak Spanish," I counter to which I receive a boisterous laugh. The man is spry for his eighties and with a personality to boot. I've laughed more in the last ten minutes talking to him and not a single chortle has been faked.

"That, you do," he says, and I follow his glance across the room. He meets Cruz's eyes—eyes that are filled with an unconditional love that makes my heart swell. At least Cruz has someone who looks at him that way. Someone he can need and admire who clearly reciprocates it.

The evening has been something of a haze. From walking in to find Sofia standing there, teeth sinking into her bottom lip as she nervously gauges if everyone's presence would be welcome.

A part of me understands her need to try and smooth things over between her brother and their father. I'm the first person to try and fix when there is any type of discord in my family. But the other part of me thinks this was the wrong place, the wrong time. This is Cruz's night to celebrate, not be on edge with a man he's currently—and to be frank, always—at odds with.

He deserved this time. To let loose. To relax. To hang with his friends. And now he's standing in the corner, drink in hand, eyes sweeping back and forth like a night watchman waiting for something bad to happen.

"It was a pleasure, Señorita Hart. Now I must get my beauty sleep. It takes a lot these days to look this good."

"Oh stop." I pat his arm and he laughs.

"And forgive Sofia for tonight. She's trying her hardest to hold these two together so she has a family. It takes nerve to do that. She's a Navarro through and through."

"There's no need for her to apologize for anything."

"Good. I'm glad you see it like I do." He motions to his nurse to come because he's ready. "I'd like you to come to the villa soon. For our family dinner. To see the other side of who we are. Next month or the month after."

A lump forms in my throat. I very much want that. To see Cruz with his family. To see where and who made him the man he is outside of his mother and father. But what will be of Cruz and me in a month or two? The deal will be done, will Cruz be done with us too? Will he miss his wild ways and the attention partying would bring to him?

"I'd like that very much."

"Good. Consider it done."

And with that, the nurse wheels el patriarca away. Cruz steps forward and squats down on his haunches to say goodbye to his grandfather. It had to have taken a lot for him to travel here to Monaco to surprise Cruz so I'm sure he's in awe that he did that for him.

Goodbyes are said and, the minute he leaves the space of the restaurant, it's like a vacuum occurs. The dynamo is gone and left in his wake are his family struggling to figure out how to coincide together with several of Cruz's friends in attendance.

Before I can make my way over to Cruz and snuggle up to him, there is a loud set of voices just outside the entrance to the patio.

And one of those voices I happen to recognize.

Oh. Shit.

If tonight wasn't weirdly dysfunctional and perfectly Navarro all at the same time—what, with Dominic's quiet, clenched jaw, with the effusive Sofia's nonstop talking as she tries to make everyone comfortable, the strained demeanor of Cruz himself, and the loud laughter from the couple of oblivious friends—it definitely became so when Genevieve Navarro waltzed in unannounced and clearly drunk.

"I'm here. We can start," she says, clueless to the fact that dinner ended well over thirty minutes ago. All of the dishes have already been cleared, and the cake has been cut and plated for those who want to indulge in it.

"Mamá . . ." Sofia says, her eyes flicking to her brother, then her dad, and then back to her mother.

By the expressions on everyone's faces, she wasn't expected to attend.

"What?" Genevieve says brashly as she walks up to a very stiff Cruz and gives him an obscenely loud kiss on the cheek. Or maybe it's only loud because the entire outside patio at the restaurant that had been reserved for the party, is dead silent. "No one is going to keep me from wishing my baby boy a happy birthday."

"Máma," Cruz says as he grimaces before taking a step back and out of her reach. "Thought we'd see you in Austin. Not here."

A light bulb goes on for me. Cruz searching the stands during testing. His checking of the guest logs. His foul mood and his request for some space as he spent the better part of a night on the roof of the hotel after the race.

"Something came up." She smiles sloppily. "You know how it goes."

"Something always seems to come up now doesn't it, Vieve?" Dominic says, stepping forward.

"Dom. Of course you'd be here. Imparting your wisdom. Holding tight with your iron fist." She picks up someone's half-drunken glass of wine from the table beside her and gulps it. "I would assume you'd have one of your trollops with you." She makes a show of looking around as my cheeks heat for Cruz and his sister. "Or is she waiting back in the hotel to suck your cock?"

"Mamá," Sofia warns, her shoulders sagging and tears filling her eyes as every non-Navarro here shifts uncomfortably.

Genevieve throws her head back and laughs like she doesn't have a care in the world while I watch Sofia shrink inside herself, Dominic harden, and Cruz disengage.

"Genevieve. Your behavior is uncalled for," Dominic says and for the first time ever, I see a flicker of emotion other than disdain on his face. Maybe it's sadness. Maybe disappointment. But I doubt it's about anyone but himself.

"Dom. Let's get real. I'm always uncalled for but considering I'm here, all will be forgiven." She turns and I wince when her attention lands on me. "Madison. How lovely to see you again. I was certain Cruz would have fucked you out of his system by now. I'm so glad he hasn't. Just another reason to piss Dominic off. But don't you worry, with time, you too can be part of this controlling, fucked-up family."

When she goes to reach for another drink, Dominic steps up and grips her wrist. "That's enough, Vieve. This is not the time nor place. See yourself back to whatever hotel you've charged to my card for the night and make sure you're out of town by morning."

And I thought he was callous with Cruz.

Is this what Cruz has had to deal with his whole life? No wonder he's so guarded about the intricacies of his family.

"You don't get to tell me what to do. No wonder you've turned our kids against me." She sneers.

There is complete sadness in his eyes when he stares at her. There is longing too and as much as I'd have compassion for anyone else in his situation, I don't for him. Dominic Navarro seemingly has none for anyone else but himself, so why should I waste mine on him? "You did that yourself and I'll never forgive you for that."

She shakes her head but then holds her hand up with a smirk on her face and begins to back away. Dominic stands like a gatekeeper, protecting all of us.

And I'm not sure I want him protecting me from anything.

But it's when I look back toward where Cruz was that I notice he's gone. Much about the same time everybody else does.

My heart sinks to my feet and my stomach pitches.

"Maddix?" Sofia asks with grief in her eyes.

"I'll go. Let me find him."

I can tell it's hard for her to step back and let me, but she does just that. "Okay." She reaches out and squeezes my forearm. "Please tell him I'm sorry. I didn't mean for any of this to happen. I wanted to do something nice. I wanted to—"

"I'm sure he knows and understands. This isn't your fault." I lean in and kiss her cheek and then leave.

The streets of Monaco are quiet tonight, the tourists busy doing other things, and the locals steering clear of them. I'm grateful for it as I make my way back to the house.

He's on the rooftop like expected. His elbows on the ledge, braced there, and his face looking out toward the ocean.

For the first time in the longest time, I don't know what to say to him. How to make it better. How to fix what his mom clearly broke tonight.

Or maybe it's always been broken and tonight was the first time the superglue failed to hold it together.

"Cruz." My voice is soft and there are questions in it. *Are you okay? Do you need to talk? What can I do to help you?*

"Please. I don't need . . . just go."

"I'm not leaving you alone." I step up behind him and press a kiss to his shoulder. "Not tonight."

"You don't get it, do you? You never could."

I get he's hurting, and I get he is looking for a fight, but the bite to his tone hurts way more than it should. "You need to stop punishing yourself for your mom. You're not why she left. You're not why she comes back when she feels overlooked or left out. You're why—"

"Why what? Why you were offered the job in New York and are moving there but didn't have the fucking guts to tell me?" he shouts, his voice breaking and the expression on his face breaking my own heart.

What the fuck? How does he . . .

"It's not like that."

"No? Then what is it like, huh? What excuse do you have as to why you accepted a job somewhere but didn't say shit to me? You going to wait till I head to the next race and then just disappear? You just going to up and walk away without saying a word? Are you—"

"What are you doing?" I raise my voice to the level of his when it all clicks into place. His thought processes. The ingrained assumption. "I'm not your mom. I'm not leaving you—"

"Could have fucking fooled me," he grits out, the words like a knife to my heart.

"Really? *Really?*" The last one comes out at a fever pitch. "How can you say that to me? We haven't discussed your deal in detail yet. We haven't discussed what happens next. But if there is anything you should have seen about me, it's loyalty. I stepped up to the plate for you to help you sign that stupid contract. And I'm the one who—" My voice breaks and the tears fall. "The one who is so goddamn in love with you, Cruz Navarro, that I love you when you refuse to acknowledge that you love me back."

The words come out like a weapon when those words never should be. Especially not to him.

Especially when love has never been a positive to him.

He stares at me as emotions flicker and fade over his features. Confusion. Disbelief. Anger. Fear.

And it's the last one that stays the longest. It's that one that makes my gut churn and the worry take root.

I reach out to touch him and he shrugs out of my touch. "Don't." The single syllable is more than a warning. It's a death knell.

"Cruz. I shouldn't have said it like that. I should have told you at my parents' house. Hell, even before then, but I didn't want to make this whole thing even more awkward than it was. You're you and I'm me and it was like we lived in the bubble where we ignored time and parameters . . . but now those are ending. For all I know, you're ready to move on to the next person because you haven't said anything and—"

"Have you said anything?" he demands. "Have you opened your mouth because, if actions speak louder than words, taking a job in New York says a whole hell of a lot."

"It was only *offered* to me a few days ago. Honestly, I was taken aback by the suddenness of it, but there hasn't been a right time to bring it up to you—"

"Yeah, there's never a right time to say goodbye. I get it. Why say it at all, huh?" He chuckles but it's ice cold. "I'm fucking used to that."

"Cruz."

He starts to stride off and I grab his bicep. He grits his teeth, but he stops and stares at me. "You know, I thought I was in love with you, but I'm not. I'm in love with the idea of you. Of this. But it'd never work because like you said, you're you—the perfect, moldable lackey—and I'm me—the fuckup you can't wait to leave. And neither of us are going to change, right? Now let me go, Hart, because I'm done playing this game."

Hart.

Not Madds.

Not Maddix.

Hart.

He's disengaged.

He shrugs out of my grasp and is at the door in seconds. I need something, anything, to snap him out of this train of thought. To make him hear me. To—

"*Cross.*" The word is out and his entire body jolts.

He turns and glares at me. His jaw ticking. Tears welling in his eyes. "What the fuck? Who told you about—goddamn Sofia. Trying to make every fucking thing right when all us Navarros can do is be wrong," he grits out. "You don't know Cross and you sure as hell don't get to call me that."

"Why? Isn't that who you are? Isn't that the man I love? The one who dances in the kitchen when he thinks I'm not watching? The one who can glance across the garage at me and I know exactly what he's thinking? The one who can't tell me the words he feels but shows me how he feels each and every day? Cross. He's the man I fell in love with. He's the man you've kept hidden from the world, Cruz, but not from me. I've met him. He's a part of you. And that man? *He's the one I love.*"

Silence stretches as seconds feel like hours. "Too bad that man doesn't exist anymore." He turns from me and walks out the door without another word. "You sure as fuck just made sure of it."

It takes everything I have not to go after him.

To beg him.

To convince him that I was going to tell him.

That I am madly in love with him.

That all he had to do was ask me to stay.

But I don't. I stand on the rooftop in the middle of Monaco with my heart on my sleeve and my emotions ground to a pulp at my feet.

CHAPTER FIFTY-TWO

Maddix

WE MOVE LIKE GHOSTS AROUND THE CONDO.

We don't exchange words.

We don't acknowledge each other.

We act like strangers who haven't been living together for three-plus months.

I give him time. I give him space.

But even with that, he doesn't react when I need him to. I have a job waiting for me. A dream on hold. A life I know now, more than ever, that I want to live, and it's a totally different one than I walked in here with. This new opportunity proves it.

But that opportunity has an expiration date on it.

"The CEO of Revive was impressed with your work when you were there," Kevin says.

"Wow. That's great." I glance over to where Cruz is leaning over the tire of the car, Otis at his side, as they point to something I'm clueless over. But I put a finger to my other ear and move out of the noise of the garage so I can hear better.

"It was more of an official call to see if it was okay to poach you from us and offer you a job."

I freeze momentarily before the excitement starts to surge through me. *"Okay."* I draw the word out, not certain what he said, if he's angry over this, or how I should react.

"I told them that it was one hundred percent up to you, but that you were a valuable asset that would be a perfect fit since you would know both companies."

A lump forms in my throat. "Thank you. I don't know what to say."

"Say yes to them, Maddix. It's a good opportunity. A huge step up that I can't offer you right now. One that will put you on a great path, with a promising future. Working with a well-known creative firm under any capacity is huge."

"I know." I still can't wrap my head around it.

"I told them what they should pay you. Moving costs. Temporary housing. I pushed hard for you, kid. The bonus? You'll still get to work with Cruz every now and again. Let's hope you don't hate him now that this is all said and done."

"No." I smile as I turn to look back at Cruz. "I don't hate him."

"Good. Be prepared for the call. It's coming within the next hour. They'll want you there by the end of next week."

The end of next week. Holy shit. That's . . . quick. Unexpected. Overwhelming.

I'm about to get everything I've been working toward. Everything. Cruz looks up across the garage at me and smiles softly before looking back at one of his crew members.

So why is the euphoria suddenly . . . sadness?

"Cruz."

"Hmm?" He doesn't look up. He's sitting on the couch, remote control in hand as he watches and then rewinds footage from the Mexico race over and over. Each overtake. Every error on the track. Each millisecond lost. His and other racers'. His need to improve with each and every race almost an obsession.

"Please. We need to talk. You can't keep giving me the silent treatment. I don't deserve it."

He stops the recording again but doesn't speak.

I step in front of the TV so that he's forced to look at me.

His eyes meet mine. "You didn't tell me." His voice is void of any emotion and I'd give anything if he would scream or yell. But he doesn't. He just sits there with his voice impassive and my heart on the line.

"You didn't give me a chance to tell you. We were busy. I was contemplating."

"And yet you accepted the job that starts in three days, and you didn't have the guts to tell me."

I move to sit on the table in front of him. This house that held such warmth is so very cold now. "I was trying to figure things out."

He smiles but it holds no warmth. "I have the jet fueled and waiting for you at the airport to take you to your new city. Your new life. Just say the word."

Ask me to stay, Cruz. Ask me to fucking stay.

"I love you."

He nods. "So you said." His words hurt more than they should. The callous nature of them just protecting the wound over his own heart.

I know that and yet it does nothing to ease the pang in the middle of my chest. "Don't do this," I whisper. "Don't end us like this."

"Like what? Face-to-face instead of running and hiding like you were planning?"

"That's not what I was doing. I was contemplating it. I was waiting to talk to you."

"I'm here." He throws the remote down beside him. "Talk."

"What do you want from me? To give up my life for you? To walk away from a dream? All for a man who can't even look at me and tell me he loves me?" He blanches at my words. "Because you do, Cruz Navarro. You love me, but if you're not brave enough to say it? If you're not courageous enough to put your heart on the line and take the risk of it being hurt like I have, then you don't get to keep me." Tears I don't remember shedding stream down my face as I stand up.

Say something.

Anything.

But his response is the pulse in his jaw and the clenching and unclenching of his hands.

"Love takes sacrifice from two people, Cruz. Not just one. It demands vulnerability from both of us. It requires us to be there for each other, to trust one another, even when we fear losing the other person. I know you expect me to leave you. I know that all you've known is for love to hurt. But that's not how it's supposed to be."

"I told you the jet's ready for you."

"And I told you I love you. I told you to ask me to stay. I told you to risk your own security for me . . . and you can't do that." My voice breaks and my body hurts from the fear that I know to be true—I've already lost him. Hell, I lost him before I had him because of his parents.

I stand there in front of him. He's like an impenetrable wall so full of scars and seams that he doesn't realize I'm standing here knocking, begging for him to let me in.

"Then that's it? All of this and we're left with nothing?" I throw my hands up.

"Isn't that what it always was? Fun? Nothing? A ruse that let us play pretend until reality set in?"

"At first, yes. But not . . . not after, no." I step forward, lean over, and press a kiss to the side of his cheek. I hiccup over the sob, but he doesn't flinch in the slightest. "I love you, Cross Navarro. I love you for everything you are and for everything no one sees." I stand back up with tear-blurred eyes. "You're letting her win. You're letting him win. Pretty ironic for a man who has spent his own life chasing each and every victory." I take a step back. "And yet you don't choose to chase me."

I turn on my heel. It takes everything I have to put one foot in front of the other and walk away, stepping over the pieces of my heart shattered on the floor at his feet.

But I do.

I pack my bags.

I stand at the door and watch him staring at the television frozen in time.

I whisper goodbye.

And when the jet takes off and we fly over the city that has been my home for several months, I press my hand to the glass of the window and say, "I'll always love you."

CHAPTER FIFTY-THREE

Cruz

THE JET RUMBLES IN MY CHEST AS I STAND ON THE OUTSKIRTS OF THE fencing and watch it take off.

As I watch the only woman I've ever loved, leave me.

My chest aches in a way I never knew was possible.

In a way that tells me I'm clearly not the man she thinks I am.

In a way that shows me I'm not the one I thought I could be either.

"You're letting her win. You're letting him win. Pretty ironic for a man who has spent his own life chasing each and every victory. And yet you don't choose to chase me."

She's not wrong. But victory on a track takes a very different set of skills and determination. I understand those. *I live those.*

"Goodbye, Madds," I whisper as I watch the jet become a speck in the sky. "I love you."

I love you so much it hurts.

I love you so much I'm letting you go.

I made a promise to your father.

One I am keeping.

Because I can't give you what you need right now. And what you deserve is the world and every fucking thing in it.

How can I promise you the world when I struggle to hand over my heart?

I clench my fingers through the chain-link fence and then turn and walk away.

Back to my condo that smells like her.

To my kitchen that has her lipstick stain on a wineglass.

To my balcony where her suntan lotion lays on its side.

To my rooftop where all I hear is the plea in her voice the last time we were up here.

She's fucking everywhere.

And I think that's what hurts even more. Because despite what she thinks, I am not a man worthy of the love of someone like Maddix Hart.

Those who say they love me, leave me.

It's inevitable.

It's fact.

No more distractions.

At least someone in this whole mess will be happy by that.

Fuck you, Papá, for being right.

Just, fuck you.

CHAPTER FIFTY-FOUR

Maddix

"ANOTHER LATE NIGHT?" HEIDI ASKS AS SHE POKES HER HEAD into my office doorway.

"It's only been two weeks. I still have so much to learn and figure out."

"At this rate you're going to burn out. Maybe you should take a day and go home at like a normal hour."

I smile at my co-worker. "Soon. Once I get caught up, I will."

"Okay. I'll let the doorman know you're still up here."

"Thanks."

But the minute she leaves, I sag in my seat and close my eyes. The past few weeks are a blur. Days filled with learning the ropes here. Feeling lost and then just when I grasp something, tumbling back into feeling lost again. Endless meetings where I have to put on an enthusiastic face to hide the fact that I feel like I'm dying inside. Lunch dates with potential clients where I hear them ramble on about things that, frankly, I've lost all interest in.

Is this my dream job? Yes. Is it full of exciting things I once yearned to learn and know? Again, yes. But my heart just isn't in it. It's been shattered. Cruz did that to me and I keep hoping I'm going to see the light at the end of the tunnel but right now, I'm not. Right now, work is the only thing that's keeping me hanging on, so I stay here as long as I can to be as busy as I can.

But then there are the nights. Because as much as I'm exhausted from working long days, I'd rather work myself to death than go home to my empty apartment where I sit and think and want. I don't have friends here yet, so

I'm always so . . . alone. Which is a strange feeling when you've been with someone almost every day for months. It's where I open my social media, noting how my algorithm has been completely curated to show me every single damn Formula 1 post known to man.

Cruz smiling as he signs an autograph for a fan.

Cruz looking into the camera.

Cruz qualifying.

Speculation runs rampant about where I am considering I've been there every race for months. We've broken up. I'm busy with a new job. He's left me because I was horrible to him.

I scour the headlines, desperate to see something, anything to either tell me to keep holding on or to tell me I'm fucking crazy for wanting to hold on. But there's nothing. No crazy partying. No cozying up to other women. It's Cruz and his racing and an occasional picture that his team has posted of him. I'm not sure if that makes things worse or better. All I know is that I scrutinize every image to try and see a sign that he misses me as much as I miss him. That he's as utterly miserable as I am.

Not even the excitement of a new job and moving to a whole new city abates the crushing weight in my chest. Not even the care packages from my mom—*gifts from home*—lessen the despondency. My parents know about Cruz and that our relationship has ended. Mom has been sympathetic, surprised, and caring. Dad has been quite silent, which doesn't surprise me. He wasn't wrong about Cruz—he was a man who could crush my heart.

Thankfully, though, there has been Tessa. And at that thought, my cell rings, right on time.

"Hey."

"Well, you sound like a woman who has been punched in the tits. Jesus," she teases. She's been the best of friends during this whole thing, and I am so very grateful that I have her.

"It's been a rough one. Not going to lie."

"Okay, so this is the part of a breakup where I tell you to stick to your guns. I know you're hurting and you're sad and everything in between but, you, Maddix Hart, deserve the *I love yous* and the whole freaking fairy tale. And oddly enough, he does too. But you can't cave now. If he doesn't see it on his own, then he'll never see it."

"I know." I rub the heel of my hand over my breastbone. "It just hurts so damn much."

"I know it does. It does him too."

I sigh. "Thanks."

"Same time tomorrow night?"

"Yeah."

But when I hang up and stare at my phone, I just want to pick it up and call him. Talk to him. Breathe the same silence as him.

Because yes, I still love him.

It would be so much easier if I hated him, but I don't.

I hate what was done to him. I hate what years of abandonment has done to his thoughts.

But I don't hate him.

I don't think I ever could.

CHAPTER FIFTY-FIVE

Cruz

"**W**HAT THE ACTUAL FUCK, MAN?" LACHLAN EVANS PUSHES HIS way past my crew and into my face. The guys go to hold him off but I just step into the space.

Maybe if he hits me, I'll actually feel something, because all I feel is numb. Nothing. Just utter white noise.

Well, all except for when I think of Madds. When I think of her, my body hurts in ways I never thought possible. Mind. Body. Soul.

I stare at the fury raging in Evans's eyes and shrug before turning and walking the other way. The fight in me is gone. It has been for weeks.

"Don't you walk away from me," he thunders as he pushes me from behind. "What's your problem, Navarro? You can impede on the track over and over, but you can't fight me in the pits?"

"It's not worth it." This time when I walk away, he lets me. But it's an hour later, after a shower and some press time, that Lachlan is waiting for me in the paddock to walk out to the parking lot.

"What do you want?" I groan when I see him.

"We go back a long way, right?" he asks, falling in step beside me.

"Your point?"

"My point is it's fucking awesome if your head is all over the fucking place like it is right now because on the track you'll slip up and I'll be able to fly right past you. And my car is a fucking train wreck—Rossi's too," he says of his teammate. "So I'll take every goddamn advantage you give me. But that also means you have half a chance of getting yourself or someone else killed. Your head's not right. It's not in it. Hell, it's not even in this fucking universe. So you either tell me what the fuck is going on, or I go to Otis and tell him you're drinking in the pits."

"What the actual fuck?" I spit the words out.

"I'm worried about you. Enough said."

"You wouldn't—"

"Try me."

I stop and stare at him. The god-awful pressure of the past few weeks is weighing down on me like the world's on my shoulders. "It's Maddix."

"Tell me something I don't know."

"She went back to the States."

"As is noted in every fucking post and article about you. Should I assume she's in the States and you didn't want her to go?"

I scrub a hand through my hair and sigh. I don't want to fucking talk about how I failed. Sofia has been in my shit since the night of my birthday, trying to get me to *talk about my feelings*. Fuck that shit. It's not going to bring Maddix back.

My sister is . . . her attempts are appreciated, but I deserved what happened to me. Not my mama's bullshit—*that's on her*. But Maddix was right. If I can't tell her I love her, then what's the point of her staying?

But I hate this. Every fucking thing about this. My empty penthouse. The silence when it used to be her humming. The empty bed beside me. The drive through town without her enamored with something trivial that makes me smile.

Fucking everything.

I could beg her to come back, but isn't that just opening me up to being told she's leaving again?

Evans isn't asking any of this. I'm sure he doesn't give a flying fuck, and yet I find myself saying, "At first, I wanted her nowhere near me. Then I thought she was a fun distraction I could get over when I needed to. But now she's fucking gone and she's all I think about."

"So you love her, then." A plain, no-nonsense, statement.

"I do."

"And you've told her this and she still left?"

"Not exactly."

"So she left because you didn't tell her this?"

"Partially. But . . . fuck, man, how do we . . . how do . . . she can't give up her life to follow me around pursuing mine."

"Isn't that up for her to decide? Women are resilient fucking creatures. Way more than men. Shouldn't that be up to her to decide what her life should be? Because I've met the woman. She's bright. She was able to work her other job while following you around so who says she can't do the same with this new job?"

I hang my head and nod. "She could. But—"

"But what?"

"But why would she want to?" I ask.

"Because she loves you."

"We haven't discussed your deal in detail yet. We haven't discussed what happens next. But if there is anything you should have seen about me, it's loyalty. I stepped up to the plate for you to help you sign that stupid contract. And I'm the one who is so goddamn in love with you, Cruz Navarro, that I love you when you refuse to acknowledge that you love me back."

"Because she loves me?" I see her standing in front of the television, eyes full of tears, begging me to ask her to stay. Fuck. I wanted her to stay. I want her by my side. "She asked me to ask her to stay."

"There's your answer. She did. You do. I mean, fuck, man, if you love her back and can't live life without her, then do something the fuck about it. You ask her to come back. You chase after her. You let her know." He pats my shoulder. "Actions, my brother. You need to say the words, but actions too."

"Fuck." The word is more for me than him.

"Yeah. I know. But if she's worth it, you better learn to grovel. Grovel but don't respond when she does. Grovel so she wants to talk to you but can't. Grovel until she wants to fly here on the drop of a dime because she can't wait another second. Women love that shit."

Grovel?

Fuck . . . here goes another thing I've never done before, let alone for a woman.

CHAPTER FIFTY-SIX

Maddix

"**W**HAT THE ACTUAL FUCK." I FREEZE IN THE DOORWAY OF MY office and take in the sight.

There has to be fifty bouquets of dahlias filling up every surface in there. It's a jaw-dropping display in every color and every species. They are simply stunning.

I move to them. I touch the petals. I remember those early days together. And I fight back the tears that threaten.

But it's the note in the card on my desk that has the softest smile forming and a surge of hope filling my heart. My hand goes to my chest as I read it.

Madds—

It might take some time. But I'm going to win you back. I'm learning to be the man you deserve.

—Cross

Every part of me who has dared to hope over the past few weeks feels like it has broken free from a glass cage with those three simple sentences.

He loves me.

He wants to make this work.

In the midst of my deepest despair, when I'd wish for sleep to come and then pray it didn't—because I knew my dreams would be filled with him— this is what I wanted.

Tears well in my eyes and a lump of emotion burns in my throat.

I clutch the card in my hand but then read it again. L _ _ _?

What the hell does that mean? Does it matter? I know what it means. Clearly, he has a plan for what it means.

I can't stop staring at the garden my office has become and once the delayed shock wears off, once this really sinks in and I know I'm not dreaming, I can't get to my cell fast enough.

I sink into the sound of his voice on his voicemail and deflate simultaneously. It's the time difference. He has to be asleep. *Pick up the phone.* "Hi. It's me." Why do I sound so tentative when this is what I want? *Because I'm scared to believe this is real.* "It's good to hear your voice even if only this voicemail. Thank you for the flowers. They're . . . gorgeous and overwhelming and—*I miss you.*" The first tear slips over. "That's the main thing. I. Miss. You."

I let the message record my silence as I try to figure out what else to say next but know that everything else left to say, I want to say it to him. Need to say it to him.

With the call ended, and as I sit in a sea of dahlias, I breathe for what feels like the first time in forever. And then I scramble to take pictures of this obscene scene in front of me to send Tessa.

She's going to have a field day with this.

I hit send to her. No words. Just the pictures. And when my phone alerts a text back, I assume it will be her.

I'm wrong.

> **Cruz:** I'll earn the O. The V. And the E. Once I do, then you can decide if you want to forgive me.
>
> **Me:** I already know the answer.
>
> **Cruz:** I'm glad. It'll make earning it that much easier. But let me earn it, Madds. Let me prove to you how much you mean to me. Let me prove that you make me a better man. You'll know when to answer me when you see it.

I reread the text exchange over and over. A part of me wants to get on the next jet to Monaco—or wherever he is—and tell him he's forgiven. The other part is standing in my office, a smile toying at the corners of my mouth, a heart bursting with every emotion imaginable, and a thought of, "yes, he needs to prove it. To earn me back. To show he values me and my heart.

But man, it would be so much easier to run back into his arms and just sink into the comfort of him.

I jump when my cell rings and I scramble to answer it. Yes, I should know it's not him, but that doesn't mean I don't hope otherwise.

"Girlfriend, that man has got it bad."

My smile goes to a full-blown grin. "Tessa."

"Did I tell you or did I tell you?"

"You did."

"Say the words."

"Oh please." I roll my eyes but it feels so damn good to smile. To laugh.

"Say it or we're no longer friends," she teases.

"We will still be friends but I'll say it anyway, because it's true. You, my dearest Tessa, were right."

"Do you know what else I'm right about?"

"What's that?"

"He's the one."

Those three words stop me as steadfast as the dahlias in my office did. Reason being? I think so too.

Isn't that why all of this has hit me so damn hard? Because I never knew I could love someone, miss someone, want to be with someone, as much as I have Cruz these past few weeks. And not just for the big things, but for the little things. The fleeting glances across the room. His hand on my lower back as he walks past me. The way he hums softly while washing the dishes. The way he takes his helmet off and looks immediately for me.

There are a million reasons I've fallen in love with Cruz Navarro yet, it's all of the little ones that mean the most.

"I know," I whisper. "I know."

CHAPTER FIFTY-SEVEN

Maddix

"**A**RE YOU WATCHING WHAT I'M WATCHING?" TESSA ASKS.

"What time is it?" I ask groggily, but know damn well what time it is. I had just dozed off in the middle of working and had forgotten to set my alarm to watch the race.

"Who cares about the time. Turn on the race."

"What? Is he okay?" I fumble with my television and find the race. Truth be told, I'm on the couch where I fell asleep as I waited for the race to start.

"He's fine." The beat my heart skipped catches up. *He's fine. He's okay.* "Actually, he's kicking ass."

"Don't scare the shit out of me like that." I half laugh, half sigh as I stare at the screen, waiting for them to show Cruz's car so I can see with my own two eyes that he's okay.

And there he is. There's his car and the flash of telltale orange. He's okay.

"And it seems he's left you a little message," she says cryptically.

"What is that supposed to mean?"

She's quiet as I search and search until my sigh in exasperation spurs her on. "Wait till they switch to his in-car camera," she says.

I wait patiently for them to cycle through the different racers and their cameras. And when they get to Cruz's, it takes me two seconds to see it.

My grin is automatic.

My hand to my heart and me sitting up straighter even more so.

There is a place on the halo that cages in the racers and protects them that they often put stickers or advertisements for their sponsors. But Cruz's sponsorship sticker is gone. In its place is a sticker that says "L O _ _ You, Madds" with a heart right after.

But let me earn it, Madds. Let me prove to you how much you mean to me. Let me prove that you make me a better man.

He's not only trying to prove it to me—declare it to me—but also to the world. Weeks ago he couldn't say the words and now he's telling everyone.

I feel like I'm floating on air. He's trying. He's proving. He's . . . *being Cross.*

"Your silence says you're caving." Tessa laughs.

"My silence says who fucking wouldn't?"

"Agreed. Any sensible woman would feel the same . . . but don't you cave. Make the man earn those last two letters. Hell, if it were me, I'd make him earn the YOU and your whole damn name, but—"

"That's crazy."

"It is."

"It's hard enough as it is waiting this long when I knew my answer before I even walked out of his place and back into this new life."

"Hmm," she murmurs and I immediately pause.

"What? I know that sound. I know you're holding back."

"I love you, you know that, right?"

"Tess?"

"How are you going to do it? How are you going to live your life, chase your dreams, be the woman you've been striving to become and be his girlfriend?"

"Where is this coming from?" I ask as Cruz fends off an attack from Spencer Riggs.

"This is coming from a friend who wants you to have it all—the man, the job, the whole fucking dream—but not give more of you than he does of him. It's just . . . I'm a little protective of you."

"Thank you. I know you are. And . . . I don't know, Tess. Have you ever wanted something so bad in your life—this job, this chance—and then when you get there it falls flat? This job is falling flat and not because I don't love it but because the other half of me is missing. So yes, I want it all. I intend to try and figure it all out. And I plan on having my cake and eating it too. I'm just trying to figure out how."

"Okay. I'm sorry for dampening the moment, but you're my person and I just want to make sure you're putting you first."

"I know and I love you for it. I also love Cruz in a way I never knew imaginable. In a way that I see in my mom's eyes when she looks at my dad. And that's strange to me because never have I ever thought that would be possible. I just thought that was something from the past . . . not something that still happens nowadays. So I'm willing to do what it takes to have that kind of love and have what I need to be fulfilled too."

"Okay. I'm glad. I just needed to get that out before I tell you that he's winning me over with each and every step he's taking."

"Are you caving?" I tease.

"Who fucking wouldn't?" she repeats and we both laugh.

But when the phone call ends and I watch the podium celebration, every bone in my body wishes I were on a flight to him.

And when the text comes across, I jump for my phone.

Cruz: That P2 was for you.

CHAPTER FIFTY-EIGHT

Maddix

"THIS IS GETTING RIDICULOUS AND AWESOME AND YOU ARE SO freaking lucky."

I look up from my seat at Heidi and narrow my eyes. "I'm not following." I say the words but I'm already standing from behind my desk and making my way toward her. "What are you talking about?"

"Look out the window of the conference room," she says drolly but her smile gives away that it's something exciting.

I make it across the opposite side of the floor in seconds and then recoil in shock when I take in the extremely large banner that has been rolled down off the top of the building across from us.

There are four separate images. The first one is of Cruz standing in a field of dahlias holding a huge sign with the letter L above his head. The second is him standing on the rooftop of his complex—a place only I'd know since I've been there with him—holding the letter O above his head. The third image is him on a Jet Ski in the middle of the Mediterranean, standing on its seat, with the letter V held above his head. And the last one is him sitting in his Formula 1 car, helmet on, buckled in, holding a blank sign above his head—for what I can assume is an E to be earned later.

"Girl, he has got it BAD for you," Heidi murmurs. "Do you know how fucking expensive some shit like that is? To rent out the side of a building in the middle of New York."

I just murmur because money isn't an object to Cruz Navarro. And it's not about the money. It's about Cruz telling the world how he feels without being embarrassed or closing up over it. It's him putting it all out there when I know he is fearful that he could make this effort, profess his love, and I could still walk away. I could still abandon him . . . I could still be his mom to him.

"He's telling the world he's not afraid anymore. He's telling *me* he's not afraid," I murmur more to myself than to anyone. "I need to text him, to . . ." I look up again and am staggered by the sight of it. By the growth of this man.

I walk hurriedly to my office and stop when I go to grab my phone because there is a small black box on top of it with an equally small card.

With a glance around and an acknowledgement that he most definitely has helpers in this building, I open the card and sigh when I see his handwriting.

Madds—
    I finally figured out a name for us. I think it fits. See if you can figure it out.
—Cross

I open the black velvet box to find a stunning diamond tennis bracelet. It's segmented with an X and then a heart, each section linked by a round diamond. I stare at the glittery diamonds and then finally get it. *CrossHart.*

Our public, silly celebrity nickname he said we had to have that first outing in Amsterdam. He's finally figured it out.

CrossHart.

I run my fingers over his handwriting, over his name, and over the bracelet, almost as if in doing so I can feel his touch.

I know I'm not supposed to call him, but I can't resist. His voicemail answers in seconds, and I imagine how hard it is for him to push me to voicemail.

"Cruz. The banner. The bracelet. The nickname. It's all too much. I appreciate it and will cherish it always, but I don't need stuff. *I just need you.*"

And then I sink back in my chair, with the greatest sense of peace I've had in forever. *He loves me. He really loves me.*

CHAPTER FIFTY-NINE

Cruz

SHE'S GOING TO KILL ME FOR THIS.

Absolutely fucking kill me.

And I couldn't be happier.

I glance at the computer again and click the button. Money transferred. Student loans gone.

Maddix Hart is a force to be reckoned with, and the last thing she needs holding her back is something I took for granted. A good education. Access to one without being tied to its debt for the rest of her life.

Loose ends.

It's what I'm tying up. What I'm trying to take care of.

And now the biggest one of all. One that has my heart in my throat and me wiping my hands on the legs of my pants.

Might as well get this over with while I can.

The phone rings several times before the gravelly voice answers. "Gavin Hart. How can I help you?"

"Gavin? Mr. Hart? It's Cruz Navarro. Do you have a second?"

CHAPTER SIXTY

Maddix

"Y OU'RE ON MY SHIT LIST, NAVARRO," I SAY AND SIGH AND THEN
smile, staring wide-eyed again at the email stating my student loans
have now been paid in full.

This is not what I wanted. Him helping me out. Him taking care of
things. I just want him and my patience is beginning to wear thin.

I pick up my phone to text him.

> **Me:** I guess I'm now making my student loan payments to you. Thank you,
> but I can't accept this generosity.
>
> **Cruz:** It was either that or buy you a penthouse in New York. I figured you
> could stomach the student loans more.
>
> **Me:** Cruz.
>
> **Cruz:** I love when you sigh out my name like that. Don't look now. Knock.
> Knock.

What in the—

"Delivery for you, Maddix," one of our interns says as she walks into my
office and places a folder on my desk.

"Thanks."

"The courier said it was urgent."

"I—oh—okay," I say, so distracted by Cruz's text that it takes me a second to realize that the folder might be the knock, knock.

And then once it registers, I scramble to tear it open as fast as I can.
Inside is a plane ticket. It's not one like I've ever seen before so I stare at it
for a few seconds before turning it over.

Your boss has approved some much-needed downtime. Take this ticket to the car waiting out front. I'm about to earn that E.

—Cross

I stand up. I sit down. I grab my purse and anything I think I need as my hands start to shake and heart begins to race. Then I run out of my office without the ticket so I have to go back in and grab it.

My co-workers give me knowing glances and cryptic smiles as I say goodbye.

The elevator takes forever to reach my floor and then descend.

The town car, with its blacked-out rear windows, waits patiently for me at the curb.

We are driving within seconds. Sure I've been living here, but I feel more alive than I've felt during the entire time. Right now I feel hopeful, excited, and ready for whatever comes next.

So long as whatever it is includes Cruz.

I don't recognize the airport as we drive into its grounds as it's definitely not JFK or La Guardia. But within seconds, we pull off to what I now know to be Cruz's jet.

"Here we are, Miss Hart. Feel free to head up and inside."

The first thing I notice is the rug beneath the portable stairway onto the jet is covered with the letter E in all different sizes. The stairwell steps are covered with large E stickers in various colors.

I take each step with my heart in my throat and a pocketful of hope.

When I step inside the jet, Cruz is standing there, holding a cardboard E.

I don't think I have ever felt so much love and relief flood through my body as I do in this moment.

It's him.

It's really him.

I think I gasp. I know I say his name as I take in everything around him. The dahlias lining the cabin. The champagne. The balloons. Cruz standing there with undeniable love in his eyes.

"Hi, Madds. Fancy meeting you here."

"What? Hi. I mean . . . Cruz."

"This is where we started. Here. On this jet. When I pulled you into my lap to prove a point—that we could pull this off. It was then I knew I was in a shitstorm of trouble. You just fit. In my lap. In my arms. In my life. You sat down and tried to pretend I didn't affect you and from then on, I spent every second of every minute of every day pretending you didn't affect me either. But I failed. Because not only did you affect me, you scared me. You made me want to be more. You made me want to be better. And I'm sorry that it took you leaving for me to realize it. For me to own it. So I'm giving you this E—if you'll have it. It stands for Everything. As in you're my everything. That I think about. That I want. That I need. Just you. Just this. Just us. Everything else is just outside noise we can figure out."

I move to him. I can barely see through the blurry tears nor breathe over the emotion balled in my throat, but I know his arms wrapped around me will fix it all. Will make it worth it.

I sink into the firm feel of him, the scent of his cologne, the sound of his sigh, the steady beat of his heart against my cheek.

And I feel like I'm home for the first time since I left him all those weeks ago.

What are you willing to sacrifice, Hart?

Anything. Everything. If Kevin only knew when he was asking me that question how my answer would change over time, I'm not so sure he'd ask it anymore.

He leans back and frames my face and kisses me. It's slow and sweet and everything I've missed and craved and wanted.

He rests his forehead against mine.

"I need you, Madds. I'll keep learning, keep trying, keep accepting that you love me and aren't going to leave me, but I might slip up at times. I might spook. And when I do, just know it's only because I love you so much it hurts. I want you to sow the rest of your oats with me. As a team. Fighting for one another. Fighting against the world—just the two of us. I never stopped loving you. I simply believed you couldn't possibly love me . . . and that was wrong of me. I just hope—"

I launch myself harder against him. My lips claiming and hands owning. "I never stopped loving you, Cruz. Not for a single minute." But it's then that it hits me. What Tessa said about caving. About giving up my dream. About the false bullshit answer I gave her. It's fine if I say it, but I need him to understand it too. "But . . ."

"But what?" Panic flickers in his eyes.

"But I still need my life. My job. My goals. I love you, Cruz, but you can't be my beginning, middle, and end."

294 | K. BROMBERG

He squeezes my hands and his smile steals my heart. "I don't want to be your beginning, middle, and end. I want to be your bookends. The person you leave in the morning and come home to at night. The person who takes care of you but allows you to be you. I want you to fit me in your life. I want you to let me be a part of yours. I want you to let me love you." Cruz's hands frame my face and he bends his knees so his eyes are level with mine. "I love you, Maddix Hart. I love your quirkiness. I love that you love your family. I love your family and how they love you. I have loved watching you grow over the past few months into the woman you are today. The woman who steps up to the plate, reaches for goals, and then smashes them. And I loved how you walked away from me to force me to face my own fears."

"Loved?" I chuckle.

"Well, not really, but you took a stand. You made me see you knew your worth. Watching you walk away was the hardest thing I've ever had to do. But in the process, you taught me more than you'll ever know." He presses a kiss to my lips. A kiss I've craved for weeks and dreamt of at night. "And while I watched you do all of this, as I witnessed you come into the woman you are, I fell in love with you. Every part of you."

He leans back, his eyes on mine, and I know he means it. I know he loves me.

And it's the best damn feeling in the world.

"Thank God you hate the color red," I murmur and press my lips against his. "Or you might have picked one of those folders."

He chuckles. "What I thought was going to be the worst day of my life, gave me the best thing ever in my life. You. So what do you say, Madds? Did I earn the E?"

"Everything?" I ask, my smile growing.

"Everything."

I press my lips to his and kiss him. "You definitely earned it."

CHAPTER SIXTY-ONE

Maddix

I MISSED THIS.

It's not like I missed a lot of races, but I missed the charged atmosphere. The anticipation. The rumble of the cars in my chest and the roar of the crowd.

And Christ, how I missed the way Cruz looks in a fire suit, walking toward me before he climbs into his car and kisses me senseless.

The funny thing is I almost missed it because I was too busy staring at Cruz's post. The one of us with me on his lap, head snuggled under his neck, sound asleep, and his caption. *Won my good luck charm back. Now all is right with the world. LOVE this woman with all my heart. #CrossHart*

How did he go from afraid to declaring it to posting it outright?

How did I go from misery a week ago to my new boss telling me to attend the race and make sure branding for Revive was present in all aspects? I'm sure Cruz gave a little push on that, but I'm not going to say I mind.

Maybe in the future I will, but not this first race with us back together.

"Wish me luck, Madds?" he asks as he links his fingers with mine.

"I don't think you need any wishing, but I'll wish it anyway." I lean in for the kiss. This time I know there are cameras around and I one hundred percent know the kiss isn't for show. It's in the tenderness of his lips. In the way he leans back and smiles gently at me. "Good luck, Cross. Come back to me safely and bring me home a victory."

"I've already won." Another press of his lips against mine and then a step back, another long look, before he turns on his heel and gets to work.

I sigh. I can't help it, but I do. How? Why? I mean . . . this is real.

"You two could make anyone believe in love," Amandine says as she steps up beside me with a dreamy look on her face.

"I take that as a huge compliment." She hands me a headset. "Thank you."

"Always."

"Uh, hey," I say as she turns.

"Hmm?"

"Is Dominic up top?" I ask, curious why I haven't seen him lurking around the garage yet. Needing to prepare myself for the dark cloud trying to dampen my sunshine.

"Nope."

"No?" Dominic Navarro not at a race? That's a first.

"He's no longer allowed in the garage area per Cruz's instruction. I guess his paddock passes somehow got mixed up." She winks and gives me a full-on grin before walking away.

I stare after her and then look back at where Cruz is getting buckled in.

He's no longer allowed in the garage area per Cruz's instruction.

Wow. It seems a lot of growing up and ownership has happened in the weeks we've been apart.

～

P1.

He won.

Cruz fucking won. He's been so swamped with the media and the podium that I can't wait to kiss him into infinity I'm so excited for him.

But his team matters. The people who got him there, who hold him, and who helped him, so I'm absolutely fine with standing back and letting them do their thing. I'll gladly settle for the stolen glances and sly smiles every now and again.

Besides, I know I get him the rest of the night so I'll bide my time.

"Team picture," Amandine says, circling everyone up to take a picture with the trophy and the sandwich board that shows the team name and finish position.

I take a step back to get out of the way.

"No, you don't," she says. "You are just as much a part of this team as anyone else, Lucky Charm."

I look at her like she's crazy. "You think I'm joking? Get in there."

And when I look up, Cruz is holding his hand out to me with a grin the size of Texas on his face.

"See?" he asks. "I told you. You're my good luck charm." He kisses me and then says quietly so just I hear him, "In more ways than one."

CHAPTER SIXTY-TWO

Maddix

CRUZ'S EYES ALL BUT BUG OUT OF HIS HEAD. "*HOLY. SHIT.*"

There's the boost of confidence any girl needs when she walks into a room with heels, a stack load of jewels on, and nothing else.

"Um," he stutters. "I thought we were having dinner. Had dinner plans. We're going to dinner." He shakes his head as if he can't believe what he's seeing.

My grin widens. "We are. But I thought we'd celebrate your new world championship with dessert first."

His eyes scrape up and down the length of me and he groans as his cock hardens within his shorts.

"Maddix." My name is a hoarse plea.

"You once told me you wanted to fuck me with just the heels, just the jewels on." I hold my hands out to my sides, putting myself on display. "Here I am. All. For. You."

His Adam's apple bobs as he draws in a fortifying breath. "You really know how to throw a man's plans off."

"Did you have something more important to do than fuck me like this?"

A shy smile forms. "Not more important. Maybe just as important," he says as he steps forward and runs his hands up and down the length of my hips. He leans in to kiss me. "I like the jewels." Another kiss. "I like the heels." A kiss to my collarbone and a tug with his teeth on the same necklace that was loaned to me for the prince's ball so many months ago. "I like you naked even more so." He slides a hand between my thighs and his guttural groan tells me he's found me wet and wanting for him. "But I think there is one more thing I'd like even better."

"This better be damn good, Navarro, if you're stalling taking advantage of me to prove a point."

His grin is lightning quick as he takes a step back and fishes in his back pocket. I assume he's digging for a condom. The quip on my tongue that he's really ready for anything dies a quick death when he pulls out a black velvet ring box.

And then he opens it the same time he says, "*This.*"

My eyes widen. A gasp falls from my lips. And my head shakes ever so slightly back and forth as I realize what is nestled in that box is not your run-of-the-mill ring.

It's a giant oval cut diamond solitaire haloed by other smaller diamonds.

It's stunning. It's overwhelming.

"It's . . ."

"It's perfect, just like you." He chuckles shyly. "I had plans. Dinner. A cruise on the boat. A moonlight proposal. But . . . seeing you standing here, like this, for me . . . I know we're not leaving this house tonight."

I chuckle nervously. "Cruz," I murmur.

"Marry me, Madds. Because you want to sow your oats with me. Because you want to be my bookend. Because you want to navigate this crazy life we have together. Because you want to be the sunrise to my sunset. The finish to my start. The calm to my storm. Marry me, because I'm so madly in love with you that there is no one else I'd rather come home to. To make a home with. To make a life with."

Tears well and spill over. I glance down at myself and start laughing.

"This isn't exactly the most conventional way to get engaged."

"When have we ever been conventional though?" He kisses me and my whole world rights perfectly. "What do you say? Will you marry me?"

"I say, thank God you hate the color red." Another kiss. This time slower. Gentler. Sexier. And when I lean back all I see is him. All I ever want to see is him. "Yes. A million times yes."

EPILOGUE

Cruz

One Year Later

P3.
Not the best day's work.
Not the worst.

But it still leaves us in the running for a repeat championship.

It still leaves us capable for good things to happen.

Amandine motions me over. "Picture time."

"Okay. I need to find mi patriarca." I'm still surprised by his appearance here today. At the race. It's been the first time he's been able to attend all year and for that I'll forever be grateful for this race. For this podium. For having him here to see and to look down as the champagne was spraying and meet his eyes. See the pride in them. Feel the love emanating off him.

"He said he'll see you back at the hotel. He didn't want to disrupt your well-deserved celebration," she explains.

I nod, my chest still bursting with pride. "Okay. Thank you. And my father?" I ask so I know. Have things gotten better between us since I won the championship last year? Since I forbade him from being in the garage? In my headspace? A little. But I also care less because I find my validation in the one and only person who matters to me, Madds.

"He is in the hospitality suite where you designated."

I nod. I saw him on the outskirts of the celebration, standing by mi patriarca. Watching everyone celebrate me—*again*. And I hate the *I told you so* pride that came with that feeling. But I felt it nonetheless.

"Okay. I'll see him after the picture." I glance up to see Maddix. Jesus, how one look from her can make every single stressful moment worth it. She's . . . *everything*. "There you are." I pull her against me and press a kiss to her lips. "Ready for the picture?"

"Yep. Sure." She worries her bottom lip between her teeth.

Something is off. "You okay?"

"Yep. I'm more than okay." She kisses my cheek. "Happy P3."

I link hands with hers and we go to take our spot amidst the team for the requisite after-podium team picture. I hold the trophy up as everyone cheers and the photo is snapped. But it's only after the photo and everyone gets up to start to go back to their collective duties that I notice them giving the sign that is beside me a double take.

Laughter rings out. Elbows are nudged. Congratulations are called out.

But they're looking at Maddix when they say it.

I stand and turn to the sign and my heart fucking stops in my chest. There's Maddix, her hands on the top of it, and her smile as wide as can be.

But it's the words spelled out on the board that own me.

"Congratulations, Daddy."

I read it several times as my tongue feels like a lead weight in my mouth. But it's the tears welling in Maddix's eyes that tell me it's right. That my guess is right.

"Congratulations, Cross."

"Are you serious?" I can barely get the words out as elation consumes me.

I get to be the father to something part me, part Maddix. I get to be the father to my child that I wish mine had been to me.

That I get to love something—*someone*—unconditionally and share something with Maddix that no one can ever take away from us.

"I am."

I think I whoop. Or call her name. Or something I can't remember because I almost knock the sign over getting to her. Pulling her against me. And kissing her senseless.

"A baby," I whisper.

"A baby," she says as I meet her eyes.

"I thought I couldn't love you more. I was wrong. You keep proving that to me time and time again. Maddix Navarro—you are everything I never knew I needed and everything I wanted."

And she is.

Time and again she keeps proving it to me.

Our love. It's unconditional. Something I didn't understand. Something I never thought could exist for me outside of mi abuelo and Sofia, but Maddix and her family have shown me differently.

They've shown me that love is about selfless sacrifice. It's not foolproof, but it is worth the effort. It's worth the risk of being vulnerable, of putting yourself out there, because the reward . . . the reward is so fucking worth it.

A daddy.

Damn. I'm one lucky son of a bitch.

Did you enjoy Cruz and Maddix's story? Do you want to meet the rest of the drivers in the *Full Throttle* series?

Be ready for another lap around the circuit in these upcoming books, available for preorder now.

Off The Grid— For Spencer Riggs, his team owner's daughter is off-limits. But weren't limits made to be pushed? Available now.

Over The Limit— The strong, silent driver in Formula 1, Lachlan Evans, is coming June 2024.

Out of Control— The bad boy of Formula 1, Oliver Rossi, is coming August 2024.

Looking for another sexy racecar driver to read until my next one comes out? Have you met Colton Donavan yet in **The Driven Series?** He's a reckless, bad boy with a good guy heart buried underneath. You can meet him in the completed series.

ABOUT THE AUTHOR

New York Times Bestselling author K. Bromberg writes contemporary romance novels that contain a mixture of sweet, emotional, a whole lot of sexy, and a little bit of real. She likes to write strong heroines and damaged heroes, who we love to hate but can't help but love.

Since publishing her first book on a whim in 2013, Kristy has sold over two million copies of her books across twenty different countries and has landed on the New York Times, USA Today, and Wall Street Journal Bestsellers lists over thirty times. (*She still wakes up and asks herself how she got so lucky for all this to happen.*)

A mom of three, Kristy finds the only thing harder than finishing the book she's writing is navigating parenthood during the teenage years (send more wine!). She loves dogs, sports, a good book, and is an expert procrastinator. She lives in Southern California with her family and their three dogs.

You can find out more about Kristy, her books, or just chat with her on any of her social media accounts. The easiest way to stay up to date on new releases and upcoming novels is to sign up for her newsletter or follow her on Bookbub.

Printed in Great Britain
by Amazon